all roads lead
HOME

A NOVEL BY BEST SELLING AUTHOR
MARY A. WASOWSKI

Copyright © 2015 by Mary A. Wasowski
Cover Design by RE Creatives
Formatting by JT Formatting

First Edition: June 2016
Library of Congress Cataloging-in-Publication Data

http://authormaryawasowski.com/

Wasowski, Mary A.
  All Roads Lead Home / 1st ed
    ISBN-13: 978-0-9896238-9-6

  1.   All Roads Lead Home—Fiction.   2.   Fiction—Romance
          3.   Fiction—Contemporary Romance:

Sometimes you will never know the true value of a moment until it becomes a memory.

PROLOGUE

...past

I'M A RUNNER. Not an athlete who competes in races. Not one who does it for exercise or enjoyment. No, I'm the worst kind of runner, you know the type. The kind that fled her life in the wake of a family tragedy, an unbearable loss that can weigh you down. What am I saying? It still does. It's a kind of loss that binds suffocating chains around your heart. Feelings cut off and numbness set in, all of which left me empty.

I chose to love my family from a distance. I chose to shut down and compartmentalize my feelings. I wrapped them up in a pretty box tied with a bow on it. I chose selfishly, and my grief paved the way to my new life. I never considered what my leaving did to my family and friends, who all remained behind when I ran and never looked back.

I said I would move forward and carry on with my life. Be happy. Marry the man of my dreams. Have babies and become a mom. Just move forward. Not carry the pain of losing the one person who knew me best and I loved the most. I promised I wouldn't live in the past and struggle to change the things that can never be changed.

I lied.

I broke my promise to him.

Yes, I promised you all of those things, but you lied too. You promised to fight and never give up. You were getting better. I felt it when I looked into your eyes. You had a future waiting for you beyond those cold, sterile hospital doors. What did you know that I didn't? You always protected me from anything that would bring me sadness. You knew this would break me, so you made me promise to not fall apart like a jig-saw puzzle. Shattered pieces of me would never heal, never allowing me to be whole again. I would be left alone without you.

When I shared my feelings with you, you laughed at the ridiculousness of it all. I smacked you on your arm and told you to stop making jokes, but you continued to laugh. In the end, I gave up and joined in. I could never stay angry with you, not even for five minutes. We were always connected, you told me this often. It was a sibling thing.

You said no matter what happens, I would always have mama and daddy, Wendy, and of course your best friends, Shane and Jagger. They were like brothers to me, but then our circle of friendship changed when Jagger and I found love. He was your best friend and my first love. *My only love . . . always.*

I never really knew if in fact that was true, because I ran. I ran across the country and convinced myself I was doing the right thing for my future. I left broken hearts in my wake. I was consumed in my own loss that I never cared to look beyond my own pain. I channeled it and used it for strength. I focused on graduating from law school and being the best at what I worked so hard to accomplish. I couldn't fight for something that was beyond my control, like cancer . . . your cancer.

It was a Monday. The sun had not risen on the new day yet. I remember having a restless sleep the night before, haunted by your image over and over again. Your handsome face was dancing around in my dreams. I wanted to reach out and touch you, but yet, you were so far away. As I laid asleep to hold onto you, I could feel your spirit leaving the physical world and preparing for what's next to come. I could hear your voice so vividly clear, but also felt your pain. Not a physical pain, but more of an emotional one. Something that no one could ever be prepared for.

I awoke and jolted out of my sleep with the piercing sound of my phone ringing. Instantaneously, my heart began to pound. I knew what I was about to be told and who was on the other end of the line.

This was my Monday, five years ago. To most it meant the beginning of a new work week. A new day. *When the life I was so certain of having just died along with you.*

I hate this day. It is the one day I allow myself to feel your loss. As I clutched your picture to my chest, my tears broke through the barriers I had so carefully put in place. They simply fell, and I did nothing to stop them. I was alone and lost in the memories of you. I felt the walls closing in around me and I needed to get out of here.

I'm a runner.

The worst kind.

The type that says . . . *I'll see you soon, I'll call you later*, but really only uses those lines to be polite.

I'm sorry I didn't keep my promise to you.

I'm sorry I ran, but you lied too.

You left me.

CHAPTER 1

Tenley

...present day

"**W**HAT ARE YOU doing here this early on a Monday?" my assistant shrilled at me as I lifted my head up from the mountain of legal briefs I was reading through.

"The last time I checked, this was my office. You see the name plate on the door?" I replied sarcastically and my tone was sounding borderline bitch.

I took a breath before speaking again to her, "Good morning, Roxy."

She half smiled back at me. Roxy, being the amazing assistant she was, read my mood before another word was spoken.

"The usual, Ms. Fairchild? No calls or visitors until you say otherwise?"

"Yes, I just need a few hours to myself. Court is at nine thirty. If all goes according to plan, we will be celebrating by lunch time."

I knew this case was already won. I worked my legal assets off for months and dazzled the senior partners. They all knew the hours

I clocked for this trial, and so did I. There was no way I wasn't going to reap the benefits from all of my hard work.

"Understood, boss. Let me know if you need anything."

"Roxy . . . " I called out.

"Yes, Ms. Fairchild."

"I'm sorry. I would love a cup of coffee . . . and please call me Tenley."

She nodded to at least two of my requests, but I wasn't sure if she would be addressing me by first name anytime soon. She was openly chastised in front of many lawyers by one of the senior partners a few months back. When I made partner, my title and stature changed here at the firm. I was friendly with most of the staff, but when I received my own personal assistant, I thought I could still maintain the same easygoing pace I always had. The higher ups frowned upon that and wanted me to behave like them. Cut and dry, black and white, no color in between. My assistant works for me, not the other way around.

I was still trying to get used to having her at my beck and call. Roxy was such a free spirit rocker chick. She had an ultra-modern haircut with purple highlights. She followed the rules at the office. Always impeccably dressed, but she wasn't budging on her hair color. I stood firm as well, and Mr. Steele finally conceded.

I think his daughter Zoey had a hand in that. She was another larger than life person and my first friend here in New York. A natural rebel, but the apple of her daddy's eye. Another free spirit who made no apologies on who she was, and another who liked a little sparkle to her look . . . I don't know what it was, but when comparing Zoey to Roxy, I suddenly felt a shiver run up my spine. It felt like I was describing my relationship with my daddy, or at least how it used to be.

"Excuse me, Ms. Fairchild." The sound of the intercom brought me out of my deep thoughts, and I was thankful for that. I had no business revisiting a past hurt that would never be undone.

"What is it, Roxy?"

"Your mother is on line three, again. She insists on speaking with you. Shall I take another message?"

"No, it's fine. I'll speak with her. Please put her through."

I counted to myself . . . *1, 2, 3, 4, 5* . . . Needing to get myself in check before speaking with her. The last thing I wanted was to forget my manners when it comes to my mother.

"Hello, mama." My voice was quiet and my accent always picked the right time to return anytime I would speak with her.

"Hello, daughter. Thank you for taking my call. How are you today?" she seemed like she genuinely wants to know.

"I'm fine, mama. How are you?"

"Your father and I are okay, thank you for asking. I received the contracts you sent over for the new horses we are about to acquire, thank you for that. You always do the best work, better than any other lawyer your daddy keeps on retainer."

"Mama, I'm due in court soon. Can I call you later?"

"That would be fine if I knew you would, but we know something will come up and you won't call. I know you're busy, Tenley, and you have no room for us in your life, but I miss you. Your daddy misses you, and I need you too. Please come home to us. Hasn't it been long enough? Our relationship with you consists of business dealings and these less than five minute phone calls. A Christmas package delivered every year right to our door step. A card containing pleasantries, but no personal attachment to the words written so eloquently on the paper. I love you, Tenley. I miss my daughter."

I tried my best to put her at ease. "Mama, that's not true. Please don't talk this way. You know my work takes up all of my time, and I know more than anyone how long it's been since I've been home. You are my mother, of course I want to talk to you, but I'm just busy now. I promise to call you later, I promise."

I tried with my whole heart to believe what I was desperately trying to convince my mother to believe, and then she hit me where it would hurt the most. "He loved you so much, baby girl. I hope you find a reason to smile today. I love you."

The line clicked off. My tears fell, and I was left with memories of him. Dammit! Not today. I'm about to hear the biggest verdict of my legal career, and my mother picks this time to throw the past in my face. Why? They have their life in Wyoming. I have mine here in New York. I don't want to hurt her. I never wanted this distance and feeling of loss between us, but it happened anyway.

"Roxy . . . " I call out to my assistant.

"Yes, Ms. Fairchild."

"Please come into my office."

She entered and took a seat in front of my desk, waiting for me to fire off my list of tasks for her to complete.

"Roxy, you are my right hand. The one person I depend on to keep me in check. I'm a very busy woman. I work fourteen hour work days, sometimes more. My entire life is work, which leaves little room for anything else. In here, I need one thing that is personal. For the last time, please address me as Tenley. If anyone has a problem with how I ask you to address me, they know where I am and can take their trivial grievances with me. Do I make myself clear?"

"Yes, Ms. . . . I mean Tenley."

I almost smiled at her slip of the tongue. Roxy was not a confrontational person, more of a people pleaser.

"Now, I need you to take care of something for me, a personal request." I enunciated very clearly to my assistant. "Please send two dozen yellow sunflowers to my mother. Address the card as follows: *'You asked me to find a reason to smile today. I'm not sure I can do that. So I'm sending you our favorite flower in hopes they bring you some happiness behind the sadness we are all feeling today. Love, Tenley,'* Please do this at once and then phone my driver. I need to get down to the courthouse." I once again was curt with Roxy. She looked at me with sadness in her eyes, no doubt after what I told her to say in my card. My mother said I never put feelings behind my words, well hopefully she would believe this one. I shut down because it's what this day represented. Usually I didn't mind having my life controlled by my day planner. If only Roxy had a magic wand to make me forget what today really meant.

Today was not just any busy work day, it represented the anniversary of losing my brother. Five long years without him. Five years trying to forget the life I loved and the people who loved me back. I left them. Fled like a fugitive on the run. I couldn't stay even to grieve with them, not when everything reminded me of the loss I felt. A pain at times that subsided, but never really went away. Today was one of the days where it reared its ugly head and I just surrendered to it.

I thought if I got to work while the city still slept, I could stay busy and forget. My mother's phone call squashed my bright idea. They grieved and moved on with their lives. I did too, but not in the way I promised I would. *I can't retreat and allow my heart to hurt.* I was stronger than that, and I had a case to win.

By the time I arrived at the courthouse, my take no prisoner attitude was back. I worked incredibly hard, and now it was time to hear the fruits of my labor. As a lawyer, I modeled myself after the fictional character Olivia Pope, gladiator lawyer. To fight tirelessly for her clients, go up against the toughest challengers, and beat their asses. To simply win and always come out stronger. The one thing in my life that I had complete control over was my career. I did it extraordinarily well, and it came before anything else in my life. It was truly all I had. *I fight for my clients and I never give up. I win for them.*

"Well done! Well done, indeed. You have done it again, Miss Fairchild." A glass of champagne was being raised up in my honor. I was being toasted by Raymond Steele, founder of Steele and Copeland law firm, where I had just won my first case as a newly appointed partner.

I was high on an adrenaline rush, the best kind. I loved the thrill of going up against the power players in the all-boys, no girls allowed club. This was a two year case in the making. My best friend Tommy, the sole owner of his construction company, was being muscled to give up controlling interest in his company by, let's just say, a more connected one. I not only exposed them for being the frauds they were, but singlehandedly took down their HUD Housing scam to cheat their way through the system. Many hardworking people who lived in those neighborhoods never saw their investments come to life because of the duplicitous acts committed by the criminals who were involved.

I knew what I could do in a court room and wasn't fazed by the looming threat of violence against me if I didn't stop pursuing the case. I would have envelopes stuffed with cash waiting for me in my mailbox, and when that incentive didn't work, they upped the ante.

One night, I received an anonymous e-mail that stated: **Go look outside at your car. We can get to you anytime . . . any place. The next time you'll be in it.**

The car detonated right in front of me. Now I was pissed, and fuck them for even trying to intimidate me.

I carried forward with my case. We won. They didn't. They went to jail, and I was still standing, enjoying a very delicious glass of champagne. Who knew where the fight in me came from? I never questioned it, not ever.

Zoey, my best friend and Raymond's daughter, was still whistling as I finished my very short thank you speech. Tommy hugged me hard and wanted to take me out to celebrate, but I refused him.

"Come on Tenley, please? One dinner, and you can be the dessert, where you're lying on my bed naked—and I mean very naked—for me to worship and devour."

For the first time today, I smiled. *You see mama? I found a reason to smile, even if it's a small one.* My friend accomplished that impossible feat.

"I love you, Tommy, you know I do," I replied. "But the answer is still no. We are friends, the best kind. Let's leave it at that."

At that moment, he seductively touched my arm and, because

I'm still a woman, react to it by stepping back but feeling the goose bumps his touch left.

"We can be so much more if you would give us a chance," he whispered.

He truly meant what he was desperately trying to make me believe, but I knew better. I'd been down this road before many years ago, and all it left me with was a heaping serving of regret. I put my champagne down and gave my friend a hug and silently wished I was somewhere else. Tommy's friendship was too important to me. I wasn't about to have history repeat itself again.

"Tommy, I know you believe that we can be something more, but this is as far as we go. Friendship is all I want with you. I have never lied to you about my feelings, but you need to stop the wanting more and just be my friend."

"Can't blame a guy for trying. You need to have another glass of champagne and stop being so serious all the time. Haven't you ever heard the expression 'friends . . . with benefits'? Jeez, you need a night out to relax."

Great diversion . . . distract me with humor when we really knew you're sidestepping the real issue here.

I questioningly looked at him, but he laughed and took me in his strong arms. I loved Tommy, I really did, but he wasn't Jagger. No man could ever be. I wasn't about to measure Tommy, or any man, to the one man who held my heart. That wouldn't be fair to my friend, and it would just give him false hope.

The celebration carried on until Zoey was hammered and Tommy was close to it. I had cars pick them up and take them home. No one would be waiting for me at my apartment, so I stayed behind to work.

As I read through case files, my private line rang. Looking at my watch, it was nearing ten o'clock. No one ever called me this late and on this line. Only a few had this number including my mother, but she knew not to call me here for small talk. Today alone should have proved that. Hopefully my flowers eased the hurt I somehow caused her today. I didn't have the ring choice on a set number, so it rang several times before I picked up the receiver.

"Tenley Fairchild speaking." I went with professional before I knew who was on the other end.

"Hello, Tumbleweed!" I would recognize that voice anywhere. Her boisterous voice carried through the receiver that I had to pull the phone away from my ear. She called me by my childhood nick-name given to me by my brother, and the only other person I could still stomach using it was her.

Placing the call on speaker, I said, "Wendy! How are you? It's been a long time."

What could I say to her? It had probably been a year or more since we spoke to each other in great length. Making partner was all I focused on, and I threw myself into Tommy's case.

"Too long, Tumbleweed, way too long. Let me get to the point of my call. I have a favor to ask of you, one I'm hoping you won't say no to."

"You know I would do anything for you Wendy, you just have to ask and even then just a look will do," I said.

"I hope that's true."

"It is. Name it. What do you need?"

"I need you to come home," she said.

The six words that I had hoped she wouldn't ask of me. *Was it possible that my heart had just stopped beating?* I actually put my two fingers to my throat to make sure. The line was silent. I knew we were still connected, but knowing Wendy, she was giving me the minute I needed to catch my breath.

"Wendy, you know I can't do that. Anything, but that."

"Tenley, have I ever asked anything of you before this phone call tonight?"

"No, ma'am, you haven't."

"Then please don't refuse me the one and only time I do ask."

"Wendy, are you okay? Can you tell me that much?" I nervous-ly questioned.

"I'm fine, Tumbleweed. This request is for someone else."

"Who?" I asked.

She didn't say.

"My parents? Are they okay?"

"They are."

"Wendy, why are you being so evasive? Just tell me why I need to come home." My voice began to rise.

"Listen here, girl. If you have to question me as to why you are needed to come home, then you've been gone way too long. Call me when you get into town, and that means tomorrow."

"Wendy, don't hang up!" I pleaded before the line went dead, and I was left to be lost in my thoughts. *God! I just want this day to end, but even after all the good that happened in my career today, I'm back to that damn fucking day that my heart shattered.* My eyes found my calendar. November 30th, five years ago . . . you died. I'm numb . . . just numb.

I unlocked my bottom desk drawer containing a precious photograph of you that I allowed no one to see. It was times like this that I needed to remember and remind myself of things that were once attainable, but were no more in reach of having. Now sitting back and staring at your face, my mind drifted back to our very last conversation we had in person.

You held my hand and smiled at me. Your smile was beautiful. A forever memory etched out in my mind and carved throughout my soul. It was the one constant that began my day. The one simple act I could count on.

You were the early riser out of the two of us, because Daddy had you do all the morning chores before sunrise. How ironic that you died before the dawn greeted the new day.

You always told me not to be scared and to not fear the unknown. I was scared. Scared to face the future without you in it. You held me through the night and woke me up with a tickle to my ribs.

"Wake up, Tumbleweed. You have a big day ahead of you. Daddy will be here soon to pick you up. You wouldn't want to miss your flight. Lord knows it will be hard enough dealing with the long drawn out goodbyes, especially from mama."

I woke to your voice and there was that smile again. How could you smile with all you were going through? I didn't move until you practically shoved me out of the cramped hospital bed.

"Don't fight me, Tumbleweed. I can't leave this earth knowing you're not happy. Promise me you will get on that plane today and keep moving forward with your life. Don't stand still because of your pain. We can't stop the inevitable from happening, so don't even try. I am your brother. I will always love and look out for you, even though I won't be here for you to see me. I promise little sister, you will always feel my love close by and watching over you. I'll be where it matters most. Promise me, Tenley! You will keep moving forward. Promise me." His voice was strong, but I could hear the sadness in his tone.

"I promise." I said weakly.

"That's all I ask. Thank you for loving me. I only hope you know how much I have loved you since the day mama and daddy brought you home. You were always shiny as a new penny. One look at you, and I was forever wrapped around your little finger. From the first moment my eyes met yours, I knew you had a fire deep inside of you. You excelled in school. Could ride a horse before you could run. A natural ability to conquer anything you were challenged with. It was an honor to be your big brother. Boy! You were a little rebel. You never did your chores. Always pushing mama's buttons, and then playing the princess card with daddy. He never could stay mad at you for too long. Hell, none of us could."

My tears began to fall, as I tried so hard to stop them, but I felt I had no strength left. "Jamie, can I ask you a question?"

"Of course, sweetheart, anything." There was that smile again as he answered me.

"If I'm so amazing, then why did Jagger give up on me? I know

I hurt him with my decision and the mistake I made with Shane, but he is so stubborn. He never really believed what I repeatedly told him. He led me to believe that my dream was our dream and that he would leave with me. But in the end, that's all it was. It was my fantasy, and not his. He should have been honest with me, but he faked it. Who the fuck does that?"

"Hey, watch your mouth. I'm still your big brother, and I will hide your ass if you speak like that again."

"Sorry." I muttered.

"That's better. Come back up here and listen to me. Tenley, I can't speak for Jagger, nor Shane for that matter. Those boys love you so much, but like the line goes in the movie, 'You can't ride two horses with one ass.'"

"You are not helping."

"Come on, now that was a funny movie. It kind of reminds me of the three of you. Listen, Tumbleweed, you have a lot in your life that most don't. You have parents who love you with all of their heart. A great mentor and friend in Wendy. Two amazing best friends that would probably lay their life down for you. I understand you're not in the best place with them right now, but give them time, especially Jagger. You think he would just give up on you when it took him so long to catch you? What happened, happened. Let it go and move on. Not one thing in this life is perfect, not even our family, but we come pretty close to it. And if I know anything about Jagger, he never faked it with you. He loves you, this I know without fail."

"Well, it doesn't matter anyway. We're over. He made his choice and I made mine," I said.

"Don't do that, not now."

"Don't do what?"

"Come on little sister, you know exactly what you're doing. You always retreated back into your private world. When things weren't the way you wanted them to be, you just put up those walls that made it impossible for anyone to get past. Please, Tenley, let people in. You need them more than you know."

"If that's true, then why are you pushing me to go? I don't have to leave today. I can put off school. I want to be here with you, Jamie."

"You don't know how much that means to me to hear that, but I can't let you do that. You need to begin the next chapter in your life. You worked so hard to get into law school, I'd never forgive myself if you gave that dream up for me."

"Jamie, please fight. Please stay with me. You've beat this before, you can do it again. There has to be another way. Another transplant, more stem cells, something dammit! Please don't leave me."

I hugged him as tightly as I could manage. Even being sick, Jamie was still so incredibly strong. It was like hugging a wall. He had natural muscle from the years of ranch life.

"I love you, baby sister. For today, I'm here, and I promise I will fight for as long as I am able to. I don't have a crystal ball. I can't see the future, but I can see today, and today I'm going to tell you that I love you. I am so very proud of you. Now go! Yale Law School waits for no one, not even you, Tumbleweed."

"I love you, Jamie. Thank you for being the best big brother in the world. I'm going to call you every day."

He hugged me back, but it felt different. He never said it, but deep down I knew. Three months later, my brother died and heaven welcomed a new angel.

Wiping my tears, I needed to get out of here. It was past eleven, and I was lost in my thoughts enough for one evening. I instructed my driver to take me to the one place I never thought I would find myself. I swore up and down I would never cross that line again, but I didn't want to be alone tonight.

I was here again in an emotional place, like I was years ago. My heart was not listening to my brain. I just needed to feel something. I needed to breathe life into this body and know my heart and pulse were still working properly.

Oh my God! What am I doing? Foolish slut. Yeah, that would be an appropriate word. I thought as I rang the doorbell. If I were in my right frame of mind now, I would turn around and run back to my car. This is not me, not by a long shot. I've done this already, and it nearly destroyed me and the two men who held my heart. One who I loved, and the other who loved me. I swayed back and forth on my Jimmy Choo stilettos while my finger lingered over his doorbell.

Ugh! This is wrong, but screw it. I'm not even out of my twenties yet, but feel like I've just aged ten years with one phone call from Wendy. Asking me to come home to the one place I no longer considered my home?

I knew better to think that way, but it was the bullshit line I fed myself daily. Once again, this was my past talking for me. I grew up there. I didn't have one childhood memory that didn't include my brother, Jagger, or Shane. Or my beloved horse who probably has forgotten me by now.

I started thinking of my parents. I missed them, of course I did. Mama didn't hold back today, not for one second sparing my feelings. She missed me and needed me to be her daughter again, but how the hell do I do that? My big brother died, and my stomach still felt the hurt from his death. My mind always retreated back to how he died and how I wasn't there to hold him. To tell him that I loved him so much, and for him to hear me say that it was okay to go. His cancer took so much from him, but you would never know it. Jamie always the stronger one.

My brother was larger than life and strong as a bull, but fearless to the very end, or so I'd been told since he didn't want me there with him in his final days and hours. I should have been with him, but he refused me. He put me first above himself. He always did.

"Go make us proud," he said, and like a foolish girl, I listened and did everything he asked of me . . . well, almost everything.

So, here I am, throwing caution to the wind, as I pushed the doorbell. Midnight booty calls weren't my thing, but there was always a first time for everything. Yeah, I was certain I would regret this in the morning, but my body needed this tonight. I needed to forget, if only for a little while, the realities of my life and the pains I struggled so hard to move on from.

CHAPTER 2

...the letter

WAKING UP TO a raging hangover was not the best way to start my day. Neither was waking up to my bed partner. Ugh . . . Another in the moment, recklessly made bad choice on my part.

What the hell was I thinking? Tommy is my friend and a current client. Good for you Tenley. A perfect way to mess up a friendship and derail a promising career.

I knew what I was doing and would have to accept the consequences of my actions. I called Tommy out of desperation. I wanted more than a bottle of wine and the thrill of my vibrator. I needed intimacy. I didn't want to be alone. I spent my life being alone, and for once I wanted something more, even if it was for only a night.

When he opened the door, he was only wearing his low hanging pajama pants. His exposed tan skin was so fucking tempting. I rolled my tongue over my lips and just wanted to lick him all over. *God! I did lick him. I'm so embarrassed.*

I practically raped him in his entryway, but he didn't stop me. If

I was playing the naughty Dominatrix role, then Tommy was my willing submissive. *Damn! I've been celibate for way too long. I'm surprised my girly parts still worked at all, I'm sore all over.*

Tommy gave me the Deluxe Special, working and spinning my body in so many positions. Crashing mouths. Hands everywhere. Tommy had my legs wrapped around him like a snake choking its prey.

He wanted more and never made a secret about his intentions. I always said no and objected about our relationship going any further beyond friendship. Well, that's all changed now. I valued him so much. Tommy and Zoey were my first friends here in New York, and to this day, my only friends. I kept them at a safe distance. Zoey was always telling me so, but it was to protect my heart and theirs in the long run. Coming here last night was a mistake. *Will he still want to be my friend once he wakes up and finds me gone?*

After Tommy fucked me and fucked me hard, I was then held. He didn't let me move. His strong arms were wrapped around my body, and I was nestled into his hard chest wall of muscles, but his skin was so soft. His chest just had a thin matting of hair, and I liked how it felt against my cheek. He was strong. Not athletic, but strong from his years spent working construction. His hands were rougher. Calloused fingers ran up and down my back, easily lulling me to sleep.

I was wide awake now and staring back at the beautiful man who slept beside me. *God, he's magnificent, all sprawled out before me in his nakedness. If only I could open my heart to Tommy, and forget Jagger.*

"I'm sorry," I whispered to him, as I placed a chaste kiss to his lips.

He moved slightly with the sheet shifting, giving me one last peek at what was beneath. *Holy shit! That thing was in me last night!* His beast of a dick was semi-hard as he shifted again, but didn't awaken. I was sure to feel the aftereffects he left on my body every time I would move today. *Good for you Tenley,* my inner slut was rooting for me, but I knew better. This was wrong. Continuing to stare at him, my fingers were itching to touch him. I wasn't much of a hugger, not anymore, but Tommy won out in the end, making sure I was secure to him for the rest of the night.

Although I knew it was wrong, I wanted to feel him again against my skin, but I stopped myself. It felt like a lifetime since I felt this way about a man. I never knew until now how lonely I was. I may have kept myself busy with my demanding career, but my body was bored and starved for human touch. Something that didn't require batteries.

My mouth tasted like cotton, and my face looked no better. I quickly gathered up my clothes and got dressed. Like the coward I was, I quietly crept out of Tommy's apartment, grabbed a cab, and walked through my own building doing the classic walk of shame. My doorman greeted me with his usual cheery tone. I half smiled back at him. He stopped me before I could make my escape into the waiting elevator.

"Ms. Fairchild, this was left for you yesterday."

"Thank you." I took the FedEx envelope from him and turned to go upstairs. All I needed was Advil and a soft pillow to lay my head down on . . . and a rock to crawl under.

Wendy's call was playing over and over in my head. Why did she want me to come home? I would do anything for her, and she knew that, but this? I couldn't. I couldn't go back there. It wasn't home anymore to me. Without Jamie, and with the way I left Jagger and Shane, how could I ever go back? I can't go back there. I will say it, repeat it, and believe it until I convince myself that I'm right on this.

I'll wash Tommy off of me—another foolish mistake. Like a phoenix, I will rise again. This is what I do. And fucking hell! I'm good at it. I phoned my office and told Roxy I would be in later this morning. I wasn't one for taking any time off, but this headache was still very strong and I would be useless until I felt better.

My cell was ringing again, and it didn't take a genius to figure out who it was. Tommy texted me six times and left two very long voicemails. He was angry that he woke up without me. I listened to only one of his voicemails. His texts messages were enough to turn my stomach. He said he was confused to why I left without waking him first and angry again because I was ignoring his calls.

I was about to call him when I was distracted by the FedEx envelope I had thrown on my coffee table. Deciding to put off calling Tommy, I picked up the envelope to see what it was.

What I found inside made my knees go weak. Thank goodness I was already sitting down. I ran my fingers over the handwriting. It was addressed to me by him . . . my brother, Jamie.

How? Who would have sent this to me? With shaky fingers, I opened the second envelope that had my brother's handwriting on it. I wiped away a tear and began reading his words to me.

Dear Tumbleweed,

If you're reading this letter, then I have been gone for five years now. Not like you need a reminder, but it is what it is. The reason why you are receiving this letter now is because you have not kept your promise to me like you said you would. How do I know this? Well, you're going to have to trust me on this. And believe the person I have put my complete faith in to help you sort it all out and get your shit together. Let me begin by saying . . .

I'm sorry, baby sis. I'm so very sorry for leaving you. It was not what I wanted, and you must believe that I did fight. I fought so hard for you, mama, daddy, and me. In the end, I just wasn't strong enough to fight my leukemia. I'm sorry I died, but you are still here. You still have a chance to live and be happy.

What about Jagger? Is he happy? If I had to guess, I would say he wasn't and just existing like you are. And Shane? They were my best friends, brothers for life. You know it freaked me the hell out when I learned Jagger had feelings for you and how they ran deeper than just friendship. I wasn't sure if I should have beat the hell out of him, or congratulate him on choosing the best gal I knew. Note to baby sister: If you didn't want to be caught, then you should have locked the damn door! Oh my eyes . . . that's an image I didn't soon forget. Okay, moving on.

When I asked you to carry on with your life, I didn't mean "Break my best friend's heart." Shortly after you left for school, he visited with me. Stayed by my side for two days straight until I forced him to leave. That man was stinking up my room and in need of a shower. All we talked about was you and how much he loved you. Shane came by too. They were trying to mend the broken fences between them. I kind of blackmailed them into forgiving each other for real and not just talk, but say the words I needed to hear. I can only pray they meant it. Bros before . . . well, you know the rest, and don't get mad, I would never think that way about you, nor would they. Baby sis, you made an error in judgment. Your one mistake doesn't mean it's not forgivable. Okay, trying to stay focused here. As hard as this is for you right now to read this, it's not any easier on my end. I want daddy to send a plane for you and bring you home, but you are where you need to be, as I am.

"Dammit Jamie! Why didn't you? I would have come home." I took a breath before reading again. This letter was tearing my heart out.

I promised the guys that I would haunt them if they didn't find a way back to being brothers. We all laughed, but I couldn't leave knowing they were hurting. It was bad enough knowing you were suffering. Why, baby sister? Jagger loved you, and I have to imagine he still does, but who knows how his life is now? I told you once that I didn't have a crystal ball to see the future, but I always wanted your future to be with him. He was the other half of your heart, and I truly hope you find your way back to each other. Okay, that's all I'm going to say on that . . . for now.

The day you left for school, you said all the right things of what I asked of you, but my big brother know-it-all skills tell me different.

19

You didn't really take my advice, did you? Sure, you did everything that was expected of you. I'm only assuming here, but I'm guessing you graduated at the top of your class, I know I'm right. So, you have this new life in a new place, but are you smiling? Are you happy? If not, then I'm disappointed. "Moving forward" meant to live your life to the fullest. Do what I can't anymore.

Once again, baby sis, if you are reading this letter, then you did the complete opposite of what I asked of you. And that makes me so very sad.

You are receiving this letter today on the anniversary of my death for one reason and one reason only. You chose wrong.

Stop hiding.

Stop running.

Come home.

I love you, Tumbleweed. I'll be watching from heaven to see if you took my advice.

Love Always,

Jamie

I whispered through my tears, "Wendy . . . " She would be the only person who would have sent me this letter, but why? Obviously I know why because I just read it, but I thought I was doing a pretty good job of living my life to the fullest. It may not be ideal to my parents or even Wendy for that matter, but it is *my* life. I've been with Steele and Copeland Law Firm since they recruited me out of Yale Law School. I've worked my way up through the ranks and last year was my biggest win when I made partner. They have been so good to me. I work incredibly hard for them. I win cases . . . big ones.

All my success comes with a price. I live alone. I bought a beautiful apartment on the upper west side with a spectacular view of Central Park. Tommy found it for me, and Zoey helped me decorate it. It's the perfect space for me. Big enough to entertain my important clients and make me appear bigger than I am.

I live alone.

My choice.

I don't even have a cat. I guess the old wives' tale doesn't apply to me. Not that I would have time to care for it anyway.

How could Wendy send me a letter from my dead brother? This hurts so much. Did he not trust me at all? I did what he wanted me to do. It was Jagger that gave up on me first and, only after losing Jamie, solidified my decision to leave and not look back.

We were in love . . . so in love. We made it through the separation of attending different colleges but always made our time count when we reunited. It was crazy, but we did it. Jagger, Shane, and my brother all attended the University of Wyoming, and I was at Creighton University in Nebraska. The guys were in their senior year while I was beginning my freshman year. Another adjustment Jagger and I dealt with, but after I graduated, we had the summer to really plan. I knew I wanted to practice law in the city, but where? I still had law school to finish. It was assumed that I would stay close by, but after a discussion with my father, I applied to Yale Law School. I couldn't have gone further, but daddy said that if I had the grades, then I could have my pick. It wasn't easy for my father to give me this much freedom. I barely made it to Nebraska without a thousand arguments. Now I was actually asking him to send me across the country to further my education.

I loved Daddy so much for believing in me. I wasn't ashamed of the life my parents led, but like Jamie always said: I was a Tumbleweed, and I chased the wind.

Sure I wanted a life with Jagger, but on my terms. Always after making love with him, he would promise me the moon and the stars. We were so in sync with one another and then at times, so very different. Like worlds apart different. He knew I always wanted to become a lawyer. I wanted to fight the injustice in the world. I thought he believed in me, but after the fantasy became the reality, I was wrong.

Jagger, like his father, wanted the ranch life, just like Shane and Jamie. He was following in my father's footsteps to one day take over for him. That dream never happened for Jamie, but mine did. And now after all this time, I receive this letter. I'm left to question all the choices I made since the day I boarded my plane and never once looked back.

On that day I took with me: Jagger's sheer look of devastation when I once again rejected him. The feeling of a father's love and adoration when he hugged me goodbye. And Jamie's smile. He was being brave for me and never allowed me to see his fear. Again, my big brother putting my needs above his very own.

I allowed my mind to drift even further back, when Jamie was alive and always wanted what was best for me.

"You know if you keep staring at the mailbox, you're going to go blind."

"Shut up, Jamie. It's coming today, I know it," I said excitedly. "It has to come today."

He smiled back at me with his dazzling smile and steel blue eyes.

"I hope so, Tumbleweed, I really do hope so. I was just making fun, don't get all upset now. Does Jagger know you applied? Oh man, sweet girl! Your eyes tell me 'No.' Tenley, I told you to tell him. He has a right to know. It's only fair."

"Jamie, don't start. If you ask me, I think Jagger is secretly hoping that I don't get accepted anywhere, and I'll just remain back here with him."

"Is that so bad? I thought you wanted that."

"Yes and no, it's complicated."

"It doesn't have to be, baby sister. You love him. He loves you. That's it."

"Jamie, you're right. I do love Jagger, more than words can say, but I'm not going to become a lawyer working a ranch. I want more, and I thought you had my back on this."

"I do sweetheart, always. I just have to have his back as well. I love you so much. I was never more proud of you when I saw you accept your college diploma. We were probably the loudest group in the place. I need you to know that whatever decisions you make will somehow affect him too. This is what you signed on for when you declared your love for my best friend, or do I have to remind you of that?"

"No." I said, sulking.

"Good! Because that's a memory I don't care to re-visit at this time. Don't look now, but here comes the mail truck."

"This is it, Bro. That truck is going to have my letter on it."

I ran toward the mail truck before he even had a chance to stop. I think Pete knew I was anxious. I had met him at the post every day for the last month. He handed me a stack of mail and there it was, my letter from Yale Law School.

I screamed so loud, I scared the horses.

Jamie walked over and lifted me into his arms. He said, "Well go on, this is what you've been waiting for."

I smiled up at my brother and ripped open the envelope.

Dear Ms. Fairchild,

Congratulations! It is with great pleasure, and my honor to inform you of your admission to Yale Law School as a member of the Class of 2009. You were selected from an accomplished and academically talented group of applicants who applied. You and your classmates are truly outstanding in your achievements, and in your diversity of interests and potential. Again, congratulations on your acceptance. Please let me know if we can be of any service to you. Looking forward to seeing you on the grounds of our exemplary school.

Yours,

Maxwell Owen Slavish

Director of Law School Admissions

"I got in, Jamie. I did it. I'm going to Yale. This is real right? I'm not dreaming."

"I don't think so, baby sis. Unless you are secretly being punk'd, this letter looks like the real deal."

"What's all the commotion about?" daddy said, as he came out, he knew just by my expression. I handed him my letter, and he took me in his arms. My daddy was a tall man. When I was little, I thought he was a giant. I still needed to tilt my head to look up at him. He was strong too, so twirling me around was effortless for him. I felt cherished when my father held me. I was his princess and today, I made him proud. His eyes were glassy, but he shrugged it off. Cowboys don't cry.

"You did it, baby girl. I never had a doubt in my mind. Maybe one day I'll hire you to oversee ranch business." He looked over to my brother, but now with a touch of sadness. I quickly brushed off the weird vibe and hugged my father again.

"Thank you, daddy. I love you. Thank you for making this possible."

"I didn't do anything, baby girl. Your determination and good smarts got you into that school. It is a check worth writing. You are worth every penny."

"Okay, okay, no need to butter me up. I'll do your work pro-bono."

"That's my girl, but you can bill me, I'm good for it," he replied.

We all laughed. This was one memory I would hold onto forever.

"Tell mama I'll be home later. I'm going to find Jagger."

"Now, honey, don't go breaking that boy's heart now."

I wanted to laugh, but my daddy and Jamie looked nothing but serious at the moment. What were they hiding? I had no time to think about it. I was way too happy to think about anything else.

Everything was perfect. I just got into my dream school. Jamie

24

was still doing great and was in remission. All was perfect in my world. I just wanted to share my news with Jagger and hoped he would be happy for me.

I drove as fast as I could to his ranch. His father ripped into me on my driving, but then he hugged me after I told him about my letter. He was a bear of a man. Muscle from head to toe from the years of working the ranch. I asked excitedly if Jagger was home, and I was told he was mending fences out on the north pasture. His father allowed me to take one of the ATVs out as long as I wore my helmet and drove safely. I crossed my heart and promised him.

The sight of Jagger nearly caused me to crash into the newly repaired fence he had just mended. He was shirtless with his Wrangler's hanging low on his hips, and his hat dipped low over his forehead. I swear he gets sexier with each passing day. Working in the hot sun with his muscles glistening with sweat, I could hardly keep my legs together. He knew I was watching him.

As I got closer, he called out to me. "Take a picture, it will last longer."

I didn't need a picture when I had the real thing to rub up against. We had sex all over his daddy's ranch, but never in pure daylight where we could get caught. I didn't know if it was all the romance novels I had been reading, but I was feeling adventurous and wanted to play with my man.

As I parked the ATV, he strutted over to me and lifted me up into his strong arms. It was like hugging a solid mass of muscle. I loved the feeling of him against my body. I didn't know if was my euphoric feeling of getting into Yale, or Jagger himself, but he was fucking hot and I wanted to just devour him. I breathed in his manly mix of Jagger. His smell was my undoing. I fucking loved it. I could lick him up and down, all day long. His eyes, alluring and hypnotizing, drew me in closer. By the way Jagger was looking at me, he was just as ravenous for me, as I was for him. I loved him . . . so much.

"For a minute there, I thought I was hallucinating. Are you actually on one of my daddy's ATVs?" he asked, as he kissed my neck and left a trail of kisses, leaving me wanting more.

"Actually, I'm in your arms at the moment and wishing we were fucking," I responded.

His eyes brightened as if I secretly guessed what he was thinking. I continued, "So, getting back to your question, I'm not on an ATV."

"I stand corrected," he responded. "Thank you for clearing that matter up for me, and yes, my love, I wish we were making love, you dirty girl. I swear you need a good hiding."

"Why? Are you volunteering?"

"Yes. So what did I do to deserve a visit from you? Or are we going to keep playing this game?"

"You know you love it."

"I do, baby, and I love you, but I don't think it's the reason why you drove out here, so what's up?"

"This."

I pulled out my letter from my pocket and showed it to Jagger. He nearly dropped me on my ass from shock. I remained in his arms, and my legs wrapped around his waist, as he silently read on.

"You got in? You really are going?"

"Hell yeah! I'm going. It says it right there." I pointed to the letter. "I'm going to Yale, and you are coming with me. Don't you see, Jagger? This is just the beginning of our new life together."

He dropped the letter to the ground and placed me down along with it. He turned away from me and walked over to the fence. With his head down low, I quietly asked him what was wrong.

"You don't know, do you? How could you stand here looking all happy about leaving our home? When you first told me about Yale, I didn't think you were serious about it. I really thought it was your way of messing with your parents. Now here you stand and show me an acceptance letter from one of the most elite schools in the country, and behaving as if I should just be okay with it. What the fuck, Ten! How could you do this to me? And more importantly to us?"

He kicked the fence post with his boot and screamed out in pain. His cries made me step back for a moment. I had never seen him angry before, not like this, and not directed at me.

"Jagger, listen to me, please. This letter represents our future. My future with you. Don't you see? It's a new beginning. A chance for us to be out on our own and living the life we want to have."

"No, Tenley. This is your life, not mine. I thought you understood. My life is here on this ranch. This is my future. The only fucking future I want. Jesus, Tenley! I had hoped you would have wanted to share it with me. This ranch is my life. You, Tenley Faith Fairchild, are part of that. How could you think for one second I would want anything else?"

His words were breaking my heart. I couldn't believe I didn't see this coming. I had a difficult choice to make here, and deep down I knew my choice would break his heart, but what about mine? I'm caught in an impossible situation, and I feel defeated. I could stay here and live his dream with him on this ranch, or I can break free and follow my dreams. If I said yes to him now, I fear I would only resent him later, and then where would that leave us?

"I'm sorry, Jagger," I said to him, "but I'm going. It's clear we want different things for our future, and it's not in each other's world. We don't fit, not anymore. We were the perfect puzzle, and now we're just broken pieces."

"You're going? That's it? You just kick me out of your life as If I never meant anything to you? I love you, Ten. You are going to stand here and say we don't fit in the other's world? You are my world! My entire world! Why can't you see that? We can have it all. I am going to take this ranch further than my father ever could, and at the top of my list is to marry you. You are meant to be a Parrish. To think anything else is just irrefutable. Don't break my heart baby. Please stay with me."

The look in Jagger's eyes was slicing my heart to shredded ribbons. I knew my decision was breaking him, but I couldn't say no to Yale, not even for him.

"I'm sorry, Jagger. I love you. Something tells me I will always love you. If nothing else, please believe that, but this is your dream, not mine. I'm so sorry."

"No! Stop saying that, Ten. This is our dream . . . and I know you want this. You're just messing with your parents to piss them off. Okay, you won. Once again you showed your mother you are so much more than how she sees you. Baby, I love you. Please don't do this. Give yourself some time to really think what you leaving means and the impact it will have on our relationship."

"You're wrong Jagger," I hissed at him. "This is not about my parents, and I have nothing to prove to them. My mother may not be on board with my choice of career, but she would never be as cruel as you are being right now. And for your information, my father and Jamie know already, and they couldn't be happier for me. I just want out. This is my life! And I will live it on my terms."

"What the fuck, Tenley! I'm being cruel? That's fucking rich coming from you. You are standing here on my ranch and telling me that I no longer have a say to anything that concerns you, or us. I am your boyfriend, your future husband who loves you. Please, Tenley, you are cutting me to the quick here. Don't. Leave. Me. You see where you are standing? Look over to the horizon, you see our spot? How many nights did we spend making love under the stars, planning our future, and chasing the dream of a life we both want? I just don't understand you at all. And now in the wake of your independence, I get left behind with a broken heart. What about Shane? Or Wendy? I guess they lose too?"

"Stop it Jagger, please stop." I held my hand over my breaking heart. "You know I love them too. It's not fair to make me feel guilty over something I want for my life. If you know Wendy at all, you would know she would never ask me to stay or hold me back from my dreams, and that goes double for Shane. Have I been that blind? I thought you would be happy for me . . . for us. Why is the one person who I've given myself over to completely and unconditionally doubting me now? You're not the only one asking why?"

28

"What if Jamie gets sick again? Would you leave him? And the ranch you hate so much to follow your dreams?" he said, mockingly. A tone he never used. The bitter taste of his harsh words was making my stomach churn.

"Oh my god! How the fuck can you even say that to me? I love my brother more than anything, even you Jagger. He's strong and healthy. You're angry, I get that, but saying these things to hurt me back is just cruel. I have faith he will continue to stay in remission. I never said I hated my family's ranch. This is the only home I know and love, but just because I want more for my life, doesn't lessen the feeling I have for my home. And for you to involve Jamie into something private between us is incredibly unfair. I'm asking you to leave my brother out of this."

"I can't Tenley. He's my best friend, and Shane too. Brothers to me, and I can't just stand here and pretend that you leaving us is okay. You're decision here today does affect your brother, don't fool yourself thinking it doesn't. I look around to this beautiful land that God has given us, and then to my hands that will work this land and make it prosper for all good things to come. This is our life, Tenley. Ranching is in our blood, and we are planning to run this ranch as partners. It's what we always wanted."

"I know, Jagger, and that's what makes what I will say next so hard for you to hear, and to accept. Please listen to me. The four of us have been the perfect shape. Once upon a time, we did fit perfectly together. Our friendship has met everything to me, and when you and I decided to be more than friends, I thought I couldn't get any happier than I already was. You were my first love, but I have to pick me now and put me first. I love you, Jagger . . . always and forever. Love doesn't come down to ultimatums. Love should be the easiest thing you do in life, and it has been for me since the day you told me you loved me. If you love me the way you say you do, then don't ask me to choose."

"How did I not see it?" he asked.

"See what?"

"You are so spoiled. So incredibly selfish and absorbed. You didn't have it that rough, Ten, if anything, you had it way too good. Your parents have given you everything you could ever want, and yet it still isn't enough for you. No one is perfect, and that is a lesson you better get straight sooner rather than later."

"Are you done?" I asked Jagger.

"I haven't even started. I love you, Tenley, so fucking much. Next to Shane and Jamie, you've been my best friend. You are the one and only that occupies space in my head and heart. From the moment you could ride, I remember your father saying you had natural fire flowing through your veins. 'A free spirit,' all the ranch hands used to call you. 'Tumbleweed' was the perfect nickname for you. You just loved to run and soar on the back of Jazzy. Why can't you feel that free with me? I love you, baby, and I thought you loved me."

"Jagger, I do love you, but I have to love me too. Why can't you understand that? I want more than this ranch. I want to see the world and live in it on my own terms."

"Fine. Go, Tenley. Go out in the big fucking world and be the selfish bitch you are. Get the fuck off my ranch. You are no longer welcomed here."

"You don't mean that. Jagger, please, don't send me away. Not like this."

My tears were falling faster than I could wipe them away. I wanted Jagger to hold me. How did we get here? We were perfectly happy a couple of hours ago, and now we were thousands of miles apart from each other.

"What other choice do I have, Tenley? You are the one that is leaving me, not the other way around. Go! Go be a fancy lawyer in your big world. I hope it makes you happy, because at the end of the day, that's all you may have left. Now. Get. The. Fuck. Off. My. Ranch."

Shattered . . .

"I love you. I'm sorry," was all I could say. I wasn't sure if he even heard me say those words to him. I was crying so loud and my voice was breaking in between, just like my heart.

Before he could say another word, I ran for the ATV and sped away recklessly, leaving my helmet to fall to the ground. Jagger screamed out for me, but I kept driving until I got back to the main house. I parked the ATV and sped off into my Jeep. I cried all the way home, and just before turning onto my property, I turned around and went the opposite direction. I had to go to my thinking place, which was still on my property but miles away from the main house. My father had a fishing cabin near the river. It wasn't a shack by any means. It was a huge one bedroom cabin that he had built when I was around ten years old. He used to tease my mother that he needed a place to go to when they argued. The only thing is . . . they never argued. They would have what they called spats, and usually over something so stupid they would end up laughing about it.

I was the fighter in our family. Constantly disagreeing with my mother about my hair, my clothes, everything. We were oil and water, my father used to say. How right he was. This cabin held the best memories I had of Jagger. I lost my virginity in this cabin. When his grandfather died suddenly, Jagger and I came here to be alone. I lit a fire and held him as he cried for hours. This is where Jagger and I declared our love for one another. Sealing a commitment between us and making a pact to be best friends forever.

I found the hideaway key under the flower pot and let myself in. I wasn't going to cry, so I decided to drink my sadness away by breaking into daddy's liquor cabinet. I had my pick. I went in hard, why settle? The more I numbed my body, I knew it would mask the hurt in my heart.

Hours had gone by, and I was alone. After my third beer and another shot of Tequila, I fell asleep for a while only to be woken up by a loud bang on my door. *Jagger!* It had to be him coming out to apologize and make us right again. I stumbled my tipsy body to the door, only to find Shane standing on the other side of it.

"Hey beautiful," he said so sweetly. One look from Shane, and I let the tears flow again. He instinctively picked me up and held me in his arms. I buried my face into the crook of his neck. My tears were like a faucet that couldn't be shut off. After how I left Jagger, I knew I shouldn't feel sorry for myself, but Shane holding me made me feel wanted and protected.

"Now, now. It can't be that bad. Dry your tears and talk to me," he said.

I stopped my crying and asked him how he found me out here. He laughed.

"Does a fish need water to survive? Of course I knew you were here. It wasn't that hard, beautiful girl. You always come here to think, or when you're fighting with Jagger."

"You can't fight with someone that you no longer have a relationship with. We broke up today. It's over. He hates me."

"Impossible. He doesn't hate you. He's just damn angry with you right now, but hate is not an emotion he knows or will ever know when it comes to you."

"So he called you after I left?" I asked him.

"He did. Jagger called me. He was pretty torn up."

"Where is he?"

"He's out. He's probably licking his wounds like you are right now. Come on. I'll take you home."

"No, Shane. I'm not going home. I'm staying here. Will you please stay with me? I don't want to be alone anymore. Please say yes, and don't leave me." *God, I sounded needy and pathetic.*

"Leaving you is the last thing I want to do, Tenley. I love you with all of my heart, I always have." The tone of Shane's voice shifted into something I had never heard before.

"I love you too, Shane. You're one my best friends." I watched him as his body language changed. He looked so serious.

"I don't think you understand what I'm telling you, baby," Shane whispered.

Baby? Why is he talking like this? Only Jagger calls me that.

"My feelings go way beyond friendship, and now that you and

Jagger are over, maybe I will finally have my chance to show you how much you mean to me. I know how I must sound right about now. How could I even think of betraying my best friend? The truth is, I can't hold it inside any longer. It's as if fate has finally stepped up and now this is my one shot to tell you how I feel. I love you, Tenley. Not a friendship love, I mean crazy, stupid love. The kind of love that I will lay my life down for you love. I can't believe I'm doing this right now, but I have to. I was so afraid to tell you the truth and fear you may reject me. I had so many chances to tell you, but once you fell for Jagger, I thought I would never get my chance. He's like a brother to me. We have an honor code, a line you never cross, but fuck it. I can't let you go again."

He loves me?! No way. My brain is fuzzy with Tequila waves sloshing around up there. Shane's my friend . . . my best friend. I'm drunk and not hearing him right.

"Shane, you're my best friend. I've already destroyed Jagger today, please don't make me hurt you too."

"You won't, baby, I promise my heart is safe. I love you. Please give me a chance to show you how much."

His hands were cupping my face and drawing me closer to his lips. As soon as I felt them on mine, electricity shocked my body, surprising me and knocking me off balance.

"Open up for me, baby. Please let me in. I love you so much."

Drunk or not, I kissed Shane.

I knew what I was doing and just didn't care.

Jagger had made it perfectly clear that he no longer wanted me if I didn't want what he wanted, so once again, I let my reckless side guide me. Jagger and I reached an impasse of our relationship I never thought was possible. His words replayed in my mind, as I took in the beautiful man in front of me. Here was Shane, willing to do anything to make me happy. I let my inhibitions go and gave him what he desired most . . . me.

He swiftly had my shirt off and slowly made his way to unbuttoning my jeans. My hands found his, and I said, "Stop!"

What the hell was I doing? I was living up to everything Jagger accused me of being. *How is this even happening?* A few hours ago, I was happy and looking forward to beginning my new adventure with Jagger, and now I'm about to bed his best friend, our best friend.

"Shane, this is wrong. We can't do this. Jagger is like a brother to you, and you to him. I love him, Shane. I'm in love with him. This is wrong. I can't do this."

He continued to kiss me, touch me, awakening all of my senses.

What he said next stunned me into silence. "Tenley, he never has to know. Please give me tonight to show you how much I love you, and if in the morning when you wake and your heart is still leading you to him, then this will be as far as it goes. It will remain between you and me. I swear I will never tell him."

"How will I ever be able to look him in the eye again? Or you for that matter?" I asked.

He ignored me and slid his hand inside of my jeans and straight toward my panties. I was wet for him. I couldn't believe my traitorous body. I belonged to Jagger, and here I was giving myself over to Shane so willingly. He never stopped kissing me. He was everywhere. His fingers were gently rubbing my clit. Every instinct in my body was screaming at him to stop, but then his fingers fucked me again, and I was screaming out my first orgasm. His lips were on mine. His tongue was invading my mouth as if it belonged there. He tasted like sweet mint and smelled incredible. I could feel his dick get harder and harder against my body. I closed my eyes and let Shane take my body to the edge again, but before I could experience yet another high, he stopped.

"Open your eyes, Tenley, and look at me. Tell me to stop, and I will. I want you so badly, but it's up to you baby, what do you want?"

Looking deeply into my eyes, he saw my answer. I kissed him back and let Shane make love to me. He quickly ripped his shirt off and his boxers and jeans followed. He undid my bra and practically tore my panties from my body.

"Condom," I whispered. He had one in his wallet and quickly covered his heavy erection with it. I closed my eyes as Shane entered me. He held my hands to the bed and parted my knees with his own. He was big. I gasped as he entered my body and then my eyes closed again and relished the pure pleasure he was giving me. Over and over again, our bodies were joined and we became one.

"Open your eyes, baby. Please look at me as you come with me buried deep inside of you," he whispered.

I did what he asked of me as he took me deeper and faster. I screamed out his name as the walls of my vagina tightened around his cock. I don't know who came first, but I was slipping into a blissful oblivion. I had just made love to my best friend and betrayed not just Shane, but Jagger. And Jamie! *What will my brother think? God! I feel so fucking ashamed.* My heart belonged to Jagger. I never questioned it. Shane was a brother to him and a best friend to me. Now this act shared between us had now changed us forever.

This wasn't on Shane. This was my fault. I could have said no, but I didn't. Did I want to hurt Jagger for rejecting me? I would hope I wasn't that cruel, but maybe I was. Shane held me for the rest of the night as I let him. Nothing would prepare us for what happened next . . .

"Get up!" I heard as the door slammed shut.

My head was spinning and my stomach was retching. I drank way too much Tequila last night. Even in my dazed state, I couldn't miss the angry form of Jagger Parrish standing above me, with a shotgun pointed directly at Shane.

"What the fuck, man? You! Here with my woman. I'm going to kill your betraying ass."

Still naked, Shane leaped out of the bed and threw his boxers on. I stayed where I was under the thin sheet that served as my only barrier from Jagger and his rage. He looked at me with disgust. How could I blame him? It's exactly how I felt.

"Calm down, Jagger. This is not what it looks like," Shane

pleaded.

"Are you fucking with me? How can I confuse what this is? I just caught you naked and in bed with Tenley, my fucking girlfriend! Am I wrong, brother? How the fuck do I confuse what my eyes just witnessed?"

"I love her, man. I couldn't let her leave without letting her know that. You said no to her. I saw my chance and took it. I'm sorry if I hurt you."

"Sorry? Oh my God! I can't believe this is happening. You love my girlfriend and you're sorry that you hurt me. Fuck you, Shane, and your apologies. We've been like brothers our whole life and for you to hurt me like this is just inconceivable to me. I can take just about anything, but you with Tenley is just something I will never be able to move past. What did you think was going to happen? Confess your feelings, pour out your heart to her, and she just magically chooses you? Well, wake the fuck up brother, because Tenley is a cold, selfish bitch. And now add whore to the list! She only chooses Tenley, and the hell with the rest of us. Fuck you, and fuck her. You two deserve each other."

Whore. He called me a whore. I stayed where I was in disbelief as to what I just heard Jagger call me. It was then that Shane charged at Jagger, knocking the shot gun out of his hand. They were entangled with each other. Fists were flying as they hit the other. Shane was screaming at Jagger to take back his hurtful words, but Jagger remained silent and continued to fight Shane. They nearly measured the same in height and weight. I doubted one could take out the other. Jagger swayed to the right, but missed the next attack from Shane. Shane lost his balance and Jagger delivered one final blow to his jaw, and slamming Shane's body down to the ground.

"Fuck you Shane! I loved you! How could you do this to me? And why my girl? Why motherfucker . . . why?" You could hear Jagger's pain with every word spoken.

At that moment of clarity, I wasn't even hurt anymore. I was everything he said I was. After what I did with Shane, I didn't deserve either one of them in my life, let alone one ounce of happiness. But after all that, I still tried.

"Jagger! Wait, please." I scrambled out of bed and quickly got dressed. I ran after him, but he was already gone.

Oh my god. Oh my god. What did I do? What the hell am I going to do now? I paced around with nervous energy. I was running on pure adrenaline now. Shane was now up on his feet and wiped the blood away from his mouth. The sight of him hurt made my stomach retch. My entire body was shaking, and then I was throwing up with Shane behind me holding my hair back. I emptied my stomach and when I had nothing left to expel from my aching body, he carried me back into the cabin.

"I'm so sorry, Tenley. Let him cool off and then I'll talk to him," Shane said.

"And what will you say? 'Sorry I fucked your girlfriend?' You'll be lucky if you get past his front door. This was a mistake, Shane, and I will never forgive myself for hurting him like that, or you for that matter. Don't you get it? I used you last night to make me feel better about my decision to leave Wyoming. I'm everything Jagger accused me of."

"Stop it, Tenley. I don't see it that way at all. I love you, and if you give yourself a chance, I know you can love me too."

"I do love you, Shane, but not in the way you want me to. I'm so sorry I did this to us. I compromised our friendship, and destroyed your relationship with Jagger. You deserve so much better than me. I'm not worthy enough to be called your friend. I hope one day you can forgive me for what I've done here today."

I left him there and drove my betraying ass home. Jamie was waiting for me with a beer in hand. I stepped up on the porch and he handed me one. He knew. Jagger must have told him, or Shane called him. The way he was looking at me made me sink lower in my shame.

Jamie said to me, "Go on. Take a sip, it looks like you need one. Or did you get your fill last night?"

Now my circle of hell was complete. He didn't say the words, but he didn't have to. I had just slept with his best friend and betrayed the other. He finished his beer and reached for my hand. I didn't take it at first, and then his eyes softened. No matter what, Jamie was my brother, my hero. He had to forgive me. It's in the handbook for siblings.

He said, "For what it's worth, I am very sorry. If I would have kicked his ass on the day I caught you two together, I may have saved you all this hurting you are going through now. I'm your brother. It's my job to protect you and defend you, even when you fuck up."

"Gee thanks, bro. You should have heard him, Jamie. Jagger said so many cruel things, too hurtful to repeat. He even talked trash about you."

My brother took my hands in his and tried to smile, but he wasn't the best when it came to hiding his feelings.

I asked, "What is it? What are you not telling me?"

"My cancer is back."

"No! You're in remission, and you've been doing so well. What the hell, Jamie? Have you been lying to me? Did Jagger know all this time? Is that why he said what he said? Oh my God! He knew. You all fucking knew, and you didn't tell me."

"Will you calm down and listen to me? It's complicated, Tenley."

"What's complicated about it? You're sick again, and I have failed you. I was the one that saved you, Jamie, and now after years of remission, you swig back a beer and tell me your cancer is back?"

"Tenley, please Tumbleweed, sit with me and we will talk this out."

He reached for my hands, but I pushed at his chest, nearly making him trip. I ran from him. I couldn't stand to look at my brother. I trusted him above all others to tell me the truth. *He was better. He looked like Jamie. How could he be so sick inside?*

I ran as quickly as my feet could take me. It was no secret what

I would do next. I saddled up Jazzy and took off like a rocket. I trained Jazzy. I taught her to know me and react the way I needed her to be. My horse knew I needed to fly, and that's exactly what we did. I worked her hard up and throughout the terrain that led me to my thinking spot. She was panting between her breaths, and needed to rest. We stopped by the river where she could get a drink, and me? Time to think.

I sat there and stared out into the darkening sky. The sun was getting ready to go to sleep for the night. I had been gone all day. It wasn't as if anyone would be concerned about me being gone anyway.

Jamie was right. *I fucked up . . . big time.* I deserve this pain I'm feeling right now. It can't even come close to what Jagger must be feeling. I was so lost in my thoughts, I didn't hear him behind me.

"You need to pick a better hiding spot."

"You scared the shit out of me."

"Doubtful, baby sister, you knew I would come for you. And I did. I just wanted you to take some time to sort out your shit. Have you done that yet?"

"Go away," I said.

"Not a chance, baby sis. Come on, let's go home. You're lucky it was me that found you and not daddy. You know the parents hate when you take off without telling them."

"Lucky for me, they have you to keep me in check."

"Are you done yet? Because I'm ready to take it. Let me have it Tenley, practice those pre-lawyer skills on me. You know you want to hand me my ass. It's not like I wanted to be sick. I'm so sorry you are hurt, but me being sick doesn't give you a free pass to be irresponsible, especially on this fucking ranch where you can get hurt."

"Watch your mouth," I retorted.

"You first."

All the fight was out of me, and my brother gave me a much needed hug.

"I'm so sorry Jamie. I know you are ashamed of me," I said.

"Never. No matter what, Tumbleweed, that is one feeling I will never have when it comes to you. They will get over it in time. You're my sister. I will always have your back."

"I know."

We rode back to the main house in silence. I was wrecked. Life pretty much continued on after that. After Jamie and I talked the next day, I was ready to simply walk away from school and stay with him, but he wouldn't hear of it.

Days turned into weeks and still Jagger refused my calls or visits, and I refused Shane's. The day I was set to leave, Shane finally managed to see me. We walked down to the barn and took the horses out for a ride.

"I'm sorry, Shane," I said to him.

"I'm sorry, too, but not for what we shared. I will never be sorry for loving you, Tenley, and finally making love to you. I'm only sorry for hurting Jagger, and that will be a wound that will hurt for a long time to come."

"Have you seen him?"

"I have, and yet I'm still walking and breathing."

"Don't make jokes, Shane."

"I'm not. He and I have talked. I told him everything and lived to walk another day. He may never get past on how much I hurt him, but he doesn't hate me. He said we've been brothers for too many years, and next to Jamie, I'm the only one he's got. That horrible scene at the cabin was just his anger talking for him. I deserved every punch to my gut, but you didn't deserve the words he spoke. They were vile, and believe me, he knows it. I reminded him with a punch to his jaw. After that, we nursed his wound with a six pack, maybe two, I lost count."

"I'm happy to hear that, Shane. He can hate me forever, but you, no way. I can't be the one responsible for tearing you apart from one another. I still struggle to look at myself in the mirror."

"You're not the only one, but please stop being so hard on yourself. Tenley, I love you. I always will. I want to be with you more than words can say, but I'm smart enough to know that you don't feel as I do. I knew that going in and I still crossed the line. Jagger was right about one thing. Ranching is our life. It flows through our veins. We know nor want anything else. I just got caught up into the fantasies I've been playing out in my head. Maybe I thought in some crazy realm of the universe, you would choose me. You can't blame me for trying. I will never regret taking my chance to be with you. No matter what happens with the three of us, please don't leave with the burden of guilt weighing you down. You will always be my girl . . . my best girl."

"Thank you, Shane. I don't deserve you, but thank you."

"Yes, you do and you'll find your way, beautiful girl. I don't know what is waiting for you beyond the protective gates of this ranch, but whenever you decide to come home, our friendship will be here waiting for you."

"Promise?"

"I promise," Shane said, reassuringly.

"Are you ready, Tenley?" Daddy asked as he took in the scene in front of him.

"I'm ready, daddy. Shane was just leaving."

I turned back to Shane and hugged him once more.

"Take care of you." I said.

"Take care of you," he repeated.

My mother hugged me and quickly went back into the house. She never allowed anyone to see her cry, but we all knew she was in her room with a box of Kleenex close by. It was her job to be strong for us. Jamie and I never teased her, we knew it was her way. I thought it was hard saying goodbye to my brother, but seeing Shane again was way worse. He just reminded me of the past few weeks and all of the hurt I have caused. That wasn't his intention, but it is what it is. No matter how hard he tried to convince me about Jagger, the truth was the truth. I hurt him . . . bad. With all communication cut off, I had to believe it was what Jagger wanted. We were over. . . really over. I didn't need any more signs to tell me otherwise.

41

My dad wanted to wait with me at the bus station, but I let him off the hook. I didn't want him to drive me to the airport. That would mean I would have had to talk and talking was the last thing on my mind. He didn't say much, but only to see the assurance in my eyes. He wanted to know if this is what I really wanted. After hurting Jagger the way I did, I never wanted anything more than to just run. I sat there alone in my thoughts and double checked my bag and made sure I had my ticket. *You're doing the right thing*, I repeated to myself.

And then he was here. Standing in front of me was Jagger Lucas Parrish. He looked as if he didn't sleep for weeks. His hair was overgrown, and he sported the sexy five o'clock shadow. I'd never seen him with hair on his face, a look I could get used to. His eyes were glazed over, but anger still was behind them. Why was he here? I thought he hated me. I remained where I was as he walked over to me.

"What are you doing here?" I asked.

He struggled for his words until he reached for my hands and looked into my eyes. He was so beautiful. His dark hair had natural shimmering highlights. Jagger had tanned skin from days of working out under the hot sun. His muscles rippled with every move he made. I couldn't help but feel a physical reaction every time he was in my close proximity.

"I've been asking myself that same question all morning, but yet here I am. I missed you at your house, and by the time I got there, your mother told me where to find you. She looked almost hopeful that I might be able to change your mind. Tenley, can I change your mind?"

"Jagger," I whispered.

"Don't say my name like that. It makes me want more. It gives me hope."

"I thought you hated me."

"I do, but deep down I love you more. You shredded me with a thousand blades when I found you with Shane. How could you so easily give yourself over to him when just hours before you were mine?"

"I'm so sorry."

"You're sorry? You better come up with something better than sorry. You ripped out my fucking heart. A betrayal that I will never forget. You hurt me in the cruelest way possible. You fucked my best friend. A brother to me. Why, Tenley? Why? Explain it to me. And if you say you did it because you were drunk, then I'm really going to lose my shit."

"Jagger, what do you want me to say here? I was drunk, yes I'll admit, but I wasn't that drunk enough to know that I didn't realize what I was doing. Shane didn't force me, and I knew it was wrong, but I fucked him anyway. Is that what you want to hear? You refused me, so I let him take my body and be in the same places you were in first. It happened, and I knew once it did, I would never forgive myself. You would never look at me the same way again. I only proved that by being with Shane, I was everything you said I was. 'Whore,' right? Yeah, I added it to the list."

"I called you those names to hurt your feelings, Ten. I was hurt so deeply and never felt so betrayed in all of my life. You are not a whore. You will never know how sorry I am for calling you that. I told my father what I said, and he just about broke my ribs for calling a woman that disgusting word. I'm sorry and feel nothing but regret. You are my world, or at least I hope you will be again. I couldn't get past the fact that you so easily wanted to leave me. I get it now. I know you were meant for so much more than the ranch, but do you have to go so far away? You can pick another school and at least we could still see each other and try to be together. We could live in the city. You can practice law, and I'll work the ranch. It can work, baby, but you have to be in this with me."

"You still want me? After what I did with Shane?"

"Shocking, right? Yes, Tenley, I still want you. I was angry beyond reason. Seeing you with Shane burnt a forever image in my brain and tore my heart out, but I can't hate him. I can't hate you. I

43

want to believe I can forgive you both, but in order for me to do that, you have to stay. I'm asking you to not get on that plane today. Please be with me . . . stay with me. You told me you loved me every single day since we decided to be together. You never stopped telling me or showing me the depths of your love. I'm asking you to prove it to me right now and just don't get on that bus to take you to the airport. Please, Tenley, stay."

He continued, "Choose me . . . choose us. I promise you won't regret it."

Jagger got on one knee and pulled out a box from his pocket. I nearly fainted when I realized what he was doing.

"Marry me Tenley. You have my heart as easily as I have yours. Please don't break me again. I love you. Marry me. Love me. Stay with me. Share my life with me. All you need to do is say yes. I swear I will love you with all that I have and promise your life will be as adventurous as you are dreaming it to be."

He asked me to marry him. He promised me that he loved me more than anything, and I was worth giving a second chance to. This is getting confusing.

"My heart says yes. But . . . " I said.

"Then that's what you need to trust. Please, Tenley . . . stay."

"I do love you, Jagger, more than myself. In a perfect world, you would be getting on this bus with me, but that's not you. I can't expect you to even change one thing in your future's plan. It would be incredibly unfair and selfish of me to ask that of you. You accused me of being selfish and you were right. Please let me prove to you that I can put you first. For that reason alone, I can't marry you, and you shouldn't want to marry me. We would only resent each other in the end, and that's something I will never be able to live with."

The bus came to a stop, and the driver stepped out. He announced to the waiting passengers to begin boarding. Jagger was still on his knee and holding the ring box in his hand. Tears were falling down his rugged and exhausted face. I abruptly got up, and he stayed where he was.

"I'm so sorry, Jagger. I'm so sorry."

I grabbed my bag and stepped onto the bus. I went to the furthest seat I could find and sat there with my head buried in my hands. *I'm doing the right thing by leaving. He deserves so much more.* I said it over and over again.

By the time I found the courage to look out through the window, he was gone. The bus began to pull away, and I was on my way to begin my new life. I was everything Jagger accused me of. I was selfish. Absorbed in only myself and not caring what I was leaving behind. No, that wasn't true at all. I let him go. I set him free to begin again with someone who would be worthy of his love and wanted the life he wanted.

I wanted to stay for my brother, but he wasn't having it. I never wanted to leave Jagger. When I received my letter, I never considered how my relationship with him would change. Yes, I wanted more, but I wanted that with Jagger, and hoped we would be on the new road to our future. *And now it's just too late. What happened, happened, and I will live with my choices.*

Wendy and I talked through the night before I was set to leave. She knew me better than anyone. There was nothing I could get past her. She tried to change my mind, but I was firm with my decision. I wasn't ready for marriage. I was twenty two. A college graduate and leaving home once again to begin law school. I wanted to leave and not be judged for my decisions. Living life on the ranch was all I knew. Did it make me a bad person for wanting more from my life? I didn't think it did. Shane promised we would always be friends, and Jagger swore he could never move past from the hurt I caused him, but yet? He showed up and asked me to marry him. How could I? I not only hurt Jagger once, but then again when I refused his proposal. I returned his kindness with saying no and by leaving him once again.

I re-read my brother's letter over and over again until my eyes were so blurred from my tears, I couldn't see the words in front of me. *How could Jamie do this to me?* He refused me when I begged him to allow me to come home and be at his side during the time he had left. He said he wanted me to remember him on the day I left for school and not as a shell of a man dying in front of me. Now I get a letter five years later to ask me if I'm happy.

"Who the fuck does that to another person? Oh yeah, my brother does!" I screamed out for no one to hear me. "Yeah, I said it. You're not here to scold me, but your letter is detailing my mistakes in living color. Thanks for that, bro. So much for having my back."

I was angry, hurt, and way too hung over to entertain this any longer. I tossed the letter and wiped my tears. I made up my mind and decided not to give the letter or my past any more power over me. I was in and out of the shower within five minutes. I spent less time on choosing my outfit for the day.

"Yes! I think today calls for Freddy Mac. He is one of my favorite designers to wear. It's perfect for what I need today."

I slipped on my matching Jimmy Choo stilettos to complete my look. Oh Yeah! I was ready. On the outside, I looked good. Power suit, killer heels, and my take no prisoner attitude.

I love my choice. I chose my choice. If I say it enough times, maybe I'll believe it.

I paused for a moment in front of my floor length mirror and silently prayed that I could pull myself out of my darkness. *Don't give up, Tenley, the beginning is always the hardest.* Daddy always used to say that when we were training a new horse. He was always there for me to catch me when I fell, but encouraged me to get back up until the reluctant horse became my friend. I took one last look, and then I was off.

I couldn't afford to waste any more time. I had a job to get to.

CHAPTER 3

...decisions

I REACHED MY office by noon. Not too bad considering the condition I was in this morning. I grappled with the hangover headache, one of many consequences I will have to deal with today due to my reckless behavior.

My phone had gone off non-stop, no doubt after Tommy discovered I was gone. He was the last person I wanted to see right now. *I'm shamed enough. I don't need any reminders.* I reached the executive floor where a trio of efficient receptionists were waiting to greet me. They liked to speak in unison, kind of creepy if you ask me, but they are perfectionists at their jobs. Like robots.

Bot number one, I know as Cheryl. She is my go-to person when Roxy is occupied with the other thousand tasks I keep her busy with. Cheryl greets me with a Mocha Latte in hand, my messages in the other.

"Good afternoon, Ms. Fairchild. May I take your briefcase and coat?" she asked.

I simply nod and hand over my things and take my coffee and

messages from her.

"Ms. Fairchild, Mr. Steele would like to see you sometime today, and your calendar is cleared for the next hour before your meeting on the Kandinsky case."

"Okay, anything else?" I said as I made my way down to my office with Cheryl following closely behind.

"Yes, one more thing. You have a visitor in your office."

I stopped and turned around, nearly colliding with Cheryl. My skin heated and my heart pounded. *Please let it not be Tommy in there. I can't face him right now.* Of course, he's a client and friend, and he wouldn't be refused.

"Who is it, Cheryl?" I bit my lip and got myself in check. *I'm the tigress around here. Claws are always out.* I can't show this side to her, nor to anyone.

"It's a woman. A friend from home. She knew so much about you, I didn't think it would be a problem having her wait in your office. Is there, Ms. Fairchild?"

I do not answer her question and get right to the point. "Call up to Mr. Steele's office. Give him my apologies for the short notice of cancelling our meeting. Explain that something unavoidable has come up, and I am needed elsewhere. I will call him at a more convenient time. Have Roxy hold my calls until further notice. Hang my coat before you wrinkle it, and do not disturb me. Are we clear?"

"Yes, Ms. Fairchild," Cheryl answered, and made a mad dash through reception.

1, 2, 3, 4, 5 . . . I took a deep breath before entering and stepping inside my office. My eyes scanned the room and saw no one. My chair was facing the window to my spectacular view of the city below. I said "Hello," but heard no response back. I reached my desk and turned my chair to find it empty.

"What the hell is going on?" I questioned, and then I questioned no more when the presence behind me scares me nearly to death.

"Gotcha!"

"What the fuck!" I screamed out, nearly spilling my coffee.

"Watch your mouth, Tumbleweed. Is that anyway to welcome an old friend?" she asked with a devilish smile running along her face.

"Wendy!!! You nearly gave me a heart attack. How are you here in my office? I only spoke to you yesterday, or was it last night?" My brain is still fuzzy from my over indulgence. "You actually got on a plane and came to New York. I don't know what I find stranger? The shock of seeing you here in New York, or just the fact that you actually flew across the country."

"You want answers?"

"That would be nice."

"Give me a proper hello, and then we will talk. We have a lot to discuss."

I put my coffee down and hugged the woman who was like a second mother to me. It was a warm embrace, the kind I cherished and took with me when I left home all those years ago.

"Please, Wendy, have a seat. Can I get you anything to eat or drink?"

"I'm fine, Tumbleweed. Let's get down to it. Shall we?"

"Wendy, why are you here? All the times I invited you for a visit, you always refused, and now I walk into my office and you're here. Forgive me if I just take a moment to process all of this."

I sipped more of my coffee and tried to push down the raging headache that was pounding throughout my head right now.

"To answer your question, I'm here because you are not where you are supposed to be."

"Which is where? Wyoming? I don't live there anymore, and it is *not* where I am supposed to be."

I picked up my phone and summoned Cheryl to bring in my briefcase. She dutifully brings it and once again caters to Wendy, but Wendy politely refuses. I opened up my case and took out the FedEx envelope that contained Jamie's letter.

"Did you send this to me?" I asked.

Wendy's eyes roamed over the envelope in my hand, and they

said it all.

"Well? Did you send me a letter from my dead brother?"

"Yes, I did."

"Why? How could you do this to me, Wendy? You of all people knew how much I loved him. How could you pick the anniversary of his death to remind me of how much I have lost since he died? I never thought in all of my wildest dreams that you could hurt me like this. Why, dammit? Why did you do this?"

I threw the letter at her, hitting her in her chest. She just sat there quiet and reserved until I was done with my outburst. A trait of hers I always hated and resented. She would always let us vent, and when it was over, she would never react, just calmly speak. She was doing it right now. Processing what I just said, and it was making me increasingly angry.

"Are you finished?" she responded and waited for my answer.

"No, I'm not. You haven't answered my questions yet, so how could I be done?"

"I will answer you when you calm down and listen . . . just listen. Can you do that? Because if you can't, then this trip will truly be a waste of my time, and I would have let down the one person I vowed to help."

"I don't understand."

"Are you ready to listen?"

I sat up and leaned forward in direct line to Wendy. "Do I have a choice?"

"No, you don't."

"I'm not a child, Wendy."

"Then stop acting like one. Are you ready to talk?"

"Fine! Let's get this over with."

"Well that's a start. I can only assume by the condition of the letter that you have read it through and through and are left with many questions. I'm here to help you. I will do my best to answer your questions. It was never my intention to cause you any pain or suffering, Tumbleweed. He didn't want that for you, and neither do I."

"Wendy, I am not in need of any help. I'm fine. What gives you the impression that I'm not what I say? I was doing just fine on my own until this letter appeared yesterday. You're right, I read that letter multiple times, and I know what it says and what it means, but I can assure you that I'm fine. You can't change the past, Wendy, nor do I want to. No, I'm wrong. If I could, he would be here right now, but that's not how my story was written, now was it? I'm sorry you traveled all this way. Please allow me to buy you a first class ticket home."

I knew how I sounded, my stomach was coiling with my words. Hurting Wendy was the last thing I wanted to do, but seeing her here was taking me down a road I did not wish to travel on.

"Tenley, thank you for the offer, but when I leave New York, you will be leaving with me. This is not your home. This is your escape. You have been in your own witness protection program for the last five years, not allowing anyone in. That stops today. You have a family waiting for you to come home. They love you. They miss you. They need you."

"You are wrong, Wendy. The family I knew ceased to exist when I watched my brother get lowered into the ground. My parents were so lost in their grief, they didn't even know I was there. My mother closed herself off, and my daddy worked his ranch. I grieved alone . . . they grieved alone. We should have been together, but it's not what he wanted for me. He wanted me to finish school and make my dream come true. I made that promise to him, and I refused to let him down. If I spent every waking minute regretting and going over what I should be doing, or should have done, I would be at a dead end with no direction. You're wrong, Wendy, I'm doing just fine. Everything I do in this life and how hard I work is for him."

"He has a name, you know. Say it. Say his name aloud, and stop treating him like he doesn't exist."

"Stop it, Wendy."

"Stop what? Reminding you of what you left behind? Say his name."

"I know what I left behind, I don't need a detailed report of it. I have my mother to remind me weekly by a phone call. Did you know she called me yesterday? Broke me down, bit by bit, until I drank myself into numbness, resulting into another catastrophic mistake. Dammit, Wendy! I'm not doing this with you. I can't do this."

"Say his name," she asked again.

I remained silent, shut down, and fought back my tears.

"Jamie!" she screamed. "His name was Jamie. He was your big brother. He loved you more than anything in the world. Jamie. Jamie. His name was Jamie. James Brockton Fairchild. Your brother. Yes, my sweet girl, Say it! Say his name. The conundrum you find yourself in is sad. Losing Jamie was sad. A sadness never forgotten, not just by you, Tenley but for all of us. Say his name. You can't, can you? Because if you do, then you are allowing yourself to feel. Feel the love you have for him, or the loss you felt when he died. The anger that still lives inside of you because you weren't there. You were living your life thousands of miles away, while he was dying."

"Stop it! I can't hear any more of this. You are supposed to love me, Wendy! Why are you doing this to me?"

I wrapped my arms around my chest and let my tears fall down in front of her.

"Please stop," I said once more.

"No, Tenley, I can't. If I do, that would mean I'm going back on my word, and I will not break my promise to him."

"Like me Wendy? Is that what you were going to say?"

"Oh Tenley? Where is my girl? Come back to us, please? Don't you see sweetheart? Why the tears? It's because you are still feeling the same guilt you felt back then. You still feel it because you couldn't save him from something so powerful beyond any of our control. Cancer. It's an ugly word, and sadly, it invaded your family and took someone you love away from you. The reason for the letter you ask? It's really quite simple: your brother knew you better than anyone else. He knew you would take his death hard, but he never gave up hope on you finding the happiness you deserve. He wanted so many things for you, but he was running out of time. So he spent his last days penning letters to you and leaving me with instructions to carry them out. He did that . . . for you. Because he loved you that much. That's why I'm here, Tenley. I'm here to bring you home. Don't make me a liar. I have never broken a promise, so please don't make me begin today."

"You said 'letters,' so . . . you have more?"

"I do."

"Where are they? I want them, Wendy."

"With all I have just said, that's all you heard? Yes, there are more letters, but you are not ready to have them. They are in safe-keeping and will remain there until I feel you are ready for the next one."

"Why are you doing this to me Wendy?" The sound of my sadness was too hard for me to listen over my tears that were falling.

"Unbelievable! You keep asking the same question over and over again. I believe I just stated my reasons in living color. You ask why I'm doing this *to* you. No, Tenley, I'm doing this *for* you. You are so lost right now, and sadly, you don't even see it. Sure you have the career you wanted. The big office to reign in, but are you happy? Really happy? These things can be achieved, but where it matters most can only be found."

She walked around my desk and placed her hand over my heart.

"Don't you see, Tumbleweed? You are so closed off in here that you never get beyond the pain. You've built a fortress around you to keep the bad from getting in. It's a hurt none of us wanted to go through, but sadly that is not our reality. You lost your brother to something so much bigger than the both of you. You lost the love of your life, because it was your loss and pain that kept you from turning around and running toward him. This is why I sent Jamie's letter to you, because it was time. How many more years are going to go by before you face what drove you away in the first place? You chose wrong, baby girl. You need to come home. Make things right with your parents. Find closure in Jamie's death. Forgive yourself for living. Forgive yourself for surviving. You saved your brother once and gave him his life back. It is not your fault that he got sick again. You need to forgive yourself and find *you* again. Not this pale version you show here, but the real you. The girl we used to know but never stopped loving and hoping she would come back to us."

I got up and threw myself into Wendy's arms. I held her so tightly and cried. For the first time in a long while, I just cried.

"Say his name." she whispered in my ear as she still held me.

"Jamie," I whispered back.

"That's a start. I love you, Tumbleweed. I always have, and I always will."

"I love you, too. Wendy, I feel it in my gut that there's more to you being here than just my brother. Why am I needed home? You stated the obvious, but I'm a pretty good lawyer and I know when someone—even you—are not being truthful. Please don't blindside me again. If you want me to come home, I need more answers."

She brushed my hair off my face and stroked my cheek lovingly looking into my eyes like a mother would. She never had children of her own. She always used to say that she would share us with our parents, but we could easily be sent home and they could do the harder stuff. I still smile at that one because Wendy was always there for me, no matter how small or big my problems were. My mother was almost jealous, but I loved them both.

I waited for Wendy to speak. I gave her the time she needed, but her expression was pained. I wiped my tears as she placed her hands on my shoulders and looked directly into my eyes. I was preparing myself for the worse.

"Jagger needs you. There was an accident, and he's in a coma."

If I didn't feel the beats of my heart under my skin, I would have believed time had truly stopped and I was dead. *He's in a coma?* I knew I heard her the first time, but I asked again.

"He's in a coma?!? What kind of accident put him in a coma? Wendy, please?"

"Jagger and Shane were driving the horses up to the north ridge of the Parrish Ranch. It was a storm, a big one, and it was fierce. Hours earlier after they finished up at your place, and by the time they got the herd in on the Parrish ranch, they were in the middle of it. They were side by side until Jagger's horse threw him. He was thrown I don't know how many feet and rolled down into the embankment below. That basin is deep and lined with branches and rocks. It literally swallowed him up. Shane tried to reach him, but he fell further. It was hours before they found him. They got lucky. Some say it was Jamie, protecting him until help could arrive. Your mother calls him their guardian angel. When the storm had finally let up the search began. He was down by the river and nearly dead. He was pretty banged up with cuts and bruises all over his body. It is a miracle his body wasn't shattered by the fall. He only sustained a broken leg and some busted ribs."

"Why the coma? Did he hit his head on the rocks below?"

"He had hematoma on his brain after the fall, but that's healed by now. He's breathing on his own, but hasn't awakened yet. That was over three weeks ago. The doctors are hoping for a miracle."

"So, what? I'm the miracle? Are you thinking that if you bring me home and to him, that he will suddenly hear my voice, the angels will sing, and he will awaken?"

"Something like that," Wendy responded, shrugging her shoulders with not an ounce of doubt in her voice.

"Oh my God! You are waging on something you will not win. Even if this were to happen, how could you think he would even want me there? I broke his heart when I refused him, not once, but twice. I am the last person he would ever want help from."

"You're wrong again. He loves you. Never stopped. He told me so."

"He told you? When?"

"It doesn't matter on the when. Just know that he loves you, and you now have the second chance Jamie always wanted for you. Take it, Tenley. Stop running. Stop hiding. And come home. My plane leaves at six o'clock out of LaGuardia."

"Wendy, before I travel anywhere, I need some time to process all of this and speak with my boss. I have responsibilities here. I just can't leave on a whim. Will you give me that?"

"I can, Tenley, but you have to give me something in return."

"Wendy, you are not being fair. You just can't expect me to walk out of my life and go back to a place I no longer consider my home."

"Why? You've done it before. This should be easy for you."

"Now you're being cruel. Don't you ever think for one minute me leaving Wyoming was easy on me. Jamie practically forced me out of the state because he didn't want me to see him die. I would have given anything to stay. A phone call was made, and I was on a plane. I cried the entire time. A ranch hand greeted me at the gate. Where the hell were my parents when I needed them! I'll tell you, Wendy, they were gone. Wallowing in their own pain and leaving no room for me. I tried to be the good daughter, do what they wanted, but I was alone. You say I have a fortress around my heart? Well it doesn't take a fucking genius to figure out how it got there."

I continued, "As for Jagger . . . you say he needs me? The same man that you say still loves me, who shunned me at my brother's funeral. I spoke maybe ten words to Shane, and then I was back on that fucking plane. Not a plea to beg me to stay, just a wave from the door. Come home? To what Wendy? We all made decisions here. Jamie chose how he wanted to spend his last days, and they weren't with me. I wanted Jagger, he wanted the ranch. What the hell was I supposed to do? Just give up law school? I wasn't ready for that, and it was selfish of him to expect me to. If Jagger truly loved me, then he would have never asked me to choose."

"Will you wake the hell up, you stubborn girl!" Wendy was yelling. "Are we talking about the same story here? You seem to forget that he asked you to consider going to a closer school. No, I'm wrong. He begged you, but you refused. Your parents begged you to come home time and time again, but you refused them too. You flew home for one damn day for your brother's funeral. You think I don't see you? I see you all gussied up in your designer suits with the accessories to match, but it's all for show. This is not you. You're coasting through your day to day acting as if you have it all figured out, but you don't. You live alone and isolate yourself from everyone who loves you. Why? I just don't understand it. A once a year Christmas card is not going to cut it anymore. You can't be a runner forever. Your presence is needed at home, and you need to face the people you abandoned and are hiding from. You are not the only one that lost Jamie. We all did."

"Abandoned? Really, Wendy? I don't need a reminder on what I've lost in my life . . . And I'm not *hiding*! *I'm living* and doing the best I fucking can. Do you want to talk about abandonment? From Jamie, my parents, and Jagger . . . they all left me on my own. What the hell do you want from me?" I hissed at Wendy.

"I guess I touched a nerve didn't I? The truth always finds its way right to one's heart. You're only reacting this way because deep down you know I'm right. I'm sorry I had to be. Like I said, I have a plane to catch and it leaves in four hours. The choice is yours."

I remained at my desk and watched Wendy exit my office. My back was against the wall and I was so lost right now. *Jagger still loves me? How? After all of this time? Can I really go back home and face the two men that I hurt the most?* Shane and Jagger were my brother's best friends. They never minded me as the fourth wheel. Then one day, Jagger looked at me differently, and we fell in love. I hurt him so much by betraying him with Shane. We both hurt him, but it was I who destroyed him. I had to live with that shame and guilt for years now. *And now I'm being asked to save him? Be the answer to their prayers. How the hell can I even wrap myself around that?* Wendy was right, for all of it. My mother was too. I am hiding. Being alone is the only way I know how to be. It is my punishment that I chose a long time ago for myself.

I loved them.

I fucked them.

I left them.

And now with a delivery of a letter, a visit from Wendy, and an in your face wake-up call, I'm about to go home to face my past.

"Roxy . . . "

"Yes, Tenley," she responded quickly. I could only imagine what she thought as Wendy stormed out from my office.

"Please come into my office and bring your tablet."

She hurried in and sat down waiting for me to tell her what I needed.

"I don't have any time to waste. Listen carefully, because I will not repeat myself. Book me on the six o'clock flight out of NY/LaGuardia. Upgrade a coach ticket to first class for passenger Wendy Ann Manning, and book me next to her. Please call up to Mr. Steele, and ask him if I can meet with him in the next thirty minutes. With the Mills case wrapped up, I don't have anything pending on my calendar other than the Kandinsky brief. Any current cases will have to be handed off to Zoey until I have a return date. Then go to my apartment and pack my luggage. This is not a formal trip, so I will not require any dresses or suits. Pack me an assortment of pants, shirts, sweaters, sleepwear, more on the casual side. I have boots, warm socks, and I will also need a heavier coat. Tell my doorman to forward all my mail and deliveries here to the office. Got it?"

"I do, but I have one question."

"And that might be?"

"Where do I book your flight to?"

"Jackson Hole, Wyoming. I'm going home."

Those words tasted like vinegar coming from my mouth. I surprised myself, but thankfully Roxy didn't question me any further on the subject. For the next hour, I cleared my desk. I answered all my correspondence, and briefly filled in Mr. Steele. He was very supportive and understanding. I'd never taken one sick day, let alone a vacation. He told me to take as much time as I needed, and for that, I was grateful.

Nearly finishing up, I thought of Tommy. All day I avoided him like the plague. He called me non-stop, filling my inbox with his voicemails. *I am such a coward. He's my friend, my very best friend and once again I've fucked up.* After what I did with Shane, I vowed never to cross that line again, but it was pain over Jamie that clouded my judgment and made me throw caution to the wind.

"Should I call him?"

"Yeah, you should have."

I looked up and saw Tommy standing in front of my desk. Looking at me with angry cobalt eyes. Moment of truth.

"I didn't even hear you come in," I said.

"Clearly from the look on your face. Your assistant wasn't at her desk, so I let myself in."

He walked around my desk and pulled me up into his arms. Caging me in with nowhere to run.

"Why Tenley? Why did you run? I woke up this morning to a cold bed. No note. No calls. Did I fuck up? Because *you* came to *me* last night."

He loosened his hold on me, and I wrapped my arms around his waist, regretting this intimate gesture, but it was what I needed.

"Tommy, I am so sorry that I hurt you. Please believe me. Last night is all on me. I wasn't thinking clearly, and I should have never brought my problems to your doorstep." I said, as I stepped back from him. It was hard to even be in his proximity. He smelled delicious, and if I couldn't drink away my problems, I certainly could see myself fucking them away, and with Tommy.

"Tenley, you are my friend. You know what you mean to me and how much I care for you. I will be here for as many times as you need me to be, but don't act like I didn't know what last night was, because I'm not that fucking blind nor naïve. My eyes were wide open, but to wake up without you this morning is what I don't understand. You completely shut me out, and I want to know why."

"It's complicated and too long of a story. Please tell me that we are fine and when I get back from my trip, I will explain it all to you."

"Trip? Where are you going?"

"I'm going to see my family out in Wyoming. I don't know when I'll be back, but I promise to keep in touch with you and Zoey. Please, Tommy, this is all I'm capable of right now."

"Come here," he said. His eyes had now softened and my friend was back.

"I can't. Please don't look at me like that." I pleaded.

"How am I looking at you?"

"Like you love me."

"I do, you know. I have for a while now, and I think you know it too. Please come here. You don't always have to be so tough."

He opened up his arms for me and I walked right into his embrace. I was thanking God I still had a friend to hug.

"I'm really sorry, Tommy." I said, as my face was buried into his soft flannel shirt he was wearing. The smell of his leather jacket alone was intoxicating.

"I know. Look at me." He cupped my face and I had no choice but to look into his eyes. "I love you Tenley. I know what we are, and that's okay. Just know I will always be here for you if you need me to be. I won't ask any questions, because I know you well enough to know you are not ready to answer them. I'll be here waiting for you to return home to me."

"Tommy, please don't."

"Now what? What's wrong?"

"Don't make promises you can't keep or expect me to. It never works out the way you see it in your head, or feel in your heart."

"Oh baby, whoever hurt you must have done a real head trip on you. I would never make promises I don't intend to keep, so my heart is safe, don't you worry. Keep in touch."

He kissed me on my forehead and turned to leave. I really could take no more today, but the flash of what I called Lightning Zoey just flew into my office.

"I just came from my father's office. You're going where?" Zoey shrieked.

"I told you, Zoe, in my message. I'm flying out today to my hometown."

"You have a hometown? I thought you eat, sleep, and bleed out the big city. So where is this *hometown?* And why haven't you ever mentioned it to me before?"

"Everyone has a hometown, Zoey. I just chose to forget mine."

"If that's true, then why are you leaving?"

"Zoey, you make it sound like I'm never coming back. An old friend asked me to come home, so that's why I'm leaving, but I'll be back."

"Sure you will. Don't you remember when we watched that sappy Hallmark movie a few months ago? The girl's father died and she had to go home to settle the will, only to reunite with her high school boyfriend? Don't bullshit me, hooker! You never talk about your past, so that leads me to believe you have a pretty complicated one."

As I typed my last e-mail to my assistant, giving her instructions for the coming week, Zoey would not let up on me. I sighed and shut down my computer. I looked around and was pretty sure I took care of all my pressing matters on my desk. Grabbing my briefcase and coat from me, Zoey stopped me at the door.

"Are you going to tell me or not?" Zoey remained firm with her questions. No wonder she was the best fact researcher we had here at the firm. She never quit until she found the truth. The problem was, I wasn't ready to tell her mine.

"Zoey, please let me pass. I really don't have time to explain my sudden trip to you."

"That's just it Tenley, you never do. You are the most elusive person I know. You never talk about your past. So come on . . . what's up? I tell you everything."

"Oh my friend, I love you, but you have no filter and wouldn't know discretion if it bit you on your ass."

"Not true, girlfriend. When the assistant to Simmons up on the 8th floor had an affair with him, I didn't say a word to anybody."

"What? Simmons is having affair with his temp? He's married with four kids. What an asshole! I only hope to be his wife's divorce attorney, so I could bury his ass in court."

"Oops! You didn't know?"

"No! I didn't know, Zoey. You see? Discretion!"

"Okay, okay, I'm sorry. How long will you be gone for? You know I can't live without talking to you at least ten times a day. Did you call Tommy yet? You know he will worry. So where is this mystery hometown located? Do you need to go to the doctor and get shots first?"

"Seriously? It's not in a third world country. I'm going to Wyoming."

"Wyoming!!! You probably won't even have cell service up there."

"I think Jackson Hole has modernized over the years. If not, I'll call you from a land line."

"What the hell is a land line?!?" Zoey threw her hands up in the air. We both laughed out loud.

I finally managed to say goodbye to my friend and escaped with four tackle hugs. I told her that Tommy already knew about my travel plans, but not to press him for information. I would call them both when I knew more.

Judging by my many suitcases, Roxy packed me enough to last me a month or more. She never mastered the art of packing. I arrived to the airport with less than an hour to spare. My bags were checked, and I made my way to my departing gate. As I got closer, I saw Wendy chewing her fingernails, probably thinking I wouldn't show, but saying no to her was something I could not easily do. Her eyes brightened when she saw me approach.

"You're here," she said, not quite believing it was me. She then wrapped me up into a hug. She grabbed her carry-on, and we boarded the plane. We took our seats in first class. Wendy was giddy with delight. At least if I had to endure a long flight, we would be comfortable.

She asked, "Ready?" as the cabin doors closed.

Not sure how welcomed I would be once I arrived back home in Wyoming, but my mother did ask me to come home to them. I miss my father too. I can't wait to hug him and then see Jazzy. *Will my horse even recognize me?* She will probably throw me off. An animal never forgets and sadly, I hurt her too when I left.

Nudging her arm, I looked back over to Wendy and whispered, "I am."

The take-off was smooth, and although I swore off alcohol, I was in desperate need for a drink, a strong one. I ordered a double Hendricks, getting a glare in return from my travel partner.

"What? I'm old enough for a drink, please refrain from the judgments," I said as my throat burned with the liquid numbing my throat.

"I didn't say anything! Oh boy, for a lawyer, you are so defensive."

"I don't mean to be. I'm just nervous. When I woke up this morning, this is not how I envisioned my day panning out."

"So what did you expect? A romp in the hay is not the answer to your problems. I would have thought you learned that tough lesson already."

"Oh. My. God." *How the hell does she do this?* I thought as she kept going on.

"Now, don't you go bringing the good Lord into this. He didn't make you give up the cookie, now did he?"

"Wendy, I am not even going to dignify your offensive and judgmental comments on my life. What I do behind closed doors and who I choose to spend time with is none of your business. You are way out of line."

"Seriously? I was right? Hell, I was just razzing you. I didn't think that actually happened, so spill Tumbleweed: Who was it?"

"I'm going to sleep. Wake me when we land."

"Oh come on, we're just getting to the good part. You can't leave me hanging now."

"Fine! What do you want to know? If I tell you, then will you be quiet for the remainder of the flight? I have a headache, and you chattering about my sex life is not helping it." I gritted my teeth as I warned Wendy off. She smiled, or smirked, either one was just agitating me even further.

"Well?" She wasn't backing down.

"I love you, you know I do, but I forgot how irritating you can be. Maybe you should have been the lawyer."

"Oh, my baby girl, I'm having too much fun playing the role of your psychotherapist. Now, tell me."

I let out a long winded sigh and answered her, "His name is Tommy Mills. He's a friend, a good one, and nothing more."

"And?" she questioned.

"And, nothing. In the wake of speaking to my mother and hurting her feelings once again, and then your call sent me into a down spiral, I was pretty much lost. So I took that loss and grief I was feeling, and add some layers of loneliness to it, and you have a classic case of falling back into old patterns. I didn't want to be alone and face going back to my empty apartment, so I went a different way and ended up in my friend's bed. Do I need to draw you a map? Or can you connect the dots to what happened next?"

"I'm sorry, baby."

"For what? You don't have anything to be sorry for."

"Yes, I do. I knew sending that letter would devastate you. You would return back to a dark place. Hell, maybe you never left, but I knew. Then I called you and pushed some more. I knew in order to get you home, I had to see you in person. So, that is what I am sorry for."

"Do my parents know?"

"Yes, they do. Connie wanted to call you first, test the waters, but you refused. Then she received your flowers, and then there was hope."

"Wendy, I didn't refuse her. Yes, I was hurting because of the anniversary, but I also was heading out to court to hear the biggest verdict of my career. You remember the case I was asked to take on when I made partner?"

"I do, but I thought you stepped down from that."

"I lied to you, but only because I didn't want you to worry. My parents already were upset after the attempt on my life, I couldn't bear to hurt you too."

"Oh, Tenley! If anything would have happened to you, they would have never forgiven themselves for not protecting you. Your daddy would have dragged you by your ponytail back home where you would be safe. That was foolish of you and you could have been hurt."

"Okay, I get it Wendy, but I'm fine, so drop it. Don't you even care that I won?"

"Of course I do, but don't you see that I love you more? We all love you more. Open your eyes and see us. If you ever want to be able to carry on with this life you say you want, then you need to come to terms with the old one first. You can have both. Loving your family doesn't have to be a choice, but it should be the most natural thing in the world to you."

"And Jagger? Will he see it that way too? You are wearing rose colored glasses, Wendy. How after all of this time can Jagger still want me?"

"I guess you're going to have to ask him."

"You're that sure I will be welcomed to just walk in to his hospital room, as If I belong there?"

"Yeah, I do. Because it's what Jagger wants."

"How can you be so sure?"

"You're going to have to trust me."

"I guess I have no choice but to trust you. I hope you're right."

I can't believe I'm back here again. How could I ever agree to Wendy's request? Too late to turn back now. The sound coming over the loud speaker pulled me out of my deep thoughts as Wendy held my hand.

"Passengers, the captain has now turned on the fasten seatbelt sign. Please remain in your seats as we begin our decent into Jackson Hole. For those who are visiting, we wish you a great time in the beautiful state of Wyoming. For those of you who live here . . . Welcome Home."

CHAPTER 4

...home

B Y THE TIME our plane had landed in Jackson Hole, it was nearing midnight. I was beyond exhausted. I didn't sleep on the plane and the past couple of days had not been the easiest ones to endure. Wendy, on the other hand was almost dancing out of the terminal. She received a massage by some therapist she met on the plane. I swear I saw her blush a few times, but she didn't pay me no mind when I was teasing her about it.

"So, where do I drop you?"

"Pardon?" I was surprised by her question.

"Where do I drop you? Do you want me to drive you out to your parents' home? Or hotel it for tonight?"

"Wendy, I can't believe you are seriously asking me where I would like to stay. It's the middle of the night, and I just can't knock on my daddy's door and yell out, 'Surprise, the prodigal daughter has returned home to you!' I don't want to go to a hotel either. Can I just stay with you tonight, and then I will call my parents in the morning?"

"Of course you can, Tumbleweed. Figured I would ask before I assume."

"Well, you know what they say when people assume."

"Watch it. You're not too old to smack."

I let out another sigh in disbelief that I was actually here. Not giving it anymore thought tonight, we collected our luggage and left the airport to Wendy's home. Her home was beautiful and rustic with the Teton Mountains as her view. They were everyone's view living up here. I used to ride Jazzy as high as her strong legs would carry me up toward the highest ridge on our ranch. I would lean back on my horse and breathe in the fresh air and feel God's presence. I was as close as I could be near heaven.

"Tenley, wake up. We're here."

I slowly opened my eyes and the familiar feeling hit me like an arrow through my chest. I was really home back in Wyoming, and standing in front of Wendy's home, where I shared many happy times here as a child. It looked exactly the same since the last time I saw it. It's only snow covered now. Tears were threatening to fall again, but I hampered them down. I was drained, and I had enough reminiscing for one day.

"The guest room is all set-up for you. Make yourself at home and get some rest," Wendy said.

I smiled. So much for asking where I would like to stay. Wendy was always a few steps ahead of us kids growing up, and tonight was no different. I brought my carry-on bag with me and left the rest in the entryway. I wouldn't be staying here for long, so why unpack? For a brief moment, I had thought I could sneak into town and leave without anyone being the wiser, but once I found out about Jagger, I knew that would not be possible.

He was all I'd been thinking about since Wendy told me the news about his accident. How and why did his horse just managed to throw him? She never said what horse he was riding, maybe it was not She-devil after all. She loves Jagger, for a horse she had a serious protection over him. Loyal to her rider, She-devil would only allow Jagger on her back. Kind of like how Jazzy treats me, or at least used to. Daddy says she's in good health, and he keeps her busy on the ranch. He uses her for tours and when the camps are in session.

For the past couple of years now, daddy changed the vision for the Fairchild Ranch. Once he changed the business dynamic of it, he also added a title underneath the Fairchild name: "Where you learn to ride and fall." How true that was. He still ran it, but appointed Shane as his manager who oversaw all the ranch business.

I was surprised when daddy phoned me and asked me to draw up the contracts. He told me that Shane's father had merged the Rhodes Ranch with ours, and we took over controlling interest. Mr. Rhodes had fallen ill about a year ago and could no longer handle the day to day. It was Shane who convinced him to sell the land to my father, but under the condition that Shane be in charge and take on more responsibility. Both Jagger and Shane earned their degrees and had of a more modern day approach on how to make the ranch more profitable in today's markets. The last time I checked the quarterly reports, they were doing more than fine.

Jagger and his father worked the Parrish Ranch together, with Jagger taking on the majority role. As everyone acclimated to the new transition of merging the ranches, Kip Rhodes did get stronger by each passing day. Daddy always said, you can never keep a cowboy down. I only wished that were true for my brother Jamie. I sent flowers to Shane's mother when I was told of his father's illness, but respectively stayed away. Shane didn't need a reminder of his past. It was hard enough knowing I was still a presence in terms of the ranch. We only spoke a few times over the phone in the last five years. It was about ranch business and nothing else. We once loved each other so much as friends, and the few words were spoken were reduced to pleasantries laced with coldness. Kept it simple and to the point, but I could feel he wanted to say more, but he held back. I did the same.

"I'm going to bed. Can I get you anything before I turn in?"

Wendy asked.

"A hug would be nice."

"That I can do. Sleep, sweet girl and don't worry your overactive brain anymore tonight. Things will look brighter in the morning."

I hugged Wendy, and she left me alone to my thoughts. Closing my eyes, he was here in my dreams . . . Jagger.

We were picnicking down by the river. My summer vacation was nearly over and I was due back at school the day after tomorrow. We spent every moment possible together. It was always hard saying goodbye to Jagger, but we always looked forward to the next time we could see each other. He didn't stopped smiling since we arrived. *What was he up to?* He placed his hands in mine and made me look at him.

"I love you, Tenley. I have something to show you. It represents how much I love you, and how happy I am to have you in my life."

"I love you too, Jagger. What is it? The suspense is killing me."

He winked and then began to unfasten the buttons to his shirt. I was clueless to what he was doing until I saw the beautiful words of endearment on his skin:

Ten, My love . . . my world.

He got a tattoo! A permanent marking on his body. I wanted to run my fingers over it, but the skin was fiery red. It looked brand new.

"Say something. Do you like it?" he asked nervously.

"I love it, Jagger. How could I not?"

"It's true, you know. You are my only love. You are my world. This is just a brief separation for us. Not a day will go by that I don't look at this tattoo—your own personal marking on my soul—and not feel your love."

I had tears in my eyes. Jagger was already prepared for this and quickly wiped them away.

"Do I have to get one too?" I nervously asked.

He laughed and kissed me passionately on my lips. His eyes were filled with sparkle as he kissed me.

He replied, "Not if you don't want to. I know you're afraid of needles."

"I am! Don't laugh at me. I probably would have to be sedated before I did something like that. I'm sure my father wouldn't approve."

"No worries, baby. I have other ways I can mark your body."

And then Jagger pressed his hardness against me and began marking me slowly with his kisses. First my neck, then down to my breasts. I wanted him and didn't care if we were caught. I may have not been ready for a tattoo, but I could show him in other ways. I bucked him off and straddled him. I touched his chest, carefully avoiding his tattoo.

"Lose the pants cowboy. This girl is about to take you for the ride of your life."

The next morning, the strong aroma of coffee, bacon, and blueberry pancakes invaded my room and senses. As I opened my eyes, my stomach began to growl. Not even sure when I had my last meal, but I was clearly hungry. I put my robe on and made my way downstairs to the kitchen to find Wendy, whistling as she poured the batter onto the griddle.

"Good morning. How did you sleep?" She was laying the cheery on a little too thick for my taste.

"As well as could be expected. Did you sleep? You sure look like you've been cooking up enough food here for an army. Cinnamon rolls too? Wendy, we can't possibly eat all of this."

"No, but our guests will." *Bam! Reality check.*

"Wendy, what did you do?"

71

"What's with the interrogation? You are a long way from New York and a courtroom. I simply invited your parents over for breakfast, which they happily said yes to."

"Do they know I'm here? Wendy . . . " I said very slowly.

"Yes. Of course they do, I told you that already. Times a wasting! You should shower and dress. I put out some fresh towels for you. Go on now, hop to it."

"I can't believe you. Did you not believe me last night? I said I would call them today."

"Well, now you don't have to, because in ten minutes they will be here. Clock is ticking, Tumbleweed. Better take that shower now."

I was beyond angry with her. How much more could I take in a twenty four hour span? First her call, then the letter, a flight home, and now my parents? *Dammit! I feel sick to my stomach. This was a mistake. I feel emotionally blackmailed not only by Wendy, but Jamie too.*

I stripped out of my robe and felt like drowning myself under the water. I foolishly allowed my heart and memories to lead me here. It's too late to worry about it now. I'm here and might as well face the past they all so desperately want me to do.

First things first, I wanted to see what Roxy packed for me. Yes, she over packed, but gave me exactly what I needed. I don't know how she found my favorite jeans, but I was so happy I have them with me. These jeans were so soft, I was surprised they still had material to them. The right knee had a hole but frayed with denim. They fit me like a glove, and I matched them up with my white cotton tee and red cowboy boots. I couldn't even remember the last time I dressed so casual before. I dried my long hair and gave myself a loose braid. A little make-up, and I was good to go.

I was still deciding how angry I was at Wendy, when I heard whispered voices coming from the kitchen. As best as I could manage, I stayed out of sight to listen. I knew this was an invasion of Wendy's privacy, but since she lacked the faith in me to call my parents, I felt this was an even exchange.

I heard my mother's voice.

"Wendy, how does she seem? I can't imagine she's all too happy with you right now."

"Connie, you can't go back and second guess us now. I made a promise a long time ago to help that girl when the time was right. Well, this is that time. She may think she's happy living in that big city on her own, but I'm not convinced. Her life is empty. It's high time for that beautiful girl upstairs to fix what's broken in her life, and that starts today."

WTH! My life is not empty. I have a thriving career. I live in a beautiful apartment which in fact I paid for all on my own. And I have two amazing best friends. How can Wendy tell my parents that my life is empty? God! I feel sick.

I continued to listen as I heard my father interrupt my mother and Wendy.

"Wendy, I know my daughter. She may be back home where we all feel she belongs, but I also know she's happy in New York and no longer considers Wyoming her home. It's her birthplace, not home."

"Hush now, Brock!" Wendy said. "You're wrong, both of you. You never forget your home. She has forever roots here in Wyoming. This is the one place she will always come back to, no matter what. We all know what drove her away, but now she has a chance to right that mistake. That girl needs a wake-up call, and we three are going to be the ones that give it to her. I know her just as well as you do, maybe even better. I'm sorry, Connie, but I do, and I love her with all of my heart. We have to try to get through to her, and if we fail, then we fail, but at least I will know I did everything I could to keep my promise to your son. Now, enough of this. She's going to be down any minute. Let's give her some room and enjoy breakfast."

I knew I probably had about thirty seconds before Wendy would call for me. I took a deep breath and tried to calm my beating heart. Daddy always said to never listen in on other folk's conversations. I wish I hadn't on this one. I guess if I wanted to find out what the hell was going on, I'd better make my appearance.

I counted for another thirty seconds and made my way through the kitchen. Through the years and a couple of renovations, one very old creaky kitchen door remained. Wendy could never bear to replace it. It had our growth charts on it. Hand prints from when we found paint and decided to make her door our latest work of art. As hard as it was being here, to look at this door brought back many happy childhood memories for me. Maybe it's what they were all hoping for. I pushed my way in to find the conspiring trio sipping their coffee. My mother's eyes lit up at the sight of me. She put her coffee down and rushed over to me. Constance Fairchild could pass for my older sister before my mother. Her skin was flawless with natural beauty. My father resembled a younger Sam Elliott.

"Oh, baby! I've missed you so much," she said as she hugged me to her.

"Hi, mama. I've missed you too."

"Now I know you're lying, but I'll believe it anyway."

"Mama, I don't lie. Just like I wasn't lying when you phoned the other day. I was due in court, and it wasn't the best time to have a conversation."

"Your flowers were beautiful. Thank you very much."

Tears were now in her eyes, as she quickly wiped them away.

She continued, "Thank you for coming home. We've missed you so much."

"Now, woman, don't go chasing her back to New York. She's home, and her daddy wants a hug from his beautiful daughter."

"Okay, okay. Go hug your daddy before we see his temper."

"I don't have a temper!" he shouted back and smiled.

"Sure you don't," mama said as she winked at my father.

I couldn't help but laugh a bit. My parents had the best banter between them. They never really fought, but it was always entertaining at the same time.

"Hi, daddy" was all I could say before he swept me up into his arms. My feet were dangling above the floor. As a child, I viewed him as a giant. And now in his arms, I kind of still do. I tightened my arms around his neck and let my reunion with my parents set in.

"Let me take a look at you. Damn, girl! You are beautiful, just like your mother."

"Daddy, why all the flattery? Some say I resemble you."

"No chance. I'm too ugly, better you take after your mama."

Now I know he was lying. If Jamie had lived, this would be how he would look, just as handsome as my father, but Jamie was more muscular as my father was leaner.

My father gestured to me to sit by him, I happily accepted. We all loaded our plates with Wendy's homemade pancakes. No one could cook like she can. I quietly ate my breakfast without engaging too much in the table conversation. I know what I overheard, and I was trying to keep my emotions in check.

"So, baby girl, after breakfast we can all go back to the ranch and get you settled in. I was down in the barn this morning, and I told Jazzy you were here. I swear that horse's eyes lit up like the fireworks on the Fourth of July," Daddy said with a smile.

"You are staying with us, right Tenley?" Mama asked me with worry in her eyes.

"Yes, mama, that's the plan."

"Great! Now that is settled, let's go."

"Mama, Daddy, would you mind taking my bags home with you, and I will meet you later? I would like to have a chat with Wendy, and then visit with Jagger. Isn't he the reason why I've been summoned home?"

I watched their faces go from bright to ashen with the mention of my former boyfriend's name. Daddy was the first to speak.

"Of course, sweetheart. You take all the time you need, and then meet us at home later on. If you need a lift, I can send one of the ranch hands to come and get you."

"I think I remember the way home, daddy, but thank you."

I couldn't help miss the sadness in his eyes when I mentioned our home.

My father loaded up his truck with my bags, and mama blew me a kiss. I waved as they drove a safe distance before I turned back to Wendy, who for once wasn't saying much.

"I'll just grab my bag, and I can drive you over."

"Not yet, Wendy. Not before you tell me what is really going on here."

"I don't know what you mean, Tumbleweed, I've told you the truth."

"Somehow Wendy, I think you left out some parts to the story. Okay, have it your way for now, but make no mistake, I will not play whatever game you three have concocted. I will see Jagger, I will visit with my family, and then I will be on the next plane back to New York."

"Are you done?"

"Actually I'm just getting warmed up. Something is not right here. Let's begin with Jamie's letter and the alleged others you still have."

"Boy, you are a lawyer, aren't you? Why can't you step out of your head right now and look beyond what you think you know? I have done nothing wrong here. When have I ever played games? You're here because this is where you need to be. Put your claws away and stop trying to be so tough. Your parents love you, and so do I. You have someone who I know you still love and who loves you back. That man is in need of help right now. So Tenley, this is not a game. This is real life, your life. Open your eyes. Open that closed heart of yours and let's go see Jagger."

Closed heart? If you only knew my friend, how wrong you are. My heart has been split wide open since the day I left here and watched my beloved brother get lowered down into the cold earth.

CHAPTER 5

...not everyone is happy to see me

WE DROVE THE short distance from Wendy's home to St. John's Medical Center. My stomach felt uneasy as we got closer. I was still trying to wrap my head around the fact that Jagger was somewhere in this hospital and in a coma.

"Aren't you coming in?" I asked Wendy.

"Not this time. I think you need to do this on your own." She handed me a piece of paper with his room number on it. "I don't have too much to do today. I'll be around if you need me."

I've always needed you, Wendy. That's not my problem.

I walked in through the main entrance and greeted the grey haired woman behind the desk. She said hello with her polite pleasantries, and I almost lost my voice returning the gesture. My throat dried up, my stomach hurt, and my brain was screaming at me to turn around and to run. I was scared, but found my voice and handed her the paper. She directed me to take the escalator up one floor and take the west wing elevators. I would find Jagger there in the intensive care unit.

As the elevator rose, so did my beating heart. *What am I doing here? How can I even think of walking through those doors?* And just like that, the doors opened, and I was slammed right back into my past. Face to face with no other than Shane Rhodes. *I've never wanted to run more than I do right now.*

"Either I need to get my eyes checked, or hell has truly frozen over. The prodigal daughter returns," he said.

Just as handsome as ever. All 6'2 of rugged, muscular manliness of him. He was sporting a five o'clock shadow on his tanned skin. His blue eyes scanned me up and down, as I fought not to bite my bottom lip. *He's just so fucking hot, but he's angry and not doing anything to hide it from me.*

"Hi, Shane."

"Hi, Shane? Hi, Shane? No! You say 'hi' when a short time has passed, not as long as a half of a decade. What the hell are you doing here, Ten?"

"Don't call me that, please."

"Why? Did I hit a nerve? Only Jagger has a claim to that? How about Tumbleweed? Oh, that's right. Only Jamie could ever call you by that name. I guess I'm out of nicknames. How about I just call you liar? Sounds about right, don't you think? I wonder what Jamie would think of his lying sister returning home? You remember him? Don't you?" Shane was purposely trying to get a rise out of me for hurting him, and using my brother's memory to do it.

"Stop it, Shane. How dare you?" I was seething with anger. I could have slapped him, but I held my own. He was causing enough of a scene by yelling at me in public. "Don't you ever say his name in a vile manner again. I mean it Shane, leave my brother out of this."

"Why Tenley? Why should I leave him out of this? He was my best friend, and we were brothers for life. I'll say his name as much as I damn well fucking please."

"Have you?"

"Have I what?" he yelled back at me.

"Have you said my brother's name through the years, or are you just using it against me now to hurt me? What happened to your promise? Why are you being so cruel?"

Please don't cry. Please don't cry. I chanted silently to myself.

He backed me up against the wall, caging me in with his strong arms. I could run nowhere, maybe he knew. Staring directly into my eyes, he said, "Here's the thing about promises, they're like hearts, and they tend to get broken."

Not backing down, I replied, "You promised our friendship would be here when I was ready to come home to it."

"I guess it had a statute of limitations on it, you know what that means, being a fancy lawyer? Now, I answered your question. You answer one for me. Why are you here?"

"Wendy called me."

"Wow! That's all it took. A fucking phone call. I guess I should have tried that too, oh right, I did. I not only called, but I sent you a letter every day for the first year after you left. And you want to know what I got back? Do you, kid? Nothing! Not one call or letter returned, but yet you stand here and dare to question me why I'm being cruel? Girl, you got that down to a science. As for the rest of us? We are just trying to keep up."

"I wasn't ready. I was too lost in my own grief to reach out to anyone. All I had left was school. I'm sorry."

"You're sorry? Two words is all you have to say to me? That's not good enough after everything you've put me through. Fuck you, Princess," Shane hissed as his eyes flared with anger.

Still trapped by him, I wanted to slide down to the floor and crawl away in shame. He made me feel so small. How could Shane do that with just a few words?

"Shane! That is enough out of you."

Kip Rhodes was here, Shane's father. Taken by surprise, Shane stepped back and let me pass. Kip looked angry and disappointed.

"Boy, where we come from, we do not speak to ladies that way. Apologize . . . now!"

"Sir, I—" Shane was stuttering over his words.

"Don't make me ask again."

"I'm sorry, Tenley."

Shane looked crushed. Absolutely humiliated to be berated in front of me by his father.

"That's better. Your mother is downstairs waiting to be taken home."

"Yes sir." He tipped his hat at his son and Shane turned away from me and didn't look back. Shane was still very much intimated by his father. A leader in the community and one of the toughest cowboys you ever wanted to know. He looked good, strong, and back to health. Thank goodness for prayers, I couldn't have taken another loss. The boys' fathers were all like second daddies to me. I loved them both very much.

"Now, Tenley Fairchild, I think a hug is in order."

"Hi, Mr. Rhodes. How are you feeling?"

"I would be better if you would give this old man a proper hello."

"Less of the old Mr. Rhodes, you look fantastic."

I hugged him back and of course, a cowboy always had to take it up a notch in their greeting. I got a lifting hug with a twirl. I had to grab onto his arms so I wouldn't fall, not that he would let me.

"You are as beautiful as ever," he said. "Wait until Kathleen sees you. I would have had Shane bring her back up, but she was tired after her therapy session."

"How is she doing? Is she seeing improvements now that she's doing the physical therapy?" I asked.

"Yeah, she's almost as good as new. That will teach her not to get tipsy and ride the mechanical bull. What was she thinking?"

"Now, I know I'm home. You cowboys never change, but you love to add layers to a story. I heard from mama that she missed a step carrying a basket of vegetables and lost her footing."

"Nah, I like my story better."

We both laughed and I hugged him again.

"Come sit a spell and let's have a chat?" he asked.

We sat down in the visitors lounge, and I was happy we were alone.

"Forgive my son and his lapse of manners earlier toward you. I don't know what has gotten into him. He's been all fired up for days now knowing you were coming into town."

What? How can that be? Wendy had phoned me, and then suddenly arrived in New York, unannounced. I knew there was more to this story. The pieces are beginning to come together.

I got up to drink some water and get my breathing under control. Shane knew I was coming into town, but how? My parents? Wendy?

I joined Mr. Rhodes, and asked him how Shane knew I was coming home.

"Mr. Rhodes, I . . . "

"Now sweetheart, you can call me Kip."

I smiled, maybe even blushed a little. Mr. Rhodes was always kind to me and so was his wife.

"Okay, Kip. If I may, may I ask you a question?"

"Darling, you can ask me anything you want. I'm an open book."

I smiled again and said, "This trip home was unplanned for me. How could Shane have possibly known I was coming home when I didn't know myself until yesterday?"

"I'm not too sure sweetheart on the how, only the why. I heard him telling his mama that he was nervous seeing you again, and every time I would ask him about it, he got all riled up. So instead of talking to him, I left him on his own, and he channeled his anger on the ranch. Again, I'm sorry he wasn't as welcoming as he should have been."

"It's alright. I probably deserved it."

"You're wrong. No one should be spoken to like that, especially a woman. I suspect my boy seeing you has re-opened a whole can of hurt. It's a past hurt, and it's one that he needs to move on from, do you get what I'm saying to you?"

His demeanor shifted into protection mode, one I understood all too well. Shane was his son, no matter what. I knew what my leaving did to not only him, but to Jagger.

"I do, sir, and I'm sorry for that."

"Don't be, sweetheart, it's in the past. He'll be fine, just give him time."

"How are you doing these days, now that the ranches have merged?" I asked him. Of course I knew the business side of it, but giving up his ranch had to be hard for Mr. Rhodes, not that he didn't profit from the sale.

"I feel good. That decision to sell to your father was a smart one. We still have our home, and about one hundred acres to do what we please. It's enough for us. After I got sick and then by the grace of God, got better, I knew I could no longer do all on my own. Sure I had Shane, but he had a different vision for his future, and I was too stubborn to change now. It's easier the way it is now. Shane is partners with your father, and I do my share for what it's worth. It's better this way, and we're all happy."

"And Jagger? Where does he fit in to all of this?"

"Sadly, he doesn't. They never could reach a place where they could be partners in anything. They tried to repair their friendship and remain friends, but in the end, they pretty much went their separate ways. Believe me, Tenley, Jagger is happy running his ranch with his father."

"Did I hear my name?" a voice called out.

Ren Parrish was standing before me.

"Mr. Parrish!" I happily screamed out. I didn't know what came over me, but seeing him here was like catapulting me back to the day I was last on his ranch. It was the day I was so happy to receive my acceptance letter and then the saddest when I broke his son's heart.

"Well, that's quite a welcome. Oh, you sweet girl. How are you? You sure look all grown up. What did I tell you about doing that? Don't go making me feel old."

I had a smile plastered to my face. Being around these two men felt right. I'd known them my entire life and loved them like my own father. It was then I felt a twinge of guilt. Here I was with Kip and Ren, when I should have been with my own father who I barely said ten words to.

"I'm so happy you are here darling. I feel our prayers have been answered and all will be okay now," Ren said as he wiped away his tears.

Kip remained where he sat and gave me a few minutes with his friend.

"Mr. Parrish, I don't know what you are expecting from me, but I'm still not sure this is the best idea to be here in the first place."

"Oh sweet girl! You are just what the Lord has told us we needed. My boy loves you and I know you two stubborn kids have been on your own for a while now, but I know you still love him. If you can tell me differently, then I apologize and won't keep you, but if you say yes, then like I said, the good Lord answered my prayers."

Looking over my shoulder to Kip, who was trying his best not to listen, I turned back to Ren.

"Yes. I still love Jagger, I never really stopped. But sir, it's so complicated and unresolved. I can't just walk into his hospital room and be your saving grace and his, for that matter. I haven't seen or talked to him in five years. Maybe he was in love with me for a time, but we're older now and live completely different lives."

He took my hand in his and sighed. "Tenley, there's something you don't know. He was on his way to New York to finally fight for you. He hoped and prayed you would come back to him, but after five years of longing for you, he had made up his mind."

"What are you saying?"

"I'm saying that my boy tried to go on without you and in the end, he was barely surviving. Sure, he works from sun up to sun down, but working the ranch is all he has. He never got serious with anyone after you. When we lost Jamie, something just broke inside of him. I was worried for a long time, but then he came back to us."

"How?"

"He sat me down one night and looked me straight in the eyes. He said, 'Daddy, I'm letting her go for now, because she has to be free. She's hurting daddy, and I can't help her right now and she can't help me. I'm going to honor Jamie's wishes and let her finish her education. Once she accomplishes that, I will know when it's time to go to her.'"

"Jamie's wishes? I don't understand this at all? Mr. Parrish, Ren, please explain it."

"After you left, sweetheart, Jagger visited your brother. He was so broken and lost after you two broke up. I knew what your answer was the minute I saw him pull up without you on his arm. Who knows what he was thinking back then with his proposal. It wasn't the right time for you, but in recent months, he said it was. Your brother asked him to give you time. Time to finish school, begin your career, and most importantly, mourn his loss. Now, I don't think you ever get over a loss like that, but Jamie felt five years would be enough time. So, sweet girl, I ask you, has it?"

"Has what?"

"Has it been enough time, Tenley? Are you ready to come home?"

Before I could answer him, Mr. Rhodes interrupted and gave me an out. "C'mon Ren, we have to be getting back now. Why don't you give Tenley some time with Jagger? We can come back later." He said to his friend with hope in his eyes.

"Sure thing, Kip. We have those new horses coming in this afternoon. Goodbye sweetheart. Thank you for being here."

He hugged me again and then Kip, getting one more hug before they turned and left me standing alone in the waiting room. I felt like I was being punk'd and was on an episode of '*This is your life.*'

Jagger was coming to New York for me? Wendy had so much explaining to do, but I can't even allow my mind to go there right now. I'm kind of stuck on 'He was coming for you and Jamie's wishes.'

I pulled out my cell and phoned Zoey. Her voicemail picked up, and I told her that I arrived safely and would call her soon. I prepared myself as best as I could before entering Jagger's room.

Please God, let him be okay. If not for me, please come back to your family.

CHAPTER 6

...scared

M Y HEART BEGAN to race, and my stomach felt uneasy. My hands were on his hospital door, but yet, I couldn't manage to make my feet move forward. This was the same hospital I spent more days than I care to remember here visiting with Jamie. The same feeling is still weighing heavily throughout my heart. I remember everything about this place. The smell, the staff, the waiting, oh how I hated the waiting.

Just go in, I kept repeating to myself, although I remained where I was. Behind this door, Jagger laid in a coma. *How am I here? He shouldn't be, and yet here we are.* Tears began to fall down my face.

"It's okay, Tumbleweed. Don't be afraid." I turned to see Wendy standing behind me.

"What are you doing here?" I asked my friend, already knowing what she would say.

"I'm here for you. Walk with me for a minute?" she asked as she extended her hand out for me to take. I did with no hesitation.

We walked away from Jagger's door and down a long hallway

leading to another waiting room. This one had floor to ceiling windows. The sun was shining over the Teton Mountains, and it was beyond beautiful to take in. She came prepared with coffee and her homemade cookies. I took a chocolate chip cookie and let out a pleasurable moan. They were still warm with the chocolate oozing out from the hand sized cookie. Wendy always went big.

She said, "Small cookies are not worth the oven temps and the gas prices. Go big or go home."

I laughed silently to myself as I took another bite. I always loved to bake with her. She said that one time trying to teach Jamie, Jagger, Shane, and myself how to make triple chocolate brownies. Oh yeah, they were big too.

"Penny for your thoughts?"

"I think you will need more than pennies." I let out a sigh and drank more of my coffee.

"Tenley, what's wrong?"

"Everything. After you dropped me off, I ran into Shane, his father, and Mr. Parrish. Needless to say, not everyone was happy to see me. Shane basically told me off, and then his father overheard him being rude and made him apologize to me. Yeah, that went over well. Mr. Parrish was over the moon to see me and believes I am the answer to Jagger waking up. Why Wendy? Why me?"

"It's simple."

"Simple, you say. Okay, why is it simple?"

"I say simple, because it is. That boy, now a man, loves you. You love him, and love is the strongest emotion in the world. It's more powerful than anything else, and yes, it can heal a broken heart. You, baby girl, need healing, and so does Jagger and Shane. Begin with Jagger, and the rest will fall into place."

"Wendy, even if I choose to believe you, it's too late for Jagger and me. It's been five years without each other, and it didn't end well for us. How can any of you expect me to just take back what I destroyed in the first place?"

"Love makes it alright for you to be here. Love makes it okay for you to take back Jagger and reclaim what you believe you don't deserve. Everyone seems to get this, but you. Even your beloved brother Jamie knew this."

"Please Wendy, don't use Jamie's memory to get what you want. You already did that, and I'm here back in Wyoming. You don't get anything more than that."

"I'm sorry if you feel that's what I'm doing, but I can assure you that I'm not. I'm your friend, and I love you."

"You love me? Is that why you believe that my life is empty? Before you say anything, I was listening to you and my parents' conversation. For the record, my life is not empty. I just took a different road, and it led me to New York doing what I love to do. I'm a very good lawyer."

"That may be true, but at what cost? Is your career worth your life?"

"You know about the car bomb?"

"Um, yes I do and so do your parents and Jagger. What were you thinking going up against known mobsters?"

"Wendy, that is just what the press played out for the public to believe. Exaggerated headlines sell papers. Yes, they were connected, but I have no concrete proof how deep they were in and what crime families they answer to." I lied, but only because I didn't want to cause anymore worry for Wendy, or my family. "Obviously I'm fine and the case carried on, and I won."

"You won. That's wonderful for you, Tenley, but what about next time? What if the stakes are raised higher? Will you once again put yourself at risk for a case? Or just to win?"

"Not every case I take is dangerous. This was my first one. I'm sure I won't be taking on anything even remotely related to this one, so please stop worrying about me."

"Can we please stop worrying about 'my so-called empty life' and start talking about Jagger? Why do you believe he still wants me after all of this time?"

"You're going to have to trust me. He will explain it all to you when he wakes up."

"Perfect. Yeah, after my magical kiss awakens him from his slumber. Thanks a lot, good old friend, but I think I'm ready to visit with him."

"Don't be cross with me, Tumbleweed. I love you, and I'm trying to help you."

"Yeah, you've said that." I was angry. She touched on a nerve that I didn't like. My life is my own, and to sit here and have to justify it to Wendy, of all people? Makes me angry. So of course, I let my mouth run her over like a freight train.

"You know dear friend, maybe you should try loving me a little less and focus on your own life and leave my life to me. It's worked out great so far for me, okay?"

Wendy being Wendy, she shook her head and gave me a little shrug. How those mannerisms irked me to no end. She knew it, and I still was affected by it.

She gave me a hug and whispered in my ear. "I think you need to work on your litigator skills. You are trying too hard to convince me how happy you are. You keep telling yourself the same old line and maybe you'll believe it. I'll see you later, Tumbleweed."

She turned and left me standing there. That went well. My coffee now cold, I tossed it into the trash. I still didn't have all the answers to my questions, but it was time to go to the source. I had to see Jagger for myself. I hurt him so badly with sleeping with Shane, and then rejecting him not once, but twice. *How is he not hogtied and married by now and with children? He's the whole package, and yet they all want me to believe that he's been waiting for me to return to him?*

This is crazy! My head is beginning to throb with beating my brain to death with my anxiety. I'm back here again. I'm in front of his door, but this time I go in. He's not alone. A nurse is with him.

"Hi," I say as I continue to enter further into the room. "Is it okay if I visit for a while?"

"Of course you can, darling. I'm all through here with Mr.

Brown Eyes. I was just changing his medicine bags. I'm Shirley, and you are . . . ?" she welcomingly asked me.

"I'm Tenley Fairchild, an old friend."

"Nice to meet you. Have a seat and take all the time you need with him. Talk to him, they say it helps."

"Thank you." I barely get out before my tears begin to fall again.

"Are you sure you're okay, sweetheart? Can I get you anything? Water or juice perhaps?"

"No thank you, ma'am, I'm fine. This is really hard for me, um, to see him this way. I'm not sure what to do."

"It's easy honey, just pull up a chair, hold his hand, and simply talk to him. He's breathing on his own. He's just being a bit stubborn at the moment by staying asleep. The better looking they are, the more attention they crave. Mr. Brown Eyes over here is doing just that, but I'll play along. He'll be alright. He just needs a little help and the good Lord above." She smiled warmly at me."

"You seem pretty certain that's all it will take to wake him from his slumber."

"Well, you see, honey, I've been a nurse for twenty seven years now, and believe me, I've seen a lot worse than Mr. Brown Eyes. Medically he's stable. His injuries are on the mend, but maybe he's just not ready to wake up and greet the day yet. Maybe, just maybe, he's been waiting for you. Only one way to find out is for you to talk to him."

"Thank you, Shirley. I feel a little better, and I will talk to him."

"Good for you. I'll be around if you need me."

"Shirley, may I ask you a question?"

"Of course."

"How did you know Jagger has brown eyes if he hasn't woken up yet?"

"Just a hunch darling, just a hunch."

She happily walked away, and I found myself smiling. Jagger did have amazing panty dropping brown eyes. They were deep brown, and some days I actually thought they sparkled. I said a silent prayer to Jamie in heaven. He seems to be behind the ruse of getting me here, so I just hope he is truly watching me now and will give me the strength I need to get through this, not only for me, but for Jagger too.

I quietly walked in and heard the beeps coming from the sensors hooked up to Jagger. His hair was longer, almost to the edge of his neck. Beautifully messy, the way I always liked it. His beard is grown in, but not *Duck Dynasty* like. Either the nurses or his father must be grooming him. As I get closer, I can see cuts and abrasions along his cheek and jawline. His broken leg was raised off the mattress in a support harness. You can tell his ribs were still wrapped through the thin hospital gown. And then my eyes found what I was looking for . . . his tattoo. I somehow convinced myself that he hated me and would probably have it removed, but he didn't. I was happy to know a part of me was still with Jagger. I carefully pulled down his gown over his heart, and that's where I saw my name. **"Ten, My love . . . my world."**

Tears were beckoning once again, but I let them fall. Here was the man who I loved more than I loved myself. I know it sounded selfish choosing my career over him, but I thought I was doing right by him by leaving. *I own my hurt. I own my betrayal. I suffer through my pain because it's what I feel I deserve. Was I wrong all of these years? Distancing myself from my family, and Jagger? I miss Zoey and Tommy. I need my crazy friends to help me get through this, but then again, I'm not too sure Tommy would be all so willing to lend advice to the woman who practically used him for some quick comfort. He said we were okay, but I'm still not convinced.*

Jagger was beyond handsome. He seriously belonged on a cover of a magazine. Even in his current state, he looked amazing. His arms were as thick as my legs. His body is layered on top of layers with muscles. You don't get this kind of body by working out in a gym, you get it by working a ranch. Unless you live the life of a true country cowboy, no one could understand all the hours it takes to keep it running. Jagger is incredibly strong in body and in mind. He has to be okay. I wanted to touch him, feel him breathe, and smell him. I was already beginning to lose my senses being this close to him again. Even in a coma, Jagger still had the ability to rouse a physical reaction from me.

I leaned in as close as I could and laid my head onto his rising chest. His breathing was steady and strong. I closed my eyes and imagined him holding me in his strong arms. I loved being wrapped around his body, especially the nights we made love under the stars. I raised my head and shrugged off those delicious memories of us. Pulling up a chair, I sat and held his hand in mine. His hands were so calloused and rough to the touch. I placed a gentle kiss on each of his knuckles and placed my cheek down on his hand.

"I'm here, Jagger. I'm home. I'm not sure if you even want me here, but Wendy and your father seem to think I am the answer to their prayers. Do you remember how the story goes? Sleeping Beauty is in a deep sleep while she waits for her prince to awaken her. His magical kiss breaks the curse, and they live happily ever after. Now in our story, you are the princely cowboy, and I'm not too sure I'm your princess, but let's go with friend for now. So like I was saying, I'm here to get you to wake up."

I continued, "Oh Jagger, I wish I had magical powers to wake you, but I'm just me. Although I can yield some power in the courtroom, I doubt I can do the same here with you. If I truly had magic, then Jamie would have lived, but that's not how our story turned out. I guess because you're sleeping, you really don't have much say in what I say right now. So I'll give you a 'this is your life,' and if you wake up, then by all means, say what you want. The sound of your voice, no matter what the tone, will be amazing to hear. I need you to wake up, Jagger. Your father needs you. You should have seen the look in his eyes when he saw me. I saw so many emotions grace his face, but the one thing that stood out was hope. How come everyone around me has it all figured out, but me?"

I ran my fingers along his jaw, his beard was coarse. I said, "Jagger, I'm sorry I hurt you by leaving. I believed by leaving it would somehow bring you peace in the long run. I did a foolish act with Shane. I knew it that night but still made a reckless decision that changed my life—our life—together. Shane having feelings for me was the last thing I ever expected him to say. Was I so deeply in love with you that I totally missed what was right in front of me? I guess so, because I never knew."

"He sure is angry with me now. His reception of my arrival was less than warm, it was downright cold. Not sure what I was expecting, but it sure as hell wasn't that. Jagger, please wake up. Open your eyes. Your nurse calls you 'Mr. Brown Eyes,' did you know that? I'm told coma patients can hear beyond their slumber, so if that's true, then make sure you bat your beautiful eyes at Shirley when you do wake. I think she may have a crush on you. It's so easy to love you, and I'm so sorry for not loving you enough. I was wrong Jagger, and I'm sorry. Please wake up."

It was late, and I was beginning to get hungry and tired. Shirley came in a few times to check his vitals and then let us be. He was lying here so still. I couldn't help but think of Jamie. There were times when I didn't know if Jamie was breathing, he was so still. I would shake him awake and then he would look at me like I was crazy. I almost wanted to shake Jagger, but I stopped myself, so I did the only thing I could do . . . I kissed him.

Ever so gently, I held his face and leaned in to place a chaste kiss upon his lips. I pushed away his hair off his forehead and kissed him there as well.

"Now, my sleeping cowboy, I don't expect you to suddenly wake from my kiss, but I pray you feel the warmth of it and know that I'm here."

"I'm so scared, Jagger. You need to wake up."

One more kiss to his lips and then I turned to leave. I watched for any signs of movement, but he remained still with his chest rising up and down.

"I'll be back tomorrow," I said.

I knew for certain I could not return to New York until I knew Jagger would be okay, but would *I* ever be?

CHAPTER 7

....where i learned to ride...and fall

BY THE TIME I left the hospital, the sun had set over the Teton's, and my stomach was grumbling something fierce. Other than breakfast and my earlier snack and coffee, I was ravenous for dinner.

I elected not to call the ranch or Wendy for a ride. I rented a Ford F-150 to take me to my father's ranch. Only in Wyoming, you can rent a truck. I had my share to choose from, but I'm sure my father would want me to drive something strong enough to get through the unpredictable Wyoming weather.

The inside temp reading said eight degrees outside. The rental agency already had the truck warming up for me, so when I got in, I was toasty warm. Thank goodness for Roxy, packing me my down coat and accessories. My boots were a little wet, not the best choice for today, but I needed a reminder of the girl I used to be and wearing my red boots would do the trick.

I came upon the secured gate of the ranch and punched in my code. It was my parents' wedding anniversary. I smiled as the gates opened up to allow me to drive through. My parents were so in love with one another. *I can only imagine how disappointed they are in me. They probably look at me and wonder what went wrong.*

Along the long road that would bring me home, I passed the cabin rentals, the horse training area, and the mini rodeo section that was always a crowd pleaser for the summer tourists. This property was huge, and now merging with the Rhodes property, my father wanted to expand even more into his business. Shane was in charge of the horses and the races they would compete in. He belonged here and was a part of it, just as much as I was. My last name may be Fairchild, but this land flowed through Shane's veins, and if Jamie had lived, they would be amazing partners.

I'll try to avoid him tomorrow and stay out of his way. I'm sure with me being here in person, my father will want to conduct some ranch business, but I will try my best to do all of that without Shane. I'm not in the mood for another confrontation with him.

I guess I spoke to soon because as I pulled up to my home, there Shane stood. I sighed in frustration because I didn't want to go another round with him. I grabbed my bag and headed up to the house. My goal was to avoid him, but Shane was right where I needed to be.

"Aren't you going to say hello to me?" he asked. I spun around and looked at him with questioning eyes.

"After your warm greeting earlier today, I felt it was best to stay out of your way, so that's what I'm doing."

I turned once again in hopes of avoiding him. He reached for my arm and pulled me close to him.

"Please Shane, let me go. I'm exhausted and can't do this with you right now."

"I know, and I'm sorry for that. I'm so sorry for talking to you the way I did today, but woman give me a fucking break. Just seeing you almost stopped my heart. Please give me a chance to make it up to you."

"Shane, I have to go. My parents are waiting for me."

"Please Tenley, say you'll talk to me tomorrow? You're not going anywhere until you agree."

"Fine! I will talk to you in the morning, but hear this, Shane Rhodes. I don't take kindly to orders, never have and never will. It's best you remember that before our talk tomorrow. Good night."

"Oh, darling! It's good to have you home. Yee-haw!!!" he screamed out into the night sky. *Oh my goodness! Only in Wyoming.*

"Well, I guess Shane had a change of heart," my father said as he opened up his arms for me to walk into.

"Hi, daddy," I whispered into his chest as he held me. I needed this hug after today's events. I was so tired, but I needed to eat before I collapsed.

"Come on, baby girl. Your mama cooked up some of your favorites."

"Good. I'm hungry."

"I figured you might be. Mama is in the kitchen. Let's go."

"I guess you'd mind if I took a plate up to my room?"

"Is that a serious question? You know the way to the kitchen. Now go!"

"Yes sir."

The sight of my mother wearing my grandmother's apron tied around her waist almost made my heart melt. The memories I tried so hard to hide away were all rushing back to me. This house and the memories it held were so strong. After all my time away from here, I could still feel my brother's presence and the love we had as a family. *Have* as a family. *I have their love, I always have. I just need to allow myself to feel it again. I'm trying Jamie, I'm trying.* My eyes became glassy as I created a new memory.

"Hi, mama."

"Oh, my sweet girl! You're finally home."

She wiped her hands and came rushing toward me for a hug. My mother sniffled a few times, but by the time she let me go, her tears were gone. She never did like crying in front of us.

"I've missed you so much, Tenley. Thank you for coming home." I gave her a silent smile.

After dinner, I was in no shape for a long talk that my mother wanted to have. I promised her a talk in the morning after a ride with Jazzy. She brightened up after hearing me talk about riding. I saw more hope in both of my parents' eyes, but I remained quiet and kept my thoughts to myself. My mother walked me up the stairs that would take me to my childhood bedroom. It's been renovated since I left home, but mama kept it personal to my liking. This room still contained memories of my life here in this house. My doll collection was beautifully displayed in a corner. Awards and photos hung above, and mama had left out my favorite pony to sleep with.

I've been away from home for five years, but somehow my mother knew exactly what I needed and maybe even secretly wanted. I hugged her, and she left me on my own.

I hadn't checked my phone all day since I called Zoey. I saw a few missed calls from Zoey, and one text from Tommy.

"If you need me, call me."

I wanted to call him, but I was way too tired. I fired back a quick text.

"Hi Tommy. Thank you for always being there for me. I'm doing okay. Sorting it all out. I'll call you when I can. Xo . . . Tenley."

He texted back. **"Ok."**

I let out a sigh and powered down my phone. Kicked off my boots and stripped out of my clothes, not bothering to look for pajamas. I wrapped myself around the duvet and lost myself into sleep.

Of course, Jagger was in my dreams. *Oh hell! I'm in trouble.* My dream took me back to a carefree time where I had no inhibitions. Jagger and I were skinny dipping in the pond on his ranch. Jagger kept assuring me that we wouldn't be seen and definitely not be interrupted. I always believed and trusted him completely. We made love in the warm water with the stars shining in the sky and the moon as our light. I could feel my orgasm again and again, and then a burst of cold air ended my bliss.

"Tenley, time to wake up sweetheart. Are you under there?"

I was having the best dream when I heard my mother over me, at least I think it was mom. I stirred a bit, then my covers were ripped off of me, and then she shrieked so loud that her screams could wake the dead.

"Oh, dear Lord! Tenley Faith Fairchild! Put some clothes on. This is how you sleep? What if your daddy came in? And you call that underwear? It looks like dental floss with a scrap of material holding it together.

"Mother! Get out. What are you fucking doing in here at this ungodly hour?"

Then I felt a stinging slap come down hard on my bare ass. It was mama's way of showing me how she felt about my choice of language this morning.

"You watch your mouth, miss, while you are under my roof. Do you understand me? It is nearing nine o'clock. We've been up for hours already, but maybe you have forgotten how ranch life works around here? Your breakfast is getting cold." And with that, she slammed her way out of my room.

After that blissful wake-up, I showered and dressed, skipping breakfast all together. I had promised my mother a talk and a ride, but after the way I had spoken to her, she was probably pissed. I crept down the stairs and grabbed my coat and gloves, only to be once again startled by my mother.

"Going somewhere?"

"Geez, Mom! Please stop doing that."

"Doing what? Catching my sly daughter sneak out of our home and without me?"

"I wasn't sneaking off, I was just going to visit Jazzy."

"Jazzy could wait, I will not. Now come in the kitchen and have some breakfast with me, please."

Following my mother through the kitchen, I felt awful. It was like I was off my game here. She was trying and I was hurting her yet again.

"This coffee is amazing. Where did you get it?" I asked as I enjoyed the strong dark roast.

"Daddy and Shane. They brought it back from Mexico."

"Excuse me? Daddy and Shane went to Mexico? Um . . . when was that?" my voice was rising at this news.

"Why the questions, Tenley? Daddy and Shane go on scouting trips all the time. This was no different. Do you even read the paperwork we send to you, or you just have your minions do it for you?"

"That's not fair, mother. I personally do all of your contracts and all of ranch business. Excuse me for one detail slipping my mind. I'm finished here. I'm going out to see Jazzy."

"Hold on a minute."

"What," I snapped back.

"Talk to me, Tenley, please? What's going on in that beautiful head of yours?"

"Okay, mama. You want the truth?"

"You know I do."

"I hope you are prepared for it then," I said curtly in return.

"Okay, here it is. Ever since Jamie died, I have been living on the outside looking in. I don't fit anywhere in this family anymore. When he died, he took the best of me with him. You and daddy were so wrapped up in your grief over losing him that you totally forgot about me. I was lost and drowning. So I buried my pain and grief and moved on without him, and you. I created a new life for myself in New York. I wanted to stay, mama, but Jamie pushed me away. So after he died, I stayed away."

I shocked myself with what was coming out from my mouth. I never shared my feelings with anyone, least of all my mother. Next to Wendy, she was the only one that could elicit a rise out of me.

"I'm sorry, Tenley. I'm so sorry, baby girl, that you ever were made to feel like less than you really were. He was my son, my first born. Losing a child is devastating. It's a pain you never get over. As time passes on, the pain subsides, but it stays with you forever and it can hit you at any time of the day. When it does, it swallows you up.

You, my daughter, are still buried so deep within your own grief and pain. It's okay to miss him, but he wouldn't want this for you. You ask why the letter? Why you're here? This is why. This long overdue talk that you and I have been running from for five years. I'm sorry I failed you. I should have been there for you. Parents are supposed to know better, but sometimes we fall, and it's hard to get back up."

"Mama, I'm so sorry I've failed you as a daughter."

"Never, Tenley! You are my daughter, my beautiful girl. I am so very proud of the woman you have become. But having said that, I'm worried for you. You're thousands of miles away from us, and you live alone in a city we don't understand. This ranch is your true home. If you have stayed away because we stopped reminding you of that, then that is my failure. And for that, I am deeply sorry. Tenley, I need you to forgive me, please."

We both stared at one another, waiting for the other to make a move. I was frozen to where I was standing. I whispered, "Thank you" to my mother and walked out, leaving her alone. I knew I should have turned around and told her it was okay and how there wasn't anything to forgive, but I ran . . . again. Her words, my words were too much to bear. She didn't follow me, this was her style. She would pile it all for me and then give me the time to process it. Jamie and Daddy were the same way. I think she was hoping for a different reaction from me, but that would be too easy, and I never do easy.

Making my way through the snow, I finally reached the stables and found my girl.

"Hi Jazzy. I've missed you. Wanna take a ride with me?" I waited for my horse to give me her answer, and I swear I saw her eyes shift into happiness that I've returned. I treated her to a good brushing, fed her some apples, and then I saddled her up.

"Come on Jazzy, let's ride." Once I was on her back, Jazzy knew exactly what to do. We trotted at a steady pace until we reached the gate. Once we were out in the open, I held tightly onto her reigns and Jazzy soared through air as if we were flying. She led me to our spot. The highest point on the ranch. We rode here more times than I could count.

"Thank you girl for remembering. I love you Jazzy." She neighed in response. I dismounted and gave her a rest. She enjoyed some more apples, and then carrots while I took in the view before me.

God's here. He has to be and so is Jamie. My brother always knew me best. Whenever I was in need of guidance, he knew I would be here. Today, I needed some help. I needed answers to my questions. I needed my brother to tell me that everything was going to be okay. Tell me I hadn't lost my family by pushing them away. Would I fit here again? And the million dollar question: Jagger . . . Where did I fit with him? He'd been invading my dreams every night for days now and to see him yesterday in that hospital nearly broke me in half. He needed to get well.

"Jamie, can you hear me? Please hear me. Watch over your brother. He needs you and so do I. Your letter brought me home, so now that I'm here, please guide me on what to do next. Because, big brother, I'm not sure what direction to take, so I will leave it up to you. I love you Jamie."

I wiped a tear and patted Jazzy. "Are you ready girl? Let's go back."

I felt invigorated by the time I returned with Jazzy. Oh my girl! I knew she was tired, but she endured it for me.

"Okay Jazzy, you get some rest. Thank you for not kicking me off. I've missed you." I held her face and placed my cheek up against hers.

"She missed you too," I heard a voice say behind me.

I turned and found Shane standing up against the door jamb to her stall.

"Is everyone around here trying to give me a heart attack?!" I screamed.

"Sorry, I didn't mean to."

"Just like you didn't mean to tell me off yesterday?"

"I guess I deserved that, but I do believe I apologized for my rudeness. Can we talk, please?" Shane looked hopeful and waited for me to agree.

"Okay. Buy me a hot chocolate."

"Nah, I know the owners, the hot chocolate is free. And I know where they hide the snacks." He smiled.

"Lead the way."

I took his hand in mine and we walked up to the house. It felt like the most natural thing in the world to do. Just like my ride with Jazzy. She knew me instantly. Followed my commands and did everything I always expected from my horse.

Shane was trying to mend our broken fences. He was also trying to break through my protective walls that shielded me from our past friendship. Everything he said yesterday was true. I should have been a better friend to him. What did I expect from Shane? His reaction was rude, but justified at the same time. Wendy was right. I wasn't the only one that lost Jamie. And when I didn't return home, they lost me too.

Still holding my hand, Shane led me into my warm house. I took in some calming breaths and silently prayed. I prayed that the friendship he promised that would be here when I was ready was in fact still real and strong enough to begin again. My eyes found his, and warmth wrapped around me.

A poster size family picture of us hung above the fireplace. Mama and daddy were holding each other and looking so in love. Their eyes actually shimmered with sparkle from the sunlight behind them. Jamie and I were on our horses. Mama wanted to have some candid photos taken of us. This one was her favorite she always said. It was the year Jamie was officially in remission from his leukemia. Mama said a blessing like this should be forever remembered in a photo.

"I'll try big brother. I'll try for you." I said to myself, as Shane called me into the kitchen.

CHAPTER 8

...friends first

"IT'S GOOD TO see you in this house, Tenley. It's not something I thought would ever happen again. Other than the few e-mails we have shared, and a call or two, that was all I had of you. It saddens me that what we had was reduced to that. Seeing you yesterday was a shock to my system. I knew you were coming, but to see you in person rocked me off my axis. And again, I'm sorry I was such a dick to you."

"It's my fault, all of it."

"No, it's not. We all played a part in it, and it's about time I own some of it. I'll never regret making love to you Tenley, not ever. I wanted you, always wanted you, and I took my chance to be with you. I was selfish and damn it hell to how Jagger, or anyone would feel about it. I'll always love you, but I know it's different on how you loved me. Deep inside I knew how you felt, and how you loved Jagger. I hurt him deeply, so deeply that it's taken years to rebuild our friendship and the broken trust that was lost. I'm telling you straight and please listen to me. He loves you, he never stopped." He looked as if he was going to say more, but stopped and reached for my hand instead.

"Shane, that may be true, but it's been five years, and I just can't come back home and take back what I chose to walk away from in the first place."

"Yes, you can. You have every right because you belong to each other. It's about time you stop running from his love and fight for him, fight for the both of you. We all see it. Now it's time for you to do the same."

"This is all too confusing. Shane, your father told me that although you tried to reconcile with Jagger, you two could never meet a middle ground. You never became partners like you always dreamed you would and basically went your separate ways. And now you are telling me something entirely different. What's the real truth?"

"The truth is that it has taken us years to find that place where we can both be in the same room without killing each other, but it's nowhere I want it to be. What you and I did, and then Jamie dying, ended our dream of being partners, but yet, we still work all of this land and do what we do best. It's just a different rhythm, that's all."

"I'm sorry." *What else could I say at this point? I was just sorry.*

"Look at me, Tenley, please."

He lifted my chin with his finger as my tears began to silently fall. He wiped them away with his thumbs and gently kissed me on my cheek. "Go to him. Jagger needs you, and you need him."

Lost in Shane's beautiful eyes, I kissed him back on his cheek and said "Thank you, friend." He smiled back at me.

"We were always friends first, right?" he said.

"No, we're not, that's not true." I quickly responded.

He looked at me with a puzzled expression.

"We're family," I said.

His smile returned, and I turned to get ready. I wasn't sure what today would bring for Jagger, and for me, but I had to try. I took a big step with Shane today. We both were on the road to healing, and

I already felt steadier on my feet. Shane was amazing. The boy I remembered showed up today to be my friend and helped show me the way. I looked out to the Teton Mountains from my window and thanked my brother.

"Mama, daddy," I called out before leaving the ranch.

Daddy came out from his office and swept me up into his best bear hug.

"There you are, Tumbleweed. Sorry I missed you at breakfast, but I heard all about it."

"I'm sure you did, daddy. Where's mama?"

"She's in town with Wendy."

"I see."

"Now don't go losing your sparkle. Your mama is fine and so is Wendy. They love you, you know this. Did your ride with Jazzy help?"

"How did you know I took Jazzy out this morning?"

"A father knows, and by the look of Jazzy a little while ago, that horse looks re-born. Thank you for giving her some happiness."

"It was Jazzy that did that for me."

"Before you go, I have something for you."

My father handed me an envelope addressed to me from Jamie. I gasped when I recognized his handwriting.

"Oh daddy! How many more are there? I don't think my heart can take much more."

"I'm not sure darling. That son of mine was a wise one with an equally wise old soul. Who knows what he chose to do in his last days here on earth. He kept us at a safe distance during his final days and never wanted us to see his pain. Even in the end, he always put us first above anything else. So it's high time you stop blaming yourself for staying away or feeling he pushed you away. You weren't the only one, Tumbleweed. He did it to us too. The only difference was? We were here, and you were at school. The distance still felt the same to all of us who loved him. We all suffered."

I hugged my father and took the letter from him. I couldn't read it just yet. *No more tears today, I can't continue to break down like this.* I stuffed it into my purse and left for town.

I loved Jackson Hole, but I could do without the arctic weather. It was just barely twenty degrees today. The town already had begun putting up their Christmas decorations, and the town square was already set to light up the tree. Tourists from all over the world flocked to this area to ski, ride, and do anything the great state of Wyoming had to offer. I checked the logs while I was down at the barn. We had reached full capacity with visitors. I was relieved that daddy had kept our part separate from the business side of it.

Before going in to the hospital, I had to check in with my office. I dialed Roxy directly, and she answered in her most professional tone.

"Ms. Fairchild's office, Roxy speaking."

I laughed silently to myself. The partners wanted her to say a whole spiel, but I kept it simple.

"Good morning, Roxy. This is Tenley."

"Good morning, Ms. Fair . . . , I mean *Tenley*. How are things going in Wyoming?"

"Hi, Roxy. I'm okay, better than I expected to be. How's the office? Anything I need to be aware of?"

I waited for her answer, and that's when I heard Zoey in the background.

"Roxy, is that Tenley? Hand me that phone," she enunciated very slowly to her. *Oh my goodness! I love that girl.*

"Tenley Fairchild! Why are you avoiding my calls? I've been calling you non-stop since you left on this mysterious trip of yours."

"You are so full of it Zoey, and check your voicemails, I have texted and returned your calls. We just keep missing each other, but I am not avoiding you."

"Well, okay then, sorry. When are you coming home? I need my best friend."

Coming home? Is New York my home? Or is it just a place I've been existing in since I lost my brother?

"I'm not sure, Zoey. I told your father that I didn't have a return date scheduled. I have a lot to work out here, and it's been a long time since I've been home."

"Wow! Tenley Fairchild is actually giving me some insight to her past. Tell me more."

I laughed and smiled through the phone. "I will, someday. I need to go Zoe, but I'll be in touch soon."

"Hey, wait a minute. Don't hang up."

"What is it?"

"What's up with you and Tommy? I saw him last night, and he didn't look so hot. And that's saying something because our boy oozes hotness."

"It's complicated, Zoe. Before I left for my trip we crossed a line that should have never happened, and one I deeply regret."

Here it comes . . . I held my cell away from my ear and braced myself for Zoey's reaction.

"Oh my God! You fucked him! Wow, oh wow, I need details."

I was imagining how many people overheard what she just screamed out loud into the phone. *Oh my crazy friend! No filter and certainly no discretion.*

"Not this call. Zoey, I have to go," I said as I hit End on my phone.

As I stepped off the elevator, I was greeted by Shirley, Jagger's nurse.

"Well, good afternoon, dear. How are you today?" She was so kind and welcoming.

"Other than cold, I'm good. How is Mr. Brown Eyes this morning?" I couldn't help but tease her about the nickname she had given Jagger.

"He's better."

"What?"

"How?"

"Did he wake up? Did he open his eyes?" I was almost shouting.

"No sweetie, not yet, but he did move his arm. He must be having some great dreams, because I saw his eyes flutter, and he half smiled. He's coming back to you. He's just taking his time."

"Thank you, Shirley. May I see him?"

"Of course you can, honey. You just missed his folks, but they already told me that I should expect you."

I smiled and went in to see Jagger. I'm still reeling from the fact that everyone in my life knows me better than I know myself. I sat gently on his bed and held his hand. His beard had been clearly cleaned up and his skin looked brighter. He still was healing from his injuries with faint coloring still lining his beautiful body.

Until he can tell me differently, I slowly began taking Jagger back into my heart. He's always been there, but now I'm actually allowing myself to feel. To remember every detail about him. To know what it is to love Jagger Parrish.

I wanted to kiss every scratch, every bruise, so I did. I lifted his gown and kissed his thigh with no cast. Ever so gently, I brushed my lips across his tanned skin and was tickled by the faint hair on him. As I got closer to his lower region, naughty thoughts invaded my mind. I wanted Jagger in my mouth. I wanted to taste him, feel him hard inside as his orgasm built and would thrust harder against my tongue. *WTF!* He's in a coma for crying out loud. My skin was on fire with fantasizing about him. I guess that would be one way to wake him up.

I quickly covered him up and began talking to him. "Some things never change. Every time I'm around you, I just want to jump you, and if memory serves, you always let me. Oh Jagger! Please wake up. I have so much to tell you. I'm hoping you will want to hear it and give me a chance to be your friend again."

Who am I kidding? We were always so much more than friends. We were each other's soul mate.

After talking for a couple of hours, he never stirred a bit. I was thirsty and got up to get a soda. I returned a few minutes later and noticed his hand had shifted. I wasn't sure if my eyes were playing tricks on me, but I was hopeful that Jagger was indeed coming back to me. I sat and sticking out from my purse was Jamie's second letter to me. I wanted to know what was inside of it, but I didn't want to hurt over it. I've cried enough in the last few days and wished to cry no more. *I can't change my past. I can only move forward.*

Another hour passed and my lip was nearly ripped open from me chewing on it.

"Screw it!" I said as I ripped open the envelope.

Dear Tumbleweed,

If you're reading this letter, then I know you're finally home where you belong. So far, you are choosing right. I knew you would, but I had two very different letters prepared just in case. I'm happy you are reading this one.

How was your ride with Jazzy? She missed you, I'm sure of it. A horse never forgets her owner, and you two always shared a special bond. I love you, Tenley, so much. I'm happy you found your way back home. Please stay this time and remember all the great things about our home. You will always find more good than bad.

When you're ready, visit my grave with mama and daddy. You three need to come together as a family and find peace in your loss. I know I'm asking a lot, but it needs to be done. You have to take the next step in your story. Tenley, it begins with saying goodbye to me. You weren't ready five years ago, but you are now. Please think about it.

Tell my brothers I love them. Even in heaven, I'll always be here for all of you. Before you chew the shit out of your lip, yes, my sister, another letter is waiting for you. When the time is right, Wendy will know what to do. Don't be mad at her. This wasn't easy on her to agree to this request of mine, but because she loved me and loves you, she couldn't deny me.

I love you, Tumbleweed. I'll be watching and waiting to see what you do next.

Love Always,

    Jamie

Wiping away my tears that have once again fallen down on his letter, I sighed and held it close to my heart.

"Oh Jamie! I miss you so much. Why did you leave me?"

If there was ever a better time for Jagger to wake, this would be it.

"Come on, cowboy! You've slept long enough. I bet you are loving torturing me with your silence. I'm strong, Jagger, I promise I can take it. You can say anything you want to me, but you need to wake up first. I totally get playing the 'hard to get' card, but come on. Even you would have to agree enough is enough. Please, Jagger . . . please. Wake up and come back to me. I'm here. All you need to do is open your eyes."

I looked for a sign, and he remained still.

...day by day

"GOOD MORNING, JAGGER." I say as I sat beside his bed. I made myself comfortable for yet another day waiting for him to come back to me. It's been more than a week, and no change. So much for waking my sleeping cowboy. I didn't really think one kiss from me would do the trick, but somewhere deep inside, I did hope.

Why isn't he waking up? Physically he is on the mend, so why this never ending sleep? Does he know I'm here?

After receiving Jamie's second letter, I decided to stay on here until Jagger woke up and we had a chance to talk. Sounds crazy, right? No crazier when I actually heard myself talking to Raymond Steele about giving me an extended leave of absence. He wasn't all that thrilled about it, but I am a partner now, and I have never asked for such a request. I was ready to throw the legal card at him. I couldn't be denied a leave of absence. This was not me on holiday in Belize, this was personal. I was home for a family emergency. Raymond was always kind to me, and I was happy I didn't have to use my usual gladiator tactic and push him into agreeing. He just wished me well and hoped I would return soon. He made me laugh by telling me that Zoey was driving him crazy.

I'm not sure what will happen when Jagger finally does wake, but I have to be here when he does. I have to see this through and hopefully find the closure to my past—our past—and finally be able to move on with a clean slate. *Is that possible? I want to believe it is, so I will.*

I began to doze in my chair when Shane entered the room. He seemed a bit nervous about something. I asked him if he was okay, and he gave me the biggest grin. His smile cheered me up, and now my curiosity was now piqued as to why he looked so happy.

"Hey, Tenley, how's our boy doing?" he asked quietly.

"The same." I replied.

"Can you step outside for a few minutes? I have someone I would like you to meet."

"Of course. Hey, cowboy, I'll be right back. You might want to think about opening your eyes. Remember I told you about Nurse Shirley, yeah that one. Well, she likes you, so do us all a favor and wake up, so you could flirt with her. You think about it, and I'll be back in a few."

I couldn't help but smile. I would say just about anything right now to get that man to open his beautiful eyes.

I closed the door behind me and stepped out into the hallway. Shane walked over to me, hand in hand with a gorgeous blonde by his side. I didn't recognize her, but why would I? I don't live here anymore.

"Tenley, I would like to introduce to you my fiancé, Shelby Morrison. Shelby this is Tenley Fairchild, um . . . "

Shane had seemed to stutter over the last part. The last time I checked, we had settled to be friends, so that's what I would introduce myself as.

"Hi, Shelby, very nice to meet you, and what Shane is trying to say is that I am an old friend. We grew up together."

"No worries. I've heard all about it," she replied.

Nervous didn't look so hot on Shane. He almost looked sick with her snide comment to me, but I shrugged it off and didn't saying anything sarcastic in return.

"Congratulations on your engagement," I said to Shelby, who never took her disapproving eyes off of me.

I couldn't help myself, so a little snarky return wouldn't hurt too much. I said, "So Shane, when we talked last week, you never mentioned a fiancé, or even having a girlfriend for that matter."

Her blue eyes darted back to Shane, as she waited for his response.

"I didn't mention it to you because the subject of my life was not the focus at the time, you coming home was. Now that you are here, it was time for you to meet Shelby. We are getting married on Valentine's Day."

"How romantic for you," I said. *Yeah, that was a bit snarky, but it's clear the girl is sizing me up. I'm not her competition for Shane's attention.*

"Shelby, would you mind going downstairs and grabbing me a coffee? I need a few minutes here with Tenley."

"Sure, baby, I'll be right back."

"Don't rush on my account," I called out, getting a raised eyebrow from Shane. He waited until the elevator door closed to begin our conversation.

"What has gotten into you? I bring my fiancé here to meet one of my oldest friends in the world, and you behave like a total bitch. What the fuck, Tenley?"

"I'm a bitch? Did you see the daggers your girl was shooting at me? She's never met me until today, and she looks like she hates me on sight. Shane, this is the last thing I need right now, a little heads up would have been nice."

"I'm sorry if she was rude. We've been through a lot to be together and with you suddenly here, it has stirred up some old wounds."

114

"I have no idea what you are talking about. What old wounds?"

"Tenley, I met Shelby about a year after you left for law school. I never had any intentions on getting serious with anyone, but she kind of nailed me right in the heart and it's been hers ever since. I struggled for a while with my feelings, not easily allowing her to get close. I thought I was so in love with you that a part me was hoping you would come back to me, not Jagger. I was so foolish to ever think that. You were like wishing upon a star. I wished and wished and then for one brief night, you were mine. The fantasy was beautiful. The reality wasn't like anything I dreamed of. The realization of losing you before I really even had a chance with you hurt me most. Then you left, we lost Jamie, and I was left here to pick up the pieces of my life without you in it."

"Shane, I'm so sorry you ever had to feel a moment of pain, but I can't change what happened between us. I can't be held accountable for how you felt about me, when it was you who never shared your feelings with me. I can only own my part in what happened after, and for that I'm sorry. Shane, I'm done saying I'm sorry. If what we talked about last week has now suddenly changed, then I will accept that and move on. Although, you will not be able to avoid me all the time. I am a Fairchild, and the ranch which you work on is my home. We still need a level of civility between us, for the sake of the business."

"Wow! You are fucking unbelievable," he retorted.

"Now what did I do?"

"How do you do it, Tenley?"

"Do what, Shane?"

"Be you. It must be exhausting being a full-time bitch. I came here as a friend and now I've been reduced to a lowly ranch hand. Well, princess, let me enlighten you. I am a partner in the Fairchild Dynasty. You may be blood, but it's my blood, sweat, and tears that work that ranch every single fucking day. So please get off your soapbox and curb your city attitude. Be my fucking friend like you used to be, because you are sure as hell not my boss."

"Once again, my dear friend, thank you for your honesty. At least I know where we stand with each other."

"Dammit, Tenley, this is not where we stand. I hate that we are fighting like this. I want us to go back to how we were before I fucked it all up. Please, can we do that?"

"*We* fucked it up." I reminded him. "Shane, we can never go back, but I can promise to try to move forward. I've missed you these last years, and I would be lying if I said I didn't. The few interactions we had were not nearly enough, but I've accepted how things were because I still felt guilty for all that happened. I don't feel that way anymore. Not since we talked. From my parents to Wendy, they have all talked to me about it. I can't live this way anymore. Holding onto the past has brought no good to my life. So Shane, it's done. Where do we go from here?"

"We start over."

"You mean it?"

"With all my heart. I love you, Tenley, but I'm in love with Shelby Morrison, and I can't wait to marry that woman."

"And I can't wait to marry you. I love you, Shane!" she screamed from down the hallway back to him. As she walked up closer to us, she said to me, "I'm sorry, Tenley, since you are starting over with Shane, how about me too? I'm not normally a jealous person, but it's been hard living in your shadow. I guess I had to see for myself what makes you so special."

"Come on, Shel . . . "

"Shane, please let me finish. I've heard hundreds of stories from Shane, your parents, everyone who knows your story with Shane, Jagger, and your brother. At times, I wasn't sure how Shane and I would work, knowing he still had unfinished business with you."

"Shelby, I can assure you, I'm no threat to your relationship or future with Shane. I want him to be happy and you seem to want that too, so do it. I won't be the one standing in the way of that."

She nearly dropped the coffees she was holding and lunged herself at me, nearly knocking me over in the process. She was crying happy tears, I think, and boy what a grip she had on me. I guess this is what she needed to hear. At least I can help someone while I'm here.

"Thank you," she whispered in my ear.

I didn't need to say anything else. I gave Shane a hug, Shelby too, and left them be while I returned to Jagger.

After another hour passed, I was so tired and that room chair was not the greatest thing for my back. I gave my body a much needed stretch and contemplated climbing into bed with Jagger. I was small enough to squeeze in beside him. So I kicked off my boots and snuggled up next to him.

This would be the first time I've actually really felt his body up against mine in over five years. I closed my eyes and got lost in my memories.

It was several days before our big fight since we last made love. I remember every detail of that night. We took out our horses, Jazzy, and She-devil, and rode through the late day hours to catch the sunset up on the north ridge. Jagger had settled the horses and then settled me. We were sprawled out on a blanket and lying on our backs, staring up to the sky. It was summer time here in Wyoming, and the skies were colored in pinks, blues, and fluffy white clouds. Jagger had his mother pack a basket for us filled with goodies to share.

Those were the perfect kind of dates. I didn't need fancy restaurants, or high priced gifts, I just needed Jagger. Even though I knew we were out here alone, I was always afraid my daddy would ride up and catch us. I wanted to make love with Jagger under the stars, but my fear of my father won out. He laughed at me in a teasing way, but agreed with me in the end. We finished our dinner and rode back to my parents' cabin. Jagger had me pinned up against the door before I could even drop my keys.

His body towered over mine. He loved to hold both my hands to his one over my head and kiss and nip at me. I loved it, and he knew it too. We always tended to fuck hard first, and then he would make sweet love to me on the bed. He was well, big, and I felt the immediate stretch of his dick as he entered me. My fingernails would dig into his cobra-like arms until I got used to the intense invasion. He would smile at me because he said my fingernails felt like kitten claws on his hard muscles. After we made love, he would always take care of me. He would run a bath for me, or just clean us both up and hold me while I drifted off into sleep.

I blinked my eyes open, and I suddenly didn't feel all that well. Remembering making love with Jagger, and to be here with him now made my heart ache. I carefully moved out of the bed and as far as I could get with my tears flowing.

"What am I doing? God, Jagger, you must hate me for how much I've hurt you. I'm so fucking selfish. They have me all convinced that this is where I belong . . . here with you. I'm behaving as if you're going to wake up any minute, take me in your arms, and we will magically get back together."

I just stared back at the beautiful man sleeping so soundly. I felt more lost than ever. I grabbed my things and bolted out of his room, not looking back at him. I didn't have the strength to stay. Here I was telling Shane not too long ago to move on from the past, but can I really do that for myself? Everyone seems to think that Jagger is just going to wake up and welcome me back. This will never work. We will still be at the same crossroad we faced five years ago. His life is here in Wyoming, and my life is in New York. Mama has already asked me if I would ever consider relocating back here or close to the nearest city. I never answered her question on account of not wanting to hurt her feelings with my answer. I simply could not predict the future and where I would fit into Jagger's life, or even expect to.

They all want me back, but the one I truly need to hear from can't tell me. I passed Wendy's house on my way out of town. I almost stopped to talk to her, but I was being led in another direction. I knew where I had to be and hopefully would find the answers I need.

I parked my truck and hiked up the hill to see the beautiful panoramic view of King Mountain. I knelt down on the cold hard ground. This would be my first time here since I lost him.

"Hi Jamie." I whispered, as I brushed the fallen snow off his stone.

CHAPTER 10

...stay

"HI, JAMIE. SO I'm following part of your letter. You have to realize how hard this is for me to be here, knowing where you are. I'm sure you already knew when you were writing your letters to me that I would eventually end up here."

"Please understand that I didn't stay away all of these years because I was punishing mama and daddy. It was more like punishing myself. I know I've hurt them with my distance, but what was I to do, Jamie? I already made so many mistakes. The way I hurt Shane and Jagger was the beginning of the end. I think back now on how I could have compromised and gone to a different school to stay closer to Jagger, but it was never about leaving him, it was more about me experiencing life away from the ranch."

"You know I loved the ranch, but I also wanted more beyond the life I was born into. I never knew how much my choice hurt others around me until mama's phone call to me last week. Now I'm home, where they say I belong, and the life I was leading back in

New York is on a permanent time-out until I figure out what to do next. I can't stay here, Jamie. I just can't leave the career I've worked so hard for to just walk away from it. I have built a life there for myself, and I'm not a hundred percent sure if I want to walk away from all of that. Don't you think if I wanted this picturesque life here in Wyoming, then I would have come back way sooner than now?"

"Jamie, I sit at Jagger's bedside day in and day out, waiting for some kind of sign that he knows I'm there. It's been over a week Jamie, and he is showing no sign of waking up. I don't know how much longer I can do this, brother. I know you are disappointed in the choices I've made, but they were mine to make and there's no point of regretting them now. It's just too late. Mama wants me to stay on through the holidays, but I'm not sure. Not a day that goes by that I don't miss you, big brother, but being back home has shown me one thing. I have to re-join the land of the living. I'm nearly thirty years old, and I'm alone. I won't sit here and tell you that my career is enough, because that would be a lie."

"I want a family to call my own someday, I just don't know if that family is with Jagger. Too many years have gone by, and he deserves to be happy and loved by someone who loves him above anyone or anything. I'm just not sure if I'm that person. You know Jamie, this would be a good time to show me a sign that you're listening to me."

"You're the right person," I heard from behind me.

"Holy shit!!! Wendy!!! You have to stop sneaking up behind me like that! My heart can't take it."

"Oh, Tumbleweed, I'm sorry. I didn't mean to frighten you. I saw you pass by, and I just had a feeling where you might be headed. I took a chance and here you are."

"So, are you my sign from Jamie? You seem to be his messenger these days."

"I can be anything you want me to be, but I'll settle for friend for now. You are struggling so much, and you don't have to be. You came home. You made amends the best way you could, and you've been with Jagger. No one could really ask or expect much more from you."

"Seriously? You don't really believe that? I know my coming home is based on so much more than you just said. Wendy, a few conversations with mama and daddy is not making amends, it's a first step. As for Jagger, I guess I didn't turn out to be the saving grace everyone was hoping for. You had to see his parents yesterday. They were going on and on about Christmas, and how great it's going to be to have me here. I'm so torn between my past and my present, my head is spinning. Everyone around me has hope, and I get within five feet of Jagger, and I'm just lost in his proximity. I'm flooded with sweet memories of us together. It takes all my strength not to shake him to wake up. Wendy, please tell me what to do."

"What's your heart telling you?"

"It's screaming from the Teton Mountains to fight for him this time."

"I do believe you have your answer, Tumbleweed. And you know what?"

"What is it?"

"I think it's high time we stop calling you Tumbleweed."

"Why do you say that? It was Jamie's name for me."

"Did you ever consider why that is?"

"Gee, Wendy, I don't know. We live in Wyoming. I thought growing up it was a cute name, and because they used it in a loving manner toward me, it stuck."

"Well, it may have served a purpose at one time, but not anymore. Some would argue that the term is meant to have no purpose. You travel down any given road the wind takes you. You see? It doesn't suit you anymore because for the first time since Jamie died, you are on the right road. The road that brought you home. The road that led you back to your family. The road that led you back to the one you love. The road that led you back here to this very place you ran from. Don't you see, Tenley? All roads lead home. You just needed a little reminding, that's all. Get out of your analytical mind and just listen to your heart. It's a good one that has been alone for too long now. You are a beautiful, smart, and incredibly accomplished young woman. We are so proud of you, but we also worry for you. If you can tell me that with all I've said here, is just an old woman hearing herself talk, then the subject is closed and we shall not speak of it again."

"You're not wrong, Wendy. It's me who's been wrong. How do I fix it?"

"I think you already know that answer. You don't need me to tell you. Just listen to your heart. It knows what to do. Come on now, it's cold up here, and I'm fixing to get some hot chocolate."

"I think I need something a bit stronger than that. Can you give me a few more minutes up here? I'll meet you back at your place."

"Okay, honey, be safe. It's beginning to get dark, and these hills are treacherous."

"I may live in New York, but I haven't forgotten my country."

"Well, thank goodness for that. I do believe you've seen the light."

"I love you, Wendy."

"I love you more," she said as she walked away.

"You heard all of that, right? Jamie, I can't promise you a happy ending for Jagger and me. It's complicated, and we have a lot to make up for. And that's only if he's willing to try with me. I can promise you this: I will for once in my life lead with my heart. I'll try. That's really the best I can promise you right now. Up to a week ago, I thought I had it all figured out, and now I'm here and my world is turned upside down. I know you're smiling, maybe even smirking. You always knew me better than I knew myself. You were downright irritating at times, but I would give anything to have you here with me now. I will love you forever and always keep you in my heart. I have to go now, but I'll be back with mama and daddy. I do believe that's another request of yours. I won't let you down this time."

As I began to make my way down the hill, a gust of wind blew in my direction and showers of snow swept over my face. I looked up to heaven and smiled up at Jamie.

"I did ask for a sign, right? Better late than never. I love you big brother!"

Although I was staying back at the ranch, I felt I hadn't been home in days. I'd been sitting vigil with Jagger and just going home to change clothes. I knew I needed a change of scenery, so I phoned my parents to meet me over at Wendy's. She had a glass of her favorite brandy waiting for me and a blazing fire to warm the house. I was cold and wet from sitting on the ground in front of Jamie's grave. Mom was bringing me fresh clothes to change into.

I cozied myself in Wendy's oversized chair she kept near the fireplace. She liked to sit here and read her romance novels. She, after all, was the one that got me into reading. We would sit for hours and just laugh over all of the hot men in the books. I used to tease her all the time that I didn't need to fantasize over a fictional character when I had the reality with Jagger.

I must have fallen asleep by the time mama and daddy arrived.

"Hey, my sweet girl, wake up now." I stirred to my father's voice. He was so incredibly handsome. He was wearing his wranglers with a red plaid shirt, boots, and to complete his look, his black Stetson hat.

"Hi, daddy. Mama is going to have to hog tie you down around the other ladies tonight. She can't take you anywhere without women swooning over you."

"Oh, my darling daughter. You are good for an old man's ego, but the only swooning I want is from your lovely mother. And don't count your mama out. She's a looker, but lucky for me, she's all mine."

"That I am, Brock, and I wouldn't want it any other way."

"Well that's good to hear, wife, because you're stuck with me."

Oh, how I had missed their banter with one another. They loved each other so much, it was a crazy, out of this world love, and they still went at each other as if they were teenagers. *I want that. I want what my parents have.*

"Are we eating, or what?" my father asked.

"Yes, daddy, we are. Can you give me a few minutes to shower and change?"

"You have fifteen minutes."

"Seriously, Brock! I can barely wash my hair in that amount of time." My mother said, as she kissed my cheek.

"Time's a wasting. Go daughter . . . now!"

I laughed all the way up to Wendy's bathroom. *For the first time in a long time, I felt really good to just let go and see where the wind takes me. Not like a no direction Tumbleweed, but for the first time, feeling some peace for a change. Yeah, I like that.*

We dined over at daddy's favorite cowboy bar and restaurant. They had all of his favorites on the menu that he really shouldn't be eating, but he said indulging once in a while won't hurt. We took separate cars on account that I wanted to visit Jagger after dinner. It would be beyond visiting hours, but Shirley had made me up a special visitors pass. Mr. Parrish also listed me as family.

I wasn't a rule breaker and didn't want to cause any trouble, but I was also secretly happy to be able to come and go and have access to Jagger.

"I'm stuffed. Daddy, those ribs were huge. How many did you eat?"

"Too many to count, so don't ask. Thank you, Tenley, for today."

"No worries, daddy. It's just dinner."

"No, I don't mean dinner, I meant to say thank you for visiting with your brother today. Judging by the condition of your clothes when we arrived at Wendy's, I figured you went up there."

My mother was quiet, but peace was written all over her face. She held my father's hand and listened as my father spoke to me.

"It's not an easy place to be, and I get that. In the beginning, I did everything in my power to evade that place. I didn't want my boy to be there, but I knew his precious soul was already in heaven and it was his body that now has returned to the earth. Are you okay? Is there anything you want to talk about?" Daddy asked.

"Do you mean the letter?"

"Yes. Wendy dropped it off while you were riding this morning and instructed me to give it to you."

"I'm okay daddy, but thank you for asking. I'm trying to understand what was going through Jamie's mind while writing those letters to me. Jamie asked me to visit and to bring you two with me. While I was there, I promised I would return with you soon."

"We will be ready when you are. Your brother loved you very much. I don't have the why to his reasons for the letters, but it's clear that your brother was thinking of you and your future happiness to the very end. We love you so much, daughter. Please understand that in our darkest hours of grief, if you ever felt that we pushed you away for any reason, I am truly sorry for that. You are our child, no matter how old you are. Grief can cripple one's soul, and it did for your mother and me for a while, but we forged ahead, and never considered how you were affected by his loss. Sure, I knew to some degree. Hell, I was the one that put you on the bus. But sweetie, I thought I was doing the right thing by you. I supported your choice of law school because we always wanted to give you anything you wanted. If I could, I would have kept you home with us."

"Daddy, where is all of this coming from? It's done."

"It's not done until I tell you the last part."

"When you were accepted into Yale Law School. I thought my heart was going to burst with joy. I was so proud of you. We were so damn proud of you. Our baby girl was going to be a lawyer. Of course, I panicked at the sheer thought of you being so far away, but your brother convinced me to support you and ultimately let you go. I'm sorry I kept his worsening condition from you. He begged me not to tell you his secret, and all I could do was give him what he wanted. I suspect it may be one of the reasons why you never returned home up to now. Jamie's funeral was a complete blur, so I'm counting this as your first time home."

"I don't think I can take a separation like that again, nor can your mother. You will always have a home with us, and please, whatever you decide for you, I hope we are included in your decisions. We need our daughter in our lives, and it's not okay to be without you anymore. You are all we have left, Tenley. I promise you with all that I am, and for the rest of my life, I will never take you for granted again."

My father's declaration had taken me by surprise. He was always an attentive father, but it was my mother who always did most of the talking. My father spoiled me, and pretty much favored what mama said, or just would give in. To listen to him speak with his heart on his sleeve broke my heart. It showed me how much I'd hurt them with my absence and refusal to come home when they repeatedly asked me to.

I wiped my tears away and held both of their hands. "I love you two so much. I'm sorry I hurt you when I should have been here with you. Can you please forgive me?"

"Oh, baby girl! There is nothing to forgive. We love you too," mama said.

"I'm not sure what tomorrow will bring, but I promise to tell you first. I have so much to work out and I'm not sure what will happen with Jagger. I know I don't ever want to disappoint you again, so please be patient with me?"

I don't know who was crying more, but the waiter broke up our group hug and delivered us three heaping plates of moose track pie with extra vanilla ice cream on top. Daddy licked his lips and dug in to his portion.

It was nearing nine o'clock, and we said our goodbyes. I promised them I would be back sometime tomorrow. I had planned on staying in town tonight. Now back at Jagger's room, I sat in my usual spot and began talking to Jagger.

"So today was pretty crazy. Shane and I butted heads, again.

Then I met his bitchy fiancé, who turned out to be a sweetheart, so I take that back. Fantasized about you. Yes, really naughty thoughts. That's another story. Anyway, I visited with Jamie. It was my first time since he died. Jagger, I felt he was with me the entire time, and he even threw snow at my face. You remember all of the snowball fights we used to have? He would nail me every time, and then you and Shane would team up and clobber him. By the time the battle was over, we were all soaked and shivering from being cold and wet. Well, I would like to think it was Jamie giving me a sign, but who knows? These past days spent here have been a revelation for me. A self-discovery of me and who I am."

"You live in a dark bubble for so long, and that's all you see. Sure I was functioning in my day to day, but not really living. I can say that now without question. Being home puts things in perspective for you. I've said more apologies this week to more people than I can count on one hand, and all I really want is your forgiveness."

"Jagger, I know I was foolish back then and so reckless, but I'm trying to move past that and begin again. The past is the past and I can't change anything about it, but learn from it and hopefully not repeat them. I've recently messed up with a friend of mine in New York. That's another story, but my point is, I now know I was allowing my past to define me. I can't do that anymore. I have to be able to let people in and embrace their love, as well as give love."

"Please wake up, Jagger, and I promise I will do everything in my power to get you well again. I promise to do anything for you. You just have to ask, and I'll do it. This time, I will put you first, I promise. Wake up, cowboy . . . please open your eyes? I'm exhausted and in need of some sleep. I will be back tomorrow, and we can pick up this conversation."

My eyes roamed over his body from head to toe. He was so tall, he barely fit into this bed. I looked over at his cast. He had so many signatures on it in all colors. Shane drew a picture of She-devil and put in a bubble . . . "I'm sorry," which reminded me to talk to Shane about the accident. I didn't want to deal with that now. Jagger needed to wake up first. There would be plenty of time to talk about it at another time.

"Okay, I really have to go now. My eyes are going to close, and I don't want to end up here beside you. I love you, Jagger."

I kissed him on his forehead and wished for him to awaken.

As my hand went for the doorknob, I heard a familiar voice call out to me. It was scratchy sounding, but it was him. I was frozen, but managed to turn around. His brown eyes were focused solely on me.

"Tenley, come here baby."

My heart was racing. He's awake. He's talking. I have to call a nurse, but he's drawing me in with just four words. I grabbed his hand and kissed it with my tears flowing, and gazed into his eyes. He struggled to speak, but managed to clear his throat. I gave him a sip of water.

"I just have one thing to say to you," he was able to get out of his dry, itchy throat.

I leaned in to hear what he would say. Now I was scared. What if he rejects me? I have to prepare myself for anything. I've been back home for days, and now it's the moment of truth. I tried my best to keep my erratic heart under control while waiting to hear his words that would decide my fate. Jagger gripped my hand and with a lone tear falling down his cheek, he whispered . . .

"Stay with me."

My tears matched his. I wanted to hold him, touch him, and scream, "Yes", but I held back and just took in the beautiful man before me. Three words that held so much promise for a new start with the man I love. *Maybe it is possible after all for a second chance for Jagger and me. If you would have asked me two weeks ago if I would be pondering this question, I would have said no. So much as changed since receiving Jamie's letter. What else did my brother have planned out in the stars for me?*

On the day I crushed his heart all those years ago, I questioned if I fit into his world. He screamed that I was his world and he wanted me with him.

Now five years later, here I am. How did I ever think I could just come home and easily leave again? Where do we go from here? Only time will tell.

CHAPTER 11

Jagger

...while i was sleeping

MY SUBCONSCIOUS WASN'T playing tricks with my brain. She was here. Tenley was here and she was real and not just a figment of my imagination. I desperately wanted to open my eyes to see her, but I was afraid.

I was afraid on what she might do once I did. The last time we were this close to each other, she turned and left me on my knees at the bus station. She said no to staying behind with me in Wyoming. She said no to my marriage proposal, she just said . . . no.

Tenley Fairchild broke my heart more times than I could count on one hand. First with applying to school so far away from our home. Fighting with me and nearly killing herself on my daddy's ATV. Bedding and fucking my best friend. Rejecting me when I chose to forgive her, and finally, just stopped fighting for us.

I stayed away because of Jamie, and what he asked of me. It was the least I could do for my dying brother, but she stayed away because she gave up. Tenley was no quitter in anything she did in her life, but after losing her brother, she lost a piece of herself too. I nev-

131

er stopped loving her. She was the sun, moon, and stars in my life, and I would not lose her again. The thought of watching her leave was just not possible for me to even entertain. No! This girl was not going anywhere this time, not while I still drew breath in my lungs and had these two arms to hold her.

She was even more beautiful since I last saw her. She still had an innocence about her, but she matured into a woman with adult features. Her hair was different. Long and pin straight, a bit darker, but still gorgeous. My fingers were itching to run through her thick tresses and wrap her hair around my wrist. I wanted to keep her as close as I can. She still had her lovely fair skin color, but I saw a hint of rosiness to her cheeks. A natural blush, I gather. She always blushed when she was happy. Her hazel eyes were glassy, but I saw a speck of sparkle to them.

Here she sat while gripping my hand and lovingly looking back at me. She was real and she was here with me. This had been my dream for the past five years: for Tenley, my girl, to come back to me.

Now all the fantasies that I had lost myself to for the years she'd been gone were now becoming a reality. She said she would do any-thing for me if I would awaken. Well now that I had, it was time for my girl to prove it. Yes, *my girl*. She never stopped being mine.

My darkest hour, finding her in bed with Shane, nearly de-stroyed me. After losing Jamie, I knew she was worth forgiving and fighting for. I would do everything in my power to keep her with me. If she needed a reminder to what we were and would be again, I would happily show her what it meant to be truly mine.

The road we were on back then was based on coming of age love. Sure, I thought I had all the answers and knew I wanted to share my life with Tenley, but I never realized how different we were until we parted ways.

She was a free spirit, where I was grounded. I wanted the ranch and all it had to offer, she wanted to go far away and experience a new way of life different from where she came from. I believed by loving Tenley, that love would be enough to change her mind to stay with me. But you can't hold down a wild horse no more than you can expect the girl you love to bow down at your feet. Not, Tenley, she's too strong for that.

Her tears had finally stopped and she was beckoning me to talk to her, but my eyes were weary. I was fighting to stay awake with her, but as my eyes closed, I heard her call out to me.

"No, Jagger, please stay with me. I need to hear your voice. Please, Jagger, don't go to sleep again."

Her words were lost on me, and I was out again. All my dreams were of Tenley. We were making love under the night sky on my daddy's ranch. Our spot that belonged to just us. Her hair swept wildly over her naked breasts as I fucked her deeply and she screamed out my name. I was awakened this time not by the sound of Tenley's voice, but to a shining light nearly blinding me.

"Hey there, son. Welcome back," said a voice I did not recognize, but assumed he was my doctor.

"Now there he is, Mr. Brown Eyes. Hello there, handsome, I'm Shirley, and I'm happy to meet you."

I tried to sit up, but the over accommodating nurse was adding more pillows to my back for support.

"There now, sugar, how do you feel?" she asked me through her smile. I think she was flirting with me. She's got to be around my mother's age if not older.

"Hi, Shirley." Was all I could say as my eyes scanned the room, and realizing Tenley has left. I felt as if I was just punched in my chest.

"Mr. Parrish, I'm Doctor Sampson. I've been overseeing your care since you were brought in over a month ago. Your vitals are strong and physically you are on your way to making a complete recovery, but I would like to run a few tests. I'm going to send you down to Radiology for a CAT scan and then we can talk some more."

"I've been unconscious for over a month? How is that even possible? Do I have a brain injury or something?" I nervously asked. The sound on the machine began to beep to a loud sound as my blood pressure began to rise.

"Mr. Parrish, please calm down. From our initial findings after your accident, you suffered a hematoma on your brain, which has now healed. With ordering another scan, I will confirm what I believe to be true. The cast on your leg can now be removed and you can begin physical therapy, as well as getting all of your muscles working again."

"If I don't have a brain injury, then why was I out for so long? Something is not right here, doc. I feel it."

"Mr. Parrish, I can assure you that you have received the best medical care, and I have no real answer to why you were sleeping for so long, but the good news is that you are awake now and all your faculties seem to be in working order. Let's thank the Lord for our blessings and not tempt fate, shall we?"

"Tenley . . . Where is Tenley?"

"I don't know any Tenley, is she a relative?"

"No, not relative, just the very reason why I'm awake in the first place."

"Mr. Parrish, let me bring Shirley back in for you and maybe she knows where your mystery woman is."

I think the good doctor was mocking and laughing at my expense. No fucking way—did I imagine her? Tenley was holding my hand. I saw her tears and felt her pain while I was in my coma.

"Hey, Mr. Brown Eyes, let's get you ready to go down for your test."

"Nurse please, where is Tenley?"

"Oh, you mean that sweet gal who's been camping out here in your room?"

"Yes, the very one."

"She'll be back handsome, don't you go worrying. After you woke up and then drifted back to sleep, she came and got your doctor. She was clearly upset and needed some air. I told her it would do her some good."

"How long ago was that?"

She looked at her watch and then checked my chart. She was flipping the pages while I wanted to just grab the chart away from her. How difficult could it be to figure out when I woke up?

"Ah, here it is. Dr. Sampson examined you around one in the morning, she left shortly after that."

"What the hell time is it now?" I screamed out as my throat burned with a sand paper- like feeling to it. I was so thirsty, I could drink a gallon of water.

"Mr. Parrish, you may have the nicest brown eyes I have ever seen, but you also need to calm down and let me talk." She put her hands on her hips and waited for me to comply.

"I'm sorry, Shirley, but I don't understand what is happening right now. She should be here with me."

"And I'm sure she will be, as soon as I call her. She left me her number to do so when you woke up."

"Well why didn't you tell me that in the first place?" I bellowed at her. It wasn't her fault, and here I was taking it out on the kind nurse before me.

"Men!!! Because you never gave me a chance to do so. And it is six thirty a.m., and I've had enough fuss from you. I need a cup of coffee first, and then I think I will have an orderly take you down."

Taking a much needed breath, I calmed myself and began again. She eyed me carefully, probably expecting me to shout again.

"I'm sorry for flying off the handle with you. You can't possibly understand what's going through my mind right about now. I thought I had imagined her being here, and when I woke to see her gone, it left me a bit freaked out."

"I understand more than you know, handsome. That girl has not left your side in nearly ten days. You have to be blind not to see how much she loves you. Take a few minutes to relax, and then you will have your test and clean up. She'll be back, I promise you. And your mama and daddy are anxious to see you too, as well as that other handsome fella, what's his name? Shane."

Just the sound of his name mentioned sent shivers up my spine. Shane was the last person I needed fucking help from. He was one that was responsible for me being in this bed. No thank you, but my so called . . . brother can stay the fuck away from me.

"Are you okay Mr. Parrish? You're white as a ghost. Someone jump on your grave?"

If she only knew.

"Yeah, something like that. Can we just get this CAT scan done and over with? The sooner I do, the sooner Tenley will be back here with me."

"Of course, let's go."

I sighed with relief, as the orderlies wheeled me out from my room. I closed my eyes and she was there . . . my Ten.

CHAPTER 12

...awake

NEARLY TWO HOURS had passed since I returned to my empty hospital room. I cleaned up the best I could with the cast still on my leg. I had all my personal toiletries here with me, so I took full advantage of using the familiar products instead of the antiseptic smelling hospital items they provided.

Nurse Shirley volunteered to give me a sponge bath, but I politely refused her. She was very sweet, but I only wanted one woman's hands on my body and lips on my mouth. I wanted her, all of her, and I was going crazy waiting for Tenley to return. My beard was a mess, my father was no barber. I took out my electric shaver and groomed my beard. I kind of liked it, so I just trimmed it to a clean cut. It was winter here in Wyoming, and the beard would keep my face warm from the brutal cold air.

I could feel my adrenaline rising as I wanted to leap from this bed. I needed to get out of here and back with Tenley. I needed her in my arms, in my bed, in my life . . . this time forever. Would she agree this time? Only time would tell.

"For a guy who's been playing the role of Sleeping Beauty, you sure don't look the part. You actually look pretty good, son."

My father was here. Gosh, I've missed him. He came over and took me into a bone crushing hug, while my mother silently wept behind him. They were a sight for sore eyes, and I was thanking God that I was back with them.

"How do you feel, son?" My mother asked.

"I'm good, mom, better than good. Have you called Tenley yet? She should be here by now. It's been hours."

"Calm down, boy, I'm sure she'll be here soon. That girl has not left your side. She's probably exhausted," my father explained.

"She may have turned her phone off to get some rest," my mother added.

"Listen, I know what you're trying to do, and I can promise you with my whole heart that I know she's coming back. She wouldn't do that to me again. You know that right?"

"Of course we do, son. Tenley has been nothing but amazing these past days. We've talked in great detail. She has a pretty incredible life in New York."

"It's not that incredible, dad," I mumbled under my breath, full knowing he heard me. He didn't have to play the buffer here, not where it concerned Tenley. He knows more than anyone what I sacrificed for her dream and my promise to Jamie. I did what I promised and waited out my time. Now it was time to take back what never should have been lost in the first place.

"She-devil. How is my horse dad?" My poor baby must be wondering where the hell I am. It wasn't her fault that she threw me. Shane lunged at me and spooked her. Then she nearly trampled me with her hoofs as I scrambled away from her. Shane was on top of me next and punching the shit out of me. When I finally gathered my wits, I fought back until I lost my balance over the ledge.

I screamed out for Shane to help me, and he froze. I begged him to pull me up and when my pleas finally registered with him, I lost my grip on the crumbling ledge. It was then Shane screaming out for me. My body tangled with the jagged rocks, brush, and the unforgiving river bank below. How I didn't die was a miracle, maybe it was Jamie that protected me while I fought to stay alive. Maybe it was my love for his sister and my determination to reunite with her.

"Are you listening to me son?"

"I'm sorry, what?"

"Just as I expected. Your head is always in the clouds. I said your horse is just fine. She misses you, but you'll see her soon."

"Dad, what happened after I fell? How much time went by before I was found?"

"Come on, Jagger. We don't have to talk about this now. You just woke up, and you need all your strength to get well. What's done is done, let it go."

"Like hell I will. How long dad?"

"Nearly ten hours before we located you son. I can't even begin to tell you the fear I had playing through my mind at that moment. I hated you for that. Don't ever do that to me again. You are my boy, my only child. You scared the hell out of us. Your poor mother cried for days. Hell, she's still crying, but I think they're happy tears now."

"Dad, I'm sorry you ever had to go through that, but it was no picnic for me either."

I was going to tell my father the reason behind my accident, when my mother walked back in with a pink box, no doubt filled with treats for me. Yup, I was right. I saw the bakery's logo on the side of the box. I had a sweet tooth and was a goner for bear claws. I didn't indulge often, but when I did, I enjoyed every bite of the delicious dessert.

"You must be starving, my poor boy. I have some donuts and pastries here for you, as well as a breakfast sandwich, coffee, and juice."

"Thanks, mama, I can go for some juice right now."

"Anything you want."

Anything I want? That should be obvious to everyone. I wanted

Tenley, and back here like yesterday. What could be taking her so long? Shirley told me that she left her number and to call her when I woke up. Something felt off, and it was getting me angrier by the minute.

"Dad, please pass me the phone? I need to call the ranch. She's not here, so that must mean she's home with her parents."

"Jagger . . . " He slowly said, and his face fell a bit. What are they not telling me?

"Dad? Where is Tenley?"

"You're right, she's home, but there's something else you should know."

"Ren, maybe this is not a good time," my mother latched on to my father's arm, as if she was pulling him away from me. Now that was all I was about to take. I was five seconds away to climbing out of this bed and crawling to find her if I had to.

"What are you not telling me?" I shouted with my father glaring back over at me. What did they expect from me?

"Jagger, now calm the heck down. You just came back to us after weeks of being unconscious. Give us a break if your parents want to just take in the miracle we've been blessed with, okay?"

"Okay," I whispered. "Dad, please hand me the phone? I want to hear her voice."

"You will son, soon. After we received the call from your doctor, we were blessing the heavens you came back to us. I personally phoned the Fairchilds, and Tenley. I couldn't hear a word she was saying through her cries, but after she gathered her wits, I asked her to stay away until we had a chance to spend some time with you."

"You did what?! Why dad? You know what she means to me," I shouted, making my mother jump at the loudness of my tone.

"I do know, son. Believe me when I say I understand perfectly what Tenley Fairchild means to you, but I also know all the hurt she has brought to your life. You say you made a promise to Jamie to let her go, but my son, really? You never did. You just said it in words, but never in your heart. We saw your pain play out every single day

140

for the past five years. We saw you hit rock bottom the day her brother died. We saw it more when he was lowered down into the cold earth and you two kids were hurting over your shared loss. She was on one side and you the other. Two lost souls fighting what you felt for each other because you were too stubborn to bend for the other."

Dad continued, "Jagger, you think we didn't see that? Do you think it didn't destroy us every time you came home drunk, or not home for days? We were out of our minds with worry over you. Then one day, you came back to us, and there was hope. It's like the light switched on, and you were focused again on the ranch, your family, friends, and all that used to have purpose in your life. You have light again in your eyes, son. I just don't want to see it burn out again."

"I promise you son, I love that girl like my own daughter. I hold no ill will against her, but you are my son first and your needs come before anyone. Do you understand what I am saying to you?" he said to me.

"Please don't be angry with us son. We needed this time with you," my mother said.

"Jagger, tell me you've heard everything I've said here today. Tell me my words have not fallen on deaf ears. I'm not trying to hurt you, I'm being your father. You are a grown man, and I certainly would never stand in your way, but I also want to protect you. Do you get where I'm coming from?"

"I do sir. I will always respect your opinions and be thankful for your wisdom, but daddy, I'm asking you to please trust me when it comes to Tenley. She's my life. I will not live one more day without her. Being angry with you two is the furthest emotion from my mind. I get it and understand, but you have to understand how I feel at the moment. I was in a horrific accident, and I didn't know if I was going to survive it. These past weeks all I've been dreaming about is *her*. I've played out every moment I have ever spent with Tenley and every feeling I experienced by loving Tenley Fairchild. Please don't look at me like I'm crazy. I know it's been a long time, but my feelings for her have not changed. I love her. I want her back in every area of my heart and life. I fully intend on making that happen as soon as I get out of here."

My mother needed no more explaining from me. She knew just by the look in my eyes.

"Okay. I'll call her." Mom said as she reached for her cell phone.

"Thank you mama. It's going to be okay. Trust in that."

CHAPTER 13

Tenley

...i'm here

I WAS OUT in the barn brushing Jazzy after our morning ride when my phone rang. It was Jagger's mother telling me her son finally had woken up. I couldn't help but shout out loud how happy I was to hear this news. I was taken back after she explained he's been up for a while, but only now calling me. I looked down at my watch and was shocked it was nearly noon.

A pang of hurt shot through my chest. What did I expect after all of this time? I had a lot to make up for, not only with Jagger, but his parents too. They loved me as much as my own parents did. The fact remains, I hurt their son and I shouldn't have expected a warm reception to my return. His father was another story. When I saw him at the hospital, he was nothing but kind to me. He was guarded, but he had to be and I would be too if the roles were reversed.

His mother, Ellen, always very kind, explained and assured me that all was alright. Ellen and Ren wanted some private time with Jagger, who by the way was hell on wheels after discovering I wasn't close by. His parents finally gave in to his demands, and that's when his mom called me. My folks were happy, and Wendy too. I'm sure now that he's awake, the onslaught of visitors will be non-stop. I ended my call with Ellen, and then finished tending to my horse. Jazzy looked well. I think my father was right when he said her spirits had brightened after we took our first ride.

I was still worried about She-devil, and how she could have thrown Jagger off of her. The lawyer in me wanted to interrogate him about his accident, but there was time for that. We had so much to talk about, and where would we begin?"

"Hey, Tumbleweed," a voice behind me called out. I turned to see Wendy, who was leaning up against the stable door.

"I thought you decided on not calling me by that name anymore. Change your mind?" I laughed.

"I guess you will always be a Tumbleweed to me, and so much more."

"Now don't go getting sappy on me, Wendy, I kind of like your street cred a little bit."

"I hear Jagger's awake and asking for you."

"Way to get right to the point."

"Is there any other way?"

"I suppose not. Yes, I know he's awake and I was just about to go in to shower and drive into town. My nerves are getting the best of me this morning, so a ride on Jazzy cures all."

"You don't have anything to be nervous about. He's probably chomping at the bit and stalking the door for you to walk through."

"Wendy, I'm scared shitless right now. I know what I said while he was in a coma, but now he's awake and probably has a hundred questions to why I'm home. What am I going to say? Being here doesn't change the fact that I still have another life waiting for me back in New York to return to. Is it fair of me to just give him false hope and break his heart all over again? I won't do that again, Wendy."

"Does that mind of yours ever just slow the hell down? You seem to already have it all figured out, and you haven't even seen him yet. Damn girl, take a step back and get yourself back to neutral. The first step is to see him, the rest? Take it one step at a time."

"How can I Wendy, when I'm waiting for the other shoe to drop? Is there another letter coming from Jamie?"

"I'm not at liberty to say."

"Yeah, that's what I thought. You're all the same, even Jamie. You say I have it all figured out, but you're wrong. I don't know what the hell I'm doing since I made the decision to come home in the first place. My heart is confused, my brain even more. I can't even decide what to eat for breakfast, let alone decide on how all of this will play out with Jagger. On top of all of it, if I choose wrong, I'm bound to get another letter from Jamie. You all think you know what's best for me, but you're all being heartless. I have to go. Please don't follow."

"Hey, Tumbleweed . . . " she called out. I ignored her as best as I could, but never to give up, Wendy called out again, this time with a loud shrieking whistle call. "Tumbleweed!"

"What?" I turned to shout back.

"Coffee, juice, and cinnamon rolls. On the table and waiting for you. You see? Breakfast is served."

She gave me a gratifying smile and then winked. God! She was infuriating at times, but damn how I loved her. I looked up to Jamie in heaven.

"Okay brother, what's next for me? Please show me the way and help me not hurt Jagger today. Keep watching."

When I got home, looking through my closet, my mother took it upon herself to unpack for me and hang all my clothes. It wasn't snowing today, but brutally cold. I felt like a teenager going on her first date with the boy she had hoped would ask her out. Now I had all the bumblebee's dancing around in my stomach as I tried to decide what to wear to see Jagger. He wouldn't care if I was wearing sweats and a t-shirt, but for some reason I want to look good for him. He always paid attention to every detail about me. Today would be no different. I didn't think he had changed that much. It was me we had to worry about.

I decided on my faded jeans with a cashmere sweater and paired them up with my brown cowboy boots. I wore my suede blazer with it and my favorite infinity scarf. Once I was dressed, I looked like a cowgirl on Fifth Avenue. Before I could second guess my ensemble, I bolted for the door, leaving my Louis Vuitton bag behind. Being wealthy was no secret, but flaunting my New York life in front of Jagger would just remind him of what I left him for. Living on the ranch, material items like bags and shoes were insignificant, but a requirement in my new life.

"Don't you look pretty?" mama said as I made my way down the stairs.

"Thank you mama."

"Why the long face? It's not even Christmas yet, and we already have been blessed with a miracle. Are you on your way to see him?" She already knew the answer to that.

"Yes, I'm leaving now and not sure when I'll be home."

"Can you give your mama a few minutes?"

"Of course, what's on your mind?"

"You. Always you, my beautiful daughter."

"Mama, you don't have to worry about me, I'm fine."

"Someday when you have children of your own, you will understand that a parent never stops worrying about their children. I can't help Jamie anymore, but I can help you if you would allow me to. You've been so distant from us for so long now. I want my daughter back. And before you say anything, I'm not talking just here in your family home, but I want back in there, where it should always matter."

She reached for me with her hand and placed it over my heart. Mama was never one to mince words. Her truth was gutting me wide open. I didn't even know how to respond to her, so I did the next best thing. I took her hand and placed my cheek on it before kissing it.

Before my tears could fall, I hugged my mother, told her I loved her, and walked out the door.

Jagger

I WAS JUST about going out of my mind when a knock tapped out on my door. Finally! She's here. I adjusted myself in bed and waited for her to enter, but it wasn't her, it was Shane.

"What the fuck are you doing here?" I couldn't help the hostility in my tone. Shane was the last person I wanted to see right now, if ever.

"Come on, Jagger. Don't be that way. Can I come in and talk with you?"

"What could you possibly say that I would want to hear . . . *brother?* You left me for dead on that ridge. Are you hear to finish me off, because I have my rifle underneath this cover, and I won't hesitate blowing your fucking head off?"

DID I HEAR him right? Shane left Jagger for dead on the ridge? No, not possible. Jagger must be confused. The hall was empty and I should have just walked right in, but curiosity won out in the end and I remained quietly listening outside. Who knew what they would tell me if I questioned them, so I waited.

"Jagger, that's not true. Please let me explain. Please just give me that?"

"Shane, I don't owe you a goddamned thing. Anything we had left of our broken friendship was destroyed in that moment on the ridge. You are the reason I'm in this bed, and you alone should be in jail right now for attempted murder on my life."

"It wasn't like that. I would never hurt you. I just lost myself for a second, less than a second, and then you fell."

"Yeah I fell Shane, and nearly to my death. Was that what you were hoping for? That I would die, and then you get to have Tenley all to yourself? Well, sorry to disappoint you, Shane, but I lived, and there is no way in the deepest depths of hell will I ever let you near her again."

"Jagger, you're talking crazy. Just shut up and listen for a fucking second. I did not try to kill you. I should have never knocked you off your horse, but I was so angry at what you were saying to me, and the real truth of it all behind your words. I am so sorry. I never meant it. It was an accident, one I will regret for the rest of my life."

"You should regret it, Shane, because I will never forget it. We are not friends, we are not brothers, and we are not anything . . .

148

anymore. I can't prove what happened on that ridge, but I know what my gut is telling me and that's all I need. You were so angry because you lost . . . again, but what you need to come to terms with is that you can't lose something that was never yours in the first place. What you think you had with Tenley is just a fantasy that you conjured up in your head. A fucking fantasy! That's all it was and will ever be. What I had, and will have again, is real. I have loved her since the moment she gave me the chance to prove to her my intentions were real. I never stopped loving her, even when she hurt me the most with you."

"If you loved her so much, then why have you waited so long to fight for her? Why didn't you fight back then? Now you're going to sit here and throw some unrequited love story in my face. It's been five years, man. You act as if this was yesterday."

"It was, Shane. I have replayed it over and over in my mind since the day I had that fight with her. A fight that should have never happened. Our fight should have never happened either, but it did, and I can't change how I feel. She's never going to be yours. The sooner you get that through your head, the better off you will be. My reasons for not going after her are mine, and mine alone. All you need to know is that from this moment on, I will fight for her with everything I have, and if she still refuses me, then I will fight harder until she sees what's right in front of her. You stopped me once, Shane. Don't even think about trying it again."

"I'm sorry, Jagger. I never meant to hurt you. I have battled the demons in my soul for so long now. I did something I could never come back from. I hurt Shelby so much with the walls I put up between us. Tenley deserves a man that will love her with his whole heart, and I wanted to be that man for her. You were right about it all, Jagger, she was just a fantasy. What I have with Shelby is real, and it's mine if I want it, and I swear to God, I do. I promise you that I will not interfere with you and Tenley again, I swear it on my life."

"Well right now, Shane, your life means nothing to me, so take your promises and get the hell out of my room before I do shoot you."

"I won't give up on us, Jagger. You are too important to me, and we've been through too much for you not to forgive me. I'm so sorry, brother . . . I'm so sorry."

Jagger

"GET OUT! GET out! I mean it Shane! Get out!" He finally turned to leave and then she was standing there with an ashen face and glassy eyes. *Fuck!* She was listening.

She looked like she wanted to run, and that's exactly what she did. She took another look at me and then left as easily as she walked in. I called out to her as loud as I could, but she didn't come back. I was trapped in this bed, and she was trapped with Shane.

"TENLEY! PLEASE, STOP for a minute." He called out to me and took hold of my arm before I could reach the bay of elevators.

"Don't you touch me! I will scream this place down if you don't let go of me."

"I'm not going to hurt you. Calm down and let me explain."

Shane implored me.

"Explain? Oh hell no! I've heard enough. How could you possibly explain to me how you chose not to save your friends life? How could you, Shane?"

I began to cry. I didn't want to be consoled, I wanted to feel this pain I was going through. Jagger could have died and once again, it would have been my fault. They were arguing because of me.

Shane backed away and sat down. He looked broken and lost, kind of like I was at the moment. He held his face in his hands and cried along with me. *How did we all get here? Once upon a time we were as close as three friends could be. We were a family, and I don't even recognize us anymore.*

The only time I ever witnessed Shane crying was at my brother's funeral, and it hurt like hell just as much as it does now. I was angry with him, but at the same time I wanted to comfort him.

"Shane, please? Tell me what happened. I have to know." It didn't matter what I overheard, I had to hear it from Shane.

With his head down, he quietly began to speak. "It was an accident. A stupid reckless accident. We were bringing in the animals and trying to get out of the storm. The wind was whipping at our backs. It was a savage storm that just landed right on us. He was screaming for me to follow, but then my mind just shifted to you. I had overheard our fathers, along with Ren, talking about Jagger and his planned trip to go to New York to see you. We managed to get some relief from the storm by seeking cover under some trees. The horses were restless with the lightning strikes hitting one after another. I can't even begin to explain why I chose that moment to ask him about you, but when I did, he immediately got angry. We began to hurl insults at each other, and then something just boiled over inside of me, and I knocked him off She-devil."

"So She-devil throwing Jagger off of her was a lie?"

"Yes, it was. I stepped out of my body and didn't see my brother in front of me anymore, I saw the reason why I wasn't with you. I attacked him. I hit him with everything I had until he fought me back, and that's when he lost his footing and fell over the edge. He called out for me to help him, but I was withdrawn. I could hear him, see him, but I couldn't move my arms out for him to grab onto. Tenley, by the time I snapped out of my disoriented state, it was too late."

He continued, "I was so scared after he fell down the embankment. I saw him fall and then he was just gone into the darkness below. I screamed and screamed for him, and then finally radioed in for help. I swear I did everything I could to find him before help arrived. We were in the middle of a storm, so the helicopters had to be on stand-by until it passed. We all searched on foot until the copter spotted him using night locating sensors. When we finally reached him, I didn't know if he was even breathing. I fell to my knees and just lost it. He was airlifted here, and after they cleared him physically, it was just a waiting game to when he would wake up."

"Were you hoping for a lesser outcome?"

"Of course not! Tenley, how could you even ask me that?"

"How?! How could you not help him Shane? And when you snapped out of it, it was too late. He could have died Shane! He could have died! And what would you have done then? Go off pretending like you weren't the one that was responsible for it? Go marry Shelby, take over my father's ranch, and live out the rest of your pathetic life into the sunset? Damn you Shane! I thought you were my friend, one of my best friends. You and Jagger were Jamie's best friends, brothers to him and to each other. What the hell happened to all of us?"

My stomach was churning with the disgust I was hearing from Shane. I could taste the acid lining my throat as my stomach retched. I ran for the nearest garbage and expelled everything I had eaten this morning. It kept coming up until I had nothing left. I felt empty and drained.

"Here, drink this, it will help."

Shane handed me a Gatorade to drink, but I refused it. I took some water from the fountain instead.

"Please, Tenley, look at me. I swear on my life, and on the lives of my parents, and Jamie's memory. I would never consciously hurt Jagger. No matter how he feels about me right now, I have to believe he knows me better beyond his anger. He's my brother for life."

"I can't speak for Jagger, but I can for Jamie. He loved you both very much, but that doesn't mean you get to use the memory of your friendship to ease your guilty conscience. This is on you, Shane, and I hope you can find your way back to the guy I once knew. Because this pale version of you is not who I know and love with all of my heart."

I continued, "You need to stay away from Jagger, and me. I have all I can handle right now. Please don't call me. I know I can't avoid you completely on the ranch, but if you see me coming, please turn and walk in the other direction. I swear to you, Shane, if I have to, I will remove you from the ranch. You may be a partner, but the Fairchilds hold the majority. It's my family's home, and clearly by your actions, it's not yours . . . anymore."

"Please, Tenley? Please don't do this to me. I know no other way of life. That ranch is my life. I will not lose it. Please?"

"What the hell do you want from me? Forgiveness? We tried that, remember? And now here we are. I find out that you are the reason for Jagger's near-death accident. And now all you have to worry about is your future on the ranch? You did this all on your own Shane. No one forced you to do what you did up on that ridge. You did that, and now you have to live with it. Get your head out of your ass, Shane, because you should be praying that Jagger will have a change of heart and not choose to press charges against you. Hell, if he does, I'll represent him myself. I'm so angry and disappointed with you, Shane. He could have died! Do you hear me? He could have died by that river with a broken body and heart. Did you think for one second how Jagger's death would have left a permanent mark on you? You see, that's what loss does. It breaks you and swallows you whole until you have nothing left. I now realize the *fulfilled* life I thought I had been living was truly empty without the other half of my heart."

"It was always him, Shane, it was always Jagger. I'm just sorry it took nearly losing him for all of eternity to get me to finally realize it."

I left him there. I left Shane alone, broken, and completely lost while I went back to Jagger. How could we all have changed this much in five years? While I was selfishly living my life in New York, the two men I cared about were struggling and fighting against a storm that was raging heavily on both of them.

For the first time, I now see what my decisions have cost the people in my life who have loved me. *Jamie was right. They all were right . . . I chose wrong.*

CHAPTER 14

Jagger

...waiting

I WATCHED HELPLESSLY from my hospital bed as Tenley walked away from me, and with Shane. If I could, I would have ran after her, but my injured leg stopped me from doing that.

Where is she? I saw the look in her eyes. I knew she heard what I wanted to share with her privately, but Shane confronting me earlier forced my anger to the surface.

I wanted to choke him for what he did to me. He wanted forgiveness for nearly killing me. I begged him to help me, but his eyes were blank as if he just checked out. He reached for me too late, and I lost my grip and fell below. How I'm not dead is a miracle. My mother believed this to be true, maybe I should too.

"Knock, knock. Are you decent, Mr. Brown Eyes?"

My flirty nurse was back. Even in the worst of circumstances, I have to admit that Shirley made me smile and laugh.

"Hi, Shirley. I don't suppose you saw Tenley out in the hallway? She's been gone for a while and I really need to see her."

"I saw her while she was talking to your friend, Shane. I don't know what happened up in here, but that boy looked like he was going to be sick or something. I almost checked in on him, but they looked like they were in a heavy conversation. I'm just saying is all."

"Yeah, I hear you, Shirley. Can you please check the hall again for me?"

"I will, but first you need to take your medicine."

"I don't want anything that's going to make me tired. My leg is fine."

"Oh really? Let's test the theory, shall we?"

"Wait, Shirley! What are you going to do?" and before I could say anything else, she moved my leg off the traction device and a sharp shooting pain vibrated through my entire leg. I gritted my teeth to not give her the satisfaction, but I began to sweat on account how much it hurt.

"You still don't want any medicine, Mr. Brown Eyes?" She waited for me to answer with her sassy attitude.

"That was a dirty trick, Shirley, and if you try that again, you no longer can call me Mr. Brown Eyes."

"Okay, I'm sorry, but I knew no other way to show you that you still need to take it easy and rest that leg. You're lucky you still have one." She reprimanded me with a stern warning.

"When am I getting this cast off?" I asked her.

"Oh don't you go worrying about it, handsome. Dr. Sampson has ordered the cast removal tomorrow morning, and then you begin physical therapy."

"I don't want that. I can do all the healing I need back on my ranch. My tests showed nothing, so I'll handle the rest on my own." I knew I was calling bullshit, but I needed to get the hell out from this bed and this hospital. I hated to be confined, and it just brings back too many sad memories of Jamie.

"Okay, Mr. Brown Eyes, let's get serious now. You do realize you are lucky to be alive, don't you? You are awake and completely alert after a month-long-plus slumber. Give yourself a minute to catch up, please? I promise you if you can cooperate with doctor's orders and follow your therapy, you will be released sooner than you think."

"Okay, Shirley, you win. Thank you."

"You're welcome." She smiled and left me on my own.

I took my pills and minutes later, I was down for the count and replaying my horrific fight with Shane.

When I was younger, I used to ride up the north ridge all the time and sometimes played chicken with my horse. The extreme side of me always wanted to take it a step further, but a near miss many years ago taught me a valuable lesson.

Daddy used to say: "You don't have control of the land. The land owns you. Go up against it and you will lose." Maybe I didn't understand what he meant back then, but I certainly did now, as once again I was faced with going up against something I didn't have control over. One: Mother Nature. Two: My deep rooted anger for Shane.

"Come on, Shane!" I called out to him as we came upon the north ridge of my ranch. It was the highest peak and the most dangerous. "We have to get back before this storm lands directly on us."

"Okay, I'm right behind you. All the horses are safe. Calm down, man! It's not like she's going anywhere. It's been five years, I'm sure she could wait one more day."

What the fuck? How did he know? I certainly didn't tell him I was leaving for New York. We decided a long time ago that the subject of Tenley was forever off limits.

"You can wipe that look off your face, man. I know where you're headed. Are you sure you want to go down that road again?" Shane asked me.

"Any road I decide to take is none of your business, so stay the hell out of it."

"Why should I do that when I'm involved too?"

"The hell you are. You have nothing to do with me and Tenley.

If anything, you were one of the reasons we were torn apart."

"You keep telling yourself that my friend, but it was you that drove her away, not me."

"Fuck you, Shane. You don't know what in the hell you are talking about."

He almost laughed as if he knew something I didn't, but that wasn't the case. He never knew what promise I made to Jamie where Tenley was concerned. This was my secret to keep, and I never shared it with anyone.

"Shane, you need to let her go, once and for all."

"I have."

"No you haven't, and that's pretty fucked up since you have an amazing woman in Shelby who would do just about anything for you, but yet you still won't marry her. You spend all your time pining away for my woman."

"What we shared that night, Jagger, you will never understand. You are just pissed because she gave herself over to me so easily."

I was on the verge of kicking his ass all over my ranch, but the storm was getting closer, and we were still a long way back to safety. We only had some trees to give us a little cover, but with the wind blowing so hard at us, it really did nothing to help us. He was just trying to rile me, but fuck me for trying to figure Shane out.

"What's wrong, Jag, nothing to say?"

"I have plenty to say to you, Shane, but once again you have proven to me that you are not worth my time. You can keep your fantasies about Tenley all tucked away in your fucked up mind, but I'll have the reality."

"She could have loved me first, Jagger, but I was too afraid of losing what we had in friendship. And then when I was ready, you came along and turned her head."

"I'm trying to figure out just how deluded you really are, Shane. She was never yours, ever. You need to get that straight. I didn't have to do anything to make Tenley fall in love with me, it just came natural for us when it was ready to happen. It is not my fault that you didn't take your shot when you had the chance, but get the fuck over it. You can't lose something that was never yours in the first place."

At that very moment, Shane charged me, catching She-devil off guard. He came at me at full speed and knocked me off my horse where I was almost toppled by her. She-devil kicked up on her hind legs and then took off into the darkened night. I was startled from his attack. Shane was screaming at me to get up. It took me a second to get my bearings, and then I was face to face with him. He shoved me with a hard push to my chest, but I stayed where I was this time.

He screamed at me, "I loved her. I still love her. She didn't love me back. Don't you get it, man? She didn't love us back, not enough to fight for what we had. We had our friendship first. The bond we all shared meant everything to me, and when she left, she fucking broke me! No matter what I assured her with, I was lying to myself and to her. Deep in my heart, I wanted Tenley to choose me, but she was selfish and left us both broken. Don't you see that? Jagger, that's why I can't marry Shelby yet because I'm still all fucked up over Tenley. Why do you think you haven't been able to commit to anyone? Because you're not over it yet. You are still so angry and living in the past that you don't want to move on from it. She's gone, man, and will never come back to you or me. The girl we loved died along with Jamie."

"You are wrong, Shane, and I am far from being broken. I'm not living in the past and I can assure you that I am over it. I loved her then, and I love her now. Do you understand me? I. Love. Her. And I will get her back. You stopped me once before, but I will be damned if I allow you to do it again. What you had with Tenley was one fucking drunken night . . . a mistake, probably the biggest of her life. She fucked you to fuck me out of her mind and heart. It's that simple, brother. Get it through your head once and for all. She will always be mine!"

"No!" He shouted over the howling wind.

Shane punched me on the side of my head. My vision blurred, but I still was on my feet to strike back. We entangled ourselves punching each other where we could get our hits in.

Shane was just as big and strong as I was, so it was like fighting myself. I finally bucked him off of me, and he came at me again. One shove later, and I missed my step and I went over the ridge. I grabbed on to the tree roots that were embedded into the side, but I was barely hanging on. I screamed for him to pull me up. He looked as if he was in an unresponsive state. Maybe I hit him too hard. My screams fell onto deaf ears, the wind was ferocious and my grip was slipping. I screamed again and again.

"Shane, pull me up! Pull me up. I can't hang on much longer."

I was praying to God for help. *"Please don't let me die. Please God, hear me please. I can't die like this and she never knowing how much I still loved and wanted her."*

"Please, Shane! Help me." I screamed as loud as my voice allowed me to.

At his moment of clarity, Shane reached down and grabbed my hand, just as my other hand slipped from the branch.

"Come on, Jagger! Grab on to my hand. Come on man!" He was screaming for me to pull myself up, but I couldn't. And that's when I was flying. Not on my horse, but falling down to my death.

I could still hear Shane's cries as I fell further down to the earth below. My body ricocheted off the mountain as if I was a ball in an arcade machine. I could feel every razor edge stab as I hit more debris going down. My body crashed into the earth below. Before I blacked out, my first thought was of Tenley. *"I love you."*

Now weeks later, I was fighting to wake and that's when I heard her soft voice begging me to open my eyes. I didn't know why I was asleep for so long, maybe it was my fear of discovering what I would find once I did awaken, but it was her voice that led me home. I was back with Tenley, back to where I was before my accident and before Shane. I talked to her parents and to Wendy. I soul searched with Jamie at his grave and then talked with my father. He never stopped telling me about his faith and love he had for my mother. He believed with his whole heart that if something was meant to be, then it simply would be. It didn't matter the timeframe of it, just the point that it existed at all.

Dad asked me if I still wanted my life here on the ranch and who I saw myself sharing it with. That was an easy answer . . . Tenley Faith Fairchild. My girl was meant to be a Parrish. I could see no one else by my side to share my life with. I had already built our home and had taken over all ranch business years ago. My father and I were partners. He was just enjoying semi-retirement, just like Shane's father. They were cowboys through and through, but it was time for the next generation to take over.

Once upon a time, my dream was shared with Jamie and Shane. We were all going to be united as brothers and partners, but fate handed us a level of sadness that we never really were able to get past . . . we lost our brother. I lost Tenley, and then I lost Shane. We were never the same as we once were, but put our differences aside and tried our best to find closure in what broke us for Jamie's sake. Now after my accident, and Shane being the cause of it, we're even more lost to each other than ever before.

Shane says he is sorry. He never would hurt me. No matter how I feel or I believe, he said we were brothers for life. He would do anything to prove that to me and make me forgive him. It took my accident to get him to finally see that he truly does love Shelby, and what he thought he wanted with Tenley was just a fantasy like I said it was. Too bad I had to pay the price for his moment of revelation.

I don't know how much time I will have with Tenley, but I have to make her see that she belongs here with me. I love her so much. My father asked me what I would give up to have Tenley back in my life. I thought about it for a minute, and then said . . . everything.

He didn't look surprised by my answer. He patted me on my back and then pulled me into one of his bear hugs.

"I love you, son. Go to New York. Go get your girl." I hugged him hard and thanked God for giving me an amazing man to call my father.

"I will, sir. I will."

CHAPTER 15

Tenley

...moment of truth

AFTER MY TALK with Shane, I just needed to clear my head. I took a walk out into the Wyoming frigid air. Probably not the smartest thing to do in December, but it did me some good. I walked only a short distance before my legs went numb from the cold chilling air, but I would take this any day over the conversation I overheard and walked away from.

Jagger accused Shane of trying to murder him. My blood went cold after hearing those words. I was frozen, and yet I stayed to listen. They were both screaming, but Shane's voice was not filled with anger, it was laced with guilt, pain, and begging for forgiveness. Jagger was another story. He sounded as if he wanted to kill Shane. The only other time I heard that level of anger was when Jagger had to witness me in bed with best friend. I would never forget the hurt in his voice or the look in his eyes.

Now we were here again. The three of us caught up in this vicious circle of anger, pain, and loss. I was here to right those wrongs, not cause more of it. I knew I had to stop blaming myself for what happened. It's in the past, my past, and I couldn't do anything to change it. Even this fight they were having, my first instinct was to blame myself and allow their fight to become my own. That wasn't fair to me, and I needed to let that weakness go. I may not be perfect, but I paid for my sins and up to the time in receiving Jamie's letter, I was still paying. No more! I'm done.

I didn't work my ass off in law school, sacrifice my family, my friends, my heart, to just come back home to be a sniveling disaster. I am way too strong to feel this torment any longer. I love Jagger, that much is true. We have a mountain of issues to work out and who knows what we will find once we do, but only one way to find out . . . I need to talk to him.

Wait . . . How is she doing this? I asked myself as I walked off the elevator to Jagger's floor. There was Wendy in the waiting room, holding a pink box and two of what I hope are hot coffees. *Once again appearing out of nowhere and saying or doing the perfect thing.*

"Are you done freezing yourself like a Popsicle? Because you have one hot cowboy in there, and he's waiting to warm you up. Please, Tumbleweed, give him and yourself this chance. You will never know and understand the true meaning behind your brother's letters, if you don't do this."

"I know, Wendy, that's why I'm here. And just so you know, I wasn't running, I just needed to catch my breath."

"I'm so sorry, sweetie. You should have never had to find out that way about Shane and Jagger."

"Wait, you know, Wendy?"

"Sadly, I do. Shane's been in counseling since the accident. I've been helping him."

"Does anyone else know? What about my parents? Jagger's or Shane's?"

"I don't think so, just me. I suppose when he's ready to do so, it will be his story to tell."

"Wendy, Shane was so angry when he saw me the first time,

and then was humiliated when his father made him apologize. He wouldn't give up until we talked and somewhat reconciled our differences, and now I find out the truth behind Jagger's accident. Why, Wendy? Is Shane sick or something? I can't keep up with his emotional mood swings."

"Come sit for a minute and warm up. I'll probably never be able to explain to you what happened on that mountain between the boys, but I do know how very sorry Shane is for his part in it. He will probably spend the rest of his life righting his wrong for what happened with Jagger. That burden is on him, and he is the only one that can make peace with it. I do believe in my heart that Shane will be okay, and Jagger too. He is so much in love with Shelby, and she is strong enough for both of them. Now, it's your turn to be strong for Jagger. He's waited long enough to have this conversation with you."

"Me too, Wendy, me too. I just can't hurt him again. What you are all asking me is just not possible without someone getting hurt. I would rather walk through fire than hurt him again."

"Some things never change," she said as she wiped a tear from her eyes.

"What do you mean?" I placed my coffee down and held Wendy's hand.

"Jagger said the same thing about you, but in reverse. When he told me his plans to go to New York and confess his unrequited love for you, he said he would rather walk through fire then miss one more day without you. God! You two are incredibly frustrating. Thank goodness companies like Clairol keep making my color, or my hair would be completely grey by now. Talk about emotional mood swings . . . you two wrote the book on that one."

"Yeah, I love you too, Wendy."

"Same here, Tumbleweed. Now get the hell in there! Go!"

I smiled and tried to hug my friend, but she just pointed her finger toward the direction of Jagger's room.

I knocked softly, not knowing if he was sleeping, and sure

enough, he was. I carried the chair over to his bedside and remained quiet, as I took in the handsome cowboy before me.

How did I ever manage to leave him? Jagger was kind, loving, and so strong in mind and body. He was probably one of the most honest men I had ever known, and if you were lucky to be loved by him, you truly were cherished. To see him in a hospital bed made me realize how close we all came to losing him.

How he survived that fall is a true miracle. I believe he had to have a guardian angel watching over him that night. Or it was a true testament to how strong Jagger really is? When I was younger and he would come by the house, I did everything in my power not to fall down at his feet. I was the kid sister who Jamie always dragged along, but he never minded. The guys were great, and then one day I looked at Jagger differently. My mama used to tease me all the time about the buzzing bumblebee's in my stomach. She would say when the right boy comes along, I would get a bee sting the size of Texas. I would know that I was in love. I was never one to give mama the credit of being right, but she was. I was completely, deeply, and irrevocably in love with Jagger Parrish.

Getting lost in the memory of him was easy to do. We had hundreds of stories between us and what feels like a lifetime of memories.

"Can we get all that back?" I didn't realize I said those words out loud until he answered . . .

"Yes, we can."

I leaned in and held his hand.

"Hi, how are you feeling?" I whispered softly.

"I'm better, now that you're here. Nurse Shirley flirted with me until I took my medicine. Who knew so much magic was in a little white pill?" He smiled.

"I'm glad you listened to her. You scared me." I bluntly confessed.

"I know. I saw it all over your face. I never meant for you to find out about my accident, and in that way. Hell, my father doesn't even know yet. I was so afraid you left and were not coming back."

"I almost did, but then I saw Shane, and knew I had to stay."

"For him?" his voice was once again angered, but not as hard as before.

"No, you crazy man, for you. Do you think I could just so easily leave after hearing what I heard?"

"I don't know Tenley, I just don't know. I was hoping you wouldn't run again, that's all. What did Shane say?"

"He didn't have to say much, I heard most of it and then he filled me in on the rest. Jagger, you may not want to hear this, but I believe him. I don't think he would have ever hurt you in his right mind. Did you know he's in therapy? He's been attending regular sessions with Wendy since your accident."

"No, how could I? I've been in a coma that *he* put me in. And no Tenley, I don't believe him after what he did to me."

I sighed in frustration and prayed for patience. "Are we going to talk, or are you going to continue to shout at me? I choose talking. What about you?" I asked him.

"Talk," he sulkily said. He wiped his eyes and moved up to a sitting position where he could look at me better when we talked. I helped him with his pillows and his leg. His leg was still elevated, making it hard for Jagger to get comfortable. Just the mere closeness to him was drawing me in where I just wanted to kiss him. He felt the electricity between us. His pupils dilated as our bodies were near each other.

"There, that's better." What I truly wanted and what I did were two very different things. I sat on his bed with my feet now on the chair. He was gazing into my eyes and drawing me in, an art of seduction.

"Tenley . . . " My name flowed off his tongue, drugging me even more.

I bit my lip in frustration and pulled back a little.

"Don't talk that way," I said.

"What way?" He pulled me closer.

"You know what way. Like the sun rises and sets with the mere mention of my name. You still have the power to disarm me with just saying my name. Jagger, just because I'm here doesn't change the fact on who I am. My life is in New York. I'm a driven worka-holic with nothing else besides my career."

He shifted again, not letting go of my hand. "Is that why you didn't stop when you could have died in that car explosion?"

"You knew about that?"

"Of course I knew, we all did. Right then, I wanted to fly to New York to kidnap you, tie you up, and never let you out from my sight again. What were you thinking, Ten?"

"I was doing my job. A job I kick ass in and win."

"Yeah I get that, but it's also a job that could have gotten you killed. You may think you do, but you don't belong in that world."

"Yeah? And what world do I belong in?"

"My world," he said without hesitation and determination in his eyes.

"And how can you be so certain of that when I don't know even know where I belong? I'm so confused."

He wasn't letting me go for all the gold in China. His grip tight-ened on me as if I was his reason for breathing. My skin began to heat with every touch. Fine hairs on my arm began to tickle while goose bumps lined my skin with every stroke of his fingers.

"Jagger, how do you know where I belong."

I asked him again because I desperately wanted to hear him say it. I can fight my reasons to why I grew into the woman I became. The career path I took. The way I chose to spend my days filled with work, and how I spent my nights alone in my thoughts. No one to hold me when I needed a hug. No one to comfort me when I had a bad day. No shoulder to cry on when I missed my brother or the family I left behind.

Now I'm here with him. He hasn't stopped touching me. My breath hitched once again. He licked his own lips and reached for my face. *Is he going to kiss me? I'm not sure. We are so close, how can he not?* My stomach was buzzing, the bees were back, and all I wanted right now was his tongue in my mouth, but he teased me instead. Holding my face in his two strong hands, he made me look up at him. I was a goner. The boy I fell in love with was now a man looking at me the same way he did back then. Pure love and devotion danced in his eyes. I say once again . . .

"What world do I belong in?" No answer? Placing his forehead to mine and then ever so gently kissing me softly on my lips, Jagger whispered . . .

"My world."

My heart fluttered with just two words he spoke. He kissed me again and ever so gently touched every inch of my face as he continued on.

"I know you are confused, but you don't have to be. All you need to do is listen to your heart and trust it, and when you finally do, please trust mine. I asked you when you were seventeen to do that for me, and you practically screamed 'Yes.' So once again I am asking you that very question and hope your answer will be the same. Your mind is beautiful, but it needs to calm a bit, don't you think? I could see the wheels turning and the conflict you are feeling. Like you're walking a tightrope, and you're afraid to fall. Baby, you never have to worry, because I will always catch you. You asked me how I know better than you, well allow me to break it down for you."

"Tenley Faith Fairchild, you belong in my world. Miles may have separated us, but you truly never left where it mattered most. Why? It's pretty simple."

"Because I love you."

"Because I want you."

"Because I want you here with me to live and to share your life with mine."

"Because I want nothing more than to marry you."

"Because I want you to be the mother of my children."

"Because . . . you're mine, Tenley. You always were. And if

you believe all that I have just said here, then we can have it all. I promise, baby, with all that I have and all who I am, we can."

"You were meant to be a Parrish. I won't stop trying to convince you until I take my last breath. The end of the love story you thought you knew is just our new beginning."

CHAPTER 16

Tenley

...if i stay?

H E WANTS ME back? After everything I put him through and the pain he had to endure, he wants me back. Why? Second chances don't always work out the way you see them play out in your mind. For years, I have secretly dreamed of this moment with Jagger, with him saying exactly what I just heard come from his mouth to my ears. But now? I'm left with another choice.

"Jagger, I know you believe we can have everything you just said, but the truth that is slamming my heart right now is that we can't go back in time. We can't erase the hurt. We can't forget the pain. I broke your heart with my betrayal. The devastation I saw on your face has haunted me in my dreams. I know what my leaving has cost you. Every time I close my eyes, I see you, but then I also re-member how much I hurt you. My heart aches and my mind always goes back to the day I hurt you the most. God! I'm sorry. You will never know how much regret I feel for the choices I made. I'm so sorry." I cried out as my tears began to fall.

He let go of me to shift again to get comfortable, never taking his eyes off of me. He's on a mission to make me realize we can, but I'm so afraid to lead with my heart. I've been closed off for so long right now. I don't even know how to even date or talk to a guy, but again, this is not just any typical guy. This is Jagger Parrish . . . *the* guy.

"Tenley . . . ," I put my two fingers to his lips. He instantly kissed them, sending shivers down my spine. I wanted more, so much more of him. I came back into reality and pulled away just enough where he couldn't reach for me. Being in Jagger's close proximity was making me lose my train of thought.

"Jagger, please let me finish. I need to say this."

He quietly nodded, but I knew he hated allowing me to voice all the reasons why we shouldn't be together.

"Jagger, like I said, we can't turn back time. I know what you want for us, but it just doesn't work out that way in real life. It's in the romance novels, but this right here is real, our reality. My heart is screaming at me right now to say 'Yes' to everything you said, but my mind is different. My conscience says, 'Let him go' and 'free him once and for all.' Jagger, you should be blissfully married to someone who loves you more than herself. You should have sons you're teaching to ride horses and dreaming of one day seeing your boys taking over your ranch, like you did with your father. A legacy already created with so much love and promise for generations to come. Jagger, you deserve a life like that. This is what I want for you, and I will not spend another day denying you of that."

My New York bravado was gone. The moment I agreed to Wendy's request, I knew somehow the walls I put up would come tumbling down around me. It was happening right now staring at Jagger, as he sat there and listened to me break his heart again. It was no use, so I didn't even try to stop my tears from falling.

"Are you done? Because if you're not, then too fucking bad. It's my turn to talk now. Come here, Tenley." He commanded. The deep timbre of his voice was pulling me in. "You are too far away from me, and me being in this bed prevents me from catching you if you run again. I see the fear on your face, but baby, you don't have to be. You never have be scared again. Please come closer."

Moments of quiet passed between us. Until Jagger shifted just enough to one side and gave me the open window to climb through and trust him, or run like I do best. Fuck it! *Trust him, Tenley, trust him.* I shuffled my feet until I reached his bed. I thought I would just sit and hold his hand, but he wasn't going for that. Jagger pulled me into his arms and nestled me close to his body. His grip tightened as my body conformed to his. My right leg was over his while his left leg was securely in the harness. I was so afraid I would hurt him because he was still recovering from his injuries, but Jagger didn't seem to care. He kissed the top of my hair and touched me gently, chasing my fear away. My tears still fell as he continued to kiss and soothe me.

"Shh," Jagger whispered, as he once again calmed me with just one word spoken. "Tenley, I know what you're thinking in that beautiful head of yours, but you're wrong. I'm not living in the same fantasy world Shane's been in since you left. I've always been real and focused on the timeline that was set in place for me."

I stayed on his chest, as if I could move anyway, but I still asked him my question.

"Timeline? What do you mean by that Jagger?"

"You know exactly what I mean Tenley. Or at least you would if you would stop overthinking every little thing. You've been home long enough now to begin putting the pieces back together of our square. Jamie may be gone, but he is still very much alive in all of our hearts, and in some way he has made this moment possible for us right now. Okay, I would have forgone the accident, but he's brought us together and given us our chance for our do-over."

"What about Shane?" his muscles tensed a bit with the mention of his name, I could feel it as much as he tried not to show it to me. "Now, Jagger, you know exactly what I mean when I say Shane. Can you finally and really put *him* and what *we* did behind you? Don't lie to me, not now after the conversation I walked in on between the two of you, and the conversation I had with your father."

"One thing you never have to worry about me is lying to you. I don't lie, and especially not when it comes to my feelings for you. As for my father, he tends to talk too much. Don't take to heart what he said. It's *my* heart that matters."

"Jagger, that's just it. His opinion does matter, as well as it should. He's just looking out for his son, the son that I hurt. Of course, he would be cautious when it came to me. They don't want you to ever go through that pain again."

"Tenley, I'm a grown ass man, and it's not like I threw myself over a cliff when you left. No! That was Shane's job, and he nearly succeeded in killing me."

"Okay, Jagger, maybe we need some air."

He held me close to him as I tried to move, but there was no way I was going anywhere.

"Hell no! I don't need space and neither do you. What you need to do is get out of your fucking head space and listen to me. Yes, I'm angry with Shane for my accident. Yes, I still doubt his sincerity. Can you really blame me Tenley? He's been harboring feelings for you for years, and it screams borderline obsessiveness to crazed infatuation. I don't believe he loved you in a way he thought he did. Once we were together, he convinced himself that I took something from him, but he's wrong. You were always mine, baby, and he has had to live with that truth all of these years. Shane is not between us, not anymore. I swear to you, Tenley, on my life. I am telling you the truth. Shane does not matter to us. If I could go back to that day when you showed me your letter, I swear I would do things differently. I know we can't go back to change our past, but hell woman! We can change our future. We can only move forward if that's what you truly want. I'm ready for all of it. Almost dying has a way of putting things in perspective. My eyes are wide open, and all they see is you."

"Jagger, go back to that day and remember what you said to me.

You said your life is here. Here in Wyoming. Here on your ranch. The ranch is your world. I can't and will not ask you to give that up to live in my world. I may be a self-absorbed bitch, but I'm not that selfish to allow you to give up on what makes you the happiest."

I took him off guard and tried to move, but he was too quick and grabbed my arms.

"Don't run, not now. Look at me, dammit, and see what is right in front of you. I love you. You are not a bitch. That was my anger talking for me that day, not my heart."

I softened a bit with his words and let some of the tension go.

"Ha! You say that now, but you haven't seen me in action in a courtroom."

"I have, you know, Tiger Lady."

No way! How did Jagger know that nickname? Only my New York colleagues reference me by that name, and it was when I was working on Tommy's case. That's when I had to prove myself the most to my firm and show them I was worth the salt of being a partner. I looked into Jagger's eyes with curiosity as his eyes looked back at me with love and adoration.

"When? How did I not know or see you there?"

"After the car explosion. I needed to know that you were safe. You should have seen yourself, Tenley. The way you commanded the room on that day, all eyes were on you, especially mine. I was in awe of your incredible ability to shock the court members, even the judge was wiping his brow when you finished with your cross-examination. I had never been so proud of you. Our Tumbleweed was kicking ass. You wouldn't believe what was going through my mind watching you. It took all my control not to charge you like a bull and throw you over my shoulder. I fantasized so many times showing up in your fancy office and fucking you ten different ways over your desk."

"Jagger! Oh my God! Where is the sweet cowboy I used to know?" My skin was flushed listening to his dirty mouth. *Who was I fooling? I loved and missed it.*

"He's still here baby, believe me, but that doesn't mean he doesn't know a few rope tricks that he could use on you." He winked at me.

"As much as I wanted to make my presence known to you, I knew I needed more time. Time to say the right things and show you how much I love and wanted you."

"You took a hell of a gamble. What if after all the time and distance between us, I would have moved forward and built a life with someone else? What then, Jagger? Where would that have left you . . . discovering the woman you have waited five years for was no longer available?"

"Like you said, gamble. I didn't know, but you are worth the risk of finding out. So tell me Tenley? Is there someone else? Because maybe you should give me his number so I could call him. He has no fucking chance at ever winning your heart and making you his. That's my job. A job I take very seriously."

I paused at his question and thought of Tommy. I could have a future with Tommy if that's what I really wanted, but he's not in my heart and not in the same way as Jagger.

"Well? Is there someone?" he asked again. I took in a few calming breaths to slow down my racing pulse before I would answer him. My mind was spinning, and my answer was right there on the tip of my tongue. All I needed to do was say the words.

Then I heard *him* . . . I heard Jamie inside of my head, encouraging me to take that leap of faith I so wanted to do with Jagger.

Are you happy? If not, then I'm disappointed. Moving forward meant to live your life to the fullest. Do what I can't anymore. You are receiving this letter today on the anniversary of my death for one reason and one reason only: You chose wrong.

Stop hiding.
Stop running.
Come home.

I love you, Tumbleweed. I'll be watching from heaven to see if you took my advice.

Okay, Jamie, I hear you. Once again I'm going to throw caution to the wind and make a choice. A choice that will not be reckless, or leave me regretting the minute the words pass my lips. For the first time in my life, I will be making a choice that is led from the deepest part of my heart. A heart that has been locked up for so long now, I was afraid to let myself feel anything good.

Jagger hasn't stopped touching me as he waited for my answer. He didn't look angry, or even nervous. His eyes were a little glassy. He was trying so hard to be strong and preparing himself for what I might say. With all of his changing expressions, I see one thing that is clear to me, I see hope in his eyes.

Five years ago he gave me an ultimatum, and I broke his heart by choosing me over the life he planned out for us. My heart was broken when I left him, his was too, but I never wavered and re-mained strong in my decision. I was good at putting up those protec-tive walls, never allowing anyone to get past them. Losing Jamie, and then Jagger made it easy for me to keep everyone at a safe dis-tance, little did I know I was never really that far away from them to begin with. Wendy, my parents, even Jagger had shown me that in the short time I've been home.

One more breath, as he placed one more kiss onto my skin. I looked directly into his beautiful eyes and gave him my answer. My choice . . . .

"Yes, Jagger, there is someone."

His softness turned to strength, as his embrace tightened, and I was caged in with no escape in sight.

"There is a man in my heart. A man who I have loved since I was a little girl. A man I gave my heart to when he asked for it. A man who I love very much, and never stopped loving even when there were thousands of miles between us. A man that I'm trusting to give my heart to now, and hope his love shows me the right road to take. That man is YOU. My answer is YES. I love you Jagger. My choice is . . . you.

CHAPTER 17

Jagger

...my ten

FINALLY! SHE GAVE me her answer after slowly torturing me with what felt like a slow and painful death. I was prepared for all of it, the good and the bad. I know Tenley, and I knew she needed a second to breathe and process all we had just talked about. The minute she said her choice was me, I pulled her into me and crashed my mouth down onto hers.

Five years has been too long to be without her. I meant every word I said to her. I will never let her go again, and she will be a Parrish.

"I love you, Tenley, so fucking much."

"I love you too. I still don't even know how we got here. My mind has fast forwarded, and I'm having difficulty catching up."

"Don't worry about anything. You saying yes made everything fall into place as easily as a round peg into a round hole."

"I thought we were a square?"

"Not anymore, baby. We are the perfect circle. It feels like that, you know. We've been through so much, and so much of it spent apart."

My leg was working my last nerve. I wanted to rip the cast off myself. I shifted again and pulled her as close as I could where I could feel her heart against my own. "Tenley, I know you probably have a million thoughts running through your head right now, but please trust me? I promise your heart is safe with me, and I will never hurt you."

"Jagger, that is one thing I know you will never do. It's me that does the hurting."

"Stop it. No more talking this way. I think we both played a hand in hurting each other. It's about time you let that go. We are starting over, sweetheart."

"Jagger, I want to believe that, I really do, but we have a mountain of issues to work out. And there's my job, and my apartment, and . . ."

I cut her off and kissed her. I knew we needed to discuss everything she just said, but not right now. My sole purpose was just to hold her and do everything in my power to keep her from running.

"I love you, Tenley. Please believe me. We will work everything out, I promise."

She said nothing, which was fine by me. We had plenty of time to talk, and just holding her right here was enough for me.

She fell asleep in my arms. I had almost forgotten how she felt. Those five years were hell on me. My father was right to call me out on my reckless and irresponsible behavior. I drank too much, I got into bar fights, and drove drunk more times than I could count. I never took in account that I could have gotten myself killed or kill some innocent driver because I was drinking away my sadness.

I hadn't thought about this in a very long time until my father mentioned it to me. He said he was never so thankful than the day his son came back to him, and once again, I had light in my eyes. I never told my father why that was. It was the night I crashed my truck coming home from another night of drinking and making bad choices. I lied to my father when he asked what happened. I told him a deer ran out in front of me and I lost control of my truck, resulting in sideswiping the tree.

I walked away from that crash unharmed, but it was during the night when I had my awakening. When I was in my right frame of mind, Tenley would always be in my dreams. I could be doing anything on the ranch, and she would be there. I would be lost in the moments we spent together, and then at night the nightmares would come. I would see Shane making love to her, and she in return enjoying every bit of him. It made my stomach turn, sometimes it would wake me with such a jolt, I would run to the bathroom and get sick. The sight of my best friend and my girl destroyed me every time I allowed my mind to go back to that day.

The night I crashed my truck and was lucky enough to walk away unharmed was the night I saw Jamie. He was angry and disappointed with me. He told me that I was letting him down and hurting my family. He reminded me of the promise I made to him, but also showed me how unworthy I was for his sister if I continued on this path. He said, "What are you doing?!"

I heard it over and over again until I woke up soaked through to my sheets. I was so hung over from hours I spent drinking that night, and then the accident that followed. It took me a while to remember my dream, and then it hit me like a kick to the gut.

Jamie was right. His spirit broke through mine and made me open my eyes. My reckless behavior was hurting everyone around me, especially my father. I wasn't the son that he raised. I was someone I didn't recognize anymore, but that ended last night after I crashed. That was my rock bottom, and moving forward, I promised myself no more drinking. No more random hook-ups to fuck to ease my broken heart. I was done with all of it, and I was ready to fight for my girl. The news of Tenley being in danger nearly gave me a heart attack. I had to see for myself if she was okay. Clearly she was, and when I left New York a few hours later, my plan was set in motion. I would go back to Wyoming, redeem myself back into my father's good graces and then prepare my future with Tenley in it.

It was a gamble, this I knew, but I had to try. Wendy was completely on board with it. She already had her own tasks to complete where Tenley was concerned, but she didn't share it with me and just asked me to trust her. It was no different than me asking Tenley to do the same by me.

Now after surviving my accident, she was lying next to me in this bed with my arms tightly wrapped around her. *This is right, I know it is. I'm going to do everything in my power to make her smile and keep her with me.*

I was about to fall asleep myself when Nurse Shirley barreled into my room.

"Okay, Mr. Brown Eyes! It's time to take that cast off," she said happily, but way too loud, which roused Tenley awake. I tried to quiet my over-friendly nurse, but it was too late. Tenley had awakened and now was sitting up and too far away from me.

"Sorry, handsome, but duty calls. It was supposed to be this morning, but they moved you down on the schedule. I'm taking you down to get that monstrosity off that leg, and then x-rays to follow. I thought you would be happier hearing this news?" the nurse asked me while winking at me.

"It does, Shirley, but the timing is off."

I tried to gesture over to Tenley, but my nurse was ignoring me and writing notes down on her tablet. Tenley was already gathering her coat to leave.

"Baby, you don't have to go. Please stay and wait for me."

She smiled and then turned back to Shirley.

"Shirley, would you mind giving me a few minutes alone with Jagger?"

"Sure, darling. I'll be right outside."

"Ten, please don't go."

"Jagger, I have to, but I will be back in the morning. I've been here all day and haven't even checked in with my folks."

"They know where you are. Come on Tenley, why are you leaving?"

"Not for the reasons you're thinking, so please get out of your head space right now. I will be back tomorrow, and who knows . . . maybe even taking you home depending on what your doctor says. Okay?"

"I guess I don't have a fucking choice now, do I?"

"Boy! You sure have developed quite the mouth haven't you? You asked me to trust you, do you remember that?"

"Yes, I do."

"Okay. Now prove it. Kiss me, watch me leave, and *trust* that I will return tomorrow."

"Okay." I growled, *but I swear to God, if she doesn't come back tomorrow like she is promising, then when I find her, I will be putting her over my knee and turning her beautiful skin to pink. Okay, that's stretching a bit, not like she would let me do that anyway, but I would certainly try.* Just looking at her trying to figure out what I'm thinking made my heart melt, and my foul mood rolled off of me.

"I love you, Tenley."

"I love you, Jagger. Do what Nurse Shirley says, and I will see you tomorrow. Good night."

"I don't know what's good about it." I said again as she reached the door.

She turned back and gave me a wink. *Now that is one that I will take.*

"I'm sure you could find ways to pass the time and make it good. Night, Cowboy!"

Yup! She was so getting spanked.

"Ooh, you have it bad. Earth to Mr. Brown Eyes." Shirley snapped her fingers in front of my face, breaking me out of my thoughts.

"I'm sorry, Shirley, what did you say?"

"Oh nothing, handsome. I just said you have it bad. Any fool can tell that you are head over heels in love with that sweet gal."

"That I am. She's my world."

"Well then, you have everything. Come on, you can tell me all about it on the way down to Radiology."

"It's a long story Shirley."

"No worries, I have time. And I sure do love hearing a good story."

We laughed and talked the whole way down. Yeah, my love story with Tenley was a great one to tell. It had years of happy memories, and then the sad parts, but now was a clean slate with new memories to make.

CHAPTER 18

Tenley

...decisions

ONCE I LEFT Jagger's room, I hurried as fast as my feet would take me out of that hospital. I called my father, and told him not to wait up for me. He of course would, but I assured him that I was fine.

All I really wanted was time to think. I just made a choice that would completely change my life—the life I was accused of living not to the fullest, an empty one, and one just existing in.

Now I have pledged my commitment to Jagger and our new life together. *New life together?* We've been apart for five years, and I've only been home for a couple of weeks now, and I've done a complete 180 of my life. I need to talk to Zoey. Normally any life altering decisions were spent over drinks at our favorite after work bar. We would talk for hours, and I would watch Zoey usually dance her ass off once we were done analyzing our problems. I would do more of the listening than talking. Zoey always had a romance crisis, where I would just vent about cases.

Now this news would send her screaming into a fit, and would leave her wanting to know every last detail. I haven't really ever shared my past with her, or Tommy. What will they think of me now when I tell them that I've come home and I just picked up with my old boyfriend after five years of being broken up? *Oh, and Tommy, you're still not pissed that we slept together a couple of weeks ago, and I've been ignoring you, are you?* Yeah, Tenley! What will they say?

I parked my rental by the stables and went to see my horse. Jazzy cured all that was wrong in my life. I had taken her out every single day since I'd been home. I loved my horse so much.

"Hey girl. How are you tonight? Feel like taking a night ride?"

"Mind if I join you?" The hairs on the back of my neck prickled as I heard his voice.

"Shane, what are you doing here?" I asked him. He was standing by the door as I huddled near my horse.

"I live here, remember? I heard your truck pull in and wanted to check in on you. Are you okay, Tenley?" He looked like he cared and wanted to know, but I wasn't sure how Jagger would feel knowing I was out here with him alone.

"I'm fine, Shane. Thank you for asking. I'm going for a ride with Jazzy . . . alone."

"It's freezing out here tonight, and it's way too dangerous for you to be out and riding alone. Please let me go with you, if anything, just to keep a safe distance behind."

"I said I was fine. I think I know my own ranch. I also have a light with me. I'm not going far. Now please move aside."

"Is this about the accident? I'm sure by now Jagger has filled your head with all sorts of assumptions about me, but I swear to you, Tenley, I told you the truth."

"I believe you, Shane. I also know you've been talking this out with Wendy. And as for Jagger, what *he* believes is his right, and no one can influence him to change the way he feels. You have to be patient and give him time."

"I swear I will. I just needed to know that you believed me."

"Shane, are you okay? I mean really okay?"

"I'm getting there. I told Shelby about what happened with Jagger, and the truth about the accident. She took it surprisingly well. She knew I was in therapy. That's not something I could have kept hidden from her, but she supported me just the same. Tomorrow, I will tell my father, and then if you wouldn't mind, please be there with me when I tell yours."

"Shane, I can't go through that again. I already heard from the two of you, down to you, and then Jagger again. It breaks my heart that you ever came to blows over me, and he nearly lost his life. Shane, do you even realize that he could have been killed? Has that thought crossed your mind and really sunk in?"

"Everyday. You can't even imagine what I carry with me on a daily basis, but telling you, and now Shelby, has made it easier to now tell my father. He's going to be so disappointed in me, and I can't have my mistakes hurt him."

"I'm sorry for that. I care very much for your father, but it's your story to tell, not mine. As for my father, I'm not sure how he will react. I guess you will have to wait and see. Now please, I'm tired and I want to take a ride on my horse."

He stepped aside and let me ride through. I knew he would follow to make sure I was safe. I'm sure my father would be angry to know I was riding alone, and Jagger too, but this is what I needed to clear my head and once again make choices. My life may have lacked in some areas, but never my career. I loved when I was arguing a case in front of a packed courtroom. The adrenaline that spiked through me when I won my verdict. I loved my friends, but I also loved what I had here.

"Come on Jazzy! Make me fly."

A few hours later, my father found me in the stables with my horse.

"You're up early," he said as he looked down at his watch and sipped his coffee. After my night ride, I ended up sleeping on the couch in the office, and then waking at 5 to tend to her, and once more take a much needed ride. I was right about Shane following me. I tried to lose him a few times, but to no avail he was on my trail. He knew the ranch just as well as I did, probably even better. This was a huge ranch to explore, but when I had a problem to work out, I somehow ended up on everyone's radar and they'd find me. I'm surprised Wendy hadn't popped up yet.

"How's your back doing this morning?" My daddy asked.

"My back? I'm fine. Why wouldn't I be?" I asked as I continued to brush down my horse.

"Oh, I don't know Tumbleweed, you tell me? I haven't seen or heard from you since yesterday morning. Your night call didn't count. Then you're off taking night rides, sleeping in the office when you could be in a warm bed up at the main house, and then you're off again before sunrise. So, daughter? Talk to me, please? I can't help you if I don't know what's wrong."

"Daddy, I know you mean well, but I need to figure some things out before I can talk to you and mama. Can you give me some time to work it all out?"

"Are you staying for Christmas?"

"I am."

"Then you have the time. Don't be too long out here, I can only hold your mother off for so long. She knows you're still out here."

"Okay, daddy. Give me a few more minutes, and then I'll be in."

"Good. Breakfast will be ready." He kissed me on my forehead and left the stables.

I returned Jazzy to her stall and fed her some apples.

"Thanks girl for putting up with me. I love you Jazzy."

She neighed in response. By the time I reached the house, I saw Wendy's truck parked out front. No surprise there. I'm sure she was waiting to hear about what happened with Jagger. No such luck sneaking into the house unseen. My welcoming committee was waiting for me in the entryway.

"Well, good morning, Tenley! Let me take a good look at you.

Yup Connie, she's doing the good ol' walk of shame this morning."

"She's doing what?" My mother wore a shocked expression all over her face.

"Oh, come on, Connie. Don't be so naïve. Let's examine the evidence. Same clothes from yesterday. Bed hasn't been slept in, and she smells like she spent all night in the stables. Now, honey, if I didn't know any better, I would think young Mr. Parrish got released last night, and you spent the rest of it romping around in the hay."

"Oh, dear Lord! Wendy, I swear. You need to go to church on Sunday and shower yourself in holy water, because your dirty mouth is going to bring your house crumbling down around you," my mother said, as she came over to me.

"Oh Connie! Where's your sense of humor? God has one."

"Never mind you. Let's leave the good Lord out of this one. Come on honey, let's go upstairs, and I'll draw you hot bath."

"I'll be down here waiting."

"Yes, Wendy," Mama said.

"Connie, enjoy the Rated 'G' version. I'll get the naughty details later."

"Oh Dear Lord! Give me strength," mama screamed.

"I thought you wanted to leave the Lord out of this?" Wendy shouted up the stairs and laughing all the way back into the kitchen.

"I swear you two. You should take your comedy act out on the road, and leave me and my 'sex life' out of your routine," I said.

"Now, Tenley, you know Wendy's just playing like she always does, but you are still my daughter, and sometimes she runs a little too much with her mouth."

"Don't I know it, but I love her anyway."

"I do too! Now, go take a bath, and I'll bring your breakfast up."

"Thank you, mama."

"No need to say thank you. You're my daughter. It's my job."

The bath did help soothe my sore muscles and clear my head a bit. I knew I had to call Jagger, and then call my office to check in. I had my laptop with me to keep on top of my e-mails, but didn't check my computer at all yesterday.

Just when I was about to, my phone began ringing. Right on cue, it was Zoey.

"Hi, Zoe."

"Hi yourself, hooker. I miss you, girl. When are you coming home?" she asked as I heard her tapping her nails. I shivered when she mentioned *home*. I wasn't prepared to answer the many questions my friend would have if I gave her the opening to do so.

"I'm not sure yet. I still have a lot of details to work out. First things first, how's the office?"

Silence.

"Zoey, are you there?" I called out.

"Yeah, I'm here, sorry. What did you say?"

"Zoey, you are a terrible liar. What's going on? Talk to me."

"Everything is fine here. Roxy still has her purple hair and is keeping things under control for you."

"And . . . "

"Nothing hooker, everything is fine."

"Zoey!!!"

"Okay, there is a teensy little thing I may have forgotten to mention to you."

"What? Tell me now," I practically shouted back at her.

"It's Tommy. There was an accident at one of his job sites, but he's okay and already released from the hospital."

"What happened to Tommy? Zoey, I swear if you don't tell me right now, I will be on the next plane."

"Okay! No need to shout. I promised him Tenley, so don't go calling him the minute we hang up, okay?"

"Whatever. Just tell me."

"His company has the contract to the new development over on Long Island."

"Yes, I know that. Our firm handled all the paperwork. Go on."

"Well, he's run into some problems securing materials and teams of workers to complete the project. He's facing delays and tie-ups with the city. He drove out to the site and came upon a group of guys loading up a truck with some of his equipment and copper wiring, I think. They got away with about $60,000 dollars of it, but not before beating the hell out of him."

I covered my mouth to hold back my tears. My friend was hurt, and I wasn't around to help him.

"Zoey, where is Tommy now?"

"That's another thing."

"What now?"

"Are you sure you want to know?"

"Fucking hell! Yes, I want to know. Where is Tommy?"

"He's with Roxy?"

"It *is* a weekday, right? Why isn't she in the office—my office—doing her job?"

I gritted my teeth. I was now under the belief that my office was not as sound as they all would like me to believe.

"She took some time off to help Tommy, and Cheryl is covering for her. Please relax, Tenley. Everything is under control."

"Why didn't you tell me this first when I called to check in? And more importantly, why is Roxy with Tommy? They hardly know each other."

"Oh, believe me, they know each other, and quite well for that matter. Tenley, they are kind of together now. I mean . . . *together*."

Now I've heard everything. Tommy is dating my assistant. I guess he got over me all too quickly. *What the hell am I saying?* There was nothing to get over. We were friends, and as his friend, I was happy for him, and for Roxy. I guess this news would have been easier to take had I not found out about his accident first.

"Zoey, I'm going to call Tommy. He's my friend."

"Tenley, I promised him I wouldn't say anything to you. Please let me talk with him first, and then if he says it's okay, I'll just pretend to tell you about it."

"Are you serious, Zoe? Tommy knows you tell me everything. What makes you believe he would think you would remain quiet over this? And especially when he's hurt?"

"Just trust me on this, okay?"

"I guess I don't have any choice, but I am calling your father. I am still a partner there, and I have to check in with my boss."

"I miss you, friend. When are you coming home?"

"I can't really say right now. Can I take a rain check?"

"You can, just don't make it a permanent one. I miss my friend."

"I miss you too! I have to go, Zoey. I'll be in touch."

I ended the call and held my head in my hands. Something wasn't right about this, and she was definitely keeping something from me. I have to go back to New York and find out what the hell is going on. But how do I explain my leaving to Jagger and my family?

"Tenley! Breakfast is getting cold." Wendy shouted up the stairs.

I stepped out from my room and told her I would be down in a few minutes. I quickly combed out my long hair and left it in a loose bun on my head.

My phone pinged a few times while I finished dressing. I looked down to it and saw Jagger staring back at me. His contact picture was of the two of us from last night. He must have taken my phone and took it while I was sleeping. I thought I was a bit old for selfies, but this one made me tear up. Jagger had his arm wrapped around me while I slept on his chest. Leave it to him to program it in my phone and surprise me with it. What I didn't like were his messages. First it was good morning, but I guess because I didn't immediately respond, he must have gotten worried. The other three were asking me if I was on my way or if I was okay? The last text messages read:

J – I miss you. Please call me when you get this.

T – I miss you too. Busy morning. I will see you soon. Please don't worry.

His response was almost immediate.

J – I'm not worried. Just thinking of you.

Liar! But I guess that's to be expected. I knew we had a mountain of issues to work out, and I can't blame Jagger for being nervous or even a little doubtful of my intentions. Words may be one thing, but actions speak volumes.

T – Soon Jagger. Xoxo
J – Love you too!

Jagger the cowboy, texting . . . who would have guessed? I looked at our picture one more time before going downstairs. He was so incredibly handsome, and the beard was definitely growing on me.

"It's about time!" Wendy greeted me with her usual in your face greeting.

"Good morning, Wendy, mama." I kissed my mother on her cheek, and stuck out my tongue toward Wendy, making my mother smile. I think I've been embarrassed enough for one morning, but something tells me Wendy had more to dish out. She looked ready to burst, wanting to hear all the details about Jagger.

"Tenley, please don't sleep in the stables anymore. I know it's heated, but still I would be happier knowing that you were in the house."

"I'm sorry, mama. I didn't mean to worry you. I just had a lot on my mind and needed my space."

"Have you had enough? Can I get you anything else?"

"No, I'm good, but thank you. I have to head over to the hospital now to see Jagger. I will call you later, and maybe we can have dinner in town."

"That sounds lovely. Your daddy will be happy to go out, but no ribs this time."

"Okay, sounds good." I hugged my mother and asked Wendy to walk me to my truck. Wendy couldn't smile large enough. She was practically bouncing all the way to my truck.

"What's on your mind, Tumbleweed," she happily asked.

"I may have to go back to New York. Something has happened, and a friend needs me."

The smile has now left her face. "No! You are needed here. What could be possibly be that important that you need to leave now? And just when you are finally making progress with Jagger?"

"Wendy, I haven't even told you anything about Jagger yet. How would you know what progress we have made?"

"Just don't worry your pretty little head about such things. You need to stay here. Your family is counting on you for Christmas."

"I know they are, and I want to be here."

"So be here. End of discussion. I'll see you later."

I let out a sigh of frustration as I watched Wendy stomp back into my house and slam the door behind her. *Well, that went well.* I thought Wendy would at least have tried to listen to my reasons, but she stopped me before I could say anything else.

I began driving along the long road that would take me back to Jagger. I wanted to see him, especially after he was so sweet by adding a photo of us to my phone. It was then that my cell phone rang, and it was Roxy calling me. I decided to hold my tongue and feel her out before I said anything to her.

"Hello," I answered and waited for her to respond.

"Hi, Tenley, it's me Roxy."

"Yes, I know. I recognized your number. Why are you phoning me from your cell phone? Aren't you in the office by now?"

"Um . . . that's why I'm calling you. I had a personal emergency that required me to take some time off. I cleared it with Mr. Steele and asked Cheryl to cover for me. I hope that's okay."

"Well I don't know, Roxy, maybe it would have been okay had you come to me first, and not Mr. Steele, being you work for me."

One business call and my curt tone is back. I didn't want to be this short with her, but now knowing about Tommy's accident, I was pissed that I was kept in the dark. Roxy knows she can tell me anything without judgment, so why keep this from me when it not only involves her, but Tommy, who's one of my best friends?

"I'm really sorry, Tenley. It couldn't be helped."

"What's wrong, Roxy? Is there anything I can do to help?"

"No, thank you, but we're fine."

"We?"

"I meant *my family*, we're fine. Thank you for offering. So I've been checking on your apartment, and all is okay. I've just come from FedEx. I overnighted all of your mail to you, and you should have it by morning. Was that okay to do?"

"Yes, that's fine. Anything else I need to know?" I questioned her again, but she wouldn't budge.

"No, I don't have anything else at this time. I have to go now, but call me if you need anything. Bye, Tenley."

Before I could say anything more, the line disconnected. Unbelievable! I feel disconnected from my New York life already, and it's only been a few weeks that I've been gone. I guess I should call Mr. Steele next, but why bother when he hasn't called me?

At the hospital, I was greeted by the ever so cheerful Nurse Shirley. Before seeing Jagger, I asked her how he's been this morning.

"Oh, you sweet gal, I am going to pray for you to have patience with that bull in there," she said as she shook her head.

"That bad?"

"I'm afraid so. He went for x-rays last night and had his cast removed. Then we were having a pleasant morning, and chatting it all up about you."

"Doesn't sound too terrible so far. So what happened?"

"Your man happened. Ooh, he is stubborn. He wouldn't wait for the orderlies to assist him out of bed, and then he went right down to the floor and screamed out in pain."

"Is he okay? Did he re-injure his leg?" I asked.

"No, he's fine, but he needs to take it easy. He has to gain some strength back into that leg, and it's not going to happen overnight. Dr. Sampson wants him to stay on here and work with the physical therapist here on staff, but Mr. Brown Eyes has refused."

"Okay, Shirley, thank you for the update, but I'll take it from here."

"Well good luck to you then because you're going to need it." Nurse Shirley said.

"I'm going to run a quick errand before I go see him. Will you be able to hold the fort down until I return?"

"I've handled bigger bears than that handsome one in there."

I slowly walked past Jagger's room, and I overheard him shouting at someone I believe was a physical therapist.

"For the last time! I. Do. Not. Need. A. Wheelchair. I will walk out of here on my own. Why is that so hard for you to understand?"

Oh boy! The poor therapist. I hope Jagger doesn't make him wet himself.

CHAPTER 19

Jagger

...she's all i need

WHERE IS SHE? It's nearly noon, and she's not here yet. I'm going out of my mind worrying about her. When she left here last night, she seemed fine, but maybe she was only acting that way to put me at ease. I can't believe she would lie to me, so this is me trusting that at any moment she's going to walk through those doors, and I will be able to breathe again.

Instead, it's Shirley. My face fell when I saw her walk in. I usually played along with her flirtatious flirting, but all I wanted was Tenley. Shirley told me that I was going down for some physical therapy. I didn't want to go, but she insisted. I was helped into the waiting wheelchair for me, and my stomach just about turned over. I hated feeling so helpless. I wanted out of this hospital and back home to my ranch.

Shirley asked me last night about my love story with Tenley. I think it was her way of distracting me when I was getting my cast removed. While the physical therapist massaged my leg, we continued to chat about Tenley. I left out the harder parts of our story, and just told her about Tenley and Jamie. Although she asked me about him, I mostly left Shane out from the story.

A couple of hours later, I was back in my room and just felt restless. I couldn't believe I fell flat on my face. Pain shot up through my leg, and I feared I messed it up again. Thank goodness I didn't. It took two orderlies to lift me back into my bed with Nurse Shirley just shaking her head at me.

"What?" I asked her.

"You truly have to be the most stubborn man I have ever met."

"I highly doubt that," I snickered.

"You are, Mr. Brown Eyes, that's for sure. You did a foolish thing by trying to walk by yourself. Do you realize you have been lying flat on your back for nearly seven weeks now? You have to give your body time to readjust. That's why I called you stubborn, because you do not want to listen to good advice."

"I am listening, but you all have to listen to me too. I will be fine once I am discharged from the hospital. My ranch offers all I need to get where I need to be. Now for the last time, please get Dr. Sampson down here. I want out of this place, Shirley, and that means today!"

"Knock, knock, May I come in?"

Finally! She's here. My eyes found her sad ones almost immediately. The light that was in her eyes yesterday has now gone, leaving me with even more worry than I had this morning.

"Hey baby, come here," I called to her. She was carrying a pink box which could only mean she brought me my favorite pastries.

She walked right over and into my arms. I kissed her lips and slowly entered her mouth with my tongue. I loved when we kissed. We could spend all night just kissing and never tire from it. I was slowly reclaiming what was mine, and that began with her delicious mouth. She felt amazing next to me, but something was troubling her.

"What's wrong? Are you okay?" I asked her. She took my hands in hers and then looked at my leg.

"Your cast is gone. How does your leg feel?" Her way of evading my question.

"It's fine," I tell her. I lied, but talking about my leg is the last thing I want to do right now.

"How was physical therapy?" she asked.

"It was fine."

"Another fine? I guess you're fine."

"Tenley, my leg needs some work, but it's nothing I can't handle once I'm released, which will be today, or I'm signing myself out."

"Jagger, you need to follow your doctor's orders. I'm sure a few days of physical therapy will get you started, and then you can finish with an out-patient program." Of course she was making sense, but I out talked her again and wanted to know why she was so sad.

"Ten, I started getting better the minute I woke up to see you holding my hand. The rest I will do on my own. Now I don't want to talk about my leg right now, I want to talk about you. What's wrong, baby?"

"Jagger, something's happened back in New York, and I have to go home."

"You are home."

"Jagger, please don't make this harder than it has to be. My friend was hurt and hospitalized, and I need to see if he's okay."

"*He*? You're not saying that the guy that cares about you is the same *friend* that now needs you? Are you, Tenley? Because there's no way in hell I'm sending you back to New York to comfort another man."

"Oh really? What are you, twelve? And please let's get something very clear. Jagger, no one tells me what I can and cannot do, so please do not even try. Yes, it's my friend Tommy, but it's not what you think. He's been hurt, and not in a typical construction mishap. I just have a gut feeling that it has something to do with the case I represented him in."

"No way, baby. If that's what it is, then absolutely you are staying here with me. I can't protect you there, but I can protect you here. Please do not go back to New York. Let me get out of here and back home, and then we can talk about this some more, okay?"

"Jagger, I've taken care of myself for quite a while now, and one trip back to New York will not endanger my life. He's been there for me, and now it's my turn to be there for him. That's what friends do for each other."

"Oh, please tell me more Tenley, how much has he been there for you?" I asked her, sarcastically. I couldn't help my anger rising with every mention of this guy's name. I wanted to put the guy through a wall and bury him in it. Just the thought of Tenley being with anyone besides me just made me sick.

"I'm not doing this with you. It's not like you've been celibate for five years, and neither have I, but that's our past and if we have a chance at making it, then you can't throw my past in my face every chance you get. Jagger, that's not fair, and I would not treat you the same way you are treating me. Remember, cowboy, I've heard some of it already, and never once called you out on it."

"What do you expect from me, Ten? I'm a fucking guy! No guy wants to hear about his woman with someone else, friend or no friend."

Fuck! The way she's looking at me tells me that I just fucked up. She's probably thinking I'm referencing her to Shane, which in a way I am. I promised her that he wasn't between us anymore, but saying what I just did has put him right back there.

"Thanks for that. Um, I need to go meet my mom now. I'll call you later. Enjoy your pastries."

"Tenley, please wait!" I called out to her, but she bolted for the door. "Dammit! Dammit! Nurse!!!"

I called out for Shirley when she wouldn't respond to me by pressing the call button.

"I have to get the hell out of here, and that's right now." I grabbed onto the side bar and got a firm grip to get out from the bed. My leg felt weak and unsteady, but the therapist left me a crutch to use for balance, because I was too tall to use a cane.

"What are you doing out of bed?" It was my father, now entering my room. "Son, you are going to hurt yourself. Come on, let me help you."

"Pop, I'm fine. All I need is to get back to the ranch and find Tenley. We had a fight and she left. Please dad, help me?"

"She didn't leave, son. She's down the hall with your mother."

Instant relief flooded over me. *She was still here, thank you God.*

"Dad, please, take me to her."

"How about this? Give your girl some time to talk with your mother. They need to catch up, and while your mama is keeping her busy, I will help you get cleaned up and dressed. Come on, son. Work with me here?"

"Fine!"

"You know, Jagger, I'm beginning to hate that word."

He wrapped his arm around me and led me into the bathroom.

An hour later, still no Tenley, but I knew she was close by. My father was watching me like a hawk, getting ready to stop me from running after her. "Dad, I'm fine. As long as I use the crutch, I will be able to walk with no help."

"Jagger, why the rush? You were more than okay yesterday with the physical therapy in place, and now I come here and you just want to make a run for the door. I know you are frustrated, but your leg needs work. Put in the work, listen to your doctor, and you will be back to where you were before the accident."

"Dad, if it wasn't for Shane, I wouldn't even be here at all. He is the reason why I'm still in this bed."

"What do you mean . . . it's Shane's fault? She-devil threw you and that's when you fell. How is that Shane's fault?"

"Really, dad? Do you not see what's right in front of you?"

"I guess I don't, son, so maybe you should explain it to me."

"When have I ever been thrown from my horse? I can tell you, never. She-devil did not throw me off of her. I was knocked off by Shane. He told you that story to cover up the truth about what really happened up on that ridge."

Of course, after I shouted out my anger over my leg, and then mentioned Shane's name, my father was relentless with his questions until I told him everything. He was so taken aback, he had to sit down to catch his breath.

"I'm so sorry, son. If I had known, I would have kept Shane away from your room. He was here every single day, sometimes more than once."

"Dad, Shane is no threat to me. He will never get another chance to hurt me again, this I promise you. He said he is sorry, and he's attending weekly therapy sessions with Wendy. He is the least of my concerns right now. I need to go check on Tenley. She's my only priority."

"I'm here, Jagger, so calm down, cowboy."

Oh thank God! She's come back and with my mother following her in. She came right over to me and whispered that she was sorry she left.

I hugged her back and whispered in her ear, "I'm so sorry baby for losing my temper. Please forgive me?"

"There's nothing to forgive. We can talk about this later when we are in private. Your mom and I talked to Dr. Sampson. He's signing your discharge papers now on the condition that you allow a physical therapist to work with you three times a week. He will come to you on the ranch, but you have to promise to do the work. Can you do that?"

"Absolutely. When can I go home?"

"Right now, as a matter of fact," Dr. Sampson answered my question as he entered my room. "Here are your discharge papers. Please follow your therapy, and come see me in about a month for a check-up, sound good?"

"It sounds great. Thanks, doc, for all you did for me."

"My pleasure, son. Just don't make me regret releasing you too soon."

"I won't, sir. I promise."

My mother hugged my father. She was so happy I was coming home. I was just about ready to go, when my father asked for a minute to talk to me. Tenley would bring the truck around front, and I would meet her downstairs. My mother wanted me to come home with them, but I refused. I knew where I wanted and needed to be.

"Dad, I don't want to talk about Shane, not anymore, not ever."

"Well, that's too damn bad, because we are going to talk about it. Do you even understand what an accusation like this means? You could have died, son, and your answer to all of it is to just not talk about it anymore? Well, I want to, and I'm going to get some answers from that boy, even if I have to beat it out of him."

"Dad, leave Shane alone. Kip is your friend, and I don't think he will appreciate you pounding on his son."

"And you're my son, so what about you? He certainly didn't care when he shoved you off your horse."

Upsetting my father was the last thing I wanted to do. He and my mother had been put through enough sitting bedside vigil all those weeks I was in the coma. I took out my frustration on them and still they showed me unconditional love.

His eyes were filled with anger over Shane hurting me. This was my father, who raised me to be strong in mind and body, and to be a good man. Today I would prove to him that his lessons did not fall on deaf ears. I would take the high road with Shane and just concentrate on my life with Tenley. We waited long enough to be together, and our time was now. I gave my father a hug, with him returning the gesture.

"I love you, son, so much more than you can ever know."

"I know, dad, and you've shown it to me every day of my life. I'm working everything out, please trust me. Shane's working it out too. Please, let's leave it at that. Now I'm ready to go. Are you going to help me or not?"

He smiled. "Lead the way," my father said.

He didn't have to tell me twice. I was ready for what was waiting for me outside of these walls.

All roads lead to my girl.

CHAPTER 20

Tenley

...possibilities

HELPING JAGGER INTO my truck was no easy task. Of course, I rented the largest Ford truck they had on the lot, which caused difficulty for Jagger getting in. Although his cast was now off and replaced with a walking brace, he was still sore. The brace kept his leg in place while he was up and around. He needed to pace himself through his physical therapy. My cowboy tried to not show his discomfort around me, but I knew better.

"Are you sure you don't want to go home and rest?" I said to him as he instructed me to turn down a private road off his property.

"I'm fine baby, stop worrying." He pulled my hand to his lips and kissed it.

"Where are we going anyway?"

"Just a few more miles ahead, you'll see."

As I got closer to our destination, I saw what he wanted me to see. It was a house, and from the sight of it, a pretty big one.

"We're here. Come on, baby, let me show you around." He practically hopped down and landed on his stronger leg.

"Jagger! Please be careful, you can't risk injuring that leg again."

He took me in his arms and kissed me soundly on my lips. He looked so happy to be here with me.

"I'm fine. No. More. Worrying. Do you want to go inside and take a look around?" he asked with hope dancing around in his beautiful brown eyes.

"Who does this house belong to?" I asked now with curiosity.

"It's mine. I've been building it for the past five years. I began designing it with the architects before you received your law school acceptance letter, and I was going to tell you about it when you officially said yes to my marriage proposal. It took me a long time to finish it, but once I did, I knew I only wanted to share this home with you."

"Jagger, I don't know what to say. I have no words. This house is . . . breathtaking."

"You don't have to say anything, baby, and I'm not pushing you to decide right now. Just come inside and take a look around with me, okay?"

"Okay." A simple agreement to a lifetime commitment. He always made everything sound so simple, whereas I overcomplicated everything between us.

The house was stunning. It was designed to resemble a modern day log cabin. It had three floors, a wraparound porch, and an Olympic size swimming pool in the backyard with the mountains as our back drop. I was right when I said I had no words. He never gave up on me, and to build this home for us was just something I never imagined would ever be.

"Say something, Tenley. Do you like it?"

"Jagger, *like* doesn't even come close. It's the most beautiful home these eyes have ever seen. I can't believe you did this."

"Well, believe it, because it can be yours with a simple answer. If not, we can live anywhere you want. I just want you. Tenley, I promise I will not be so selfish again when it comes to us. You choose me. I choose you."

"Jagger, don't you see? We are still back in the same place we were all those years ago. I expected you to leave with me, and you expected me to stay. I love you. I've always loved you. How can I not? You are amazing in everything you do. Look at this house."

"I am looking, and all I see is you in it. Tenley, I want to marry you. I want our kids to grow up in this house, and I want to sit right there on that porch and hold your hand when we watch our grand-children play out on this beautiful land. I'm not asking you to give up your law career to be a rancher's wife. Just be *my* wife. I don't have a ring for you, not the one I want you to have, but I will."

I don't deserve him. He's painted the perfect picture for us and for our future, and I still can't say yes to him, at least not complete-ly. He hasn't wiped his smile off of his face since we got here. I can see the pride in his face as he takes in the house he built. This is his land, his house, and his dream.

"Hey," he said, as he lifted my chin so I could look at him. "Talk to me. Is this too much, too soon?"

I let out a sigh as he held me.

"Yes, it may be. Jagger, this trip was never supposed to be per-manent for me. I came home to find closure in Jamie's death and the wreckage I left behind. To make peace with my parents while trying to find a little for myself. To see you again has brought it all back for me. The feelings are still there. It's like time has just stopped, and we were on a holding pattern. Now we've been cleared for take-off, and it's just a matter of what direction to take. I just can't see myself giving up everything I've worked for in New York to come back here and start over. I know, selfish, right?"

"I wasn't going to say that. It makes you honest. You were hon-est then, and you're still honest now. But who says you have to start over? I can move to New York. I'll follow you this time around."

"No! I will never ask you to do that."

"You didn't. I offered."

"Jagger, please don't do this."

"Don't do what? Love you? Want you? Don't you see? It's impossible to move on without you. I tried that once, and I epically failed. Every woman I fucked in the last five years paled in comparison to you. All I saw was you. I want no one else. When Jamie listed all the reasons why his best friend shouldn't date his kid sister, we proved to him that he was wrong. I knew I loved you way before you ever told me how you felt. I was scared and didn't want you to laugh in my face. When you finally took a chance on me and trusted me with your heart, I did the same. Please, baby, trust your heart now, and I'll trust mine. This right here is where we can start over, or we can have that in New York. I can do anything as long as I know you'll be waiting for me when I come home."

"You would really give up everything you have here in Wyoming to move to New York to be with me? Your ranch. The beautiful home you spent five years building. Your family. You would say goodbye to all of that for me?"

"In a heartbeat," he answered with no hesitation. "I let you go once because I refused to see no other way of life beyond what I was living. In the end, I had no life without you. I don't want to feel like that again. Having you here with me now almost feels like a dream. I'm afraid to wake up and realize that's all it was, but then I touch you, I feel your skin against mine, I feel how your body reacts when I do and the loss it feels when I stop. We were just on a break, baby, a long vacation, but it's time to come home now, and my home is where you are. Ten, just think about it, please? Take the time to really think about it, okay?"

"Okay." He accepted my one syllable answer, and we drove the rest of the way in silence. As we pulled away, I couldn't help but look at the massive work of art Jagger had built, and most of it with his own hands. He never ceased to amaze me and what he could do once he made up his mind. Although this home was technically on the Parrish Ranch, it was far away from the main house where his parents still lived. Jagger had it built on his own acres that was separate from the rest of the land and properties.

He told me that once he cleaned himself up and refocused on the ranch, that's when his father signed over the deed to him. The house was always Jagger's, but now the land was his too. This was his dream, it always was.

Jagger, Jamie, and Shane were natural born cowboys following in their father's footsteps, paving the way for their own legacies to be passed down. Jamie never lived long enough to see his dream and what would come for him, but he made the most out of the time he did have. Every day he worked the ranch side by side with my father, along with the other ranch hands. My father's ranch was considered the crown jewel of all of Wyoming. It was the top grossing ranch in the state, and one of the top ten in the entire country.

Now Jagger has offered me his crown jewel to share with him. His home, his land, his heart. All I have to do is say "Yes," but I'm still struggling and I don't understand why.

We were at the main house, and I had not yet put my truck in park, Jagger leaned over and did it for me. He wanted me to stay with him tonight, but I needed to get back. I still had so much to talk to him about, but my head was pounding and I just wanted to go to sleep.

"Tenley, will you look at me please?" his voice sounded so small.

Don't cry. Don't cry. I was barely holding on to my resolve with Jagger slowly chipping away at it. I was helplessly falling back into our old rhythm we once shared. He held my face where I could look at him.

"Will I see you tomorrow?" he asked.

"Yes."

"Good, I was hoping you would say that. I kind of feel like I have to ask. You're not giving too much away right now, emotion-wise."

"Jagger, that's the problem. All I'm feeling is emotion, and I don't know how to put my feelings into words."

"That's okay baby, I don't need to hear them right now, just show me."

"How?"

"Kiss me. Kiss me like the first time you knew you loved me. Is that what you want?"

"Yes." I said, almost breathless.

"How much do you want it, Tenley?" He leaned in and stroked his fingers along my cheek, inching closer to my mouth.

Oh if he only knew how much. I was about five seconds away from pouncing on him.

"Please kiss me, Jagger." I whispered. He did with so much love and passion. I wanted more, but I pulled away.

"I love you, Tenley. Don't run, please. Just have faith this time around."

He kissed me again and then hopped down from my truck. His father greeted him at the door and waved goodbye to me.

I don't deserve him, I thought as I made my way home.

My house was dark when I arrived back home. I had totally missed dinner with my parents, but thankfully they understood why. I made my way into the house and found a note waiting for me on the entry way table.

Dear Tenley,

We're staying in the cabin tonight. Daddy will be with Sky. She's about to deliver her new foal, and I'll be helping him. See you in the morning.

Love,

Mom

Relief washed over me after reading mama's note. With all that was thrown at me today, I had just enough I could take. I made my way upstairs to my room, and all I wanted to do was fall asleep and think of nothing until morning.

But that's when I found it: another letter addressed to me on my side table. *Another letter from Jamie. How many more are there?*

Wendy must have left it for me when she was here earlier. I sat with my back to my headboard and turned on the radio. Rascal Flatts was playing, "Here." I held Jamie's letter and listened to every word coming through the radio. My tears flowed like a faucet. If there ever was a perfect song that described Jagger and me, this was it. I ripped open the letter and began reading my brother's words.

Hey Darling,

How ya doing? I swear to you these letters are not meant to hurt you. They are to help and guide you. You're probably thinking why I've taken on the role of knowing what's best for you better than you do, but as your big brother, it's kind of my job. We had that special connection between us, little sis. I always knew what you were thinking before you usually shouted it out. Do you still do that? I'm actually smiling right now because you would go from 0 to 50 in a second. It's no wonder why you chose law to pursue as a career. My natural born fighter, you always were. Which brings me to my next question: Are you still fighting? Fighting that impossible wall that you've put up? It doesn't have to be that hard, especially when it comes to love.

This letter is just a reminder for you to look at what's in front of you, who's standing in front of you with his heart in his hand and waiting for you to take it. You don't always have to have all the answers to your questions. It's like a roller coaster. Do you remember when we went to Disneyland, and you wouldn't go on Space Mountain? I practically dragged you onto the ride— your tears nearly broke me sweet girl —but then I held your hand and promised you there was nothing to be afraid of. You trusted your big brother, and you had so much fun, you begged me to go back on. It was the first drop that you were most scared of. The part where you are on the edge and once there, no turning back. You just have to go for it. You gripped my hand and shouted as loud as you could, but then you let go and allowed yourself to feel the rush of the excitement flow through you. Well, baby girl? That's what love is, and if you're on the roller coaster ride right now, then open your eyes, let go, and allow yourself the ride of a lifetime. Do you want that? I hope you do, sweetheart, because I want that for you and my best friend. Let go and just love him.

Let him love you back, and see where the wind takes you. Listen to your heart this time. Follow your heart and don't question it. I love you, little sister. Remember, I'll be watching.

Love,

Jamie

"Oh Jamie! How did you know? How could you have known that this is what became of my life? I have everything I could want in this lifetime and the next, but I sit here and question every thought. I feel strangled by my fear. Am I afraid to take this risk with my heart? This is what I keep asking myself. Why am I making it so hard? I think you're wrong, Jamie, you did have a crystal ball and saw my future before I could actually live it. These letters are a big 'I told you so' in-your-face reminders of how I chose wrong."

"Please Jamie, your words may not be enough, I need a sign to lead me in the direction I need to walk toward. Do I take a chance and try with Jagger again? Could I easily just fall back into step with him, and so casually walk away from my life in New York? This is what I need concrete proof on. I need to know that I'm choosing right this time."

"I miss you so much, Jamie. Your smile, especially your smile. Your faith in me is so strong. You always knew how I ticked, and which way the wind blew in my direction. I wish I had that now. It just doesn't seem fair. Our time together was not long enough, big brother. I know I can't blame myself for you dying. I wanted to be your savior, the hero that saved her big brother from his big bad cancer. For a while, I was, but I guess God had another plan. I don't blame him anymore. I don't think I really ever did, it was just my grief talking for me."

"I don't know what tomorrow will bring, big brother, but I

211

promise to *try*. I promise not to stay trapped in my past and concentrate on my present. As for the future? You have to be patient with me and give me some time. Good night, Jamie. Keep watching me from heaven."

I tucked his letter under my pillow, and tears poured from my eyes. These were the times where I missed my brother the most. If I closed my eyes, I could picture Jamie smiling and practically see his faith in me materialize. He was my hero, my big brother. I fell asleep to the sounds of Ed Sheeran. Listening to love songs and dreaming of Jagger, finally lulled me into a much needed slumber. I was on Space Mountain again, readying myself to let go. The screams from the other riders accelerated my own adrenaline as I looked over to Jamie.

"Are you ready, Tumbleweed? Here comes the drop."

I had no time to think and raised my arms up to the sky and screamed out my excitement. I felt so alive on that ride, and with Jamie by my side, I felt protected. It's what Jagger was asking of me now. He wanted me to let go and take the ride with him.

CHAPTER 21

Tenley

...leap of faith

THE MORNING LIGHT was slowly brightening my room as the day met the dawn. Surprisingly, I was feeling better. I must have cried for hours after reading Jamie's letter, and then listening to sad love songs on the radio. I finally shut it off, and my mind too.

I gave my body a deep stretch, then opened up my laptop. I probably had hundreds of e-mails to go through and a much needed phone call to make. I knew I had to speak with Tommy today, then Mr. Steele. I had this strong feeling something wasn't right back in New York. I mean, Tommy getting attacked on his own job site? He never had to deal with any kind of trouble for as long as I've known him. Sure he would have run-ins with work crews, but it never reached a physical beat down like Tommy endured. And this whole Roxy/Tommy love connection? Where the hell did that come from? He was always kind to her when he would stop by the office. I would see them chat and Roxy flirt a little, but how could she not? He was gorgeous and very available. My initial reaction surprised me, but maybe because I recently slept with him and compromised our friendship. He assured me that we would always be friends, and he would always love and care for me in that way. It was me that never wanted anything more because that was always what I wanted with Jagger.

I can say that in my head and feel it in my heart, but why can't I say it out loud to him? He needs to hear my answer and will proba-bly not relent until I give it. What the hell am I waiting for? Just go to him you foolish woman and take back your man. Oh god! I can't wait to tell this story to Zoey. She is going to flip out, but let me talk to Tommy first.

I dialed his number before I chickened out, and I thought his voice mail was going to pick up, but on the final ring, he said hello. Just the sound of his voice put me at ease.

"Hi," was all I could manage before he spoke again. "Are you okay? I heard about your attack. Please tell me that Zoey is not lying to me, and you are as well as she implored me to believe. Please tell me you really are okay."

"I'm on the mend. Not as pretty as you remember, but I'll heal."

"Tommy, no jokes right now. Please tell me what happened? I need to know. If you don't tell me now, then I will get on a plane and come to you, but I need to know."

"Coming back to New York is the last thing I want you to do." His words hurt.

"What is it, Tommy? Please tell me."

"You're in danger, Tenley. We all are. Beating the hell out of me was the first message. The second was your apartment being ran-sacked. Whatever they were looking for, they didn't get, but they promised they would be back until they right the wrong and seek jus-tice for their fallen soldier. By the way, all has been cleaned up, and your apartment has been returned to its pristine manner. Roxy took care of it for you."

"I don't understand. Fallen soldier? What does this even mean? And why my apartment? I can't believe my building manager didn't call me."

"Your apartment has been locked down. It's part of an investigation. I have a security detail on me, as well as at my job sites and crews."

Now it all makes sense. Fallen soldier? This has to do with Tommy's case and the players involved who I sent to prison. "Tommy, I'll be on the next plane out of here. I have to get back to my office. No way in hell are these bastards going to get away with this."

"No, Tenley, you can't. The FBI has already been called in. I suspect you will be hearing from Agent Paulson soon. Please stay where you are. You are safer there, and if they haven't found you yet, then it's a good chance they don't know. The minute you step back into New York, they will, and I can't risk you getting hurt. Please promise you will stay where you are."

"Okay, I promise. Are you going to be okay?"

"I will. Like I said, it was just a warning. It could have been way worse. I have Roxy staying with me. She's been great."

"How great?" I couldn't help to ask.

"I know what you're thinking, and you have a right to. We are probably the most opposite pairing you ever want to meet, but she just kind of happened when I didn't see her coming."

"Will you tell me about it?"

"Not much to tell. A couple of nights after you left, we were at a bar with mutual friends. We got to talking, dancing, and then, well you know what happened next. I thought it would be just a hook-up and then nothing, but I discovered that I really liked her. She's so cool, funny, and free. She has no hang up's about anything. She's just staying, and what surprises me the most is that I want her to. Who knows what will happen, but I'm not questioning it. Are you okay with this?"

"Why wouldn't I be? You have always been there for me, and I love you. You deserve to be happy, and if Roxy makes you feel all those feelings, then go for it. I will not stand in your way."

He let out a sigh so loud that I could hear it on my end of the call. Tommy didn't need my approval for anything, but for some reason he asked for it anyway.

"Thank you, friend. I love you. Please be safe and keep in touch."

"I will. And Tommy . . . ?"

"Yeah."

"Be happy. I love you too." I disconnected my call and looked up to see Jagger standing before me.

"Hi, what are you doing here? I can't believe I didn't hear you come in," I said.

"I'm not surprised, on account how you were just saying 'I love you' to some other guy."

"Jagger, it's not what you think, so please let me explain before this gets out of hand."

"Okay, explain."

I almost laughed, but that wouldn't be the right thing to do right about now, not when Jagger was breathing fire. I'm always being accused of flying off the handle going from 0 to 50 in a heartbeat, Jamie even said it. But here stood Jagger, looking like he was ready to explode, and here I was the calm one.

"Tommy's my friend, and yes, I told him that I loved him because I do, as a friend. He's been hurt, physically hurt, and I had to know he was okay."

"Is he okay? Will you tell me what happened?"

"He's healing from his injuries and should make a full recovery. He's back home and being nursed back to health by my assistant who works for me."

"And the story gets better and better."

"I wish it was a fun story, but it's more complicated than that."

"Tenley, you keep dancing around your relationship with him. Did you have something with this guy? Something more than friendship?"

I so didn't want to have this conversation with Jagger, but he was not giving up. I guess this is where the trust part comes in. He can't hold me accountable to who I slept with when we were apart, just like I would never hold him to his past. I pushed my laptop aside, and asked him to sit down beside me. He shrugged his jacket off and slowly came over to the bed.

"How's the leg this morning?"

"It's okay. I tried to ride She-devil, but it was hard mounting her, even with the help from the block."

"Jagger, I know you must be itching to get back on your horse, but please give yourself some time."

"You're right about that, and I will. You had to see her Tenley, she came to life when I walked through the barn. I had to let her know it wasn't her fault for throwing me off of her. It was like she needed my assurance or something. I don't know how to explain it."

"I understand more than you know. It was the same for me when I saw Jazzy. In my case, she probably felt abandoned by me, but didn't hold any grudges against me. She welcomed me and took me for the ride of my life. It was like returning home."

"Yeah, I get that baby, because you are home. When are you going to realize that?"

"I'm getting there, I just need more time."

"Time I have, patience I don't. Now tell me about Tommy."

"Wow, I thought you may have forgotten."

"Not a chance."

"Tommy's a friend, nothing more. He and Zoey were my first friends in New York, and have been in my life since day one. They are both very special to me. Tommy is also my client. I represented him in a land deal that he was trying to acquire, but he was getting muscled by some shady characters. They wanted to take over his business, and I stopped them. We got closer with all the extra time we were putting in, and I guess I wasn't paying attention when his feelings changed for me into something more. I never saw it, kind of like what happened with Shane. I told him we would only be friends, and he accepted that until one night a few weeks back where I crossed the line."

"What happened?"

"It was the biggest win of my career at the firm. It was also the anniversary of Jamie's death, and then add a guilt trip of not just a phone call from my mother, but Wendy too. I felt like I had a vise around my neck and I just didn't want to think or feel anything. I showed up on his doorstep, and well, do I need to paint you a picture? You know what happened, please don't make me say it. I was ashamed and felt so small afterwards. I left him there and went back to my apartment, only to find a letter from my dead brother. He listed everything in great detail how disappointed he was in me for the life I'd been living and how I broke my promise to him. I proved him right by making yet another reckless choice that not only hurt me, but my friend too. It wasn't fair of me to treat Tommy any less than he deserved. Reading Jamie's letter nearly gutted me. To read his last words to me, and then having to be reminded of the life I walked away from, hurt like hell."

"I'm so sorry you had to go through that, Ten. As for this guy, Tommy, it was just one time?"

"Yeah, one time, and once again a very big mistake on my part. It was stupid and reckless, and I should have known better, but I fucked up. What else is there to say?"

"Nothing baby, nothing. Thank you for telling me and I'm sorry I even asked. I just need to know where your head is at. I know I'm asking a lot of you right now, but that's only because I believe with my whole heart that we have a chance this time. I just need you to believe it too."

I did believe it. Maybe it was Jamie's letter or me voicing the words out loud, but I did believe it and now I was going to show Jagger how much.

"Make love to me, Jagger. Right here, right now. I want you to make love to me."

"Are you sure? Because once you say yes, I swear baby, I will not be able to stop."

"Yes. Jagger, my answer is yes."

Jagger walked back toward the door and locked it. He told me we were alone in the house. *Thank God!* I thought as I watched Jagger begin to take his clothes off. I was already wet between my folds as my body achingly craved for Jagger to be inside of me.

He asked again, "Are you sure?"

"Yes! Jagger, I'm sure. Please fuck me." I blurted out.

"Oh I intend to, but I will make love to you first."

"I don't care, just please don't make me ask again."

I was only wearing a camisole and panties. It wasn't hard to remove me from my clothing, but Jagger took his time. He pushed me back to the bed and parted my legs with his hands. He leaned in and kissed me first on my lips and then to each breast before making his way down to my already drenched sex.

He buried his face between my legs and inhaled my arousal for him, and only him. He seemed pleased with himself, as I began to flex my pelvis up toward his mouth. I couldn't be clearer of my intentions. I wanted his mouth on me, deep with his tongue thrusting inside of me.

Removing my panties with his teeth, he inhaled once more and entered me with his finger. I cried out, and he entered a second finger as my hands latched onto his hair and pulled him closer down on me. He didn't disappoint. I calmed myself and waited for Jagger to take me.

"Yes," I cried out as my first orgasm hit, and then quickly a second. Jagger would not stop. He thumbed my clitoris and continued to finger fuck my throbbing sex. Proof of my orgasm was all over his face, but it turned me on more. I reached up and grabbed his face and took his mouth on mine. Tasting myself was so fucking erotic, I wanted more. I wanted Jagger. He kissed me savagely as we crashed our mouths together.

With one tug, my camisole top was ripped from my body as he tasted my breasts next. He sucked hard on my right nipple, pulled and twisted until I screamed his name. Not letting me catch a breath, he gave the left the same treatment. My nipples were on fire, a feeling coursing through my body. He bit, licked, and raked his teeth over my sensitive breasts once more until I came again.

His steel rock hard cock was pressed against my entrance, teasing me with every move he made. Jagger reached for his pants and retrieved a condom from his wallet. Now was not the time to ask about each other's health records. I knew I was clean and didn't doubt him. I took the condom from him and ripped it open with my teeth. As I kept the condom on my lips, I slowly and sensually slid it down his hardness and just about made his eyes roll behind his head.

To see Jagger come undone like this was a beautiful sight to witness. I'd missed this so much. Our lovemaking was never awkward or complicated. We just fit with each other. He positioned himself on top of me with his knee parting my legs. He took in my wetness as evidence of my arousal glistened visibly.

"You are so beautiful. I can't wait to be inside of you. I love you, Tenley. I am never letting you walk away from me again. I swear it baby, never again."

I said nothing as he pushed deep inside of me. I felt the instant burn of his thick cock, as my body got reacquainted with his. He moved effortlessly in and out, continuing to thrust harder and faster. I was aroused as my muscles tightened around him, my body climbed higher and higher as my orgasm intensified. I was close and so was he.

All of our time apart and I never felt more connected with Jagger, as I was here with him now. His hands clutched against the sides of my head, pulling lightly on my hair, just enough to make me feel it. He dominated my mouth and called out my name. He held on tightly, as my fingernails clawed his tight, round ass. It was my turn to scream his name, and then he flipped me over and took me from behind.

"Tenley, I'm clean, I swear it. I need to take you bare. I need to feel my dick inside you as I fill you up with my come. Please baby, let me?"

I cried out, "Yes" and the condom was gone, and he took me again. I was face down onto the mattress with my ass in the air. He fucked me so hard, I thought I was going to go blind. His fingers pressed into my hips. He pushed harder, faster, and was now pulling me up with his arms engulfing me. He was strumming my body like a fine musical instrument, controlling every note he played. I was completely lost to his touch.

"I love you. I love you forever, Tenley Faith. Please, baby, be mine, and this time, make it forever." His words were sincere and laced with so much love.

I spoke in an unrecognizable dialect as my orgasm exploded. My body was full with Jagger still connected with mine. He poured every last drop of his essence inside of my heated sex. I felt like I was on fire. Flipping me over, he commanded me to look at him.

"Open your eyes, baby. I need to see you and I need you to see me. This is us, right here, right now. You are my world, my reason for waking up every day, and I swear it with all of my heart that I will love you with everything I have. It's yours, baby, now and forever."

These rawest of words and emotions had the power to yield their magic and heal what had been broken since the day I left him. My empty heart had now been replaced with Jagger's love and promises. I trusted him and knew he would never hurt me, and I prayed I would never hurt him again.

My greedy body desired more of him, but I was spent. We were both coated in each other's sweat. My room smelled like sex, and fucking hell, it was turning me on even more.

Jagger pulled out of me, making my legs close together. I felt the ache between my legs, as his come spilled out of me. He kissed me there and got up to grab a towel off the dresser to clean me. Then he raised the towel to his nose and inhaled my scent. Holy shit! He was hot and so inviting for me to take again. Instead, I just took him in my arms and we held each other.

"Are you okay? I wasn't too rough, was I?"

"No, and I loved your version of rough. Jagger, that was . . . amazing. I may not be able to ride my horse for the next few days."

"That's okay, baby. The only thing I want you to ride is my dick."

"Jagger! Oh my God! You sure do have a filthy mouth on you."

"Yeah I do, and one I want to use on you again. You taste delicious, and I love how I taste on you baby."

"Jagger, I was being serious. I may not be able to get out from this bed."

"Good. That was my intention all along."

"What? You knew I would ask you to make love to me today?"

He smiled wickedly. "I was hoping. Making love to you again is all I've been thinking about. I want nothing more than to have your body under mine. So yes, you're not getting out of this bed anytime soon."

"I think my daddy may have a thing or two to say about that."

"I think you're right, but he's not here right now, so don't worry about it."

After an agonizing night of overthinking every aspect of my life, I'm here now with Jagger. Reconnecting with one another has been as easy as riding a bike.

I've come home for the first time in five years. A place where I'm loved, protected, and wanted. It took Jamie's letters to make me see what I was trying so hard to forget. All those feelings were always right in front of me, I just needed to open my eyes to see it, and open my heart to feel it.

Jamie's words were my awakening. Jagger's promises of a future together are my truth, my reality, and all I have to do is say *yes* to him, and it can all be mine.

He continued to draw out circle eights along my skin, as I gathered up my courage to turn over and say the words he was waiting to hear from me. His movement slowly stopped, and I shifted to look at him and saw that he fell asleep. *God, he was beautiful.* So I kissed his lips ever so gently.

As I watched my handsome and rugged man fall deeper into a sound sleep, my mind calmed and my heart raced. He was the only man I have ever loved. Every girl fantasizes about the man she will marry. The perfect guy with no flaws. The perfect guy who will never hurt you and vow to love you to the end of time. Some girls say they don't exist, but I never doubted my prince or my cowboy . . . not ever. Jagger won my heart the day he opened up his for me. Even at seventeen, I was an over thinker, but somehow he managed to get around that and made me his.

To lay so close with him now, I don't know how I'm not crying my eyes out. Everyone who knows our story may believe it was easy for me to walk away from the life I had here. My future with Jagger, and what I chose instead, but they would all be wrong.

When you lose someone you love, you do lose a part of yourself. Daddy was right about grief swallowing you up. I'm living proof of that. I buried my hurt, masked my pain, and created someone new. One who on the outside looked happy and confident, one who had her shit together. My inside looked way different, and I allowed no one to see it, not even Zoey and Tommy.

I loved what I did for a living. It fueled my competitive side with adrenaline and fire, but Wendy was right, it didn't keep me warm at night. Now, I get that second chance to begin again with Jagger. All I needed to do was say the words. Was there ever a doubt? I didn't think so. I didn't think I could be here with him now if there was. I kissed him on his lips. His beautiful swollen lips from kissing me. He twitched slightly when I did it again.

"I love you, cowboy. My answer is yes, to all of it. I'm ready to let go and take that leap of faith with you. All I ask of you is to please catch me, and don't let me fall. I love you, Jagger . . . my answer is YES."

CHAPTER 22

Jagger

...i'll always catch you

I SLOWLY OPENED up my eyes as I felt her heart beat slowly next to mine. She had fallen asleep, whereas I had not. I was completely awake and heard every word she whispered to me, even the thoughts she didn't speak out loud.

Tenley said *yes*. One word to simply change the hands of time, and me, for all of eternity. This right here is what I promised myself I would have again. To not follow her when she left five years ago was the hardest thing for me to do. A promise between best friends sealed my fate, and I let her go. I don't know if I could have done it had Jamie lived, but I wasn't a man to ever go back on my word and wouldn't begin with Jamie. He trusted me. He also knew his sister and the battle she would wage within herself. How right he was, but it changed when she came home.

I had to prove to myself that I was worthy of Tenley. Sure I knew I could provide for her and the family we dreamed of having. But I needed to be confident that I was worthy as the keeper of her heart.

For a time, I wasn't sure and doubted myself after what happened with Shane. I never felt so betrayed in all of my life, but Jamie made me see reason and find the understanding under the convoluted situation I was in.

I'll never forget my last day with Tenley, and how I begged her to stay, but she still got on that fucking bus. I watched her get on that bus and retreat to the back. I stayed in the shadows, only to catch the last glimpse of her as she peered out the window.

I saw the devastation of her choice written all over her beautiful tear-stained face. She never knew that I got into my truck and followed her bus to the airport. Then stayed hidden and watched her nearly stumble through the crowd through her tears. The pain of my broken girl before me ripped through my soul. It would take seconds to just catch up to her and take her in my arms, and hold her. To soothe her and tell her that I was in love with her. To promise to wait for her, and to forgive her. When I watched Tenley board her plane, that's what I saw and heard myself doing, but I knew the forgiving part would take some time. Driving back to the ranch seemed like the longest drive of my life. I couldn't hide my hurt from anyone, especially my father, who knew the second his eyes met mine.

He said nothing and handed me an ax. For the next hour I chopped blocks of wood, hundreds of them, to beat the pain out of me, but it was not to be found, not today. I needed to feel it, to remind me that she was real and what we had was not a dream I created in my mind.

My muscles were on fire, but I took the burn and continued to chop the wood until the last block was split in half, kind of like my heart. I fell to my knees and leaned against the ax handle and . . . cried.

The following days were a blur after she left. Jamie had been released from the hospital and now was home for good. My father told me that Brock had told him about Jamie halting his treatments, and I should be a friend and go to him. I was so lost over losing Tenley. How could I have offered any solace to Jamie, when I was broken myself?

Jamie had chosen to live the time he had left on his ranch. To return to the land he gave his life for. I felt detached from mine, and I don't even know how I got there, but I was on his doorstep, the same doorstep I visited thousands of times throughout my entire life. He opened the door and invited me in. Just seeing my best friend already was helping in picking up the pieces to my shattered heart. The same heart his sister had broken.

Jamie looked like Jamie, and at the time, I had thought maybe my father had bullshitted me just so I could get out from the rock I had climbed under. The house was quiet, too quiet without her voice resonating through it. He handed me a beer and he said his peace.

"You look like shit," Jamie said to me as he raised his beer to his lips.

"Gee! Thanks a fucking billion for that." I said and gulped my beer down. He handed me another and asked me to listen to him. I thought I may have needed a few more beers to do that, but I didn't. Talking to Jamie was as easy as breathing. He never minced words and always spoke from his heart. He asked me to listen to him, and I gave him my word I would. But then . . . what he said next would shatter me even more.

"Jagger, I'm dying. Not the type of dying we will all face some day, but dying and I mean soon. My leukemia is back and my doctors have exhausted every idea to cure me. It's just too strong, and I don't have too many more days to fight it, which is why I need you to hear me out and promise me something."

"Anything." The one word that easily rolled off my tongue. Here was my best friend, my brother, asking me a favor with what he was facing. My personal pain felt small compared to what Jamie was going through. I put aside my feelings, and put my brother first, and was willing to do whatever he asked of me.

"I was hoping you would say that because what I'm about to ask of you to do will be a true test to our friendship and the love you have for my sister."

"What are you talking about? What does Tenley have to do with this?"

"Everything. Jagger, she is the sole reason for the promise I am going to ask you to make."

"Which is what?" I asked him. His dancing around it was pissing me off.

"Let her go," he quietly said.

"I have, Jamie, or do you see her here somewhere? I watched her board that fucking plane and walk completely out of my life and the life we were going to have together. Let her go? Yeah, that ship has sailed, and it's headed for the other side of the country."

"I'm sorry, Jagger. I think I've wasted your time here today, and wasted mine as well. For me, time is precious. You take care, man, I believe you know the way out."

He got up and began walking toward the stairs that would take him up to his room.

"What the fuck, man? That's all I get after everything we've been through? You just up and leave like your fucking bitch of a sister did?"

In my moment of anger, the words slipped out from my mouth, words I would never truly mean, but to Jamie, I crossed a line that made him see red. He charged me like a bull and pinned me up against the wall fireplace. The hard bricks were piercing my back, as his bear claw hands gripped my shoulders.

"You fucking asshole! As long as I draw breath, no one, and I mean no one, will ever speak of my sister like the way you just did. Do you hear me, Jagger? Because I'm not a man that will say it twice. If you dare to be so careless and free with your mouth again, I'll be putting my fist in it and break your fucking jaw. Get the hell out of my house!"

He screamed at me and released his hold. I crumbled to the floor and called out for him to wait. I begged him to talk to me. I would agree to anything he asked of me. I couldn't lose Jamie and our friendship, not when I knew I would lose him forever to his cancer.

God would be calling him home soon enough, and I couldn't waste one more minute with him.

"I'm sorry Jamie, please forgive me. I don't even know what I'm saying right now. I'm so hurt over losing Tenley, I can't think straight, let alone see what's right in front of me. You are my brother, my best friend, come on, man. Can I stay?"

"Get up off your knees and have another beer. I'll be right back."

I watched him go upstairs and come back down a few minutes later carrying what looked like a shoe box.

"Jagger, first off, I can't even begin to know how you feel about what happened with Shane. It's a hurt I wouldn't wish on anyone, and for what it's worth, I am very sorry you ever had to go through that. For the record, my sister is faring no better for her part in it. I've had to watch her for weeks now retreat deeper and deeper into a dark place. It nearly broke me every time I would see her cry, which was all day, every day."

"You haven't lost her, not in the way you think. I know how much you love her, but this is not your time, I know this because I know her. She loves you, Jagger, more than she loves herself, but even knowing that, she still had to choose her own heart and where it was leading her over you and what you wanted. If she had stayed, she would have resented you in the end, and the future you want with her would cease to exist."

"Jamie, what are you talking about? She left. We have no future. You can sit here and tell me otherwise, but the fact remains is that she didn't love me enough to stay and try. She took that bus and then boarded that plane without me. How can you say I haven't lost her?"

"Jagger, you're going to have to trust me. I was the one that pushed her to leave. She had to go and finish what she started. Do you even know how much she sacrificed to earn her degree? Taking double the course load for all four years? It's an incredible accomplishment, and what a bad ass my little sister is. You only remember the good times when you reunited and just had each other. Do you even know what it meant for my sister to receive that acceptance letter from Yale? Yale, Jagger! Fucking Yale Law School. It's mind blowing. I was never prouder to hold her in my arms and be her big brother. All she wanted to do was tell you, and hope you were just as proud. You didn't listen, did you? All you saw was Tenley moving on with her dream of becoming a lawyer and leaving you behind."

Jamie continued, "Maybe it was selfish on her part, but no more than you asking her to give it up for you. Don't even go there because I know what you are going to say. You did ask her, but she said no. What did you expect? She loved you, but to give up Yale would have destroyed her. Your lack of faith in her nearly did, and when you kicked her off your property, you might as well kicked her right through her heart and led her straight to Shane."

"Stop it, Jamie! I can't take it anymore. Why are you making me relive this? You know how much I love her."

I wanted to hit something, I was so angry. I loved Jamie, but hearing him remind me of the pain I had to endure for the past few days was destroying me.

"I can't brother, not yet. You will never know how much she regrets and blames herself for hurting you, and Shane for that matter. Tenley always put us first, you know that Jagger, and if she could go back in time, I know with my whole heart that she would have never traveled that path with Shane, not for all of the gold in the world. Please tell me you know this?"

I said nothing, just nodded. He went on.

"You need to forgive Tenley. I'm not asking today, but someday when the clouds part and you let the sun shine down on you, forgive her and truly mean it, my brother. And that goes for Shane too. We have been best friends since we were in diapers. You need him in your life, and he needs you. Now, back to Tenley. She's going to put herself through an unimaginable amount of pain as she struggles to find the reasoning in why I died and left her. She will retreat and shut everyone out who loves her. Although she promised me she wouldn't, I don't exactly believe her either. It's just a feeling, but for now I have to trust her. She needs to finish her education and see where it leads. That's another three years or so, and then to begin her career will take even longer."

"Jamie, my head hurts. Please man, what are you asking me to do?"

"Okay, here it is. Don't give up on her. Love her from a distance, but love her. Believe in the stars and hope that your love story is written in them. Your love story is not over for you, or for her. What's meant to be will be, and I promise you that if you believe in the love you have for one another, it will lead her home and back into your arms. I may not be here to see it, but I promise you, my brother, I will be always watching over you from the sky and helping you any way I can along the way."

"Here in this box, I have laid the path down for Tenley to return home to you and all who love her. The only thing is that she will not travel on that path for another five years. Five years is your time to wait for her to come back home. In that time, you will have to rediscover you, Jagger, and what you truly want for your own life. It just can't be about a dream we all once shared. It has to be more than just the ranch, it has to speak to you from your heart, to the deepest depths of your soul. If it's not Tenley who is the beginning and ending with every breath you take, then please move on with your life. And I truly hope you find happiness and all life's blessings you deserve."

"I love her, Jamie. She's all I want since the day I bravely whispered the words to her, and patiently waited for her to say the same back to me. I love her, and I feel so lost without her. I'm so sorry for pushing her away. I should have listened, but I was hurt. I swear I will wait forever if it means she will come back to me."

"That's what I thought you would say. Thank you, Jagger. I love you both very much, and I will not leave this earth believing you won't find your way back to each other."

"You're so sure, aren't you?"

"I am."

"How?"

"You're going to have to trust me brother, I just know. When one is facing the end of his life, things become simpler and clearer. It's another sense mastered, but never questioned. I just know, and for now, Jagger, that's what I am asking you to trust."

"I do, Jamie, always. Can I ask what you have in the box?"

"Like I said Jagger, it's Tenley's path back home. When the time is right, you will know."

Those moments spent with Jamie, I would never forget for the rest of my life. He was my age, but so deeply spiritual. He always had an old soul that spoke to you, I know it did for me that day. We spent hours laughing, crying, and our friendship was never stronger than at that moment.

Three months later, I said goodbye to him, and shunned Tenley when my eyes found her mourning for our fallen brother. I was lost and didn't trust myself back then. I once again let her go, but vowed to keep my promise to Jamie. I had to travel my own path of self-discovery and to grieve for all I have lost. My friendship with Shane, my best friend, to something greater than all of us, and the love of my life.

Now, after it all, she was here with me. Her beautiful, naked body was perfectly aligned with mine. I memorized every curve, every part of Tenley that nearly made my heart stop. She was gorgeous, probably too smart for a guy like me, but she was still here and she said yes.

I heard the fear in her voice when she asked me to catch her if she fell, oh hell! I would never let that happen. *She's here with me because this is where her heart has led her. It doesn't matter how it happened, all it matters is what Jamie promised me would happen. Tenley came home, not only to her family, but to me. No man will ever love and protect her like I do. I will prove my love and never take our second chance for granted.*

I'm not sure what's waiting for us beyond her locked door, but I do know with my whole heart that she will not walk it alone. I will be the man that makes all of her dreams come true, and she will be the light that brings sunshine to my cloudy days. We will stumble, but never fall, never again. I'm going to marry her someday. I will carry her over the threshold of the home I built for us to share our lives in. I will bow down at her feet with the sight of her swollen belly with our child. I will be everything she needs me to be, and make love to her under the stars. Our stars. The ones our story is written in. Yeah, that's exactly how it will happen.

She began to stir a bit, and I wrapped my arms around her even stronger than they already were. She opened her eyes and smiled back at me. We slowly made love again, sealing our newfound commitment to each other.

"I love you, Tenley Faith Fairchild. You were meant to be a Parrish." She smiled and let a tear fall down onto my chest. I wiped it away, kissed her passionately, and waited for her to respond to my very bold statement. It shouldn't have surprised her, I'd always said it to her, and now what I saw on her face was all the assurance I needed. She believed it.

"I love you, Jagger Lucas Parrish, and yes, my love, I was always yours. Thank you for loving me enough not to give up on us when I so easily did. I swear it with all that I have that you will never have to miss me again, because I'm home and there's no other place I want to be."

Her words consoled me. Every bit of pain in our past was dissolved. I never felt more in love with her than I did here now. I was a lucky son of a bitch. My girl straddled me and rode me like I was a mechanical bull. I never came so hard in all of my life. I held her face in my hands so I could look deep in her eyes. She was the window to my soul. My reason for existence was in her hands, along with my heart.

CHAPTER 23

Tenley

...new beginning

    "JAGGER, TIME TO wake up," I said as I kissed him along his chest and made my way down to his perfectly sculpted abdominal muscles. I stopped myself right before the danger area where I could easily take him in my mouth and have my wicked way with him.

We stayed in the privacy of my bedroom all throughout day. My muscles were sore and definitely overworked from consummating our reunion. We couldn't get enough of one another. We were back together and stronger than ever. *How did this even happen?* For so long, my faith in getting the fairy tale with the only man I had ever loved was lost. I would never allow myself to believe in second chances or even chance encounters where one could so easily pick up with someone after years apart, but that is exactly what happened with Jagger.

I gave my body one more stretch, and then my cowboy was awake and looking right at me.

"Hey, baby," he crooned. His voice alone made me wet between my legs, but I needed a cold shower to calm myself down. We needed to get up before we were discovered by my parents. As Jagger continued to kiss me, I glanced over to the side table and noticed the time. It was nearly six, and a weird feeling came over me. My body tensed and Jagger stopped.

"What's wrong? You look like you've seen a ghost?" he asked anxiously.

"Jagger, we need to get up." I practically shoved him off of me, and he pulled me back to the bed.

"Hey, talk to me. What's wrong? We were fine a few minutes ago, and now you're upset."

I took a few breaths to calm myself and reassured Jagger that we were still okay. I kissed him quickly and explained.

"Jagger, I haven't seen or spoken with my parents since yesterday. We've been in here all day. I guess I just got scared for a minute. If I'm even late for breakfast, my mother barges in, most of the time without knocking. Don't you think it's strange that we have had an uninterrupted day?"

"No, not at all. They weren't here this morning when I arrived, but some of the guys were talking about the new foal being born. They were probably still busy with the vet. No worries, baby, this is how ranch life works. The animals always come first. Now, come here and let me love you."

"Jagger, I'm serious. We need to get up. Aren't you hungry?"

"Not for food."

His hand were at the nape of my neck, and I had no escape of his mouth on mine. I was relaxing and feeling my body meet his when I heard noises outside of my bedroom door.

"Tenley, are you in there?" I heard as the door knob jiggled. Oh shit! My mother.

"Jagger, you have to hide."

"Where?"

I looked around and pointed to the closet. He put his boxers and jeans on, but his shirt and boots were still out in the open. I tried to kick them under the bed and shove him into the closet.

"Be quiet and don't make a sound." I put my fingers up to my lips, but he grabbed them and kissed them.

"Will you stop? If my father catches you in here, you don't have two good legs to run with."

"I have something that is good and working just fine."

"You ass! Be quiet."

Oh my god! I am a grown woman and he's got me behaving like a lovesick teenager.

"Tenley, open the door," mama said, as she now was knocking. I quickly threw my robe on and checked myself in the mirror. I looked thoroughly fucked, and I had skin abrasions all over my jaw and neck from Jagger's stubble. *Way to go being discreet, Tenley.* Zoey would be loving this right about now.

I opened the door to find my mother standing there, and of course Wendy, grinning from cheek to cheek. They both barreled in my room, nearly knocking me over in the process.

"Okay, Tumbleweed! Where is he?" Wendy asked as she looked around the room. I saw Jagger's boot sticking out from under my bed, and I shoved it out of sight before they noticed it. I tried to play it cool, but I already knew there was no way out of this.

"What are you talking about, Wendy? No one is here, just me. I've spent the day catching up on my e-mails and work I missed while being here."

"Connie, do you believe the line of bullshit your lovely daughter is trying to make us believe?"

My mother began to smile. She said, "No way, Wendy, my girl is knee deep in bullshit and slowly sinking."

Wendy said, "Tenley, we know Jagger is here. Did you forget that we know what he drives? His truck is parked right outside."

Oh shit! I could hide him and his clothing, but I forgot about his truck. Yeah, we were caught.

Wendy was laughing so hard, her cheeks began to redden. She said to my mom, "Okay, Connie, time to pay up. Oh, I love being right. So let's break it down. You owe me one hundred big ones. Never bet on a sure thing, I'm always right."

"Okay, Wendy, here you go. You don't have to rub it in."

"Oh, Connie, I'm just having fun with you, and this is a good thing, so smile."

I watched them both laugh and give one another a hug. My heart loved them so much, but also hurt a little that I pushed them away for so long.

"Okay, Jagger, time to come out. I hope you are decent because Tenley's father is downstairs, and you know the gun cabinet is fully stocked," my mother said as she looked around to where Jagger could be.

He slowly came out of the closet with cheeks as red as strawberries. He was so incredibly handsome and now he was blushing too. He looked around for his shirt, but I had it under the bed. My mother, knowing me all too well, pulled it out along with his socks and boots.

"I do believe these belong to you."

"Yes ma'am."

My mother and Wendy were having way too much fun at our expense.

"Jagger, why don't you take a shower while I speak with Tenley, and then we will have a talk downstairs."

Jagger nodded and turned to go into my bathroom when Wendy said, "Um . . . not that bathroom, cowboy. The one down the hall."

"Yes ma'am."

He quickly left and closed the door behind him. Nothing worse than getting caught with your pants down, especially in front of my mother and Wendy. I'm sure I will not be living this one down for a long time to come.

Now the playful Wendy was gone. She had tears in her eyes as she pulled me into a hug. She said, "I love you, Tumbleweed. I knew you would follow that heart of yours. You just needed a push in the right direction. I know he's smiling down on the both of you right now."

"Thank you, sweet girl, thank you."

She placed a kiss to my forehead and said she would be down-stairs waiting for us. I didn't know what to say to my mother, so I remained quiet while she smiled at Wendy.

"Mama, I'm a little confused on what's going on here. Wendy goes from nearly jumping up and down, to crying and falling apart."

"Come sit with me, and I'll explain it to you." I held my mother's outreached hand and joined her on my oversized chair. God knows I didn't want my mother to sit on the bed after all the naughtiness Jagger and I did today.

"Wendy loves you so much, as if you were hers. I do love all sides to my dear friend, but seeing her cry is one emotion that gets me every time. Tenley, you must understand how hard it has been for Wendy to undertake such an emotional request with what your brother asked of her."

"You knew about the letters?" I asked my mother.

"Not at first. Your brother was very private and even more so in his final days. I can only guess from the moment that you and Jagger broke up, and with everything that happened with Shane, he decided to put his plan in motion. Jagger was the only one that spent the most time here with your brother. At the time, Shane was on the outside looking in, but your brother never shunned him. He just spent time with him without Jagger being here. It was very hard for him to know his best friends were at odds with one another."

My tears began to fall after hearing that. My mother quickly wiped my tears away.

"Oh my sweet girl, please don't. Your brother loved you very much and although it has been hard on you to receive his written words, I truly hope they have brought some comfort too."

"Not at first, mama. His first letter hurt very much. No one likes to discover what a disappointment you are to your family."

"Oh no, Tenley, that's not what your brother was saying to you. He only wanted the very best for you and feared his death would be incredibly hard on you, and he was right."

"It was, mama, but I still managed to finish school and become a lawyer. It wasn't that bad, it was just . . . "

"Lonely?" she answered for me.

"Yes, it was. And now I'm here in my home, reunited with the man I love, and I still feel like I'm being pulled in a hundred different directions. Mama, what road do I take? Do I just say goodbye to New York and my life there to come back here and begin again?"

"How does your heart react after you say those words?"

"What words? Like 'home' and 'love'?"

"Yeah, those words."

"It feels complete and full. Like it was hollow for so long and now it's put back together again. I know without any more doubt that it wants Jagger, and it would nearly destroy me to walk away from him again."

"Then, my darling daughter, you have your answer. Everything always seems to work out the way it is was supposed to, and when it doesn't, life leads us down another road. Sometimes it may not exactly be the right one at the time, but we work it out and hope it leads us to better things. Your heart guided you home and to Jagger. Listen to it. Trust it, and just have faith. Did you ever wonder why your middle name is Faith?"

"Not really? What's so special about it?"

"Your name represents complete trust in God. When Jamie was born, then diagnosed with Leukemia, I thought my heart would completely separate from my body. I never expected to hear those words from the specialist. We knew nothing about this cancer and the survival rates for the patients who had it. Jamie was diagnosed with Acute Monocytic Leukemia. It was an extreme cancer, and your brother was now facing the fight of his life. He was only three, and as his parents we were preparing for the worst, and then I found out I was pregnant with you. Another miracle from the good Lord, but also a very scary one. With what we were facing with Jamie, the thought of you being born sick just scared us to the brink of constant worry."

"We discussed our options with the specialists and how to proceed once you were born. Stem cells were taken from your cord blood and tested. You were an identical match for your brother, and it was you who saved him. You, my Tenley Faith, gave our family a miracle not just with you being born to us, but you also saved your big brother. This is why your middle name is Faith. We trusted God with everything we had. This is why your brother knew you better than anyone else because you two were completely connected. He loved you with all of his heart, and in the end, he was going to protect yours and bring you back home."

"Oh, mama! I miss him so much."

My mother held me as I cried and cried onto her shoulders. She lovingly comforted me and quieted me down. I had grieved for so long for Jamie, and felt his loss daily. To hear this story for the first time made me feel so blessed to have had him as my brother and for as long as I did. God gave us our time with Jamie, and we spent every day of it loving each other and being happy as a family. I had the best childhood here on this ranch, and now for the first time since leaving home, I could picture myself back here and sharing my life with Jagger and the family we would make together.

"Thank you, mama. I love you so much," I said with the last of my tears falling.

"I love you too, Tenley Faith. Please don't ever question it again. I will always miss your brother, but it was you that I missed more."

"How?"

"Because you were still with us, but yet so far away not only in miles, but in your heart. Our children are our greatest accomplishment in this life. We want nothing more than to see you happy. I see it now, Tenley, and I will thank God, Jamie, and Jagger in my daily prayers for making that happen for you. You deserve nothing more than all the love your heart can hold."

When mama first came into my room, this was not the conversation I thought we would have, if ever. But once again, she surprised me with her words of wisdom and complete declaration of love.

"Okay, daughter, we've been up here long enough. You need to clean yourself up a bit, and then join us downstairs for a talk. Your father and I have been with Shane for most of the day with his parents as well. We all need to clear the air, and that begins tonight."

"Mama, I'm not sure this is the right time for Jagger and Shane to be in the same room with one another, there is so much you don't know."

"I know everything, and so does your father. Get ready, and I'll see you soon."

My mother kissed me on my forehead and told me all will be okay. Jagger was standing on the threshold of my bedroom when mama placed a kiss on his cheek. She told him thank you and said to meet them downstairs.

Jagger smiled at her, then came in and closed the door. He took one look at me and held me in his arms. He had heard it all and was crying along with me.

"I love you so much, Tenley. I am going to make you so happy and never allow you to ever regret taking that leap of faith with me. I swear it on the blessed memory of your brother, I will never stop loving you. You are my life."

He held my face and kissed me gently at first, and then passionately as our emotions got the best of us.

"And you are mine. I love you cowboy. Let's go greet the parents," I said through my smile.

As we made our way into the living room, his hold on my hand tightened as he saw Shane leaning up against the mantle. He was standing by his father, Jagger's father, and mine. Generations of cowboys in my house and all looking very serious. I rubbed my thumb over his hand to calm him. My father invited us to join them. We followed my father into our large dining room. We all took a seat at the table with Jagger's hand still connected with mine, sending Shane a very clear message.

My father began. "Welcome home, Jagger. From the looks of it, you seem pretty happy with yourself right about now, and my daughter's smile matches yours. For that, I am a very happy father today. I love you both."

We both said thank you, and he slapped Jagger on his back, but also sending his future son-in-law a message. He whispered for only Jagger to hear. "I don't see a ring on her finger yet, so no more coupling under my roof, okay son?"

Jagger was silent and just nodded in agreement. My father was not someone to rile up, none of them were. These men were all very protective and scary as hell, but I loved them all.

Daddy continued, "Now, let's get down to why I have gathered you all here. It's very clear that Jagger and Tenley are back together, I can only hope for a wedding to happen very soon. It would bring us complete joy to know that our kids are finally getting their happily ever after. Right, Ren?" Jagger's father agreed with a smile lining his face.

"Having said that, we now have a situation that needs to be addressed."

My father turned to Jagger, and spoke only to him. "Jagger, we all know the truth about your accident up on that ridge. We have spent the better part of the day speaking with Shane and discovering the real story behind your accident. I believe I can speak for all of us on how sorry we are that you ever had to go through that, but thankful all the same to the good Lord for saving and bringing you back to us."

We sat in silence and hung onto every word my father had spoken. Shane, along with his father, and Ren remained quiet as well. It was clear my father was in charge here.

"Now as you all know, the Fairchild Ranch is the top grossing ranch in all of Wyoming. Everyone here in this room has contributed to the success of this ranch. It was these hands, Kip and Ren's, that worked this land with our fathers, and they passed it down to us, and then we passed it to our sons." I watched my father bow his head for

Jamie, and then continued on.

"Generations have worked incredibly hard with their blood, sweat, and tears and have given themselves to this land. I am forever thankful in this ever growing legacy we have all had a hand in. It was my late son's dying wish to continue on through the bonds of our friendship. He loved this land and from the time he could run amuck with you two boys, this was all he ever dreamed of. You three would be partners like your fathers before you. Now that partnership has been strained and tested. I am finding myself at a crossroads and not sure what path to take. Jagger, you chose to run your portion of it with your father, and alone, where Shane and Kip joined me here on our combined land."

"It saddened me when you made your choice, but we respected it nonetheless. With you marrying my daughter—am I right to assume this son?" my father asked Jagger.

"Yes sir, absolutely."

"Okay. Tenley is a Fairchild, and marrying you will connect our families as one. We always felt we were, but you two will now make it official. Where does that leave Shane? And his role here?" My father asked as he looked directly at Jagger.

You could hear a pin drop in the room. My father commanded us all to sit in full attention. Jagger looked like he would throw up at any moment. I rubbed his thigh and encouraged him to talk. He took in a deep breath and surprised me with what he said.

"Sir, everyone in this room can attest to my love for ranch life. It's in my blood and I know no other way of life. You're right, it was my dream along with Jamie and Shane to take over for you all one day, and make our businesses even greater and prosperous, but when Jamie died, that dream died with him. I respect you, Brock and Kip. You are like second fathers to me, but I no longer see Shane as my brother. I don't know if I will ever be able to move past what happened between us, but I will not hold it against him either. My life is my own, and it will not be guided by holding a grudge. My new life began here today in this house with your daughter, and I promised her a lifetime of happiness. I'm not sure where that will begin. Tenley and I have to discuss our future in private. All I know is that if this life here in Wyoming is not what she wants, then I don't want it either, and this time it will be me following her."

"Jagger . . . " I said.

He kissed me to silence my objections.

My mother and Wendy were wiping their tears away, while Kip patted his son's back. Ren looked over to his son with nothing but pride showing over his rugged face. My father appeared to be at a loss for words, but he just shrugged back his shoulders and looked right at us.

"Jagger, you are a good man, and I trust you completely in your promises to my daughter. You have our blessing to marry her and join our family . . . officially. It is my hope that you and Shane will reconcile your differences and renew your once strong friendship, and bind yourselves back to this land. This is truly where your heart lives, and it will bring me great sadness to see it be destroyed. I know you're hurting son, but life is too short to hang onto a past hurt. You know what I'm saying son, and it will only hurt you more to carry it with you in your new life with Tenley. Now, my partnership with Ren and Kip will remain. We will run our cattle and horse business just like we have always done. The lovely ladies in our lives will still handle their roles in our family's ventures. It's up to you cowboys to really decide what to do about your roles. Shane has offered to relinquish his partnership back over to me and walk away clean with severing ties to the ranch."

We all looked at Shane as daddy continued, "This is not what I want, but in life you have to make some tough choices. Jagger, I'm not going to make it. No matter where you are with my daughter, this ranch is still her home, and you, son, are going to have to decide if you want Shane to be part of it. This is his home as it is all of ours, and he's willing to give it all up for the sake of righting his terrible wrong. I know this is an incredible decision I am laying on your lap, but again, it's yours and Tenley's to make. I truly hope whatever you decide will bring you peace. That's all I have to say and will say until Jagger gives us his answer."

My father dismissed all of us, and we watched one by one as everyone left the room, leaving us behind. Jagger's expression was carved out in stone. I wasn't sure if I should even touch him, so I began to get up from my chair and that's when his hand reached for my arm.

"Where are you going?" he asked coldly. This was not Jagger, his voice was laced with anger.

"I'm going to fix myself a drink, and I think you could use one too."

"I don't want a drink, and seeing you drink is the last thing I ever want to witness."

"Jagger, a glass of wi . . . "

"No! Do you hear me, Tenley? No drinking for us, not now, not ever. People make bad decisions when they drink, and I need my head clear, okay?"

Right there I was taken back to the night I was drunk and betrayed Jagger with Shane. *Oh God! Will he ever truly forgive me for that?* I didn't have the strength to call him out on it, so I did the next best thing . . . I ran. I grabbed my coat and made my way to the stable to see Jazzy.

Jagger called out to me, but I ignored him. My tears were falling rapidly, and my heart was breaking. No matter how far Jagger and I came today, there would always be my mistake with Shane hanging over our heads. He swore to me years ago that he would never forget what I did to him, and clearly he never did.

CHAPTER 24

Jagger

...no more running

"FUCK! DAMMIT TO hell!" I couldn't stop her with my hurt leg. Declaring war on the liquor cabinet showed her my biggest regret. I meant every word I said to Tenley. I was no longer living in the past, but having to sit here and listen to her father go on about family, friendship, and most of all Jamie, nearly broke me in half. My father watched my every move while I sat and listened to Brock.

After my collision with the tree, I swore off alcohol and bad decisions. Once in a while, I would still have an occasional beer, but it had been so long going without it that I don't even miss it. I saw the look on Tenley's face when I said it. She had to be thinking about Shane, assuming I still blamed her. I didn't, and hell, I didn't even blame him anymore. It was a part of me, and my wounds were still raw from my accident and knowing Shane was the cause of it. After I vowed to never hurt her again, it's exactly what I just did.

"Go away, Shane, you are the last person I want to see right now," I said, as he made his way over to me. My leg was so stiff, I couldn't walk another three feet in front of me. I sat on the porch freezing, knowing my girl was out there somewhere and alone.

"Too bad, Jag, but I'm not going anywhere. What are you doing, man? What will it take for you to forgive me? And her? You finally have her back. Don't fuck it up by throwing her greatest mistake back in her face every chance you get. If you truly can't move on, then you don't deserve her. Let her go back to New York where she may have a shot at being happy with someone else."

"HELL NO! Do you have a fucking death wish Shane? Why are you trying to rile me up right now? You want off this ranch? Get the fuck off it and take a long walk of a short cliff. Hey, I tried it and looky here . . . I'm still alive!"

"You're an asshole, but you're my asshole brother/best friend who I love. I know you're mad at me, but I also know that buried under all of your hurt is forgiveness. It's there, and when you're ready to give it, I'll happily accept it. I'm so sorry, Jagger. You will never know how sorry I am for all of it. Please don't let your stubborn pride get in the way of being happy with Tenley this time. I've learned so much from my therapy sessions, and the wisdom from our fathers. A man's pride is just as important as the air in his lungs. No man escapes taking a fall in his life, but it's what comes next after the man gets up that matters. Be that man to get up, and go get your girl. Get the fuck up, and go get your girl!"

I looked at Shane, I swear he was going to punch me while I was still down. When I got up, he wore a shit-eatin'grin that I just wanted to punch, but he knew I wouldn't.

"I really fucking hate you right now, you know that, right?"

"That may be, brother, but I know you love her more. Now for the last time . . . GO. GET. YOUR. GIRL."

I wanted to say thank you to him, but I think Shane knew it. I got in my truck and drove down to the stables. I called out to her, and no one answered back. Jazzy was still in her stall, and I saw no other horses missing.

"Tenley! Where are you?" I voiced out loud.

"Oh boy! Will you and my daughter ever get it right? Hell, my son up in heaven must be knocking back a Tequila shot by now," Brock said as he made his way over to me.

"How did you know, sir?"

"Know what, son? How the minute we all left you would once again fuck up and hurt my daughter?"

"Yeah, something like that."

"We had hoped you would have been the bigger man about it, but clearly you still are fighting that internal war within you. Son, you're not going to get many more chances to be with her. You take a foot forward only to be catapulted three feet back with your stubborn pride. It's over, son. That thing with Shane and her . . . Let it go once and for all. Did anyone really ever stand a chance against what you and Tenley have? Please be the man I know you are and go find my girl. Love my daughter with every fiber you have, and marry her. Make good on all those new promises, and be happy with the one you love. That's being a man, an honorable one who I can respect as my son-in-law. If you can't be those things, than please walk away."

"Never sir. I will never let her go. I swear I will make this right."

"Good man. She's at the cabin."

"Thank you, sir."

"You're welcome, Jagger."

I never drove so fast in my life. I hit every bump on the road, causing painful spasms through my leg, but I didn't care. I needed to get back to my girl and grovel at her feet.

"I swear it, Jamie, I swear it. I will never be so careless again with your sister's heart. I'm sorry, brother, please help me make this right again. After all we've been through, I won't lose her now."

The cabin was dimly lit with the fireplace roaring. I could see the smoke coming from the chimney and knew she was in there. I saw not her rental, but one of the jeeps they used on the ranch.

I didn't bother knocking and just walked in where I found her in deep thought in front of the fireplace. I closed the door behind me and kicked off my snow covered boots. It was warm in here and my girl was surrounded by ice cream and tissues.

She was quiet. Who could blame her? I sat beside her and turned her to me. She didn't flinch with my touch and that was a sure sign that I still had a chance here.

"Baby, I am so sorry for what I said back there at the house. I know what you must be thinking, but I swear it was just a knee-jerk reaction to all your father hit us with. I swear to God that I am no longer holding onto that past hurt. I will never ever bring it up to you again. Please talk to me. I will do anything to see you smile again and hear you say you forgive me. Please Tenley, please?"

"Ice cream?"

"What?"

"I said ice cream, do you want some?"

"Um . . . sure. What kind do you have?" My heart was pounding in my chest and here was my girl offering me ice cream.

"The freezer is stocked up good." She got up and walked over to the refrigerator and told me what she had. "We have Chocolate, Strawberry, Vanilla, Rocky Road, and my personal favorite, Chocolate Peanut Butter. What will it be?"

Fucking hell! She was teasing the hell out of me right now and making me sweat. Tenley was wearing skin tight dark denim jeans, with a sweater only reaching her waist and giving me a clear picture of her perfect round ass which she was taunting me with. Her sweater was thin with only a tank top underneath. I could see her nipples hardening in front of the opened freezer door. My dick was so hard it was causing me pain against my zipper.

"Well? I don't have all night."

She winked at me. And right there, I knew we were okay. I made myself comfortable up against the floor pillows she placed in front of the fire. I spread my legs for her to see my hard erection, and her eyes widened. Licking my lips, and so ready to play this game, I said, "Chocolate Peanut Butter."

She grabbed the container and a new spoon and slowly walked

over to me. Popping the top off, she dug in with her spoon and brought it to her mouth, spreading the ice cream all over her lips. My dick was so hard, if I didn't take her soon, I was going to explode right in my pants. Knowing my girl, this was exactly what she probably wanted to happen. It would serve me right for being a stubborn ass.

"Hmm, this is good. Want some?" she teasingly asked.

"Only if you feed it to me."

"I don't think that will be a problem."

"Take off your jeans and sit on my lap, then you can feed me," I requested.

"I don't think so."

"Are you saying no?"

"I'm saying no, but would be willing for an even exchange. Let's call it 'What will Jagger say next?' "

That hurt and went right through my heart. She was clearly playing with me, but remained guarded at the same time. I deserved it and would take anything she threw at me.

"An even exchange? Okay, go for it," I said.

"Take off your clothes, Jagger," she said without batting an eyelash.

"Where would you like me to begin?"

"I would start with your pants," she said, taking another bite of ice cream and licking the spoon clean.

Yup! I was about to shoot right in front of her. I kicked off my jeans and then slid my boxers down my legs with my dick springing free. I then lifted my t-shirt from the hem and whipped it over my head. I was completely bare in front of her, waiting for her next command.

"Very good. You may have a taste."

She spooned out some ice cream and I opened my mouth to take it, but she slowly and teasingly ran the spoon down her neck.

"Oops, I missed. Whatever shall I do now?"

She didn't need to say another word, I leaned in and licked up the fallen ice cream with my tongue, leaving not a trace behind. She squirmed under my touch, I could feel her legs rubbing together. She wanted me, that was clear, but I knew I needed to be patient and have her lead me where she needed me to be.

"I'm sorry I ran," she said.

"I'm sorry I was the cause behind it."

She spooned another serving and placed it in my mouth, then a scorching kiss followed. I relished the decadent flavor and wanted more.

"I love you, Jagger."

"I love you too, Tenley, so much."

"Will you ever truly forgive me for Shane?"

"I already have. I swear to you I will never bring it up again. I know it hurt you, and I instantly felt the pain in my gut when the words left my mouth."

She took in another spoonful of ice cream and then dropped to her knees, taking me in her mouth. I wasn't going to last long with Tenley making a meal out of my dick. I was so turned on by her assault. She dropped the container and put her hands behind her back with just her skillful tongue working me over. I instinctively held her head and pushed my hardness further down her throat. She moaned out her pleasure, and I was five seconds away from erupting into her hot mouth. I warned her before, but she didn't release her hold on me. I arched my head back while still holding hers, and I came so fucking hard down her throat. She took all of me, and I was a bastard to allow her to. She licked me clean, and not a drop was spilled. She got up, looking pleased with herself. Placing the ice cream back into the freezer, she turned and slowly removed herself from her clothing.

Her flimsy sweater and top went off together. Next was her jeans she shimmied out of. Tenley was standing in front of the fireplace with just her bra and panties remaining. Her eyes invited me closer, and I took it from there. I unfastened her bra and let it drop to the floor, kissing her mouth and tasting the remnants of my come mixed with ice cream.

"I love you. Relax, baby, because it's my turn to show you how much."

I kissed my way down to her dripping sex and ripped off her panties, if you even want to call them that. My tongue pushed into her folds, and immediately Tenley's pelvis rocked against my mouth. I fucked her with my mouth. I could feel her legs weakening with every thrust of my tongue inside of her. She dropped down into my arms where I placed her on the pillows and blanket. I didn't stop, I would never stop pleasuring her. I parted her legs and stretched her to the brink of pain. She cried out over and over again as her orgasms ripped through her body. At the height of her climax, I plunged deep inside of her swollen tightness.

"You feel so good, baby, wrapped around my dick. Let me hear you," I commanded her.

"Holy hell, Jagger!"

"That's right, baby, scream my name. I fucking love it and love you so much."

We were on the brink of pure ecstasy. I fell to my back with Tenley riding my dick even harder than before. I sat straight up with my arms wrapped around her. I pushed harder, she rode me harder, and then we came together. Our bodies were slicked in sweat mixed up with both of our juices. She collapsed onto me, and I held her with the intention of not letting her go.

Somehow we made it into the shower to clean up. I washed her from her hair down to her toes. All I wanted was to make her feel good. I was so done being an asshole that throws her past in her face. Tenley's past was mine as well. It didn't serve either one of us any good to keep living there. We had an amazing future to look forward to, and I wasn't going to tempt fate again.

"I'm starving," she said as she snuggled up against my side.

"Wait here, and do not move. I will make us something and bring it back here to bed."

"I won't move a muscle," she quietly said. I gave her about two minutes, and my girl was down for the count. I cleaned up the floor a bit, and then gave her some time to rest.

I went outside to gather some firewood, and found a note taped to the door. I looked around for anyone in sight, but saw no one. I saw tracks that matched the ones from Tenley's jeep, so I wasn't worried that it was someone we didn't know. I shoved it into my back pocket and gathered up the wood. The fire was blazing again and warming up the cabin. I made us omelets with toast and fruit on the side. I clipped a sunflower from the arrangement on the table and placed it into a single vase. I double-checked everything I placed on the tray and carried it over to my sleeping girl who was beginning to stir with the aroma coming from the food tray.

"That smells delicious. What are we having?" she asked playfully.

"Breakfast for dinner."

"My favorite" She winked.

We talked while we ate and cleared the air from the heavy conversation back at the house. I wasn't ready to make any decisions about Shane, or my future role on the ranch. I was happy with the horse business shared with my father which blended into Brock's business he conducted with the summer tours he hosted. I also needed to feel out Tenley and where she wanted to be. I was absolutely serious when I said I would follow her this time.

My father was already prepared for me to leave if it came down to it. He was still worried for me, but he also knew my heart was forever aligned with Tenley. The rest was only details.

CHAPTER 25

Tenley

...what lies ahead?

I T'S BEEN THREE days since Jagger and I officially reunited. The morning following our amazing night spent at my cabin, I sent Jagger home to begin his physical therapy. He wasn't a great liar, and clearly was having some issues with his leg. Dr. Sampson assured him that with the proper physical therapy, he would return to where he was physically before his accident.

He already had a home gym designed and set-up in the new house, so he opted to work out there versus going into town to the hospital. On the ranch is where he felt most comfortable, and deep down I knew that. After we cleared the air about everything, I told Jagger that I needed a few days on my own to think and come to some decisions that would affect my career and where I wanted to live. Of course to everyone involved, the obvious answer was Wyoming, but Jagger would agree to New York if it meant being with me.

We already made the decision to be together, so now it was up to me to decide the rest. No matter what Jagger has promised, I would never be able to live with myself if I forced his hand and self-ishly chose my career again over him. His heart was in Wyoming, and my heart was entwined with his, so there was my answer.

Shane was keeping a low profile around the ranch. He kept himself busy with his daily work while waiting for Jagger's decision. I didn't want Shane to dissolve his partnership with my father. This was his home, and he belonged here just as much as I did. I wouldn't be the one to hurt him like that, and I prayed with great hope that Jagger would feel the same. It certainly didn't serve us well to keep holding onto a past we could not change. The life I'd been living was proof positive of that. Jagger needed to be shown the way, just like I did. I believed in his good heart, and I was confident he would find his way back to Shane and renew their friendship as the brothers they once were. I knew Jamie never stopped hoping for that to happen.

After a morning ride with Jazzy, I took refuge in my father's private office. I'd been home for about a month now, and Christmas was just about a week away. The ranch was in full swing with vacationers, and the town was hosting a tree lighting spectacular with a winter carnival to follow. It had been years since I'd gone to the winter carnival. The last memory I had was with Jamie, Jagger, and Shane on my last holiday break before I graduated college the following spring. I wanted those good memories again. I was hoping the ice melted a bit with Jagger and Shane, and we could all go as friends.

My father's office was cozy and warm. I lit a fire and sat beside it with my laptop and phone. It was time to make a difficult call, one I'd been avoiding, but no longer saw the point of putting off. It was time to pull the Band-Aid off and take yet another leap of faith. I called Mr. Steele directly on his private line, but it went straight to voicemail. I hesitated and disconnected my call. I then called his assistant and left a message with her. He was tied up in meetings across town and would not return to the early evening. What I said would be difficult enough, so waiting a few more hours was fine by me.

I then called my own office where Roxy was still on leave. Cheryl had taken over her duties and was managing the day to day tasks. She answered in her most professional tone.

"Good Afternoon, Steele and Copeland Law Firm, Ms. Fairchild's office."

"Hi, Cheryl, it's Tenley."

"Hello Ms. Fairchild, how are you doing?" She sounded a little off, but I shrugged it off at first."

"I'm fine, Cheryl, thank you for asking. How is the office? Anything I need to know about?"

"All is great here, Ms. Fairchild. Roxy is having a great vacation, as I'm sure you are too. Where did you say you were again? Would you like me to forward any mail to you?"

"That won't be necessary, Cheryl. I'll be in touch."

I quickly disconnected my call with her, and realized she was probing me for information. I never disclosed my itinerary with Cheryl or the other administrative assistants. Only Roxy knew along with Zoey and Mr. Steele. My travel plans were password protected with only Roxy and Mr. Steele having access to it.

After the car explosion during Tommy's trial, Jacob, my friend and the agent who worked with me, advised me taking extra security precautions. He had a private security firm work with me to secure all my personal and business dealings. It was also strange how Cheryl just assumed Roxy was on vacation, but what assistant takes weeks off? I needed to speak with Mr. Steele right away, and I decided to phone him on his cell phone.

He answered right away and was comforted in knowing I was safe. His concerns about my safety raised alarms with me especially after Tommy was attacked.

"Mr. Steele, please level with me and tell me what is going on. I already know about the assault on Tommy Mills. Zoey filled me in, and I know Roxy is on a leave of absence, with Cheryl filling in for her. Have there been any more threats?"

"Yes, Tenley, there have. An unmarked envelope was messengered over to your office with a letter of threat made against you. The second was a flower delivery, but when it was opened, the boxed contained snakes."

"Oh my God! Did you phone the police? Is everyone safe at the office?" I was pacing my father's office and contemplating getting on a plane to fly back tonight.

"Tenley, we are all safe, and no more threats have been sent. I did contact Agent Jacob Paulson directly, and he told me he would be in contact with you."

"Mr. Steele, I haven't heard from him yet. When did you last speak with him?"

I spoke to him four days ago. I would have thought you would have heard from him by now."

"I have not. Mr. Steele, are all my files still secured?" I questioned.

"Absolutely. We just performed an office sweep last night when everyone went home. We told no one of this, and we also tapped your phone. I already knew you checked in today, as I have to imagine so does Agent Paulson. Stay where you are, Tenley. I will sleep better knowing you are safe. I almost want to put Zoey on a plane to join you, but she compromised and moved back into my home until we figure out what the hell is going on. Agent Paulson suspects this all has something to do with the Mills case."

"I think you're right about that, Mr. Steele. I had a bad feeling since hearing about Tommy."

"Please, Tenley, call me Raymond. You've earned that right."

"Thank you, sir. Sorry, old habits die hard. Thank you, Raymond, for giving me this time. I will be in touch soon."

"My pleasure. If any developments arise, I will call you immediately."

I ended my call and then phoned Jacob. If anyone could help me, it would be him. His office told me he was out on assignment and I could leave a message. I then phoned Tommy to check in on my friend. He was doing much better, and his ribs were completely healed. He still was hot, he said as I heard Roxy laugh in the background. They both sounded really good, and I was happy for the two of them. Tommy deserved to be happy, and I had good feelings about his blossoming romance with Roxy.

"Okay you two, have fun and please be safe," I said to them.

"You be safe too, my friend. I love you, Tenley."

"I love you too, Tommy. I'll speak with you soon."

As soon as I ended my call, I noticed Jagger standing in the doorway.

"Hi, I didn't hear you come in," I said to him.

"How could you when you were telling another guy you loved him. It feels like Déjà vu all over again."

"You're right, I do, but just as a friend."

"I know that, sorry."

"It's okay, I'm getting reacquainted with your jealous side."

"I'm not jealous, baby. Just protective of what's mine. I trust you completely with my heart. I know you love me."

"I do, Jagger, I love you so much. I just can't have you doubting that love."

"Never again, I promised you that. Now come here, and give me a kiss. I've missed you, and I've been going crazy without you."

I walked into his arms where Jagger hugged me with all of his love for me. He made me feel so wanted and cherished.

"Did you take care of all of your work?" he asked.

"For the most part, yes, but I still didn't speak with Raymond about my future plans."

"Which are?" he looked nervous.

"Jagger, do I really need to say it? My life is with you, and you're here, which means I'm here."

"Tenley, I'm not asking you to choose. This is how I lost you the first time. I want it to be different for us this time, and whatever you decide will be okay with me. As long as we are together and married, I will be fine anywhere."

"Thank you for that, but I'm ready to walk away from my life in New York and begin my new one here with you. I will still practice law, maybe even open up my own practice. I haven't had much time to really think that far ahead, but I'm not ruling it out either. Would you be okay with that?"

"Baby, I would be okay with all of it. You have made me so happy."

He crashed his mouth down onto mine and demanded entrance. I opened for him and he kissed me with such passion, I began to feel dizzy. We were interrupted by a knock on the door.

"Come in," I called out to whoever was on the other side.

"Hey there, Fairchild," Jacob Paulson was entering my father's office. He was a monster of a man, having played professional football in the NFL. His build matched Jagger, but my guy was leaner in muscle and just as intimidating.

Jagger still had his hold on me as he glared at Jacob. *I guess this would be the perfect time to test the jealous theory.* I knew my cowboy. They always protected their own, and by the looks of it, Jagger was not happy with Jacob at the moment. Did I mention he looked like Chris Hemsworth? Yeah, he's that hot, but was only a colleague and friend.

I nearly jabbed Jagger in the ribs to release me. He did, and I walked over to greet Jacob, who of course picked me up and caged me into his wall of muscles he called his chest. Jagger cleared his throat in the most obvious way. *Here we go . . .*

"Jacob, put me down." I laughed as he smiled back at me.

"Sorry, Fairchild. It's a Paulson thing. We tend to do that a lot." He winked at me.

"So I remember. Jacob, this is my . . . " Not sure how to address Jagger, he made it easy and did it himself.

"Jagger Parrish, Tenley's fiancé. And you are?" He shook Jacob's hand in a tight handshake and waited for him to respond.

"I'm Jacob Paulson, Federal Agent Paulson, and it's a pleasure to meet you."

"Likewise. So what brings you here to Wyoming, and without any notice?"

"Jagger . . . " I interrupted him, but he had the balls to put his hand up to silence me. *Oh hell no, cowboy!*

"Fiancé you say?" Jacob looked over to me. "I would think your man here worked for the agency, on account of the twenty questions," Jacob replied.

"Not really twenty questions, just two," Jagger fired back.

"Okay, Mr. Parrish, not that it is any of your business, but since Tenley here seems fond of you, I'll answer you. I am here on official FBI business. I did in fact wire a message to this ranch several days ago, and when my message was not returned, I decided to fly out here personally to check in and status with my colleague. Satisfied?"

I had just about enough of the "who's dick is bigger contest" with Jagger, who promised me he would not behave like this. "Jacob, will you excuse me for a few minutes while I speak with my fiancé?"

"By all means. Is there somewhere I can make a few calls in private?"

"Yes. You can make your calls down the hall, the last door on the right." I pointed down the hall to show Jacob the way.

"Thank you. I won't be too long."

"Take your time," Jagger called out.

I waited for Jacob to close the door behind him, and then I turned back to Jagger, who was practically foaming from his mouth.

"What the hell was that? I have never been so humiliated in all of my life, and this is not just any guy off the street. This man, Jacob Paulson, is a highly decorated federal agent, who lucky for you has a sense of humor. And do you care to explain to me what the raising of the hand was? Oh, cowboy! If you think for one God loving second that I will just transform into the good little woman who fucking bows down to your feet, you have another thing coming. I am not that girl. I was never that girl, and I will never be that girl. Got me?"

"Oh, my Tumbleweed! My wildcat. You drive me fucking insane. I love your dirty mouth, and I love how you work it on me. I want you so bad right now. Keep talking that way, and I don't care who he is, I will take you right here, right now."

I was shoved hard up against the wall, knocking down the pictures that my back banged into. Jagger had my legs wrapped around his waist and was kissing me savagely on my neck and chest. I kissed him back with the same intensity. We pressed our foreheads together and took in some calming breaths.

"I'm not sorry," Jagger said. "Be angry with me, but don't shut me out. Punish me the way you see fit, preferably on my body, but don't leave me. I love you, Ten, and I'm just out of my mind that I have you back. Maybe back then I never had a reason to be jealous because I was this overconfident guy who thought what you just accused me of doing. Now my innocent spitfire has returned as this hell on wheels woman that has the ability to bring me down to my knees, and I'm smart enough to know to remember that. I love you."

"I love you too, and you are forgiven, even though you're not sorry. He's a friend and a colleague, nothing more. Please do not be rude to him. Obviously Jacob's reasoning must be pretty important if he took the time to fly out here. I just wish I knew what happened to the message he said he sent."

"Wait a minute, didn't he say about four days ago?"

"Yeah, he did."

"I think I know what happened to it. We were at the cabin, and you were asleep. I went outside to get some firewood and found a note tacked to the door. I shoved it in my pocket and haven't looked at since. I guess I forgot about it until now."

"Where is it, Jagger?"

"I have it here. I put it in my jacket intending to give it to you, but then I haven't been back here since I left you a few days ago."

Jagger handed me the telegram, and sure enough, it was from Jacob, asking me to call him as soon as possible, and from a burner phone. It's not something I advertise, but I do carry one for emergencies like this one. I knocked on the closed door as Jacob was finishing up his call.

"Can I come out now? Or is the caveman going to club me over the head?" Jacob asked.

"You may, and he only uses the club on me." I tried to make light of the tense situation, but neither guy was laughing.

"Okay, can we start over? I'm sorry, Jacob, for all of the confusion. I did after all receive your message, so what is this about?"

"It's federal business, Tenley. We need to discuss this in private."

"You're out of your mind if you think I'm not staying. If this involves my girl, it involves me," Jagger once again interrupted, staking his claim.

Jacob sighed in frustration. "Fine! At least allow me to finish a full sentence before you rudely interrupt me again."

I looked over at Jagger, and he had his arms crossed over his chest and nodded at me. I mouthed back, "I love you" to calm and reassure him. *Honestly! What is it with men and their pissing contests?* I asked Jacob to take a seat, and we got comfortable to hear him out.

"Tenley, the reason for my visit is simply to bring you back to New York with me."

I grabbed Jagger's knee to silence him. He gritted his teeth while his jaw clenched in vexation.

"Why? What's happened?"

"Roberto Bornarelli has made his presence known, and we now can tie him to Tommy's brutal attack. All the video footage has been analyzed, and there's no doubt it was him that ordered the hit on your friend. The threats at the office have also been linked back to him. He wants revenge on you for putting his father away. His father wants peace and no more bloodshed in his family. The take-down not only brought down their housing scheme, but it also cost the lives of two captains, and more than six men who proved to have failed the family."

"Wow! I spoke to Raymond today, and he mentioned the threats, but not all of this."

"He doesn't know all of it, just what we feel is enough for him right now. We also have your phone tapped. One of the assistants there, Cheryl, is a mob plant working for Bornarelli. She's a single mother with college loans to pay off. He got to her and will take her out if she doesn't give up your location. I'm guessing that's why she asked you about it today. Up until now, Cheryl has been a loyal employee. I've heard the rumors, all true by the way. You scare the hell out of half the staff in your office. She didn't do this on her own. She's being threatened by Roberto."

"I knew it right away just from her tone alone. She has never been so casual with me on the phone."

"You have to come to New York with me. Once they know you're back in the city, they will make their next move against you, and then we will move in and arrest them."

"No. Fucking. Way. Is Tenley going back to New York as bait," Jagger blurted out as he stood to face Jacob.

"I can't protect her here. It's too open and vast," Jacob responded, now facing Jagger, towering over him.

"If anyone is going to protect Tenley, it will be me. She stays here."

"Enough! Back to your neutral corners and let me talk. Jacob, do they know where I am right now? Is my family in danger?"

"No. As far as anyone knows, you are on an extended holiday and very far from New York."

"Okay then. That will be the story that will continue to play out. We can create a false paper trail and send them to the office. In the meantime, you place a twenty four/ seven protective guard on Cheryl and her daughter."

"Tenley, security measures are already in place for her and the child. Roberto's getting ready to make his next move. I need you back where we can draw him out into the open. His father doesn't want him harmed. Roberto is a loose cannon who shoots first, never questions. He did this all on his own without the approval from his father, so if this goes bad, he may have to be taken out before he tries again to get to you, but it won't be from us. His old man will order the hit himself. If that occurs, then you are still in danger because we will not know if any other threats exist. We need to draw him out into the open. It's the only way."

"Fine, I agree."

"Tenley!" Jagger shouted. Ignoring him completely, I focused on Jacob.

"I will agree to this plan, but not before Christmas. I'm safe here on my family's ranch. We have state of the art security systems wired all throughout our properties. I have a dozen or more ranch hands that live here on this property alone, and if memory serves, Jacob, I'm a damn good shot. You can thank my daddy for teaching me."

"I guess there's no point in arguing with you after that list of valid points, counselor."

"You can try, but I'm not only a good shot, but a damn good lawyer too! So pick the battles you can win, Paulson."

And with that, the tension that filled the room a few moments ago had been replaced with Jacob laughing and Jagger undressing me with his eyes. His eyes were blazing with feral desire for me. It'd been a long time since we had a good tongue lashing with each other, but now we would continue it in the bedroom. It took all my control not to pounce on him. He got me so turned on, my panties were dripping wet.

He knew what I was thinking and nodded in victory that he had the ability to affect me without even laying a finger on me. I offered my parents' cabin to Jacob to stay on here while I celebrated Christmas with my family. He only stayed the one night, and then flew back to his office. He would return to Wyoming on the 27th, and we would fly to New York together.

Jagger was adamant about going with me, as if I could stop him.

I explained in the shortest detail possible to my parents why I needed to go back to New York, but since Jagger was accompanying me, they didn't worry. For the first time in many years, I was home and I was determined to give my family the best Christmas they had ever seen. It would never be the same without my brother with us, but I knew he would be watching from the night sky above. They needed this moment with me, just as much as I needed to share it with them. I even convinced Jagger to have Shane and Shelby join us at the winter carnival.

I didn't care what I had to do to help my man mend his broken fences with Shane. Life was too short, we all had a hard lesson in realizing that. They both meant too much to me not to at least try to help them find their way. It was my way of honoring Jamie's wishes for his brothers. No matter what danger lied ahead for me back in New York, Christmas here in Wyoming would be beautiful, and it would be shared with the man I love, along with my family and friends.

CHAPTER 26

Jagger

...my heart is yours

THIS WEEK HAD been one surprise after another with Paulson showing up making the decision to take Tenley back to New York. Some fucker was gunning for my girl and would not stop until he succeeded. Going with her was the only way I could keep her safe. He would never have a chance to harm one hair on her beautiful head.

She could brag all she wanted to Paulson about her skill when it came to firing a gun, but I'm praying it would not come down to that, and Jacob's guys can take him out. This was my first Christmas with Tenley in over six years, so I was kind of nervous about it. I had her ring, and I wanted to choose the perfect time to present her with it. Wendy already told me to make a big production out of it and get on my knee in front of the entire town, but that wasn't my girl. Her career may be fast paced, but never the girl. Tenley would always choose simplicity over the grand gestures. I was sure of it and knew exactly how I would do it.

It'd been a few days since I attempted to ride my horse. She was itching to get out of the stables just as I was to ride her. I fastened the last strap on her saddle and had a chat with my horse.

"Okay She-devil, we're going to take this slow, and I'll let you know when we should fly."

I fed her some apples and she nudged my shoulder for more. I was just about to mount her when Shane walked in.

"Hey, man, mind if I join you?"

"I don't know, Shane, going to throw me off a cliff again?"

He looked defeated, and I knew I was being a dick to him. After Paulson left us, the conversation shifted to Shane. Tenley wanted me to try and work at letting go of my anger and to find the forgiveness to move on from the pains of the past. She wasn't taking no for an answer until I promised her I would try. I conceded and said I would. Judging by the way he was looking at me, Shane was pissed.

"Sorry, man," I mumbled.

"Yeah, I think that is the most overused word in my vocabulary. I'm sorry too, man, but I'm done saying it. I've been apologizing to you for over six years now, and I'm done. I swear to you that I never meant to hurt you, and I will regret my actions for the rest of my life. These past years have not been easy for me, and they don't seem to be getting any better. I've paid over and over for my sins, brother, and I'm so fucking over it."

"Want to talk about it?"

"Are you fucking serious, man?"

"I know, shocking, right? Yes, Shane, I am. I was just about to take a ride. Saddle up and join me. We need to talk, or maybe I just need to listen for a change."

He didn't hesitate and grabbed a saddle. The sky was clear, and the temp wasn't too bad. We took the horses out to where I built my home for Tenley. Shane had never seen the house before today, and his eyes brightened in amazement. It was stunning, I would have to agree. I personalized every last detail with Tenley in mind as I designed it. It was always my dream to share it with only Tenley, and now that dream is coming true.

"Wow, man! You truly outdid yourself. The house is gorgeous."

"Thanks man, I love it. I can't wait to carry my girl over the threshold to our new life together."

"That's all I want for you two," Shane said. "I hope you know that. You can never go up against fate and win. You and Tenley are two halves of each other's soul. I'm happy you two made it."

You could see the sincerity written all over Shane's face. For the first time in years, I saw who my best friend used to be, and it hit me hard through my chest. I wanted our friendship back. I looked up to the sky and tipped my hat. *This is me trying, Jamie.*

I gave him a tour of the house, and we talked for hours. I told Shane I no longer wanted to live in the past. Words hurt just as much as actions did, and I knew I was doing both. When I was choosing the bottle of Jack to make me forget my girl and the betrayal I felt, it was only breaking me down more, until my crash. Hitting that tree was probably the best thing that could have happened to me. I was at my lowest point in my life, my rock bottom. I walked away from that unharmed and with new resolve to straighten out my life and pave the road back to Tenley.

Every single role model in my life has always preached the saying, "Everything happens for a reason." During the harder days, that was tough to believe, but now without a doubt, I will never question it again.

We rode back to the stables a little lighter than we started out. The subject also came up about Shane continuing working on the Fairchild Ranch. After our talk, I already knew what I should have said a long time ago.

"Shane, this is your home. You belong here."

"Are you sure, Jagger? Because if you're not, I meant what I said to Brock. I will walk away and just start over."

"You do that, Shane, and that would hurt Tenley more than you could ever know. It would also hurt me. I'm not saying we will return to the brothers we once were, but we talked more today than we've done in years, so it's progress man. This land is big enough for the both of us, and it's ours to run together if you want to."

"It's all I ever wanted, Jagger. Thank you."

"You're welcome."

On cue, my beautiful girl walked into the stables with her meg-awatt smile. She walked right into my waiting arms, where I kissed her senseless.

"Hey, you two. How was your ride?" she asked with hope in her eyes.

"It was good," I replied.

"Better than good," Shane added.

"I'm happy to hear that, and I know Jamie would be too."

With the mention of Jamie, we each had our moment of silence to always remember how much he meant to each of us and the hap-piness he brought to our lives. Tenley didn't look sad, she just glowed. I saw peace on her face with a hint of the sparkle dancing in her eyes. I would do anything to forever keep her looking that way.

Over dinner, we shared the good news with her parents, who were relieved with the decision I made. Our ranches were without a doubt a living legacy for generations to come.

"What are you thinking about?" I asked Tenley, as she stared up to the ceiling.

"Nothing in particular, just happy as all."

"I'm happy you're happy, but I know it's more than that. You're worried. Baby, I will never let anyone hurt you, I swear it."

"I know that, and believe it or not, I'm not that worried. This New York guy is just a two-bit thug who hides behind his father's power, money, and muscle. I'm not scared of Roberto. If anything, he should be the one afraid of me. I know what happened with the car explosion, and it scared all of you. But it was just smoke and mirrors."

"I'm sure your friend Tommy doesn't feel that way."

"He probably doesn't, but it wasn't Roberto throwing the punches either. He's a weasel, and I am not afraid of him. I also in-tend not to drag this out either. I'm not going to put my life on hold for him and his bullshit threats. I spoke to Jacob today. Cheryl is still feeding information to Roberto. He seems to be buying it so far."

"Once I arrive back in New York, Cheryl will alert him, and we will wait for his next move. Jacob has him under surveillance."

"What about his father? If something happens to his son, won't he seek revenge?"

"Once upon a time he may have, but Roberto has proven to be more of a liability than asset to the Bornarelli Family, so he may just be waiting back to see how it all unfolds. Even discreetly assisting Jacob with the investigation will not lessen his sentence."

"What happens after this is all over? What then?"

Up until now, Tenley has made it clear of her intentions, but I still needed to hear the words that would put my mind at ease.

"I think you already know," she said as she kissed me soundly.

"I still need to hear it baby."

She sighed animatedly, but smiled back at me.

"Once the threat is neutralized, I will have a conversation with Raymond, and will hand in my resignation with the firm. Zoey will be heartbroken, but I guess she called it all along."

"Will it be that simple to just walk away from that life?"

"It will. I was only living a half-life. Professionally speaking, I had it all, but personally, I was a disaster hiding in the shadows with sadness all around me. I was angry when my hand was forced and I came back home. But Jagger . . . I will never regret my decision getting on that plane, not when it led me home to you."

We made love all throughout the night with the stars shining through the skylight. She said this was her favorite feature of the home I built for us. I knew when I designed the skylight, it had to be as big as a picture window. Making love under the night sky was a special memory for us. Every time she looked up, I saw the happiness on her face.

Her answer set my heart on fire. It was now the perfect time to ask her to marry me. She slept peacefully beside me as I ever so gently left the bed. I retrieved the ring from my pant pocket and climbed back into bed with her.

"Tenley, baby, wake-up." She stirred until her eyes were completely open and staring up at me. I swear she brought me to my knees with just one look. All I saw was love and desire.

"I need sleep, you animal!" she said as she tried to close her eyes again. I laughed and pulled her closer to me.

"Open your eyes, baby, I have a story to tell you."

She sat up and positioned herself against the headboard, and I turned to face her.

"A long time ago, a boy fell in love with a girl. The thing is, he just didn't know it at the time. The boy, along with the girl's brother and best friend, used to call her their tag-a-long. They could go nowhere without their shadow, but they didn't seem to mind it either. The girl was a free-spirit. She could run, ride, and pretty much do everything the boys could do, and sometimes even better. Her brother called her 'Tumbleweed,' always flying through the air with no end in sight. We all loved and protected her very much."

"Then one day she suddenly looked all grown up, standing before the boy who loved her. He truly saw her beauty for the first time and was lost to her kindness and passion. Little did he know that she loved him too, but was afraid to confess her true feelings. So the boy took a shot of courage and a leap of faith in hopes she would love him back."

"He took her for a ride on his horse, and they sat down at his favorite spot on his ranch. They sat hand in hand, looking over the highest peaks, with the sun shining down on them. The boy was scared, probably more than he ever had been in his life. His hand was sweaty, but she didn't seem to mind. His stomach was doing flips, for this would be the first time he would ever tell a girl he loved her. He gave her a sunflower, which reminded him of her innocence and beauty. Taking her hands to his lips, he placed a chaste kiss upon them and whispered the words he would hope she would return back to him.

"I love you, Tenley. Will you be mine?" He never broke eye

contact with her until he saw a tear fall down her lovely face. He wondered if he was wrong, but then her tears turned to smiles and she said, 'I love you too, and my answer is yes.' "

"On that day, the boy gave his heart to the girl he loved. He promised she would always be safe with him and she could trust him always. She promised the same in return, and they sealed their commitment with a kiss to end all kisses."

I paused to look at Tenley. She never took her eyes off of me, as tears rolled down her face. I wiped them away with my thumbs, and her breath hitched with my touch as my skin touched hers. She was heart stopping beautiful, and she was about to be mine forever. I straightened my shoulders back and continued pouring my heart out to her.

"Their newfound love sustained over the harder times when distance was between them. The times they reunited was never taken for granted, and they spent every minute recommitting the love they first promised to each other. Through their years of sunshine and bliss, they were also faced unforeseen sadness and heartache, a pain he didn't see coming, but endured all the same."

"The girl, a natural free-spirit, never denied who she was and what she wanted for her life. Although she loved him, he could not make her stay, so he watched her board a plane to her new life. Through the years and on their own, he never gave up hoping for the one day she would come back for him. If ever granted this chance with the girl he loved, he would vow never to be so careless with her fragile heart. He would promise to love her for all the days of his life."

"The boy who trusted the girl all those years ago is now a man asking for that same promise of the beautiful woman in front of him. Tenley Faith Fairchild, I love you more than any man has ever loved a woman before. You are truly my soul mate, the one that I love, and will continue to love until I draw my last breath. Today, I unconditionally give you my heart, where I'm asking and trusting you to always cherish and protect me with your love, as I will do the same for you. I'm asking you to marry me and share your life and heart with me. I swear it on the heavens above that I will make you so very happy for every day you allow me to. You were meant to be a Parrish, as I always knew I was meant to be your husband. Marry me, Tumbleweed, and we will fly together, hand in hand . . . always."

I opened the black velvet box and presented her with a ring I had designed especially for my girl. It was a two carat yellow diamond halo set stone. It was surrounded by rows of diamonds, and on the outside was a sunflower etched out onto the gold band. She always loved sunflowers, something shared with her mother.

The girl I fell in love with had grown into a sophisticated woman. Back then, my girl never needed what money could buy, and she always appreciated the simple things. I knew I needed to present Tenley with a ring that would make her feel special and wanted. I could buy her the biggest ring in the showcase, but that was not Tenley. The ring I had designed for her was perfect and was waiting to be placed on her finger. Her mouth was covered by her hands as I waited for her answer. She wiped away her tears and pulled my lips to hers, kissing me with all the love she felt for me. My heart was beating, my temperature was rising, I wanted her with me forever, and all I needed was her answer, the one word that would turn my world right. The one word that would erase all of our past mistakes and replace them with new memories to make.

This is all I want with Tenley. It's what I have always wanted but was too stubborn to realize. The pain of losing her, losing Jamie, and losing myself in the process has shown me how precious life truly is.

I'm not a patient man. I want nothing more than to make love with my girl and lose myself in her for hours, but I won't until I have her answer. God! She's killing me. I have never loved her more. Please, baby, say yes.

CHAPTER 27

Tenley

...love is my guide

"YES. MY ANSWER is yes. You're the one, it was always you Jagger. You say our story is written in the stars, that may be true, but it so much more than either one of us ever realized. It took leaving you to discover what I had all along, but my foolish choices and maybe even stubborn pride held me back. You will never truly know how sorry I am for ever getting on that bus that day instead of dropping to the ground and wrapping my arms around your neck. When you asked me to stay, I thought my heart would stop beating. How is it that after all of this time, you still wanted me?"

"Maybe it took me leaving to grow up and be worthy of your love. I believe I am so ready to become a Parrish. When I look into your beautiful eyes, I see the boy now a man who will fight, protect, and love me always. You loved me through it all in spite of myself, and you never gave up even in the darkest hours when you thought you did. When I returned and saw you again, I felt at that moment complete. I no longer had shattered pieces, I was whole again. Your love brought me back to life and back to where I belong."

"I trust you with my heart, Jagger Lucas Parrish, today, tomorrow, and always. I promise to never break your heart and cherish every minute spent with you. I'm looking into your eyes, and all I see is **HOME**. You. Are. My. Home. My answer is yes."

I held out my hand for Jagger to take. He slid the ring onto my finger and placed a kiss upon it.

"Thank you for saying yes. I love you, Tenley. I'm going to make you so happy."

I kissed him back and said, "You already do. Now, may I ask you a question?"

"Anything."

"I would like my future husband to make love to me. Please, Jagger, make love to me, with me, and never let me go."

"Always, baby. Always and forever."

Jagger and I made love until we literally passed out in each other's arms. I dreamed of becoming his wife as I soundly slept, and saw my brother with tears in his eyes. He whispered to me . . .

"You. Chose. Right."

We kept our "official engagement" a secret until Christmas day where we could share our news with our family and friends. Wendy knew instantly from the expression I wore. Our home was bursting with sounds of laughter and new memories being made. As a Christmas gift to Jagger, myself, and Shane, my mother presented us with a photo collage of our life shared with Jamie.

The frame was double the size of an average poster frame. Wendy laughed and called out to us before we knew what was inside. "Go big or go home," she said. Leave it to our friend for always saying how it is. I loved her for that. My mother gave a short little speech before she allowed us to open our gifts.

"Merry Christmas. For the first time in a long time, this house is no longer silent. It is loud, and I wouldn't want it any other way. I will always remember the good feeling I have in my heart when my eyes scan this room and see all of you smiling back at me. Brock and

I are truly blessed to have you all in our lives, but I would be remiss if I didn't thank the one person who truly never gave up on reuniting all of us here today. To our son, James Brockton Fairchild. He is our guardian angel in heaven who looks out for us all. Not one person in this room hasn't stumbled a time or two, maybe even fallen so hard it took a long time to get back up."

My mother paused and smiled at me, as Jagger leaned in and kissed away my tears.

She continued, "Each and every one of you meant so much to our son, and mean so much to us. We are a family forever, and just know that whatever road you find yourselves on beyond the gates of this land, always remember . . . all roads lead home. Home to the ones who love you. Your family. Let's all raise our glasses to Jamie and to each other."

"To Jamie!" We all toasted together. Not a dry eye in the house. Wendy was passing out tissues to us and using some for herself. The three of us looked at my mother, and then my mother waved us off and gave us permission to open our gifts.

I waited and allowed Jagger and Shane to go first. Shane got his open first and took a step back to admire the living memories in front of him. Jagger did the same and both men were speechless. My mother, along with Jagger and Shane's mom, all pulled pictures of the guys from their childhood. Shane and Jagger's collages were filled with pictures of Jamie, and all three of them together. From their toddler years, to school years, to adulthood. Every box told a story about the trio of cowboys whom I loved very much. All I could do was smile and close my eyes where I could see Jamie smiling back at me. *Okay, brother, stop showing off.* I smiled and wiped away more of my tears. Wendy called out to me.

"You're next, Tumbleweed. We're all waiting."

"Okay Wendy, hold your horses."

I slowly opened my gift, and my collage was my life in pictures. My birth picture where I made my entrance into the world, and one of Jamie holding me when mama brought me home. Jamie always said it was his favorite one of us together, it was our first. Of course my collage wouldn't be complete without pictures of the guys and me. We were the perfect square. All of us had a side that completed our perfect shape. My eyes found the last picture we all took together. The guys had this one too. It was the summer I graduated college. Three cowboys engulfed me as my mother snapped the picture. It was a perfect day, kind of like this one right now. I hugged my mother and thanked her over and over again for the best gift I could ever receive.

"I love you, mama."

"I love you, daughter. Thank you for coming home."

"Thank you for still providing a home for me to come back to. I swear it, mama, I'll never stray so far away again."

It was the perfect day spent all together. I would never forget this Christmas for as long as I shall live. Jagger and I spent the rest of our time together locked away in my family's cabin. We tried to forget about our upcoming trip to New York and the problems that were waiting for me to come back to.

Jacob messaged me on the new burner phone he left when he was first here. Cheryl did what was asked of her. The trap had been carefully set, and upon my return, we would wait for the rat to take the bait.

"Are you ready?" Jagger asked me as I looked around the room. My stomach was tied in knots. "Wipe that worry off your face. We will see this cabin again, I promise you, baby. Nothing will happen to you."

"I know that. I'm just allowing my mind to get the best of me."

He held me in his arms and the knock at the door alerted us that our car was here. I opened it to find Shane standing there with a bag in his hand.

"What are you doing here?" I asked, surprised.

"I'm coming with you to New York."

Jagger didn't look all too surprised by this news, and then Wendy walked up behind him. I was the only one that didn't know what was going on.

"Wendy . . . " I said very slowly. She was the only one that I trusted to keep our secret and know what to do in case our plan did not work out the way we hoped it would. Wendy had made enough promises to see two lifetimes, but she never complained. It was her love for all of us that guided her to do what always came natural to her. She loved us unconditionally like we were her own.

"Now, Tumbleweed, don't go looking all snarky at me. You need all the help you can get. Those macho whatever hood rats you call them will not see these boys coming. You don't mess with a cowboy and get away with it."

I told the driver to wait and gave a look to Jagger and Shane who were completely ignoring me. I took Wendy's hand and pulled her into the bedroom.

"Wendy! How could you tell Shane about New York? It's hard enough I have to involve Jagger, and now Shane too? What were you thinking?"

"I was thinking with my heart, and my love for you. What have I always told you? You don't always have to be tough, and you should know by now that those men out there will walk through fire for you. You need their help, and they need to be allowed to do so."

"Wendy, Shane is about to marry Shelby, so she should be his priority, not me. I can't risk him getting hurt."

"Don't you worry about Shane and his love life. You need to concentrate on putting the bad guy away and come back home here to stay."

"Wendy, has something happened with Shane and Shelby? I know she wasn't able to join us for Christmas with her visiting family out of town, but is there something else I should know about?"

"Don't worry about Shane. He's fine and happier than I've seen him in a long time. Please focus on what you need to do, and come back home to us. Now go!"

"Where have I heard that before? I love you, Wendy."

"I love you too, Tumbleweed. You will never know how much.

Be safe, and call me as soon as you can. I'll take care of everything here, no worries."

"I never do, Wendy, especially when it comes to you."

I made my way out to the room, where Jagger took me in his arms. He whispered in my ear to not be mad. I wasn't. I grabbed my bag, and the guys followed me to the car.

"Hold onto your cowboy hats! New York, here we come."

Shane let out a big whopping "Yee-haw," and then grabbed his bag to follow us out.

CHAPTER 28

Tenley

...never bet against the queen

NOTE TO SELF: Leave the never-flying cowboy home on the ranch. It was a hellish flight I had to endure, with Shane vomiting all over first class, to Jagger nearly having an anxiety attack once we took off. Although Jagger had flown before, he said the take-off always gave him the jitters. Once we were in the air, he calmed. Shane was another story. Jacob's pant leg took the most damage when Shane didn't reach the bathroom. He was beyond livid that they had to travel with us at all, but try telling Jagger to stay behind.

It would prove difficult enough for me when I would have to ditch my security team and take matters in my own hands. While Jagger and Shane were doped up on Dramamine, I used the quiet to devise a new plan. One that would require some means of persuasion, an insurance policy to use when it was absolutely necessary. This would be one of those times.

Convincing Jacob of my new plan would be another story. He and his team were already in place to take out Roberto if necessary, but this capo was delusional if he thought for even a second that he was the one calling the shots. The boss was no other than Anthony Bornarelli, and he was currently sitting in a New York State Correctional Facility awaiting relocation to a Federal Prison. I realized the plan in place was wrong. To take out his son would only ignite a mob war. I knew I had to go directly to the top of the food chain, and that would bring me to Anthony himself. Jacob would be furious with me for not disclosing what I had on certain city officials, but their hands were just as dirty as Roberto's. The only difference . . . They were still operating in the appointed positions they held and were walking free as if they didn't have a care in the world.

I was going over my case file when Jacob approached me.

"Tenley, I need a minute, and in private," he said.

I looked over to Jagger who was sleeping soundly. I closed my laptop and followed Jacob through the cabin where we could speak freely without being interrupted.

"What is it, Jacob?"

"You tell *me*, Fairchild."

"Ooh, using my last name can only mean one thing: You're pissed off about something, but for the life of me have no idea why."

"You know why, so drop the act. Other than the vomiting episode, all of your attention during this entire flight has been spent on your computer. What are you looking for that we don't already know the answer to? Be straight with me, Fairchild, or I will throw your ass so fast in protective custody that your head will spin."

"Keep your voice down, please? Jacob, I am not hiding anything from you. All I was doing was going through some of the court transcripts from Tommy's case."

"What are you hoping to find that we haven't gone over a thousand times already?"

"Jacob, I think I've come up with a way to neutralize Roberto without the threat of violence."

"I'm listening."

"Will you promise to keep an open mind?"

"Tenley, my patience is running thin, and I'm in need of a shower. Let's hear it, or any bargaining chip you may have will not even be considered."

"You're right about my chips. I have many to use and will use if necessary. I want a meeting with Anthony Bornarelli."

"Out of the question, my superiors will never grant you access to him."

"I wasn't asking your superiors. I have my own connections to get to him."

"Like hell you will! Tenley, we're supposed to be partners on this, and there is no way I'm going to stand back and let you take the lead on this case."

"Jacob, no one lets me do anything. I say. I do. And I will let you know when."

I watched his jaw tick with anger. Jacob was always cool and collected, but this conversation with me had proven to be a bit tasking even for him.

"Jacob, Anthony is still the boss of his family, no matter his current location. His son has gone rogue and needs to be reeled in. If his hand is forced, Anthony will take him out. Roberto has proven to be an embarrassment for his father. No man in his position of power will stand for public humiliation, especially from his own son. I need a sit-down with him."

"I think you've been watching too many Hollywood movies. Tenley, this is the real life mob, not a group of actors portraying one. Roberto vowed vengeance against you when his father was sentenced. That psychopath will not stop gunning for you, and he feels entitled because of his name and will use that as a way to get to you with any means he can."

"I disagree, and will prove you wrong once I meet with his father, which by the way will happen, so save the effort and don't try to stop me," I said.

"What if I try? Will I be wasting my effort? Or is my fiancé not worth the risk?" Jagger interrupted, as he made his way over to me, clearly overhearing my conversation with Jacob.

"Hey, how are you feeling? We should be landing soon," I asked him.

"I'm better, so what's this about a prison meeting with the mob boss?"

"Jagger, I'm not going to discuss this right now with you, and in front of Jacob."

"Why the hell not? You had no problem when you thought I was sleeping."

Jacob took that as a clear sign to give us some privacy, but his eyes told me that our conversation was far from over.

I placed my arms around Jagger's waist and pulled him closer to me. "Baby, this is my job, and it's a job I do very well. I can take care of myself. I have been for a very long time."

"That's just it, Tenley. You don't have to do that anymore. You have me, and no one is going to hurt my woman."

"I love you for that, I really do, but you need to stay out of it, Jagger. I've got this, and I will win."

"You know, Ten, you don't always have to list your accomplishments every time we have a conversation. I know you are a somewhat of a badass. I watched you in action, remember? But this is me and you here, and you don't have to put the walls up and shut me out, not after all we've been through to be together. Please let me help you?"

Jagger looked at me with sad eyes, imploring me to lean on him for support. I knew I was responsible for the hurt he showed me, but he was in my world now and this was what I did. This need for control fueled me to take on the injustice of the world and fear no one. I wasn't afraid of the looming threat, they should be afraid of me.

The flight attendant announced over the intercom that we would begin making our descent into New York and for us to take our seats. I was literally saved by the bell, and Jagger dropped the subject for the time being. I gave Jagger my best reassuring look and kissed him quickly on his lips before returning to our seats. Poor

Shane was still knocked out from getting sick and then having to take the Dramamine. I took out my phone and snapped a few pictures of him. A picture says a thousand words, and I was sure the guys on the ranch would love seeing their leader drooling from his mouth.

Jacob leaned in and whispered in my ear, "We will continue our discussion when we have the private time to do so."

"Tomorrow morning in my office," I replied.

"No, tonight in my downtown office along with my team from my FBI task force."

I said nothing more to him. My silence was not me acquiescing to his request. Jagger was upset in his own right, and with Shane sick, my plate was already too full. I needed to get settled back at my apartment, and then I would decide what to do next.

Our landing was smooth, and we deplaned rather quickly. Shane was feeling better and excitement took over as he took in the city before him. This was his first time ever in New York City. For just a minute he had forgotten the real reason we were all here and his smile faded. I looped my arm with his and promised him that I had everything under control and soon it would all be behind us.

Jagger overheard me talking to Shane, and both men gave me a look as if I was crazy to think the sweet Tumbleweed from Wyoming could handle the bad guys on her own. It was frustrating to no end that they still viewed me as Jamie's little sister who they always protected. I loved them for that, but I could always take care of myself. Now even Jacob seemed to be doubting me, which was making me very defensive and more determined than ever to see this through and handle it my own way.

The limo pulled up in front of my building, as my doorman greeted us. Jagger tried to be a gentleman and help me out of the car, but my doorman was quicker, receiving a glare from my already stressed out man.

"Hi, Charles, how are you?" I greeted him as he took in my guests.

Jagger and Shane were wearing almost identical outfits from their black Stetson hats down to their cowboy boots. I introduced them to my doorman. "Charles, these are my friends, Jagger Parrish, and Shane Rhodes. They will be staying with me during their time here in New York. Please make building passes for each of them."

"Yes ma'am, right away."

"Thank you."

Charles began collecting the luggage when Jagger and Shane took the bags from him.

"I got it," said Shane.

I sighed, but remained silent as we all stepped onto the elevator that would bring me to the top floor. Jacob was agitated and wanted to talk, but Jagger didn't give me a minute to breathe. He was annoyed how I introduced him to Charles. *Um . . . when I left here over a month ago, I was single. I didn't feel it was appropriate to discuss my relationship status to my doorman, or anyone for that matter. Having a conversation with Zoey and Tommy will be difficult enough, and I still need to resign my position with the firm.*

I was exhausted, and they were exhausted. I was craving a soak in my oversized tub with bubbles all around me. Maybe that would soften my angry cowboy.

Jacob entered the apartment first, having a key and the alarm code. This was news, but he explained it was necessary to secure my protection. The apartment had been checked just hours before our arrival, and Jacob did one more sweep before giving us the "All clear" to enter.

Shane's eye's popped out of his head as he took in the luxury before him. My apartment was decorated very uptown chic, nothing that screamed home where you could snuggle on a couch or put your feet up on the coffee table. The apartment was meticulously kept with everything in order.

"Make yourselves comfortable, I'll give you a tour in a minute," I called out from the kitchen. I kept a bottle of Vodka in my freezer. I wanted a drink to take the edge off, but was nervous about how

Jagger would feel about it.

I casually retrieved a glass from the bar and fixed myself a drink. He raised his eyebrow at me, but said nothing. I enjoyed the cool liquid coating my throat and the burn it left behind. I certainly needed it after the last few hours being closed up on a plane with Jacob, Jagger, and Shane. I took Jagger's hand and showed him my apartment. His eyes brightened when he took in my bedroom. I had a California King Canopy style bed. It was quite big and decorated with plush pillows. Jagger's eyes blazed with desire as he cupped my face and kissed me.

"I want you . . . now," he voiced ever so slowly, but we were interrupted by Jacob.

"What is it, Jacob?" Jagger shouted as Jacob walked in to my room.

"We need to go, Tenley," Jacob said directly to me, ignoring my fiancé completely.

"Jacob, I'm tired, and as I explained earlier on the plane, we will discuss this in the morning."

"No, we will discuss it now, and down in my office."

"Will you kindly step out of my bedroom and wait for me in the living room?"

"Don't be long. You have five minutes," he replied and closed the door behind him.

"What the fuck, Tenley! That guy is a dick, and he's one step away from getting my fist in his mouth." Jagger balled up his fists and paced my room.

"Jagger, first off, no one is punching anyone, so get that thought out of your head, and second, Jacob is not a bad guy. He's just a little mad at me right now. You must understand how it works in my world. We spent thousands of man hours on this investigation. This goes way beyond land deals and muscling in on someone's business. Jagger, we are talking city corruption, back room mob dealings, and with the head of a crime family now in jail, it just made our jobs even more tasking than ever before."

I continued, "I need to see this through, and I've come up with a solution that I think will work. The crux of the problem right now is that Jacob disagrees with me, and I will not relent on my decision. You and Shane being here is also a complication, but please do not mix my words. I love you, and I want nothing more than to walk freely around the city and show you the sights and have an amazing time with you, but my work has to come first. Please tell me you understand this? Jagger, this is all I know. And I know how it makes me sound, but you know the real me behind the wall. I'm still the same girl you fell in love with, and the same girl you gave this ring to."

I showed him my beautiful engagement ring, as he placed a kiss down on it.

"I love you baby, so much, but I'm also so worried for you. Please let me help you?" he said.

"I'll be alright, I promise. I have to go with Jacob, but I will try to wrap things up quickly and be back soon. There's take-out menus in the kitchen, so order anything you want and charge it to me."

"I think I can pay for my own meal," he said in a clipped tone.

"Okay then. I love you." *Please tell me you love me too.* He was silent for a minute, and I turned to leave when he pulled me back to his chest and hugged me.

"I love you too. Please be careful."

"I will."

Shane settled into the guest bedroom and was watching a game on my big screen. He was in his glory as he stretched out on the bed which also happened to be a King size. My apartment was huge, and although I really didn't entertain too many overnight guests, I decorated it in hopes that maybe my family from back home would have visited me. But they never did.

That's my fault for distancing them, but no more. We have come full circle in our relationship, and now with me engaged to Jagger, my parents were in complete bliss. I was happy and in love with Jagger Parrish. He soon would be my husband, something I have dreamed of since I was seventeen years old, but thought I lost when I left him.

"I'm sorry, Tenley," Jacob said as we entered the waiting car.

"For what?" I say, as I roll my eyes at him.

"I guess I deserved that. But your safety is everything to me, and I will not risk you getting hurt because you are too stubborn to ask for help."

"Jacob, I appreciate your concern, but . . . this is me. When we first met, you seemed to not have a problem with how I operated, and now you do. So what gives? Why the sudden 180 on me?"

"You've changed. It's so obvious that you don't even see it."

"See what?"

"A year ago, you were focused, driven, and commanded a room to bring the biggest men to their knees. And now . . . "

"Now what?" I demanded to know.

"Now . . . You have something to lose."

"I don't understand, Jacob. Where are you going with this?"

"Exactly my point, Tenley. You're in love, and the minute I saw you in Wyoming, I knew it. You found the other piece of your heart, and that's a beautiful thing, but it also makes you vulnerable and an easy target."

"Jacob, I think the conversation has just shifted. This is not about me, but maybe more you. I'm a lawyer, not a big, bad FBI Agent. Yes, I'm in a dangerous situation right now, but that's not how it normally is. I just happened to get caught up in something bigger than any of us ever realized, but just because I have a personal life does not mean I have lost my drive. I know exactly how to handle Bornarelli, and I will stop him. Are you in? Or are you out? Because I need to know now before we go any further."

"I'm in, but you have to be straight up with me and not go out on your own, deal?"

"Deal," I said. He smirked at me, and I wasn't too sure if he completely believed me, but I didn't say anything more on the subject.

After hours of discussing our plan with Jacob's field commander, I was more than ready to return home to Jagger. Jacob was close by in a nearby apartment that the agency was using for surveillance to watch my apartment. It was after midnight, and my home was dark. I peeked in on Shane, who was out cold. I saw a few beers next to his side table with popcorn and chicken wings. *Oh, my poor linens!*

Jagger appeared to be sleeping, so I tried to be quiet. I changed in my bathroom and got ready for bed. He was sitting up when I came back into the bedroom.

"Hi," I said shyly, as his eyes roamed over my body. I was only wearing sleep shorts and a camisole top. My nipples were already erect with how Jagger was looking at me. I was exhausted, but I wanted him as much as he wanted me.

"Come here, Tenley."

I didn't hesitate and quickly walked over to the bed, where Jagger's strong arms pulled me up to straddle him.

"I love you so much," he said as his hard length pressed against my entrance. I rocked back and forth on top of him until he flipped me over to my back, hovering over me.

"I hope you're not too tired, baby, because I want nothing more than to bury myself deep inside of you and fuck you harder than ever before. Can you handle that?"

I stuttered in my response, but it was clearly a "Yes."

I was suddenly wide awake and would take all of him. Jagger pulled me up into a sitting position while he lifted my top. My panties were another story. One flick of his finger and they were ripped and thrown over his shoulder. He held my hands over my head with one of his, but not too tightly where I was restrained. He was so damn sexy, I couldn't stand it. Jagger pelted my neck with wet kisses that he trailed down between my breasts and made his way to my heated core. I was on fire. Fuck the foreplay, I wanted him inside . . . and now!

He tortured me with every lick, kiss, and bite. Was this his way of punishing me? Men could use sex as a weapon just as much as a woman can, and right now with Jagger, I felt I was being punished. He slowly entered my sex, taking in a breath and entering me with his tongue. When I was close to climaxing, he withdrew and took a breath. My legs were pulsating, my sex was dripping with arousal. He leaned in again with me, this time latching onto his thick hair. I even pulled a bit to let him know how frustrated I was with him holding back.

"Fuck me, Jagger. Stop this now, and fuck me," I all but screamed at him.

He wickedly smiled back at me with his perfect white teeth.

"Problem baby?" he asked.

"You can say that. Why do you keep stopping?"

"I'll get you there baby, don't worry. I just need to explore your body, taste every inch of you, and drive you to the brink of insanity. Kind of how you made me feel when we were on the plane."

"Jagger, please fuck me," I was almost whimpering, as he entered me again with his two fingers.

He said nothing as he continued to fuck me with his tongue and fingers. I was just about to come again, and he stopped. I was out of my mind. I wanted to claw his back with my fingernails and probably draw blood. I was so pent up with sexual want for him.

My face was heated as my sex was too. I placed my hands on his face and looked intently into his eyes, showing him how much I loved and wanted him. I was begging him to love me back. He kissed me, as I tasted myself on his tongue.

I let out moans of pleasure as Jagger finally entered me. I was swollen to the point where I felt every delicious inch of him piercing through me like a razor edged sword. He was strong, feral, and pounding into me with perfectly tuned thrusts. I was so close to coming, I thought I would pass out.

"You are so mine baby. I love you, and I need to hear you say it. Scream it, and don't hold back." He clutched my face as he pounded harder into my sex.

"I love you, Jagger! I'm yours, only yours. No man will ever fuck me. My body is yours! Make me come!"

"Yes!" he screamed out as my words tipped him over the edge and he exploded inside of me. He stayed connected with me and didn't move for a few minutes.

I feared I may not be able to walk in the morning. My pussy was still vibrating as he pulled out of me. I clutched my legs together on account of how sore I was. I've had rough sex before, but this went way beyond anything I have ever experienced. This was Jagger unequivocally marking me and making my body his.

I couldn't move and had no want to do so. Jagger placed a warm scented washcloth on my sex as he cleaned me. I was already asleep when he climbed back into bed and held me for the rest of the night. He whispered he loved me as I fell deeper and deeper into a sound sleep. He took over my dreams as I pictured him riding She-devil along with me and Jazzy, but we were not alone. Our son was nestled in front of him, as Jagger was teaching him to ride. My heart was bursting with love for the two men in my life.

Marrying the man I love was a dream I never thought could happen, and now I'm dreaming of having babies with him? How did I get here? I thought as I settled back into sleep, thanking the heavens for giving me another chance with Jagger. I was already in over my head and so much in love.

CHAPTER 29

Tenley

...the meeting

"**A**RE YOU READY?" I asked Jagger as we were about to step off the elevator to the executive floor at my law firm. I quickly kissed him on the lips before the doors opened. He wanted more, but this was not the time or place to begin something we couldn't finish. He always looked at me with passion and love dancing in his eyes. I looked over to Shane who was trying to ignore us, but smiled at our public display of affection. I looked back at Jagger, and my eyes showed him how much I loved him.

"I am. Show me your world," Jagger said as he kissed my forehead.

He looked at me differently this morning, like he finally got it. Little did he know that after my dreams last night, I was so ready to walk away from this life and ready to begin my new one with him.

"Good morning Ms. Fairchild," Angela greeted me as I made my way toward my office, walking with Jagger. Shane was following behind us and taking in the loud and busy office. The females were all gawking at him. He was a sight to take in, but my eyes were solely focused on Jagger, who gave me the sexiest grin I thought would literally make my ovaries burst.

Now was not the time to lust over my hot cowboy, but the electricity was so alive between us. It always was, and I'd never wanted him more. Gathering my wits, I shrugged off my naughty thoughts and reserved them for later when I could be alone with Jagger.

I entered my office to find Cheryl waiting for me. I placed my coat and briefcase down, walked over to my desk, and gave her a questioning look to why she was behind it. I already knew, but something told me to feel her out at the same time. She'd been a trusted employee, but even the best could be persuaded to the dark side if enticed enough.

"Welcome back, Ms. Fairchild. I was just going over your messages."

"Hello, Cheryl," I curtly greeted her and gave her the look to get the hell out from behind my desk. As if my standing in front of her didn't already send her a clear message. She was nervous, a bit too much. To my understanding, she was briefed on all that was going on, so why the ruse?

She quickly came to her senses and gestured for me to sit. She eyed Jagger and Shane rather suspiciously, but remained silent until I introduced them. Before we left this morning, I already explained to them the back story I would tell my office, and they went along with the plan. I had Jagger and Shane dress in matching suits, wearing ear pieces to look like part of my security team. Jagger looked incredible in Hugo Boss. He sure didn't look like a rancher. He looked delicious and hot and certainly could hold his own with any cover model. Shane too!

"Cheryl, I would like you to meet Agent Parrish and Agent Rhodes. They will be shadowing me. Give them anything they request, understand?"

"Yes, Ms. Fairchild. Can I get you anything? A latte perhaps?"

So you can poison me? Um . . . don't think so. I declined and dismissed her. I pulled out my burner phone and dialed Jacob immediately.

"Jacob, I'm here at my office, and something is not right with Cheryl. I thought you debriefed her and all was okay."

"I have. Any new developments? What's going on?"

"I think you need to delve deeper into her past. Something is off with her. I just have a gut feeling, and I'm usually never wrong."

"Okay, I'm on it. Are we still meeting in an hour?"

"Yes, just let me take care of a few things here first, and then I'll meet you downstairs."

"Okay, see you then."

Before I could say another word, my door burst open, and Jagger nearly covered me with his body.

"Hooker! I have effin missed you," Zoey shouted.

Oh, how I have missed my friend! Jagger's heart was beating so fast, I placed my hand over his chest to calm him and then kissed him on his lips.

"Jagger, this is my very best friend, Zoey Steele. Zoey, this is Jagger Parrish, my fiancé."

He smiled with how I introduced him to Zoey. He kissed me soundly, as Shane just stayed back and rolled his eyes.

She was bouncing on her heels in excitement. "Fiancé? For real? I knew it, Tenley! Just like the Hallmark movie. I should have placed money on this one. Oh my God! Tell me everything."

"Zoey, why don't you say hello first."

I couldn't help but smile at my friend. Her energy and zest for life was amazing, and she was drop dead gorgeous. I couldn't help but notice how Shane was looking back at her. He certainly didn't look like a man in love, about to get married. His eyes were filled with lust as he extended his hand out for Zoey to shake. She returned the gesture, but Shane lifted her small delicate hand to his lips, making my girl swoon like never before. Her cheeks were blushing as she flirted with Shane. Jagger and I cleared our throats to bring her back to the present.

I quickly filled Zoey in on what was happening this morning.

She already was up to speed, but never expected the added company in my office. I owed her a long overdue conversation and promised we would catch up.

I left the guys in her company while I went upstairs to speak with Raymond.

"Absolutely not!" he bellowed at me about my plan.

"Raymond, it's the only way I can see this playing out. Why are you not agreeing with me on this? I thought we were on the same side?"

"We are, Tenley, we are, but you cannot use what you have on the assembly members. It's too dangerous, and I will not put you in that position."

"No worries Raymond, I'm putting myself on the line, and I have plenty of coverage watching my back. I may have been away for weeks now, but don't think for a second that I'm out of the loop. The most powerful player in the state's assembly has just been taken down, so a few cabinet members is easy. Besides, I don't plan on exposing them. I just need to shake them up a bit and gain access to Bornarelli."

"I can't give you my blessing on this, Tenley. I'm sorry, but my answer is no."

"Well, I'm sorry too, but I'm moving forward no matter what, and I have an entire task force behind me. I will not hesitate to use them if it deems to be necessary."

"Tenley, you are playing with fire. Stand back before you get burned."

"Raymond, are you threatening me? Because that's what I'm hearing. Unless you're on the take as well? And if I bring them down, then you go down as well."

He held his face in his hands and was silent. Running his fingers through his hair, he got up and fixed himself a drink. It was just past nine in the morning, and to see him knock back hard liquor concerned me.

"What is it Raymond? Please talk to me?"

He took a key out from his pocket and unlocked a drawer in his desk. He handed me an envelope, and I gloved up my hands before touching it. I already knew it could be evidence and didn't want my prints on it. I pulled out and read a threatening letter addressed to him. It contained picture after picture of Zoey, his wife, and one picture of a badly beaten Tommy. I took in a few calming breaths after seeing my friend in that condition. A note was attached to the photo that simply stated

Your daughter is next. It would be a shame to cut up something so beautiful.

It was unsigned, but I knew instantly who it was from.

I kept the envelope, while he drank another drink. This was my mentor, founder of this firm. I had never seen Raymond Steele succumb to anyone for anything, but this situation was different, and very personal. This was for his daughter, and she was in danger.

"Raymond, I swear to you that no harm will come to Zoey. I have a twenty four/ seven team on all of you. This shit ends today!"

He got up and hugged me as if I was his daughter too.

"Please be careful, Tenley. If anything were to happen to you or my Zoey . . . "

I quieted him down and assured him we would be fine. I already had my bag with me and what I needed from my safe, so there was no need to go back downstairs to my office. I didn't have my coat, but one of the girls from Raymond's office offered me hers. I appreciatively accepted it and left to meet with Jacob. Zoey was keeping the guys busy, and I quickly texted Jagger.

T- Left to meet with Jacob. Please don't worry. I will see you soon. Xo

J- What?

I powered down my phone and stepped into my waiting car. I handed Jacob the file from my safe, as well as Raymond's threatening letter, and he was stunned with what it contained.

"I can't believe he kept this from me" Jacob cursed under his breath. "What the hell was going through his mind?"

"Probably the same thing that was going through yours. He wants to protect his daughter, you want to protect me. This asshole has tried my last nerve. It's time to go meet with Oliver. I want that meeting . . . today. Young Mr. Bornarelli needs to be shut down one way or another."

"I absolutely agree."

Jacob and I walked into the downtown offices where Oliver Michaelson worked. He was also the state attorney general. His assistant told us he was in meetings and would not be able to see us today. But Jacob flashed his badge, and we were quickly granted entrance. I led the way, making my presence known. Oliver was on the phone when I slapped down Raymond's envelope on his desk.

"What the hell! You just can't barge into my office!" he shouted and slammed his phone down onto the cradle.

"I can and will, Mr. Michaelson," Jacob said.

"And who the hell are you?"

"I'm Federal Agent Jacob Paulson. I head up a specialized Mob Task Force, and this badge right here gives me access to anything I want in this office. So now that we've been introduced, you will sit back and be quiet. I believe my colleague over here would like a word with you."

Oh, he was good. Michaelson looked as if he was going to be sick. He was a man who held a powerful office in the State of New York, but was allegedly just another weasel whose hands were in too many pockets.

"Thank you, Agent Paulson," I said. "Oliver, I will get right to the point. Roberto Bornarelli. He needs to be shut-down, and I mean today."

"And what, pray tell, do you expect from me? You already got his father. What, you didn't get enough press already? You want more?" he said, mocking me.

"Feeling a bit insecure, Oliver?" I hit him back. "You're just pissed and clearly not over the fact that my case was stronger than yours, and let's face facts . . . you dropped the ball. It's called research, Oliver, and you clearly didn't do enough of it to prove your case against the Bornarelli Family. Here I come along, thinking I'm taking a simple case over a land dispute, I never imagined it would lead to bringing down a major head of a crime family—the same family you lost against . . . unless you planned it that way."

"How dare you fucking come into my office and imply that I'm on the take! Fuck you, Fairchild. I am the New York State Attorney General, for cripes sake! I am not dirty, and I resent it to hell for you even going there."

"Okay, maybe not, but you know the players and so do I. I have a file layered with evidence that will take down an entire cabinet. It's my insurance policy if something were to happen to me. You're not invincible, Oliver, and neither am I, but they ignited a war against me. And now I have to finish it."

"What do you want?" he asked in defeat.

"I want a meeting with Anthony Bornarelli, and it has to be today."

"And what will you do once you are in there?"

"Negotiate, plain and simple."

"Well, good luck, because you're going to need it."

Oliver made some calls, and soon Jacob and I made our way to the correctional facility where Anthony was being held. We took back entrances where we would go unseen.

Jacob said to me, "You had to see yourself hammering away at Oliver. I was in awe of you. You sure you want to be a lawyer? I could use someone like you permanently on my team."

"Jacob, that's a great offer, but the only team I care to be on is one with my name matching Jagger's."

"I thought you would say that."

"Jacob, I don't need to know about your past and why you seem so closed off, but you can let people in and still do this job."

"You're wrong Tenley. A long time ago I believed that, but I was wrong."

Jacob shut down after making that revelation to me. He refocused himself, and we walked through the meeting room, where a shackled Bornarelli was waiting for us. He looked surprised, but welcomed us to join him.

"I never thought I would see you again, Ms. Fairchild. So what do I owe the honor of your company today?" he questioned.

"I think you know, Anthony. Your first born, Vincenzo, the prince of your organization was gunned down in cold blood. And now your less than worthy other son has been running amuck around New York City, causing quite the uprising in your organization . . . as if he were planning a coup or something."

"My son is an idiot, and will be taken care of."

"Well, that's why I'm here. Your son will be taken care of one way or another. I would prefer he be in an adjoining cell next to yours, but we know that's not how this will play out, now is it?" I said.

"I'm not ordering a hit on my own kid! He's not right in the head, he never was. He's a loose cannon and needs to be taken care of in a different manner, not a bullet to his head."

"He's been threatening members of my law firm and is responsible for the beating of Tommy Mills, and we know he likes to tinker with car bombs. Anthony, you must tell me where I can find him. If we find him without your help, then I may not be able to guarantee what happens next. He is a threat, and threats need to be neutralized. We are prepared to do so if you do not cooperate."

"I'm fucking locked up, lady. How the hell can I help you?"

"This is how," Jacob told him. Jacob pulled out a burner phone from his pocket and handed it to Anthony.

Anthony dialed his son. Once Roberto answered his call, the FBI was able to triangulate the signal. From there, we had his location locked.

"He's there. Don't hurt him, please? He's all I have left."

"Anthony, I don't want to hurt him, but if it comes down to it, I may not be able to stop it. You must agree here to not retaliate or seek anymore vengeance. This is what he signed up for, you must know this. You're a smart man. I also know you are dying of stomach cancer, so maybe you have three months tops, maybe six. I can make your remaining days comfortable if you cooperate with us. If not, then you will die in this prison and not in the comforts of a hospital."

"Do what you have to do," he said. "He's dangerous, and I can't stop him. My second in command is already in position to take over and will not partake in any further acts of violence against you or anyone close to you. This was always on Roberto. Had I not been incarcerated, I probably could have contained him, but seeing me in here drove him to snap and make careless decisions. I'm lucky he's not dead yet."

"I will try to prevent that from happening at all costs. You have my word."

We left the facility and drove back in silence. Jacob was in deep thought. I turned my phone on, and my inbox was flooded with messages from Jagger. I didn't bother to listen to them, already knowing he was furious with me. He had to know I was safe with Jacob.

"Any new information on Cheryl?" I asked Jacob, as he was scrolling through his phone.

"Nothing yet, but hopefully soon. No red flags were raised during our initial findings. She lives with her daughter in a Brooklyn brownstone. Her only income is what she brings in from the law firm. She has no offshore bank accounts. The brownstone she rents in was originally owned by her grandmother and was left to her, so that's probably why she can afford it. It's located in Park Slope."

"You said she was a single mother? Who's the father? Do we know?"

"The records came back listing a Thomas Daly as the father, but he died in a car accident before the kid was born."

My mind was spinning in a thousand directions. I had a strong feeling that something was not right here and was staring us right in the face. They say if you're too close to an investigation, sometimes the most obvious clues were the hardest to see.

"Dig deeper," I said to Jacob.

"I'm already on it," Jacob said as he texted a message to one of his men.

"Great! Let's get back to the office, where I can face off with my angry cowboy."

"This I have to see."

I half laughed at Jacob's remark. Fighting with Jagger was the last thing I wanted to do. I hoped he would understand and just kiss me madly. Calming the beast was one skill I could do and do very well when it came to my man.

CHAPTER 30

Jagger

...holding on to you

I WAS GOING out of mind with worry over Tenley. I swear she was going to get put over my knee, and get spanked when I could get her alone. I didn't need another lesson on how strong she was, and how great she was at being bad ass lawyer, but ditching me without a word for hours was not sitting well with me.

Why the hell was I here if she was going to keep me in the dark? *Get a clue, genius! You know why you're here, because she's your woman and you vowed to protect her even if she doesn't think she needs you to.*

Well at least Shane is having a good time. Zoey took him out sightseeing all around the city, and then brought back her friends Tommy and Roxy, who works for Tenley. He seemed like a cool guy, if not for the fact that he slept with my girl. I wanted to hate him for that, but I couldn't hold that against Tenley. We weren't together, and she owed me no explanation to how she lived her life when I wasn't in it.

Her assistant Roxy was quite the firecracker. She was very outgoing and seemed to be into Tommy. They never stopped touching each other the entire time they were here. I felt my girl's office was turned into a frat party. Zoey was making up drinks, and Shane had food delivered. Her father peeked in on the commotion, but seemed okay with it. I introduced myself to him and took him by surprise with news of our engagement. I guess that would be the general reaction around here. Tenley was very private when it came to her personal life, so showing up suddenly with a fiancé on her arm would be shocking to all who knew her. I didn't care who knew about it. I just wanted her safe and back here with me.

A few minutes later, in walked Tenley with Paulson. She immediately scanned the room and locked eyes on me. I didn't need to even blink, that's how quickly she was in my arms. I held her closely to my chest and breathed her in. The thought of being away from her today hurt more than I realized. I needed to get her out of this city and back to our ranch where we belonged.

"Can we go somewhere private?" I asked her.

She had a connecting door off of her office that led to a back conference room. I followed her inside and locked the door behind us.

Not wasting another second with my girl, I had her against the wall with her legs wrapped around me. I wanted nothing more than to make love with her, but I knew we didn't have the time I wanted to show her how much I missed her. I kissed her repeatedly all over the sides of her face and down her neck. She was out of breath, but I continued on with my onslaught attack on her neck. I nearly gave her a hickey, I was so turned on.

"Jagger, stop. We can't do this in here," she said as she caught her breath.

"Baby, I'm sorry. I don't know what came over me. I have never been so stressed out before and not knowing where you were all day freaked me out in more ways than you can imagine."

"I think I know, but I love hearing you say it," she said, as she kissed me again. "Don't be angry with me, please. My heart has no room for arguing with you, I love you too much."

"Okay, tell me more?"

"I'm sorry I couldn't tell you where I was going today. It was strictly confidential between Jacob and me. I trust you completely, baby, but this was work."

"I get it, and although I wasn't happy about it, I do understand. Besides it's not like I wasn't entertained. Your friends are really great. Zoey is the spunkiest woman I have ever met in my life. She can go toe to toe with the best of them, and bring the strongest of men down to their knees."

"Oh yeah? Sounds like you paid attention today, maybe a bit more than I would have liked."

"Jealous?" I asked.

"Absolutely. You're my man, and the only eyes I want on your body are mine."

"Then we agree, because that's exactly how I feel about you. Anyway, can we get out of here? I'm starving, and I don't mean for food."

"We can, but can you give me a little while? I need to wrap up a few things on my desk before I head home. Tomorrow is going to be a big day. This case could be wrapped up by then if all goes the way I have planned it out. Jacob is pretty confident as well. He's looking into a few tie-ins to the case for me. I should be hearing something soon."

"Music to my ears. I can't wait to get you home."

"Home to my apartment?"

"No baby, home to *Our Home* in Wyoming."

"I know . . . just checking," she replied.

My heart almost ached. I couldn't wait to marry her.

CHAPTER 31

Tenley

...more than meets the eye

JAGGER AND I made our way back into my office where our little group was still laughing and getting to know one another better. I hugged Roxy, then Tommy next. I was so happy to see him better. The images of his bloodied body still gave me the chills.

"You look happy, really happy," Tommy said to me as he hugged me again.

"I am my friend. So much has happened in the past month, I wouldn't know where to begin."

"Well, I think I've been properly brought up to speed. Your friend Shane can talk with a few drinks in him. And don't worry, he didn't say anything I already didn't know about you. He seems to really genuinely care about you."

"He does, and I care for him, but . . . "

"He doesn't hold your heart like the big guy over there does, right?" Tommy finished my sentence and nailed it right on the head.

"Exactly. Are you mad at me?"

"Now what kind of question is that? I could never be mad at

you."

"I guess what I'm really asking is that what happened between us will not affect our friendship, and we are okay?"

"Always, Tenley, always. I already told you how I felt about our night together, but I now see why you could never move forward with me. You love Jagger, and that's okay. As long as he treats you in the manner you deserve, you have my blessing friend. Be happy, that's all I have ever wanted for you."

With tears in my eyes, I hugged Tommy and wished him well with Roxy. He told me that she had completely taken him by surprise. Once he allowed himself to feel something for someone besides me, it was like fireworks on the fourth. They had an instant connection and they both appeared to be happy.

After Tommy and Roxy left, Zoey was not too far behind them. She had asked if I would mind her taking Shane out to the local hotspots. Shane seemed to be interested in Zoey, so what the hell?

"Go have fun," I told them both, and no sooner than I said it, they were out the door.

"Holy shit! My boy moves quickly, doesn't he?" Jagger said as he watched them getting a little too close for comfort and smiling as they looked at each other. We heard their echoing laughter as the doors to the elevator closed.

"Jagger, I'm all for Shane having a great time, but is there something I need to know? He is still engaged to marry Shelby next month, right?"

"As far as I know, baby, the wedding is still on."

"I hope you're right, because I don't want Zoey getting hurt. She deserves happy, not heartbreak, especially from a cowboy from Wyoming."

"Hey now, what's that supposed to mean? A cowboy from Wyoming?"

"Now don't get all twisted up in your Stetson. What I meant to say and should have said better was that cowboys from the west are supposed to be charming, born with ingrained manners, and know how to treat a lady. I wouldn't want Shane shattering that image for Zoey."

"I think your friend is safe, and Shane will be on his best behavior."

"Let's hope so." I smiled and kissed Jagger.

The office had pretty much been abandoned by now. It was nearing seven, and I was just about to wrap things up when my private line buzzed. It was Raymond phoning me from his office.

"Hi, Raymond. You're here late tonight," I said as I double checked my clock. He never worked past five on any given day. He asked if I could come up for a few minutes to speak with him before I left for the night. I agreed and said I would join him in a few.

Jagger was just finishing up with a call from his father. All was well back home, and they just missed us and wanted to know when we would be back.

"Are you okay?" I asked him.

"Yeah, I'm fine. My dad was just checking in. She-devil has been restless without me. He took her out for a ride this morning, but she wasn't her best self, so she's grounded to the stables until we return home."

"Oh, poor She-devil! Your horse misses you." I hugged my man and kissed his nose.

"Can we get out of here?" he said very slowly.

"Yes we can, but not before I take one more meeting. I promise it will be a quick one," I said with my fingers crossed behind my back. Any conversation with Raymond was never quick, more like an hour plus, and that's *before* he got to the point.

"I'm coming with you this time. No more ditching me."

"No need to follow. I'm only going two flights up."

"I'll always follow you, baby, remember? That's our deal and how we roll, got it?"

"Got it. I won't be long. I'm waiting on news from Jacob. I'm going to leave my cell with you in case he calls. Tell him I'm with Raymond, and I'll call him back as soon as I can."

"Okay, boss."

"You know baby, I kind of like the sound of that. Maybe that will be my new nickname?" I said.

Jagger leaped from the chair and scooped me up into his arms.

"I like the sound of that too! You can boss me around anytime the mood strikes as long as it takes place in our huge, bigger and better bed than you have here in New York."

"I like my bed," I said as he still held me in his arms.

"Yeah, baby, I do too. But I'd much rather prefer you in *our* bed."

"Soon Jagger, I promise," I said as he placed me down. I kissed him again and practically skipped down the hall to Raymond's office.

"Knock, knock. Raymond, are you here?" I called out to him as I walked into his office.

The door slammed shut, and I turned around to come face to face with no other than Roberto Bornarelli, Jr.

"Hey, whore! Remember me?" he said, as he punched me, landing a hit onto the side of my head. I was taken by complete surprise and his assault had me spiraling down to the floor.

After he cowardly sucker punched me, my natural instinct was to lash back and defend myself, but I was too dizzy. I blacked out for a couple of minutes, because when I came to, my hands were bound to the chair with cable ties biting into my skin. My vision was blurred as I struggled to take in the figure before me. He was licking his lips and touching my hair.

"Do not touch me!" I screamed out. He manically laughed at me and touched me again, this time flicking open the buttons of my blouse.

"Oh I'm going to have fun with you baby . . . that is, *before* I cut you up. You have been nothing but a trouble making bitch and have messed with me for the last time. Yeah, I know you made a deal with my old man, but fuck him, you deal with me. Did you honestly think I didn't know what you were up to? They all think I'm crazy, but that's what I let them think so I can play behind the scenes and get what I want."

"And that is . . . ? What do you want, Roberto? How do you see this playing out for you?"

He didn't answer my question and got up to grab the Scotch bottle off of Raymond's bar. My eyes were back into focus and that's where I saw his body, motionless on the floor near his sofa.

"Roberto, is he dead?" I screamed out, but he still ignored me.

Oh, please Jagger. Please find me. I was praying that Jagger would crash through the door at any minute, but then I stopped because Roberto would not hesitate on killing him if given the chance.

"Roberto! Answer me. Is he dead?"

"Calm your skirt, he's not dead, just knocked out. He's not the one I want, but I can put a bullet in his head if that will make you happy."

He took out his gun and aimed it at Raymond.

"NO!" I screamed. "Please don't hurt him, your fight is with me."

"You bet your sweet ass it is. Why couldn't you have just left things alone? Your pal got his land back and we backed off, but you just had to keep digging until you came up with something to use against us. That fucking housing project was mine! I owned those people and now Ms. Nosy bitch of a lawyer gets involved and shuts me down. You know how much money I've lost because of you? Now how do you think I'm going to get that back? Hmm?"

"Roberto, all you are is a small time capo who doesn't know his head from his ass. You've been living in your brother's shadow and memory for so long now, you don't even know who the hell you are anymore. He was the one that everyone followed, not you. You're not worthy enough to even be second choice. Your father is dying and will die in prison. You are not his heir to the throne. You are nothing and will never be more than just a hood rat who deals with bookies and takes advantage of innocent people trying to earn an honest living."

"Shut up!" he screamed.

He threw the glass down onto the bar with shards of glass going everywhere and one piece landing at my feet. I slid it toward me and hoped I could use it to break free. *Thank God, he didn't see that.*

"You're the one who doesn't know anything," he said, walking towards me.

He slapped me again and again, until I was spitting blood from my mouth. The metallic taste made my stomach nauseous, and the pain from his assault made my cheek throb.

"You think you're so smart, bitch? My brother is dead because he got soft and led with his dick before his heart. He chose some slut over loyalty to his family. He thought he could get out? And try to go legit? Wake the fuck up, Vincenzo!"

Roberto had become enraged and was screaming up toward the ceiling. His brother was dead, and Roberto was trying to move into his position of power, but was always held back by his father.

"You see, Ms. Fairchild . . . oh I'll miss saying that name once I kill you. Did you ever look in the mirror and say it out loud? 'Fairchild' . . . sounds so classy, don't you think? Damn! I'm starting to love that name. It's too bad I have to kill the whore that it belongs to. Okay, you see how you distract me? Anyway, like I was saying, my brother was an idiot, and he was killed for it. My father thought it was a contract hit from the Carlucci Family, but wrong again. I took him out myself as he begged for mercy. I almost changed my mind at the very last second, but then he reminded me of something. It gave me great pleasure to torment him until I fired the shot into his brain. I took what was his and now plan to take what belongs to my father as well. Do you want to see what I took? Do you, whore?"

Oh, he was losing his grasp with reality. He was sick and so deluded within his own warped mind.

"What in the hell are you talking about?" I asked.

"Oh, it's good, wait for it. Hey, baby! Come on out. Someone wants to say hi."

If I hadn't been tied to the chair, I may have just fallen over from the shock. It was Cheryl who walked into Raymond's office, but it was her eyes that painted a different picture than the one Roberto wanted me to believe. I saw fear in her eyes as he grabbed her and started kissing her neck. She looked as if she was in pain and would do anything to stop him from touching her.

He stepped in back of her and pushed her toward me.

"You see baby? I got the bitch for you. You've loved me so good lately that I'm willing to let you do the first cut. Would you like that baby?"

She looked at me and nodded her head, but it was not in agreement. *At least that's how it looked. It seemed like a hidden message to me. . . . God, who's side are you on, Cheryl?*

He grabbed her face and held her forcibly.

"Answer me, Cheryl? Do you want the first cut? You want to make me happy, right? Well, this is what I want. I want you to pick a spot on her body and make her bleed."

"Just one spot? I can't cut more than one?" she questioned, as Roberto's eyes lit up as if he just won the lottery. He was beyond insane. He gazed into her eyes and evilly smiled at her.

"I knew it. I knew you would perfectly fit with me from the very first moment I laid eyes on you. I kept thinking, why you would want to be with my weak brother when you could have been with a real man like me? Then he fucked you up when he knocked you up with his bastard kid. I wanted to kill him then for that, but I waited for the perfect time. He should have married you and told my father the truth about you and the baby, but he had you name some nobody as the kid's father to save face. That's what I don't get, Cheryl? Why did he do that? He was the prince of the family, right? So why did he hide you? Oh, so many questions but no answers, because I *killed* the fucker and the poor sap you named as the baby daddy. Hey! Cutting a break line was easier than blowing up a car, right, bitch?"

He looked back at me and laughed again. He was so twisted in his mind. I had to get out of here. It felt like hours, but in reality it was the longest thirty minutes of my life.

"So the clock is ticking, baby. Are you going to do the honors? Or shall I?"

Cheryl said to him, "It would be my pleasure, Roberto. You're absolutely right about this one. She's a cold hearted bitch, always has been the way she struts around the office as if she was a Steele herself. I want to take my time with her. Will you give me that?"

I couldn't be sure what side Cheryl was playing on, but watching Roberto get excited over her words was scaring the hell out of me. I was defenseless against the two of them because I was in this chair. Maybe this was her way of giving me a fighting chance. If she distracted him enough, I could try to get free.

He then pulled out a shiny silver blade from his coat pocket and handed it to Cheryl. It looked big and heavy. She took it with ease as he licked her face and then kissed her hard, smearing her lipstick. If she truly was playing a part, then she did it quite well. He looked pleased with himself and grabbed the Scotch and sat down on the couch to watch.

She slowly stalked over to me and leaned in to my ear. I could see Roberto gulping the liquor and wiping his mouth. She seductively caressed my face and then stroked my hair and wrapped my pony tail around her wrist. She yanked on my hair and pulled me closer to her. Roberto yelled out and began rubbing his hand over his dick. The sick bastard was actually getting off on Cheryl touching me. He was so lost in the way he was looking at her, he didn't see her cut my ties and free my hands.

"Can you stand?" she whispered. My eyes told her yes.

"Okay, when I give you the signal, you need to strike, Tenley. You will only get one chance, okay? One chance, or we both die."

I nodded my head, and she handed me the knife. The intricate edges that lined the blade were sharp and would have the power to easily rip through his skin. She looked at me again and told me she was ready. I was ready. If I was going to die by his hands, I would go out fighting to the end.

For a second, my mind went to Jamie. If I died here today, I would be seeing my brother again, but I wasn't ready to leave Jagger. We had an amazing future waiting for us to begin. I wasn't going to allow Roberto to rob me of my life with the man I love.

I promised Jagger I would not run again and would stay this time. I knew I had to fight with every last fiber in my soul to make it out of here alive.

Please, Jamie, watch over me. I prayed silently as Cheryl gave me the signal.

"You bitch!" she screamed at me as she slapped me across my face.

"What the fuck!" Roberto screamed back. "What are you playing at Cheryl?"

He tucked himself back into his jeans and walked over to us.

"I was just having a little fun with her, you said I could baby, and then she bit me! The bitch bit me," Cheryl said to Roberto.

"I guess she didn't like how you tasted. Step aside and allow me to show you how it's done."

Cheryl did what she was told and our eyes locked. She mouthed "now," and I knew what I had to do. I didn't have a second to think.

My memory jumped back to when my father and brother taught me how to fire a gun. My father always instructed me to envision the target, feel the distance between your weapon and then strike when the moment was right. *Okay, daddy, I'm taking my shot . . .*

"Bitch, where'd you put the knife I gave you?"

Please God! Let me be mightier than the sword. Jamie, give me strength . . .

Roberto looked so confident, as if he had won and now would finish me off.

Hell No! I am no one's victim. I am a gladiator. I will win, and he will lose. With all my strength and courage . . .

I strike!

CHAPTER 32

Jagger

...no more waiting

I PACED TENLEY'S office, anxiously staring back at the clock. She promised she wouldn't be long, and it had been nearly an hour. It wouldn't be difficult to find Raymond's office and go and find her. I was about to leave when Jacob came rushing in through her office.

"Tenley! Tenley, where are you?" he screamed for her.

"What's going on man? What's happened?" I asked him.

"Where is she? Where is Tenley?" He barely could catch his breath.

"She's not here. She left about an hour ago to meet with her boss."

"And you didn't go with her?" he shouted back at me. "She's in danger. I just got all the reports on Cheryl Lockwood. She is Roberto's girlfriend, and her daughter is a Bornarelli, but Roberto is not the father. She was with his brother first. Now it makes complete sense. Tenley was right not to trust her, because Cheryl was a plant here to get closer to her. She was playing both sides, but really her

313

loyalties lied with Roberto. The girl went off the grid earlier today and has not been seen since. Once I pieced it all together, I had her daughter placed into protective custody along with Cheryl's mother in one of our safe houses. This has been one revelation after another. Your girl was right all along."

"Do you know where Roberto is right now?" I asked with panic in my voice.

"He's either on the run or making his way here."

"What if he already is?" I asked Jacob, who didn't waste another second.

We both took the stairs to Raymond's office. My gut was telling me that my girl needed me. I was just praying that we reached her in time.

He radioed for back-up, and I swear his men reached the top floor before we did. They were all in position, waiting on Jacob's command. He reached for his gun and counted down. I thought my heart was going to stop beating. He raised his hand to his team.

"1 . . . 2 . . . . 3 . . . . GO!"

Jacob led the team and crashed through Raymond's door. We came upon a bloodied scene, and my world went dark.

Two women and two men were all on the floor. The older man, Raymond Steele, was unconscious and next to the couch, while the other guy was lying in a pool of blood.

My eyes found hers, and I fell to my knees not knowing if she was alive or dead. Agents were shouting over their microphones and calling for medical assistance. Jacob was securing the room and identified the dead man as Roberto Bornarelli.

My hands were shaking as I crawled closer to her body, and then she opened her eyes and smiled at me. She was alive and smiling at me like she was looking at me for the very first time. I reached for and held her in my arms.

"Oh, thank God, baby, thank God. I thought you were dead. You were lying so still. Are you hurt?" I asked her as I scanned and touched every inch of her body. Her wrists were sliced open with abrasions, and bruises were beginning to line her skin. As I took in the marks, tears fell from my eyes. All horrid scenarios had been running through my mind. She was calm, too calm for an ordeal she just survived through.

The other woman was coming to. Jacob identified her as Cheryl. The EMT's arrived and were treating Mr. Steele, while the other worked on Cheryl. She was bleeding from her head, but appeared to look like she would be fine. She was visibly shaken, but alive just like Tenley.

My hold on Tenley's tiny frame tightened as my anxiety and fear took over. *I could have lost her, and I wasn't even here to protect her.*

"Jagger, too tight. I can't breathe," she mumbled into my chest.

"What?" I questioned.

"You're. Holding. Me. Too. Tight. I can't breathe," She almost laughed.

"Oh, I'm so sorry, baby. Are you okay?"

"I'm better now. I love you, Jagger. Thank you for finding me."

"No need to thank me, baby. Looks like you did all the work. You must have been so brave."

"I was only brave because I had my brother watching over me, and your love leading me back to you. I promised I would never leave you again. I couldn't let Roberto win," she said. Then she began to tremble and close her eyes.

"Tenley, baby? Open your eyes, open your eyes!" I screamed as one of the EMT's rushed over to examine her.

"Sir, let us through. She seems to be in shock. We're going to take her to the hospital to be looked at. Sir, she's going to be okay, please move aside."

I didn't respond or let her go until Jacob put his hands on my shoulders.

"Jagger, let them take her to the hospital. You can ride with her," he said.

I blinked, and I was back. To hear her talking to me one minute and then out cold the next made my heart stop. I let the paramedics take over, and they gently lifted her onto a stretcher. I needed a minute to catch my breath.

I watched Raymond get wheeled away as well. Cheryl was next. She reached out her hand to me and pulled her oxygen mask off to say something to me.

"She was so strong. I didn't know if we would make it out alive, but she saved my life."

I had no words. I remained still while they were all taken from the office. I stared at the blood soaking into the expensive carpet and covered my mouth. I felt sick. This could have been so much worse and that blood could have belonged to my girl. Jacob walked over to me and told me the ambulance just left and I could ride with him.

"It's over, Parrish. He will never hurt her again. She's safe now."

"You don't know that, Paulson. What if his father retaliates or any other member of their family?"

"I don't think so, especially when it was all captured on voice recording."

"What do you mean?"

"This office was wired for sound just like Tenley's. Everything that happened here tonight has been recorded. We have Roberto Bornarelli on tape, admitting he murdered his brother Vincenzo in cold blood, and how he took out Thomas Daly, who was simply an innocent bystander. Daly lived in the same neighborhood as Cheryl, a friend only. I guess when she got pregnant, she named Daly as her daughter's father to ultimately shield her from the crime family. If Anthony Bornarelli had known the child existed, he would have never shunned his grandchild, especially the child of his first born, who he worshipped. He was never the same after Vincenzo died, and now we know just how sick Roberto was."

"What about the girl, Cheryl?"

"It appears that she was under Roberto's control and pretty much did his bidding until her daughter's safety was in question. She helped us through the entire operation, but she hasn't been cleared yet."

"I need to see my girl. I need to see my girl." I just kept repeating that to Jacob.

He led me away from Mr. Steele's office, as his team was already combing through the crime scene. I didn't even know where Shane was. I had called him earlier while I was waiting for Tenley, and my call went straight to voicemail.

Minutes felt like hours as we made our way through the city traffic. We walked through the emergency room and were taken to a private triage room where Tenley was being examined. A doctor dressed in scrubs walked out from behind the curtain to speak with us.

"Hey, is she in there?" I asked him.

He looked at me with reassuring eyes. I was waiting to hear the worst, but he looked too calm to deliver bad news.

"Sir, I'm Dr. Cross. Ms. Fairchild is resting comfortably. She's suffering from a mild case of shock. I administered a sedative to let her sleep. I've cleaned and bandaged her wrists, which should heal rather quickly. She's going to be taken upstairs to a private room where you could join her soon."

"Thank you, doc. Thanks a million." I shook his hand, nearly breaking it, I was so nervous.

He nodded and gave Jacob an update on Raymond and Cheryl. Raymond was already in his room upstairs, resting soundly. His major injury was a concussion after Roberto attacked him. The doctor said he should be fine with rest. Cheryl was recovering from her head wound, but stayed under police guard until she could be cleared or charged.

I didn't have any phone numbers, but I was told that Zoey, Raymond's daughter and next of kin was notified and that she was on her way to the hospital. I could only assume Shane was with her.

I couldn't stop shaking, and I didn't want to fall apart in front of Tenley if she woke up and saw me like this. I had never wanted a drink so much than I did right now, but I didn't want to fall into old patterns, so I shoved that thought out of my mind.

Jacob was in conference with a man I'd never seen before. When the doors burst open, I saw Shane with Zoey, and he was holding her hand. She was in tears. He didn't even blink. He held her close to her side as if she belonged to him.

"Hey Jagger, we just heard. Where is Zoey's father? Is Tenley okay?" he asked. "I'm so sorry I wasn't here for you both. I came here to help, but instead I take off to party."

"It's okay, Shane. No one could know this would happen. Raymond is fine and resting in a room upstairs. Tenley is going to be fine too, that's all that matters."

"Damn straight. Can we see her?" Shane asked.

"Not yet. She's getting settled up in her room, and then I will join her."

"She's the strongest person I know," Zoey told me as she left Shane's side to give me a hug. "I'll check in with her later after I visit with my father."

I said my goodbyes to her, and then Shane took her hand and led her away down the hall to the bay of elevators. I didn't have time to think about him right now, but I sure was curious about the two of them. He did have a fiancé waiting for him back at home, and Shane was acting like that wasn't the case anymore.

After a few hours, it was way past midnight. I sat beside Tenley in a lumpy chair while holding her hand. I was thinking back to the moment when I was in the hospital and opened my eyes and looked into hers. Her stunning beauty captivated me, and all the love I ever felt for Tenley Faith Fairchild hit me straight through my heart. I was in a deep sleep for weeks, and then the beauty who was holding my hand wielded a powerful spell over me and I was awake. This was what I needed to do for her.

She needed to wake up and look at me. I needed to hear her voice and feel her heart connect with mine. I needed Tenley always. I got up and kissed her lips, hoping it, too, would magically wake her up. *Please, baby, open your eyes. I'm going to stay awake next to you until you open your eyes.*

"Hey, cowboy! Time to wake-up," I heard Tenley say, but I must have been dreaming because I knew she was still asleep. I heard her voice call out to me over and over again until I was jolted awake with something hitting my head. I sat up straight, and she was covering her mouth to keep down her laughter. She hit me with a tissue box to get my attention. I guess I was more tired than I realized and fell asleep.

"Oh my baby! You're awake, thank God," I screamed.

I kissed her all over until I rested my forehead against hers and breathed her in.

"I was so scared, Tenley. Please do not ever scare me like that again. You nearly aged me ten years, and that would have been years without you. I swore on the day you accepted my marriage proposal that I would not waste a minute with you. Any moment spent with you is a blessing I will never take for granted. You are my entire world."

My hands touched her face, neck, arms, and every inch until I was reassured she was okay. I hated the fact that that bastard had his hands on her. She had a faint marking of bruises on one side of her cheek. The corner of her mouth was split open, but already healing with the ointment that was on it.

This could have been an entirely different outcome if it wasn't for Cheryl helping Tenley. While she was asleep, I had spoken to Jacob in great detail about his findings.

Roberto had every intent to kill Tenley tonight. Jacob confirmed that Cheryl was truly under Roberto's control, but she was just caught in an impossible situation. Jacob ultimately cleared her in the investigation, and Cheryl, her daughter and mother would be placed into witness protection to begin a new life far away from New York and the Bornarelli Crime Family.

The sun was beginning to rise on the outside of her hospital window. You couldn't see the sky to greet the day. All you saw were buildings instead of mountains. I missed our home. All I wanted to do was to take Tenley back to Wyoming and forget the last years of our time apart. I never wish to live like that again. The days were long, and the nights were colder and lonely. *Tenley lit up my world.*

She looked beautiful having just experienced what she had gone through. A thought came to my mind, and I was hoping she would agree to my plan.

"Tenley, tomorrow is New Year's Eve, and there's something I want you to do for me."

"Anything, just say the word."

"I was hoping you would say that. I've always wanted to see the ball drop and feel what the other millions of people feel the moment it drops and a new year begins. A new year filled with so much promise and wishes to dream on."

"Sounds perfect Jagger. Was there a question somewhere in there?"

She held my hand, and when Tenley looked at me with those sparkling eyes shining back at me, I just fell in love with her even more.

"I was getting to it, I swear."

"It's okay, take your time, I'm not going anywhere."

"As I was saying, I would like to spend New Year's Eve with you. Anytime I would watch that on television, you would always see lovers kissing passionately in the middle of Times Square. I want that baby, but when I kiss you, I want it to be after we say . . . I do."

She tilted her head to one side. Did she not hear what I said? She was smiling and probably processing what she just heard.

"Jagger, are you saying to me that you want to get married tomorrow night? In Times Square? On New Year's Eve?"

"Yes to all of it. Tenley Faith Fairchild, will you marry me tomorrow and make me the happiest cowboy alive?"

"Yes, Jagger Lucas Parrish! I can't wait to be your wife, your world, and to be a Parrish."

"You have made me so happy. Before my accident, I knew I

was on my way to New York to fight and do anything necessary to show you that you belonged with me, and to give us another chance at the fairytale. In my wildest fantasies, I never knew how much fate would play a part in reconnecting my heart with yours. I promise you here today that I will never doubt the stars again, especially when we have Jamie looking over us."

CHAPTER 33

Tenley

...i do

I T WAS NEW YEAR'S EVE, and later this evening I would be saying two words to the man I love: "I do." I was about to become Mrs. Jagger Parrish. I'm still pinching myself at the fact that this was really happening.

After my release from the hospital, I visited with Raymond, who would be discharged later in the day. My heart nearly stopped when I saw him in the condition Roberto left him in after his attack. All I kept thinking of was Zoey, and how she loved her father so much. Her world would be shattered if she lost him now and in this way.

I was still giving thanks to God for sparing his life, and my own. Anthony was delivered the news about his son, and the truth behind Vincenzo's brutal murder was also disclosed to him. Jacob kept the agreement I made with Anthony, and he was transferred to a facility that housed a more comfortable hospice wing for prison inmates. He would die alone knowing his two sons were gone. One son murdered by the other, and the other murdered by me.

I would never forget the moment the blade pierced his heart, and the look in his eyes when he saw death was coming for him. He deserved no less than what he got. I did what I had to do to save not only my life, but Cheryl's life as well. She was caught up in a world that she never belonged in, but stayed in because of the man she chose to love. She bared his child and was held captive by his murderous brother, who nearly destroyed her. I'd never been so relieved to be able to walk away from this nightmare. My friends were safe, and their lives would resume again, as well as my own. *My new life begins today . . . with Jagger.*

I was nervous and feeling guilty for not including our families in this joyous event. Jagger assured me that once we returned to Wyoming, we would marry again and host the biggest celebration Wyoming had ever seen.

I called my parents to wish them a Happy New Year, but I could not reach them. I called the main house and was told by their housekeeper that they were traveling.

Traveling? Her answer was vague, but what did I expect? Their lives went on as much as mine did in New York. I still would have liked to talk to my mama especially on the day I was getting married, even Wendy was not around. My heart hurt, but this was for Jagger, and I wanted to make him happy.

The guys were out with Tommy, while Zoey and Roxy helped me get ready. Along with Raymond, I pulled some strings out of my "use when necessary" hat and fulfilled another wish for Jagger. The mayor of New York City, a good friend to Raymond, would be marrying Jagger and me, fifteen minutes before the gorgeous ball of thousands of Swarovski crystals dropped down and the New Year began.

I was lost in my thoughts as I stared at a framed picture of my parents with Jamie and me making silly faces behind them. I never wanted to disappoint my family for the choices I made for my life. I couldn't be second guessing this choice with Jagger. After all, this was what they all dreamed for me. To be happy with the one person that made my life better, gave me a thousand reasons to smile each day, and to just share my life, and to grow old with. I had that with Jagger, and I couldn't help but smile every time I thought about how we got here to this day.

"Hey, hooker! It's almost time to leave," Zoey called out to me.

"You know, Zoey, I do have a name other than 'hooker,' and I would so appreciate you not using that word on the day you eventually meet my parents."

I hugged my friend.

"Okay, I'm sorry. I just can't believe you are getting married, and to one hell of a hot fucking cowboy!"

"Zoey! Discretion. Language. In that order, please? And yes, I am marrying a very hot cowboy, he's just as beautiful now as he was when I was seventeen years old."

"Hallmark movie," she laughed.

"Exactly, Zoe, but even better," I responded. "Before we go, do you mind if I ask you a question?"

"Of course, I'm an open book," she said as she retouched her lipstick. She looked beautiful with her long hair layered in curls. She added a few streaks of pink and purple. I laughed when she said she needed her sparkle. Roxy was no better, but she only went with purple.

"What's going on with you and Shane? You seemed pretty cozy and then left together."

"I only borrowed your cowboy for the night. You can have him back."

"He's not *my* cowboy. He's my friend, and he's also a taken one. I'm sorry Zoe, but he's getting married next month. I love you, and I don't want to see you hurt."

"Freaking double d's, Tenley! Did you think I met him, fucked him, and sent him back to his fiancé in a pretty package with a bow on top?"

"You didn't sleep with him?" I was almost surprised with my reaction to this news.

"No, I did not. Damn! We just hung out and had a good time.

He wanted to see what the city was all about, so in the short amount of time we had together, I took him around town. He seemed to have a blast and didn't mention anything about a girl back home."

"I'm sorry, Zoey. Please don't be angry with me. I just heard how he took care of you when I was in the hospital, and Jagger said you two seemed close."

"No worries, hooker. I'm good. Shane is great, but I have another type in mind, and he's packing some serious heat."

"Oh, my ears are just about to bleed out. Do I really want to know this?"

"Would you settle for a rain check on the story? I want to see how it goes before I get my hopes up."

"You got it, Zoe, and I hope it does work out for you because you truly deserve some happy in your life."

"I can't argue with you there, but for now, what do you say we get you married so the world can see the New Year's kiss that I'm sure will be on the cover of *The New York Post* tomorrow."

It was exactly thirty minutes before the ball would drop and fifteen before I married Jagger. We were met by security and escorted to a location unseen by the press. Jacob was leading the team to ensure our safety. I was surprised he hadn't returned to Washington yet. He said he couldn't leave without seeing me get married.

"You look stunning, Tenley. Absolutely beautiful. Your guy may just pass out when he takes in the gorgeous beauty in front of him," Jacob said to me.

"Thank you, Jacob. You have been such an amazing friend, and even better partner. I'm very proud of the work we accomplished, and I wish you all the best. Where will you go from here?"

"California. I just caught a case, and I'll be leaving the day after tomorrow. I was hoping to take some time off, but duty calls."

"Vacation? You? I don't see you relaxing on a beach kicking your feet into the sand."

"You got me there. That's more my kid brother's style. Simon lives out there with his wife, Nicolette. I haven't seen them in a while, so at least I get to visit while I'm out there. My parents live there as well. It will be somewhat of a family reunion minus my other two brothers. Who knows? Maybe this case will wrap up quickly, and I can have some fun. I sure could use some of that in my life."

"I hope you keep in touch, and don't drop off the grid. You tend to do that when you are working a case."

I wasn't sure if he was exactly listening. Jacob's eyes were scanning the room and his eyes found hers over my shoulder. He was staring at Zoey. I smiled and kept my suspicions to myself, but wished upon a star for my two friends.

"I promise you, Tenley, you will see me again." He kissed my cheek and escorted me to another room, where I was welcomed with the best surprise of my life.

My family is here! Wendy, the Parrishes and the Rhodes, all here to see me marry Jagger. I took in a deep breath to halt my tears, but it was no use, I was a goner. My mother quickly rushed over to me with a tissue in hand. Of course she always came prepared. My very handsome father swept me up into his arms and kissed my cheeks.

"Did you honestly think that I would miss handing over my precious daughter to her future husband?" my father said as he lovingly held me in his arms.

He set me down and I was engulfed with hugs from my mother, and the rest of the parents. The only one I still needed to connect with was Wendy. She was patiently waiting her turn.

"You look beautiful, Tumbleweed, probably the happiest you've been in your entire life. This is what he wanted for you. I only hope you now understand the path I was on and the choices I had to make for you."

"I do, Wendy, and if it wasn't for you and the unconditional love you always had for us, today would be a very different day. This moment I get to have would not have been possible without you. Thank you for charming your way into my office and forcing me to see what I so desperately gave up of ever having again . . . "

"Oh, sweet girl, what is it?" she asked as she dried my tears.
I simply replied . . . "LOVE."

Jacob was right when he said Jagger may pass out when he saw me walking toward him down the aisle. My father's protective hold was entwined with my arm as he escorted me to the makeshift altar. Jagger was heavily breathing when I reached him. My father placed a kiss on my cheek and then to my hand before passing it to Jagger. Daddy put his hand on Jagger's shoulder and looked at him with the adoration of a proud father.

The mayor began with the traditional vows, and then we would say a few of our own. We knew how much we loved each other and vowed to live up to our sacred commitment all the days of our life. Jagger and I discussed what we would say, and we agreed to recite one sentence to each other before being pronounced husband and wife.

The mayor gestured to Jagger to recite his words to me. Jagger smiled before unfolding the piece of paper he held in his hand. I peeked, and it was more than one sentence which made me so happy because mine was too.

"I love you, Tenley Faith. I've loved you for what feels like a lifetime spent in your beauty, wonder, and light. Through the good times, the bad, and the sad days in between, you were never too far from my mind and my heart. I made a promise to your brother, my best friend, that I would love you until I take my last breath, and even then I think the good Lord negotiates. Today is the day I make you mine and give myself completely over to you. You are not only my lover, but my very best friend, and today my sweet Tenley, we simply begin anew. I love you."

The crowd beneath us at Times Square was hooting and cheering. Our ceremony was being filmed and transmitted on the big screens! We were minutes away from not only our big moment, but the world's moment too! The mayor gestured to me to begin. I looked over to Wendy, the one who got me here. She blew me a kiss of encouragement, and I sure needed it now more than ever. I didn't want to stumble over my words, but what could I say to Jagger in such a short length of time?

"Jagger, I gave you my heart at seventeen. You asked me to trust you, I did with everything I had. We had our good moments and sometimes bad ones too, but the hardest ones were the roads traveled on without you by my side. It took me putting my trust in others to help me come back to you. I thought I had lost my way and would never get that chance again to have this day with you, but then you said . . . stay. I love you."

Our families were crying tears of joy, as our union was about to be sealed forever. The mayor held our hands and recited his closing words:

"Now that Jagger and Tenley have given themselves to each other by solemn vows, with the joining of hands and the giving and receiving of the blessed rings, and with all of you to bear witness, then by the power of the great state of New York, I pronounce that they are husband and wife. You may kiss your lovely bride."

Jagger winked, took my face into his hands, and wiped away my tears with his thumbs. We both smiled along with our family and friends to begin the official countdown to the New Year and begin our new life together.

"10, 9, 8, 7, 6, 5, 4, 3, 2, 1 . . . .Happy New Year!!!"

The cheers erupted as Jagger's lips touched mine and kissed me so lovingly that it sent electricity down to my toes. I'd never felt more alive than in that moment with my cowboy. Jagger was not only my best friend and lover, but now he was my husband.

"Happy New Year, Mrs. Parrish."

"Happy New Year, Mr. Parrish."

We kissed and kissed. It was the kiss seen and captured for all of the world to see. It was a magical moment, one I could give to Jagger, and to Jamie who was sure to see our love story from the stars.

CHAPTER 34

Tenley

...what's next to come

THE DAYS FOLLOWING our New Year's wedding were spent in complete bliss. We celebrated with our family and friends until the morning dawn, and then did some private celebrating of our own. We chose to spend our honeymoon in the penthouse suite of the Park Lane Hotel. The views were incredible, looking over the city we just married in. I didn't know why we needed this luxury, as we didn't leave our bed for the next three days. It was truly magical as I was lost and wrapped around Jagger's protective love. He was mine, and I was his.

I couldn't stop laughing at what he said as we checked out. We were holding hands and walking toward our waiting car when he said, "I told you so." And then he leaned in and kissed me.

I wasn't sure what he was referring to. A strong minded woman like myself especially in gladiator mode doesn't like to hear when she's wrong, but for this, I would gladly be reminded of for the rest of my life.

"And that means what, my love?" I asked.

He kissed my hand and then each knuckle before crashing his mouth down onto mine. Jagger's kisses were addicting that I craved him again and again. I had almost forgotten what we were talking about.

"Never doubt a cowboy. You were meant to be a Parrish, and now you are my love. My wife. My life. Keeper of my heart and guardian of my soul. I love you, baby."

"And I love you."

"Are you sure you don't want me to come with you?" He asked me again, but I was more than okay going back to my office. Jagger didn't want the flashbacks of that horrific day to enter my mind, especially after our wedding and honeymoon. I assured him that I was okay and owed it to Raymond to personally resign my partnership with the man who had given me the opportunity of a lifetime. Zoey and her father knew it was coming, but I never actually said the words until now.

I was welcomed back with hugs and congratulations. My heart skipped a beat when I passed the administrative counter and saw a new assistant in Cheryl's chair. I shrugged it off and kept walking toward my office where Raymond and Zoey were waiting for me.

My career began here with Steele and Copeland Law Firm. A spunky free spirit with crazy hair barreled through my office one day and promised we would be sisters forever, and how right she was. And then my life changed the moment I walked into my office only to be shocked by Wendy's visit. She rocked my structured world and turned it inside out, and I couldn't be happier. And now I will walk through these doors for the last time. Again, I couldn't be happier with the choice I have made.

We reminisced and laughed for hours while Zoey and Tommy helped me pack my last box. They hugged me fiercely and promised to visit me in Wyoming soon. Tommy was still happy with Roxy, who was practically bouncing outside at her desk. She was in love, as was my friend, too. As for Zoey, who knew what the future would bring for her, but I knew it wouldn't be boring.

I took a minute to look around my vast office and commit the happy moments to memory. I had many.

"You know when I recruited you out of Yale, I thought to myself: *Now this girl is tough. She's raw and gritty and will command a courtroom with an iron fist, and a voice to match.* I never thought you would give all of this up for love," Raymond said as he walked over to hug and say goodbye to me.

"I'm still going to command a courtroom with an iron fist, but it just won't be here."

"Things won't be the same without you around here. Hell, Zoey is leaving me too!"

"Where is she going? She didn't tell me." Now that was new information I wasn't aware of. My voice almost sounded offended that I didn't know something so important about my best friend.

"All I know is that she's taking a page out of your handbook. She told me that she's going to chase the wind to the west and see what happens when she gets there. Don't ask me what that means, because I don't have a clue. I always said she was her mother's daughter and not mine."

He gave me one last hug and held my hands as we both took in my now empty office.

"So once you leave here today, what will you do next? What will you become?" Raymond asked me as he closed and locked the door.

It was the easiest answer I could say.

"Happy. I will be happy."

Saying goodbye to one life and beginning a new one was easier than I had thought it would be. Jagger made it easy by simply loving me. The night we arrived back home in Wyoming, we spent our first night as husband and wife in the home Jagger built for us. He was true to his word and carried me over the threshold, promising he would do this for as many times as I wanted him to. A rugged cowboy and a natural born romantic.

He made it his mission to christen every room in our home. I swear my man had stamina and never stopped worshipping my body with his. There would be no lovemaking under the night sky due to the season we still had to endure, so we settled under our skylight in our bedroom. Jagger made passionate love to me all throughout the night and held me for the rest.

I watched Jagger gaze up toward the stars that were shining brightly tonight. Jagger always said it was a good sign to have the stars be your light. He repositioned himself to lean on his elbow and looked directly at me.

"I want babies with you. Carry my child, Tenley, and make us a family."

He said nothing more and put his cheek to my stomach. I wasn't sure if I was ready to give Jagger what he wanted. Our reunion was nothing short of a miracle, and I wanted time with him before we committed ourselves to having children. He didn't push, he just wanted me to know where his heart was leading him to next. He said he would be patient and wait for me to get there. He fell asleep soundly with his body wrapped around mine. I let out a breath and made a wish of my own and then joined my husband in sleep.

The next day was spent settling in and unpacking. Jagger was up before the dawn to begin the daily chores. He kissed me goodbye and told me that he loved me. I slept a few more hours before beginning my day.

My boxes had arrived, and I had chosen a room that would be my office. Time had flown by and it was past noon. Wendy called and asked if she could stop by. I told her yes and how I was looking forward to her visit. I managed in just a few hours to completely set-up my office. Jagger had built in bookcases that completely lined one wall. He had built me a customized desk, big enough where I could work freely with books and my computer.

"How did I get so lucky to have found him?"

"Well if you ask me, I think you both got lucky," Wendy said.

"How are you always here when I'm talking out loud to myself, and it seems you are the only one I do this in front of?"

"I guess I'm just lucky that way, Tumbleweed."

"I guess you are. I'm so happy to see you, Wendy. Thank you for stopping by."

"You look good, sweet girl."

"I'm more than good, I'm . . . "

"Happy?"

"Yeah, something like that."

"Well, that's good. I truly hope you stay that way once I give you what I have here in my bag. Come and sit with me."

She took my hand and we sat down by my huge bay window. It would be a view I would take in every single day.

"Is everything okay, Wendy?"

"Oh yes, honey, don't you go worrying. It's a good thing, I'm sure of it."

"Well if anyone knows about being right about such things, it's you, dear friend."

"I'm not the only one," she said as she handed me a letter, and not just any letter, a letter from Jamie. With all that had happened since Christmas to now, I had forgotten that more letters may have existed. Wendy had said there were others, but never said how many. Now once again, my friend is passing me more words from my brother. I was almost afraid to take it, but she assured me it was something worth reading.

I ran my fingers over his handwriting. His penmanship was flawless, and I could almost picture Jamie sitting at his desk and chewing on his pen. He was the wordy one and could turn a simple sentence into a ten page essay.

My brother was known for making his point very clear until I understood the hidden messages behind his words. These letters were filled with them.

"I'll leave you to it. See you soon."

"You're not going to stay?" I questioned Wendy.

"This is not my only stop. I have a few more deliveries to make."

I started a fire and made myself comfortable on the floor surrounded by pillows. I so wanted a glass of wine right now, but we had none in the house. Jagger was adamant about me not drinking. It reminded him of a dark time in his life. I knew what he was referring to and always respected his wishes. For all that he had done for me, this request was easy.

A letter from Jamie
For my sister

Dear Tumbleweed,

If you're reading this letter, then you must know it will be the last one you will receive. Don't cry, baby sister, it's a good one, I promise.

Happy Wedding Day! You see, sis? Everything always has a way of working out to God's plan for us. I always knew you would find your way back to Jagger, and he would find his way back to you. You two are your own shape now. Fill it with happy memories to pass onto generations to come.

Writing these letters to you brought me much comfort in my final days. It was my way of saying the words I no longer could say to you in person. It would be too hard for me and even harder for you.

I was angry with God for my cancer returning, and then I quickly dismissed my anger and prayed for his mercy. God doesn't want any of his children to suffer, and when they do it is hard on Him just as much as it is on the family the cancer affects.

I would have given just about anything to not have this happen to me, but it did and I made my peace with it. This letter would have never reached you if it wasn't for Wendy. Wendy Ann Manning is a living Angel, and she does selfless work for others who need her. I needed her to carry out my last wishes, and she never hesitated with her answer.

Always keep her close to your heart, she deserves nothing less. She loves you Tenley as if you were her own and would do anything for you. Next time you see her, please give her a hug from me and tell her how much I love and miss her . . . and her pancakes!

I'll always be watching over you. If you should ever need me, just look up to the night sky, and I will be shining on the brightest star.

One more thing . . . say the words I wasn't strong enough to say to mama and daddy. Please tell them how much I love them. It is my honor to have been blessed with amazing parents. It breaks my heart to leave them and you. I love you all very much. You have made me the happiest big brother. You Chose Right!
    Jamie

A letter from Jamie
For Jagger . . . my best friend

Jagger

WITH THE EXCITEMENT over the past few weeks, I had almost forgotten about my leg and the rehab I was supposed to be doing for it. I totally skipped out on my therapy sessions, but I knew my body better than anybody. Well, that wasn't exactly true. My girl quickly got reacquainted with it, as I did with hers. I had messages on my voicemail from Dr. Sampson's assistant asking me to call to reschedule an appointment that I missed. I hardly felt any discomfort until today when I put in my first real day working the ranch. I was hurting pretty bad and needed a hot soak to ease the stiffness in my muscles.

I was just settling She-devil into her stall and shutting down the stables for the night when I saw a truck approaching. Other than staff, only a few people knew the gate code to enter my property, and one of them was Wendy. She beeped the horn to get my attention, but I already heard her beast of a truck a mile away.

"Hey there, cowboy, want a ride?" she called out.

I couldn't help but laugh.

"Hey Wendy, that would be great."

I climbed into her truck and she gave me a big welcome home hug. This was the first time I had a chance to catch up with her since our wedding in New York.

"Um . . . Wendy? Are we going to go?" I asked her. She looked deep in thought, and it was never a good sign when she clammed up on us. That was a sure sign that something was weighing heavily on her mind.

"Hey girl, what's on your mind? Are you okay?" I asked.

"Oh, I'm sorry, sweets. I'm okay. I've had a long day myself, and I visited with your lovely bride earlier today."

With the mention of Tenley's name, I broke out with the biggest smile. I missed her so much today, and I couldn't wait to get home to her.

"Did you all have a nice chat? And how many times did my name come up in the conversation?"

She smiled and I laughed with her. Women and their talks could last for hours and most of the time, they centered on men.

"Now, Jagger, you can't expect to be the center of her universe all the time. Let the girl come up for air once in a while."

I knew she was kidding, but her words stung a bit. Tenley was the center of my world, every last part of it, and when we married, I became hers in all ways that mattered most. Now more than ever, I wanted to see her.

"What's up Wendy? You look like you're a million miles away. You can tell me anything, you know that right?"

"I know that, Jagger, and please forgive me for beating around the bush. It's just that I have something to give you."

"Okay, what is it?"

"A letter from Jamie." She quietly answered my question.

I knew from Tenley that Jamie had left some letters for her, and I never pressed her about them. I figured when she was ready to share them with me, she would. I never thought he would have left one for me.

"Do you have it with you now? If so, may I have it please?"

She opened her bag and handed me my letter from my best friend. I didn't know how to explain it, but when she handed me the letter, I felt an immediate connection to it.

"Thank you, Wendy."

"You're welcome, Jagger, and I want you to know I gave a letter to Tenley as well. It was the very last one he had written for his sister."

"Was she okay after you gave it to her?"

"Yes, I believe so. I gave her privacy to read it on her own, and then I came here to give you yours. I hope whatever it contains will bring you closure, peace, and understanding."

"Thank you, Wendy, so much. You don't know what this means to me."

"I think I do, son. This letter is just a small part of who Jamie was. Whether it was here on earth or up in heaven, your brother will always be looking out for you. He loved you very much, and he just wanted all of you to move forward with your lives and never allow the sadness you felt over his death to hold you back. You see, Jagger, everything in this life happens for a reason. Some things we will understand and accept, and the others we will be mad as hell over. You all had to go through what you did to get here now. I'm not sure what his final words will say, but if I know anything about Jamie, I'm sure he wrote down exactly what he felt you need to hear. I was just honored to be asked to carry out his wishes. I love you, Jagger. I love my Tumbleweed, and Shane too. You are my kids, and like Jamie, I always wanted the best for you. And now that you all have it, I can finally rest easier too."

I said goodbye to Wendy and walked back into the stables and sat with She-devil. I sent Tenley a text telling her I would be home soon. She responded back a few minutes later telling me to take my time, and she would be there waiting when I got home. Her words alone had the ability to make me weak in the knees. I didn't know how she was feeling after reading Jamie's letter, or maybe she didn't read it at all. No one knew more than I did how Tenley felt about Jamie. They were extremely close and protective of one another.

With another deep breath let out, I tore the envelope open and began reading my letter.

Dear Jagger,

Let me begin by saying Thank you. Thank you for loving and not giving up on my sister. If you're reading this letter, then I'm going to say congratulations, brother, on marrying the love of your life. I always believed in my heart that you two would find your way back to each other. I know what I asked of you all those years ago, and I know what it cost you, but you're a good man, Jagger Parrish, and I am very proud to call you my brother in law.

If I could ask one more favor of you, I swear it will truly be my last. I know I don't have to give you the big brother speech: "If you hurt her, I'll kill you and make it look like an accident." I won't be around for that . . . but my daddy will, and you know what an extensive gun collection he keeps at the house. Okay?! I hope you know I'm kidding. You love my sister too much to ever hurt her, at least not intentionally. She's an amazing person who lost her way after I died. It wasn't too hard to figure that would happen if you knew the true Tenley. I'm just forever thankful that she found herself again, the real girl that she closed off for too many years to count.

Am I a mind reader? No, I'm not. I'm still very much alive as I write this letter to you, but my time is short, Jagger, and I feel God all around me. The letters I wrote to Tenley, it was me being hopeful and just wanting the very best for my sister. If Wendy carried out my last request in handing you this letter, then know, my brother, I am at peace and will be up here in heaven keeping protective eyes on the ones I love. You are my best friend, and it was an honor to be yours. Be happy, Jagger. May you and Tenley be blessed every day of your shared life together.

    Yours,

      Jamie

I folded his letter and placed it in my coat pocket. Here I was, a grown man never one for crying, but after reading Jamie's letter that's all I could do. He'd been gone for more than five years now and his words felt like he was still here with us.

We were the same age, but his soul was older and filled with wisdom beyond his years. On the outside, Jamie was pure cowboy. He worked from sunrise to sundown every single day on his ranch and side by side with his father. On the inside, Jamie spoke as if he was a philosopher of a different time. He was smart as a whip and got straight A's. He saved our asses more times than I could count when Shane and I decided to party in college, where he stayed behind to study. I got my share of good grades, but Jamie was the most responsible one out of our group, and when my eye turned to Tenley, I'll never forget what he said to me.

Tenley and I were keeping our new relationship a secret until we could figure out how we would tell Jamie about it. It was mine and Shane's job to keep all the assholes away from his sister within a 50 mile safe zone. He never expected one of his closest friends making a move on her, but she wasn't just any girl, Tenley was *the* girl, and I was going to make her mine. I wanted to come clean, but she wanted to wait. He was her hero and she didn't want to disappoint him.

It all changed the day he walked in on us making out, yeah it was quite the compromising position. I was never so scared in all of my life. We matched in height, but Jamie was a bear and could do some serious damage if he wanted to.

Tenley worked her magic on him and shouted out that she loved me. I nearly passed out upon hearing the words. I loved her too, but to actually hear it was an amazing feeling. The shock wore off, and he gave us his blessing. Tenley and I had been through so much to be together, and here was Jamie helping us all along. His friendship was a gift. Our brotherhood was a blessing.

I made my way to my truck and looked up toward the sky. I saw a shooting star and felt the wind blow on my face.

"A shooting star? Seriously bro? You were always a show-off."

I smiled as I thought of my friend. I took out my letter and held it in my hands pointing to the sky.

"Thank you for this, Jamie. Thank you for believing in us. I promise you, brother, I will never let you down and will love her for the rest of my life."

I tucked the paper back into my coat and made my way home . . . home to Tenley.

CHAPTER 35

Tenley

...where you learn to ride and fall

THE DAY I read Jamie's last letter was the day when I closed the page to the living diary of my past. When I was younger I thought I was somewhat invincible. I could saddle my horse and ride like the wind and chase the blue sky looking over the Grand Teton Mountains. I never felt more alive than when I was riding and never felt so alone after Jamie died. Time had stood still the morning of his passing with the ring of my phone and the shrilling cries I let out after I hung up on my mother. That was the day I had fallen and didn't rise again until five years later when his letter arrived.

It took reading Jamie's words and deciphering the messages to get me to open my eyes and take a real hard look at myself in the mirror, and an even harder look at the life I had been living. My brother's life was tragically cut short from something greater beyond our control. He made me promise to move forward with my life and to live every day to the fullest. To not get lost in my grief and to celebrate life and his memory, but I didn't keep that promise. Career, money, fancy clothes all looked great on the outside, but if your spirit had no light shining through it, you truly had nothing.

My daddy always used to tell me that he was the richest man in the world, and I would say to him, "Because of where we live and what we have." I was young at the time, my answer was appropriate for my age. He shook his head and laughed at my answer. My father was just as strong in his thinking as Jamie was. You could stare at a painting all day and just see the image, but they would always look beyond the canvas. They looked at what the artist was trying to convey in his work and the meaning behind it. After a few moments of pause, my father lifted my chin so I could look into his eyes and he said:

"I am the richest man in the world, because I found love here on this land. I found love with your mother, and then I found love again when we were blessed with the most amazing children. Love is the strongest emotion you shall ever know in your lifetime, and it's one I hope my little Tumbleweed will find one day. It will confuse you, make you crazy, and then incredibly happy all at the same time. You will know it when it happens, and then, my sweet baby girl, you will be rich too."

I could feel the heat radiating all over my face from smiling and remembering one of many beautiful moments spent with my father. I kept my word to my brother and took my parents along with Jagger to visit his grave. It was a beautiful sunny summer day in July. The flowers were in bloom and not a cloud was in the sky. We all joined hands in a circle and prayed together. We each shared a story about Jamie, and then laughed together, smiled together, and then shared a few tears too, but all happy ones.

As my family and Jagger made their way back down the mountain, I stayed behind to have a private chat with my brother. I could not see him, but I felt a strong presence surrounding me, and I knew he was watching from heaven. I had written him a letter and I read it out loud, hoping he would hear my words to him.

Dear Jamie,

To say thank you to you for everything you did for me doesn't even come close to the thousand words I want to say. You always believed in me even when I didn't believe in myself. You said you didn't have a crystal ball to see the future, but you were wrong, you did, big brother. Your amazing, beautiful heart served as your magic window to all of our lives. Through your words, you gave me the greatest gift one could ever receive, and that was giving me my life back. I will always be grateful to you Jamie for the gift you gave me. I will never waste a moment, and I promise to live life to the fullest. To be happy with the man I love. To have babies with the man I love, and move forward hand and hand with Jagger, always and forever. This I promise you, brother, with all of the beats in my heart.

I'll love you always and smile every night up to the stars where I know you're shining brightly.

Love,

Tenley

I folded the letter and placed it in a tin box. I wanted my words close to Jamie, so he would know that I was okay and would be for the rest of my days. I buried it under a bed of flowers, where it would always remain.

My new life began the minute Jagger asked me to *stay* with him. I could never go back and change my past, I could only live in the present where we spent our days working the ranch, spending time with our family and friends. We witnessed another love story on the day Shane married Shelby. Our friend finally got his happily ever, and we couldn't have been happier for him.

I looked at the calendar, and it was once again the anniversary of my brother's death. There would be no sadness today, only tears of joy when I would share my news with Jagger. I had gone into private practice and worked from the comforts of our beautiful home. I wasn't sure if I would ever be the gladiator I once was, but it was okay because I was happier with the person I was now and the life I had made here with Jagger.

I asked him to come home early, and he did with no question. He thought I may have been sad because of the day and what it represented, but no, I wasn't. Today was for Jagger. When he walked through the door, my knees went weak at the sight of him. He was just beautiful . . . my husband, my world. I watched him hang his hat and kick off his boots, and then he saw me and caught me staring. He winked and asked me if I liked what I was looking at. I winked back, and I told him I liked it very much. He picked me up and lovingly kissed me and twirled me around until we were both dizzy.

He put me down, but not until he showered me with kisses and told me how much he loved me. I took his hand and asked him to follow me. He said, "Always love. You lead and I will follow."

Damn! My cowboy sure knew what to say to make my heart melt. We sat in our favorite spot in the living room. Our view was spectacular with the mountains in our backyard. I handed him a note, because I didn't trust myself to be able to say the words without falling apart into a heap of tears.

"A note? What's this?" he asked as he began to unfold it. I took a deep breath and answered him.

"A gift." Just two words was all I said.

"Oh, sweetheart, don't you know I have everything I could ever want here with you? You don't have to give me anything."

"It's not just for you, it's for us." I whispered. Jagger smiled and read my note.

Dear Jagger,

I'm pregnant with your child. I love you so much, husband, and I thank you for loving me.

Tenley . . .

His brown eyes filled with tears as he read the words out loud.

"You're pregnant? We're going to have a baby? And I'm going to be a father?"

"Yes, Jagger, you are. Are you happy?" As if I didn't know, but asked anyway.

"Oh my love, I think we need a new word for happy. I am so beyond happy and so in love with you."

He took me into his arms, where he kissed me until my eyes rolled back into my head. I was drunk on Jagger. He carried me up to our bedroom, and we made love until the night was upon us and the stars were shining through our skylight.

As Jagger held me in his arms, I reflected on this day a year ago where I was feeling the loss of my brother and the pain I still carried with me. Now, one year later, my life was completely changed. It took a letter from beyond the grave to help me stop drowning and come up to the surface. To breathe life back into my lungs, and to feel love again in my heart.

Jagger always told me that our story was written in the stars for us. I believed that with my heart and soul. My eyes found my star, and I knew it was Jamie once again shining down on us. My parents always told me that home would be here waiting for me when I was ready to come back to it. No matter what road I would take in my life, all roads would lead me home. It took a letter to make me finally believe what I tried so hard to forget. I wasn't the same girl I was when I left all those years ago. I was found again through Jamie's hope and Jagger's love.

I'm not a runner anymore.

I was . . . **HOME.**

EPILOGUE

...the doctor appointment

TODAY MARKED TENLEY'S twentieth week in her pregnancy. We were halfway there and so ready to find out what God had blessed us with. We debated back and forth on not finding out, but I knew a baby shower was in the works, and from her mother, to Wendy, they begged me to find out.

Wendy would leave messages on my voicemail and simply say . . . "Will your colors be blush and bashful or rugged and suede?"

I didn't have the faintest idea what she was referencing to until I came home early to walk into a room full of crying women. They were all watching a movie called "Steel Magnolias," one of Wendy's favorites. My girl had crumpled up Kleenex surrounding her as she sniffed and hiccupped through her tears.

I knew it was just a movie, but it still hurt my heart to see my girl cry. Then I laughed when Wendy handed her a bowl of ice cream and said, "Here, honey, Chocolate Peanut Butter cures all."

Now *that* I can agree with as my eyes went back to our night spent in her daddy's cabin. I blew my girl a kiss and let them finish up with their movie.

As we drove into town for our appointment, my girl never stopped smiling. She was rubbing her belly, and then bounced a bit when she felt a kick. She quickly grabbed my hand to feel our baby inside of her. I was just now beginning to experience what she had been feeling the past couple of weeks. It was a feeling like no other, I was truly lost to the miracle growing inside of her.

"Are you sure you want to know?" I asked her one last time before walking through her doctor's office.

"I am one hundred percent sure of it. Mama is chewing her manicured fingers to the cuticles and Wendy calls me every day to make sure I didn't change my mind. They really are very sweet."

"They are love, but this is our baby and I think we should leave the decision up to us, don't you agree?" I asked her with hope that she would have a change of heart and side with me, but I could read her like a book and I knew she wanted to know. I finally conceded, and she kissed me.

My girl was ready to burst with all the water she had taken in while preparing for the ultrasound. We were going to be seeing our baby through a 4-D image. Not only would we be seeing the baby's body, but actually see what he or she was going to look like. Tenley's doctor said we would have a better idea further along in her pregnancy, but it didn't matter as long as the baby was healthy, and my girl could safely deliver him or her when she was ready to.

The tech got Tenley prepared as I sat beside her and held her hand. Dr. Tillman walked in a few minutes later and greeted us.

"Well, kids, are you ready to see your baby?" he said as he began placing the cold gel on her belly.

"I know I am, but Jagger is being a bit stubborn. He doesn't want to know."

"No, baby, I do want to know," I said as my eyes stared at the screen and I took in my child staring back at me. Dr. Tillman snapped picture after picture while doing his necessary measurements.

I held onto Tenley's hand with my tears falling down. I had never been happier in all of my life. She looked over to me and winked. "Are you ready?"

"So ready," I whispered.

She gave Dr. Tillman the go ahead and he said, "You're having a boy. Congratulations Jagger."

"A son? I have a son." I whispered as my tears fell and my legs turned to jelly.

Dr. Tillman printed out our photos and handed Tenley our baby's first pictures. I was so happy I almost stopped breathing when I heard the doctor's words. We were having a son.

We drove back to the ranch, and I knew what I wanted to do next. I wanted to build my son's nursery furniture and set up what would be his room. Dreams of me teaching our son to ride took over my thoughts. *How could one man be blessed with so much good fortune in one's lifetime?* I thought silently as I held my beautiful wife in my arms throughout the night.

My eyes found the stars that shined through our sky light every night. I wished on them. I prayed on them, and was so thankful for my brother who was our guardian angel. This moment, and all the moments I have with Tenley, were made possible through Jamie's love for us. How I would ever thank him, I wondered, and then I knew.

On July 4th, we welcomed our son into the world with the sounds of fireworks outside of our hospital window. For some reason my girl had a feeling, and I knew better to never question her.

We spent the holiday in town with our families and Wendy. This way if my girl was right, then it would be an easy drive to the hospital. I was still smiling at the memory of Tenley's water breaking in the middle of the town square. My girl was amazing throughout it all and nearly broke my hand with the last hard push. It was then our son screamed his way out and we welcomed him into our hearts forever.

After the last visitor left, my lovely wife was finally able to get some much needed rest. I didn't let our son out of our sight, and kept him with us in her room. As Tenley soundly slept, I held our son protectively in my arms. He was absolutely beautiful and all mine. He had a crown of thick dark brown hair that matched mine. He was a bundle of joy at eight pounds and six ounces. His eyes were blue, but I'm told they would probably change.

For just hours old, he was bright eyed and looking up at me. He squeezed my finger and my heart nearly stopped. He was our miracle that our love made, and we were a family. I knew what I had to do next. I lifted the blinds and looked out to the night sky. Man! The stars were bright tonight. I looked for his star and when I found it, I told our son about his amazing Uncle Jamie who lives in the stars. Our son had fallen asleep, but I kept on talking.

My heart was so filled with love for my wife for giving me the best gift I could ever receive. "Hey Jamie, I have someone here I would like you to meet. He's so beautiful. Our little cowboy with the perfect combination of Parrish/Fairchild in him."

"Please shine brightly and watch over him. I would like to introduce you to our son, and your nephew: James Lucas Parrish."

The End . . .

a note from the author

THANK YOU, READERS, for taking the time to read *All Roads Lead Home*. Please consider leaving an honest review.

When I began writing this book, I had only one person in mind while doing so: my sister Jeanie. I lost my sister to something that was bigger and beyond our control, and sadly, her voice was silenced nearly six years ago. Losing her unexpectedly left a profound pain in my heart and unequivocally changed my life. She is now a spirit in the sky, and I hope she's laughing, dancing, and smiling with the angels.

To remember her is easy; I do it every day. The difficult times come when I'm doing something and wishing she was here to share it with me. Losing a loved one is hard. Sometimes it can be so painful that you never believe you will be able to move forward on the darker days, but then the clouds part, the sun shines, and you just do.

Writing had always been a dream of mine, and I feel so incredibly blessed that I had finally found the courage I needed to take the leap of faith to pursue it. Jeanie would have loved everything about it, this I know without a doubt. Although she is not here to share it with me, I know she's watching from the heavens above. Thank you, Jeanie, for inspiring me to keep chasing my dream . . . one book at a time. I love you always.

A true Thank You would not be complete until I thank the angels that live in my life every day . . .

Henry: thank you for loving me. It's been an amazing 25 years sharing my life with you. You are a forever romantic, and not a day goes by that you don't make me smile or laugh. I love you, husband.

Mindy: thank you for taking the time to read my words. Your feedback is instrumental. I'm never worried when I receive your critiques. I trust you completely, and I am so lucky to have your support when it comes to my writing, and even more in friendship. I love you more.

Alice: thank you for your words of encouragement and the virtual slap to my head when I was scared and had doubt. I appreciate your valuable advice and thank you for breaking down my words that became my awesome blurb. You rock!

Wendy: you make an amazing character. Thank you for inspiring me.

Joe: the other guy in my life. You are not only my editor, but my very dear friend. Thank you for inspiring me and listening to all my crazy book ideas. You. Get. Me. And I love you for it.

JT Formatting: thank you, Julie, for all you do. You are my forever rock star.

RE Creatives: thank you, Renee, for designing a breathtaking cover.

For the bloggers: thank you to Kylie McDermott of Give Me Books. You did an amazing job spreading the word for *All Roads Lead Home* to the blogging community. Everyone who participated has been so supportive, sharing my cover and spreading the word.

Lastly, to you, my readers: I hope you enjoyed reading Tenley and Jagger's story. Whether the story comes from real life to a fictional one, I want to give you a piece of my heart on every page. That's one of the amazing things I get to experience every day as a writer.

Writing *All Roads Lead Home* was very personal for me. Authoring this book gave me closure to many chapters of *my* own story. In some small way, I finally felt free from the pains of my own past. It's scary when you close one door and walk through another to begin the next chapter of your life. You learn to accept the things you've faced and know sometimes can never be changed, but then look toward the future for brighter days to come.

Thank you for traveling on this road with me.

Sparkle on loves,
　　　　　Mary

coming in 2016

BEST SELLING AUTHOR Mary A. Wasowski brings you an exciting new book that will take you back to characters you fell in love with in *A Changed Life*.

You will meet Agent Jacob Paulson again, as well as Uncle Jack, in *An Unfinished Life* . . . the story after Nicolette and Simon's happily ever after. Two very different men will struggle to find the balances of their pasts, come to terms with what connects them with their present, and ultimately change their future.

Stay tuned . . .

XOXO . . . Mary

other books by
Mary A. Wasowski

A Changed Life (**standalone**)

Forever Series:
Forever: Book One
Second Chance at Forever: Book Two
Our Forever Promise: Book Three

about the author

MARY A. WASOWSKI is a Best Selling Author who writes contemporary romance and is best known for her *Forever Series*. This is her fifth publication.

A romantic at heart, she's reading when she's not writing. Her Kindle goes everywhere with her! Born and raised in New Jersey, she shares her life with her husband, Henry, and three sons. The story of her life will soon continue . . . in North Carolina.

I would love to hear from you. Please feel free to reach out to me:

EMAIL:
AuthorMaryAWasowski@gmail.com

FACEBOOK:
https://www.facebook.com/pages/Author-Mary-A-Wasowski

INSTAGRAM:
https://instagram.com/authormaryawasowski/

WEBSITE:
http://authormaryawasowski.com/

GOOGLE +:
https://plus.google.com/+MaryWasowski.

TWITTER:
https://twitter.com/wasow6